Ms. Kontolios

FALLING IN LOVE

WITH NATASSIA

A N N A   M O N A R D O

Falling in Love
with Natassia

a novel

DOUBLEDAY

New York

London

Toronto

Sydney

Auckland

PUBLISHED BY DOUBLEDAY
a division of Random House, Inc.

Copyright © 2006 by Anna F. Monardo

Published in the United States by Doubleday,
an imprint of The Doubleday Broadway Publishing Group,
a division of Random House, Inc., New York.

DOUBLEDAY and the portrayal of an anchor with a dolphin are registered
trademarks of Random House, Inc.

This book is a work of fiction. Names, characters, businesses, organizations,
places, events, and incidents either are the product of the author's imagination
or are used fictitiously. Any resemblance to actual persons, living or dead,
events, or locales is entirely coincidental.

Portions of this work appeared in the Fall 2000 and Spring 2004 issues of
Prairie Schooner.

Library of Congress Cataloging-in-Publication Data
Monardo, Anna.
    Falling in love with Natassia : a novel / by Anna Monardo.— 1st ed.
        p. cm.
    1. Young women—Fiction. I. Title.
    PS3563.O5164F35 2006
    813'.54—dc22

                                                                2005053748

ISBN-13 978-0-385-51466-8
ISBN-10 0-385-51466-2

PRINTED IN THE UNITED STATES OF AMERICA

10 9 8 7 6 5 4 3 2 1

First Edition

to Leo,

son and sunshine

ACKNOWLEDGMENTS

The Dance Collection of the New York Public Library for the Performing Arts was a tremendous resource as I did research for this novel, as were the dancers I took class with at Dance Space in New York City, the Omaha Modern Dance Collective, the Omaha Academy of Ballet, The Moving Company, and the Fayetteville (AR) Dance Center. Kelly Holcombe Hanneman, former Pilobolus and Momix dancer and currently Omaha-based choreographer and yoga teacher *extraordinaire,* was a meticulous reader and an inspiring consultant. My talks with Shelley Freydont, former member of Twyla Tharp Dance, were informative. I thank the Center for Psychotherapy and Psychoanalysis at the Creighton University Department of Psychiatry for welcoming me to their seminars. My visits to the studios of painters Scott Neary, Bosiljka Raditsa, and Lanny DeVuono were informative, as were my visits to Barbara Collier's collection of vintage clothing; and also, Lanny, thanks for being a willing and kind early reader of this manuscript. Nancy Tosone, A.P.R.N., Marilyn Lowe, C.N.M., Shun Kwong, M.D., and Richard Fleming, M.S.W., generously shared their time and professional expertise. For helping me with publishing-related questions, both big and tiny, I thank Marianne Merola, Liza Dawson, Dianne Choie, and Joanne Brownstein; and I thank copy *x*

editor Terry Zaroff-Evans for bringing a reader's sensitivity and a detective's thoroughness to these pages.

I am grateful for the support I received from the Nebraska Arts Council and the University Committee on Research at the University of Nebraska at Omaha. Residencies at Yaddo and the MacDowell Colony were invaluable.

For years of fine camaraderie, I thank my students and colleagues, present and past, at the University of Nebraska at Omaha and at Eastern Washington University. For their excellent care of my son at various times during the years of rewriting, I thank the wonderful women at the Child Development Center of the University of Nebraska Medical Center, The Montessori Children's Room of Omaha, and also Melissa Schutt, Jen Hermanitt, Liz Stefaniak, Meagan Lloyd, Nicole Kulper, the Enright-Chouinard village, and Nonna Catherine.

Finally and especially: To Gail Hochman, thank you for making so much possible; your continued faith in me and my work is a gift. And to Deb Futter, *you* are a gift. First of all, for your friendship, but also for your brilliant hard work, your deep commitment to the work, and your willingness to join me in caring for these difficult characters, all I can say is *grazie. Mille mille grazie.*

. . . solos can be elaborately designed

but ensembles cannot be very complex

and retain their clarity of focus.

—Doris Humphrey,
THE ART OF MAKING DANCES

part
ONE

CHAPTER 1:

1973

Mary and Ross were in Rome on a junior-year-abroad program when they had their baby, Natassia, who was conceived on a dare: "Do it with no birth control," another couple challenged. "We'll do it if you do it." The guys dropped acid, the girls said they didn't need to, then both couples went to bed, in Ross's dorm room, on single cots pushed right up next to each other. It was 1973, September, their first month in Rome. Italy was still as hot as summer, and the semester felt more like a vacation than school. The dorm they were living in was a run-down palazzo with windows too huge for screens, so, during their first days in Rome, Ross had hung mosquito netting above the beds. Now, for privacy, the two couples pulled that sheerness between them, the only thing dividing them. Mary got pregnant, the other girl did not. Every morning that hot October, Mary threw up in the cracked marble toilet before leaving for dance class. Ross, awed by her as always and now a little afraid of her, too, watched and felt helpless. Years would pass before either of them would even begin to understand why they had done this.

MARY'S POWER as a dancer was her ability to fly. Most of her action happened a few inches off the ground. Beautiful, this flying, but it gave Ross the unsteady sensation that Mary would one day get away from him.

"I want you to have this baby," he told her. It was a chilly late-October night. They were shuffling through Piazza della Rotonda, past the Pantheon, kicking street trash back and forth between them. They'd been in Rome almost two months and Ross still had no desire to explore the place. He said it smelled just like home, like New York. He'd pretty much stopped going to classes. Lazy in the extravagant way of the very brightest college students, Ross spent his days in bed getting high on hash from Piazza Navona and reading *The New England Journal of Medicine.*

Sometimes, though, on clear nights like tonight, Mary got him to walk the streets. As they walked, they were always, always touching. In the year they'd been together, Mary's body had become the current that connected Ross to anything outside his head. Right now, her fingers were in the back pocket of his jeans, scratching.

"I found out how I could get an abortion," she said, "but I'd have to go to Florence for a weekend. I'd miss a couple rehearsals. They'd be pissed."

"You've had two abortions already." She'd had five, three before she met Ross, but Mary decided he didn't need to know that. "I think we should have a baby, see what happens." He said it casually, as if it were nothing, trying to keep the hope out of his voice and the fear out of his heart. He had no idea why he was pushing for it, he was just full of some quiet panic telling him, *Do it.*

But there was no way. Why would Mary do this? And why with *him*? Ever since Ross had known Mary, she'd been headed toward a serious career, and it was no pipe dream. She'd been performing, even soloing, with not-shabby modern-dance companies since she was fourteen. Taking up that no-birth-control dare when she knew—absolutely *knew*—she was ultra-fertile had been a kind of Russian roulette. For Mary actually to have a baby would make no sense.

But here she was, flattening her palm inside Ross's back pocket to stop him. She turned him toward her. They stood in the empty piazza, and she looked up at him. She was so tiny and he so tall, six-foot-two and stooped, with width in his shoulders and baby fat around his middle. Ross's black beard was thick enough to shave twice daily, but he got to it only a few times a week. He was just eighteen and she was almost twenty, but he felt older and responsible for her because he was so much bigger. He looked down through heavy, dark eyelashes into her hidden, lidded Korean eyes.

Often when Ross looked at Mary, he tried to picture what her birth mother might have looked like—probably young and tiny and gorgeous and roughed up by war—and it saddened him deeply that nothing would ever be known about that woman. He felt the same aching frustration now, as he stood in the lit-up dark streets of Rome holding on to Mary's shoulders, leaning over so her face was just a breath away from his. He never would know exactly what happened inside Mary the moment before she said, "Okay. Yeah."

"Yeah?" Ross smiled.

"Yeah."

So—they were having a baby. "You're sure?" he asked. "I don't want this to change things."

She pulled her hand out of his pocket and slapped his butt. "Jesus, Ross, of course it's going to change things. I'm going to get huge and fat. I'm going to have to dance lower, stay closer to the ground. I already found an African class. See?" she said. "Watch."

"Ah no, come back"—but she was off, doing some hyped-up, jumpy thing across the piazza. For Mary, the only point to Rome was these big empty spaces at night, where she could move all around however she wanted. "Ma-r-r-ry," Ross called, his voice an icy echo in the chilly night. He noticed two businessmen stop to watch her. They reminded Ross of his father, the way the men pushed the fronts of their trench coats open and shoved their hands into their trouser pockets, the way they hit that proprietary stance, watching her as if she were dancing just for them. "Mar, come back here. I was talking to you."

"Just a sec." Her voice came out breathy, from inside some spin she was doing in a far corner of the piazza. The Italians applauded, buttoned their trench coats, and moved on.

Yeah, sure. Pregnant, she was closer to the ground, but those African steps had her moving fast; her boots on the stones of the piazza were rattling like Ross's teeth. It was almost November now and it was cold.

THE WOMEN Mary met in the African class realized early, before anyone in any of her other dance classes, that she was pregnant. Mary and the African women spoke to one another with gestures and with the little Ital-

5

ian they had. The basic words of music and dance: *piano*, slow; *più presto*, faster; *forte*, hard. The women were impressed that Mary learned so quickly how to listen to the drums, that she understood how the drums were telling her to move. After a month, one of the women, an older woman called Mama Ci-Ci, looked a long minute at Mary's stomach, then put her hand there and asked, *"Grassa?"* Fat?

Mary took Mama Ci-Ci's wrist and pulled her hand out a couple of inches, to where the baby would be in a few months. *"Più grassa ancora,"* Mary told her.

Mama Ci-Ci and the others around her smiled. Mary laughed. They all laughed. Another woman took Mary's left hand, her ring finger, and asked, *"Marito?"* All the women, seven or eight of them, were listening now, and Mary said the Italian words to let them know there was no husband, there was a boyfriend, there would not be a wedding or an abortion. A few of the women shook Mary's left hand and insisted that if the man would not marry her she should not have the baby. Then Mama Ci-Ci talked fast and long in her own language, explaining to the others, it seemed, that Mary might have religious reasons—Korean reasons—for not wanting an abortion. She asked Mary this by making the sign of the cross and raising her eyebrows. Mary nodded yes. Why the hell not?

The women never guessed that Mary was American. They assumed she was like them, an immigrant, maybe working as an illegal domestic until her papers were in order, a girl just passing through Rome.

The skin of all the women was very dark. Ama was large, with hefty firm flesh on her arms; Sula, skinny like thread. Esi had hair cropped to almost nothing. Lulu and her sister wrapped their heads with big bright cloths to hold up their many braids. Mama Ci-Ci and her young niece were modest and changed for class behind a screen. All the women had tired feet. They kicked off their shoes—sandals, high heels, tennis shoes—as soon as they got in the room, and sat for a minute or so with feet exposed, toes flexing. Mary liked that. Even though they had only the two-hour lunch break, they took time for that reverent moment with their feet. Then Mama Ci-Ci called out a few loud words—Mary could never unscramble the sounds—and the drums started going, never to stop the whole time. The drummer, Ama's brother, wore sunglasses and eased down over his drums in such a sleepy way you couldn't tell if he was awake or if maybe his hands were moving through a dream. Even after Mary had been in the class a while, she still felt that rush with the first drumbeats, the sound of something big beginning to happen, a thunderstorm or some kind of ceremony, a parade.

This class was held in a tiny dark garage.

With the drumbeats, the feet dug down. Stomps, fast and syncopated. Knees bent, elbows bent, arms swinging, back leaning over, not straight. The movement was much like modern dance, and Mary caught on quickly. But this dance was new for Mary, too, and reminded her of being thirteen and standing for the first time in a modern class after years of strict classical ballet training, that stunning moment when she was told, "Go ahead, let your shoulders roll, let your wrists go limp. No need to point the toes, flex your feet. Looser arms! Swing! Bend! Melt! Roll up slowly— just in your own time." Mary still remembered every minute of that two-hour master class taught by Tim Dillon Dancers, a modern-dance company from Albany; it was like finally having your straitjacket unlocked, like getting permission to rip masking tape off of your mouth. It was like food; Mary couldn't get enough. At that point she had already been a performing ballerina for six years, but that first modern class was her birth as a dancer. Now, years later, pregnant, with the African women and the drums telling her to bend over, curl in, Mary was born into her body again. She felt her blood traveling, felt the energy moving in and out of the rooms of her heart. Mary had never had anything so lively inside herself to protect before. Rolled up, she felt as tight and compact as a nut, some perfect hard skin holding in its precious fruit.

ROSS HAD TOLD Mary there was a theory that you find what you need whether you're aware of your need or not. He said it happened to him sometimes in bookstores—his eyes would catch a title, he'd pull it off the shelf, and, bingo, he'd be holding in his hands exactly what he needed to read right then. Mary figured it was by that same principle that she had come to be with the African women.

Mary had never known her own mother, a Korean prostitute whom her father, Jerry Mudd, had spent a few nights with in a village south of Seoul in the early spring of 1952. On a hunch, Jerry had gone back to the woman nine months later, toward the end of his tour of duty, and he'd found Mary, three days old. He cried the night he told Mary how easily her mother had given her up. It was just after Mary's birthday dinner. She was five and had been asking a lot of questions about her birth. Finally, after she blew out the one candle on her Hostess cupcake, Jerry told her how much he loved her, and told her how the Korean woman had handed Mary over to him wrapped in a cotton shirt, then tossed over a necklace of braided silk thread.

"Where's the necklace?" Mary asked.

"Trash," her stepmother, Dorie, said, and walked out of the kitchen.

Jerry always followed Dorie when she walked out of a room.

They never worried about leaving Mary alone. Especially after the three boys were born, each fourteen months after the brother before him. Mary wasn't in kindergarten yet when Dorie discovered a ballet academy two blocks away. For Dorie this was better than a babysitter. The more classes Mary took, the cheaper they were. Plus, the dancing kept Mary out of the house.

One Saturday morning, Mary stood in ballet class looking at herself in the studio mirrors. She was the youngest and smallest in intermediates. The class was learning *rond de jambe en l'air*. The teacher demonstrated how they were supposed to keep the body straight, lift the right leg to the side, bend it at the knee, and circle the bottom part of the leg, keeping the rest of the leg and the body perfectly still. This required you to pull all your strength into your abdomen. "Now you try." The teacher came by and patted Mary's middle and said, "For such a skinny tummy you have a lot of strength pulled up in there. Very, *very* good. That's it! Pull everything *up*. Make yourself taller."

You were supposed to make your middle strong as iron. Make your arms light as nothing, graceful as air. Keep everything straight. Keep your hips square. Keep your shoulders square and lined up with your hips. Pull all your energy into your stomach and *up* so high you created space between your ribs. With head and hips and shoulders aligned, could you raise your leg without shifting anything else? Could you keep that leg in the air? Could your leg make circles in the air? Could you keep those circles perfect and slow?

Mary saw in the mirror she was the only one in class who could do it.

Everyone else wobbled. In the mirror she also saw that her features made her face different from all the white faces around her. That day, for the first time ever, it occurred to Mary that this difference was interesting.

"Now, everyone, stop," the dance teacher said. (Because she couldn't pronounce the woman's complicated Polish surname, Mary never addressed the teacher directly and was always nervous when the teacher spoke to her.) "Legs down. All of you, please, turn to watch Mary. Mary, dear, would you demonstrate the *rond de jambe en l'air*? Class, all eyes on Mary." With everyone watching her, Mary did the difficult step. She had no choice but to watch herself in the mirror. And though she saw she was doing the *rond de jambe* perfectly, she felt no pride, just a detached curiosity. Mary felt no more connection than that to the image in the dance-studio mirror. What she felt strongly, for the first time ever, was the gap between what she saw of herself on the outside and what was inside her—a landscape as bleak as the upstate New York town where the Mudds lived.

Mary had always known she had something special about her. The story of the miracle of her father's finding her newborn had proved that. Just that he'd gone to the trouble of looking for her made it clear to Mary that she was worthwhile. But her father was so weak, crying often, so nervous around Dorie, Mary couldn't love the spots on her face where she saw she was like him—his skinny nose, his soft chin. She preferred to focus on all the ways in which she was different from the other Mudds and everyone around her—her narrow, uplifted eyes; her golden skin; her coarse dark hair; her smallness; her perfect dance form. And yet the gap. There was nothing inside her that matched the outside of her. Mary was exotic even to herself.

At the end of class, the teacher held Mary back and asked her, "Mary, for a minute there you looked like you were almost going to cry."

"No!"

"You can be a ballerina, my dear. Surely you can have that, but you will have to work, yes? Toughen up!"

Mary never knew what had made the woman think Mary wasn't tough, that she was going to cry. Mary had already trained herself not to cry.

Years later, in Rome, dancing in the garage with Lulu and Mama Ci-Ci and Sula and Ama and the other African women, surrounded by all their dark, warm flesh, Mary felt the gap within her being filled. She felt in the presence of what she imagined when she imagined *Mother.* It was here, pounding the floor, not flying, staying in one place, digging in as if to claim a spot of earth, pound it down, making wild noises, that Mary began to believe she was going to have a child.

AFTER THE AFRICAN CLASS—even in those sleepy first months—Mary ran to a different part of town to do an hour of barre work, then she rushed to Via del Gesú to rehearse with Teatrodanza. They were the only professional modern-dance company in Rome—maybe in all of Italy— but Tim Dillon had given her a contact, and Mary had auditioned and got in. She danced full-out in every class and rehearsal; no way was she letting them know she was pregnant, not until she really had to.

When she finally got back to the dorm after all those hours of dance, Ross loved the scent on her. Early evening, he'd be sitting by the window in his stuffed armchair, writing in his journal, entries of self-analysis to send back to his psychiatrist in New York. As Mary walked in, Ross put aside his notebook and his pipe, pulled her onto his lap. "I adore you, do you know that?" Talking to Mary, talking about her, he often used the word "adore."

"You're so comfortable," she told him, "like a piece of furniture."

"Climb onto me, baby. Climb all over."

YOUNG AS SHE WAS, Mary didn't kid herself. She knew she didn't adore Ross. But she had never known anyone—no friends, no family—she liked so much. He had tried to ask her a few times, in quiet middle-of-the-night moments after making love, "Why're you having a baby with a loser like me?" and all Mary could do was turn away from him. The dare still con- founded her, both in its stupidity and in the power it had had over her: a se- duction she hadn't managed to steer clear of. When, of course, she got knocked up, an even scarier thing had happened—Mary could find nothing inside herself to help her turn away from this particular pregnancy. After each of her abortions, there had been a feeling of relief, a release, when she got her next period; now that same easier breathing came to her each month when she saw there was no blood. *What* inside her was insisting on this baby?

Ross kept telling her, "Everybody thinks this is the coolest thing."

"Yeah, well, they're morons." The kids they were in school with knew nothing about dance. Having a baby at twenty was, basically, a dancer's death wish (and years—years—would pass before Mary would begin to have even a clue why she'd decided to do it). Back then, when Ross asked her, Why?, the only thing she could think of to say was "So she'll have a chance for nice long dance legs, like yours."

"So she's going to be a dancer?" Ross asked, and, "She's going to be a she, huh?" Mary turned toward him, nudged him onto his side, and for the rest of the night pressed her fattening self up against his back. With her body growing right out of her leotards, as out of control of herself as she was, what could she tell Ross? In her way, as best she could, she cared for him.

He didn't have the body intelligence she had, but Mary loved it that Ross could do with words what she could do with her body: create illusion, convince, transport, seduce. She loved him a lot the day they were called in to talk with Dean Margaret Greco about Mary's pregnancy.

The word in the pipeline was that Mary and Ross were going to be kicked out of school. "Nervous?" everyone asked them.

"No way," Ross said. "This is our ticket to ride."

The two of them stood at the closed door of the ballroom that was the dean's office. Ross was carrying his backpack like a briefcase. He leaned down and kissed Mary for good luck. She slipped him the tongue.

They knocked. The heavy door opened. Dean Greco stood there dressed in her signature white, lots of pearls. "W-e-l-l," she said. She was a Southern belle gone awry—an expatriate, divorced from an Italian diplomat she'd met during her debutante tour abroad in 1958.

"Please, have a seat," she said, and motioned for them to take the reconstructed Louis XIV chairs in front of her desk.

"We're glad you called us in," Ross said. "We'd been hoping to get a chance to talk to you."

"Why, I'm always available to talk," she said, "you *know* that. You just know that. Anytime." Mary smiled. It came up often—how Greco wasn't available for students. Ross had her on the defensive already. Mary just had to sit back and enjoy.

"I'm sure you've heard our news," Ross began, "that Mary is expecting our child."

"Yes, I heard. In fact—well, first, have you told your parents about this development?"

"Absolutely," Ross said.

In a lower voice, the dean asked, "Mary?"

"Yeah," Mary lied. Her family didn't even know she was in Italy. A couple years had passed since she'd talked to them. She'd been too busy trying to do two things at once: have a dance career and prep for some non-dance career that would inevitably have to follow. College was barely paid for by scholarship and loans and money she earned dancing Fosse-style jazz on a Caribbean cruise ship during the summer. Mary had been in the dance program at SUNY Purchase for two years, but the academic stuff had just not worked for her. She'd gone on the junior-year-abroad program because she could be with Ross and get college credit, and Teatrodanza liked foreign dancers and the company was getting attention. If she had the chance to perform with them for a year, Tim Dillon Dancers might have a spot for her when she went back to New York. Even if they didn't, she'd be way ahead of where she'd been before. Already Mary was paranoid about the shelf life of her career. Her parents were the least of her problems, but the dean kept pushing.

"So—your parents, they do know?"

As she sat in the tall, ornate chair, Mary's feet didn't touch the floor. She pulled them up under her, like a kid at a movie, and yawned. She really was sleepy these days. When Mary said nothing, Greco looked at Ross. "And your families' reactions?"

"Joyous," Ross said, "as expected. As the occasion demands."

"You do understand, don't you, that your families will have to help you with the medical arrangements." Ross nodded and let there be a long beat of silence.

"W-e-l-l." The dean was pushing away from her desk, giving them a full look at her long white-stockinged legs. "Is there anything else you-all'd like from me? Besides, of course, giving you my very best wishes, is there anything I can do?"

"Yes," Ross said, "there is." Mary knew pretty much nothing about the publishing business Ross's father was in. She did know, though, that he was a major operator, and now, seeing Ross cross one leg over the other and lean forward, a gesture that was both intimate and businesslike, Mary knew she was seeing David Stein, New York book editor, at work. It came naturally to Ross, that instinct to look in the eye, keep the voice down, concede a few points—he had that innate savvy.

"This pregnancy," Ross said in a voice gilded already with the sobriety of fatherhood, "we see it as an important opportunity toward growth for us. We want to make the most of it." Reaching down into his open backpack, he looked away from Greco, and the dean followed him with her eyes. Mary saw that Ross had the power of a lodestone. He pulled out a manila folder thick with papers, held it in his hand, not giving it up yet, making Greco lean forward, reach for it. Then, for a second, he hesitated, so the dean's hand was suspended there, empty.

"Why, what is it?" By the time he gave it to her, she couldn't wait to have it in her hands.

It was a twenty-page outline for an independent study that Mary and Ross privately called "Fucking for Credit," but the title on the cover sheet was "An Interdisciplinary Exploration of the Prenatal State as Experienced Through the Prisms of Science, Dance, Art, and Literature." What the paper proposed was that Mary and Ross would chart the pregnancy and get a bunch of credits.

"My," the dean said, "this is different."

"We knew you would connect with it." Mary got such a kick out of watching Ross, how he kept that sincere pinch between his eyes, even while they were talking total bullshit. He was like Twyla Tharp choreography, witty. Ross turned to Mary. "See, Mar. I told you we could depend on Dean Greco to back us up."

Greco blushed, Mary winced. Greco really did have a thing for Ross. Mary had always suspected it, that's why she'd worn her peasant dress with the deep U-neck. It showed cleavage. Mary was starting to have cleavage, and though she was terrified by her new heft, she did know how to use her body to get an important point across. Greco leaned forward, her blouse dipping open a bit farther, as if on cue, and said, "W-e-l-l. Well, I just need you to explain to me a bit what exactly you-all've got in mind here."

"Well, it's simple—"

"Yes, I'm just a little—"

"No, you're right. We should explain. What we are proposing is that

13

through the varied and layered lenses of physiology, psychology, movement, dance, poetry, folklore, photography, and personal journal we will trace the development of the embryo now firmly planted in Mary's uterus and—"

"Yes, well." After "uterus," Dean Greco wasn't going to ask anything more.

"There's just one last point we feel is important with this independent study."

"Yes?"

"What we're proposing here is extensive." Ross spread his wide hands on the desk in front of him. "It's big. And as I said, it means a lot to us. Heck"—Mary loved that, "Heck"—"it's the birth of our child. We want to give this program of study our full attention." Ross's fingers tapped the desk, as if he'd just completed a difficult task there. "Naturally, we're going to have to drop our other coursework."

It was only a matter of time—less than a week—before Dean Greco approved Fucking for Credit. When Mary and Ross got the word, with a note brought to them in the dining room at dinner, Mary went after Ross with a heat that surprised them both. She made him leave his tortellini, made him go upstairs to their room, pulled a mattress onto the floor, and tied his wrists lightly with scarves to the legs of his desk. She slipped her hands inside his jeans and slid them down over his hips, over their firm skinniness. God, how she loved the taste of his skin. "Yes," he moaned. "I love this."

Maybe then, that one night, after the meeting with Greco, Mary adored Ross. She was flamed up to realize how good he was at what he was good at. And heating it up hot-white that night in Rome was the dash of jealousy, the way the dean was so willing to melt for Ross.

What Mary didn't know was the thing Ross had never told her, because, in ways, he was older than his age, already practicing the discretion he would be a master of years later, when he was a doctor. Ross knew how to use people's weaknesses to get what he wanted, but he also knew it was important to handle any weakness of the soul gently. What Ross never told Mary or any of the other students was that occasionally Dean Greco handed him a fistful of lire and asked him to go to Piazza Navona to buy her any numbing shit he could find. He brought her small amounts and gave back her change. "Oh, Ross, this is all you got?"

"That's all they had this time," Ross lied. More than supplying her, he was medicating her. The semester after Mary and Ross graduated, while she was relying on another student, Greco overdosed. Years later, Ross would remember the dean as the first and only patient he ever lost.

THE AGREEMENT was that Mary and Ross would drop all their classes but one. Mary stayed in art history, since the course was mostly just going around to churches to look at art. Ross stayed in European Novel, because he'd already read everything on the reading list. They lived then in a state of perfect freedom. They didn't have to do anything they didn't want to do. There was more time for Mary to dance, more time for Ross to read and take drugs. The drugs helped him keep up with her energy, and at the same time Mary was getting bigger and a bit slower. Before, she'd always kept her thick blue-black hair short, a fringe, but now she was letting it grow longer. Ross liked that, he could hold on when he was inside her. She stayed still longer, she didn't mind the anchor of him so much. Some mornings, he woke and found Mary sleeping with her face on his stomach.

"Hey," he'd whisper, "hey, Mary, come on up here."

"Not yet." Was it because of his scent, Mary wondered, that she wanted, *needed*, to latch on to him?

There was hardly any distance between them now. Years later, when they were separating, both of them made a point of telling Natassia that the time in their history when they were most completely together was those months in Rome when they were waiting for her.

FOR THE INDEPENDENT STUDY, Mary choreographed her first solos for herself. At SUNY Purchase, she'd choreographed a duet and an ensemble piece and got good grades, but it had all felt like homework, which is what it had been. Now the impulse to create dance came from within her as, week by week, her body grew. Fairly early in the pregnancy, her center of gravity began to shift, causing Mary to lose balance, even fall. Quickly, privately, she made small adjustments to the pieces she was performing with Teatrodanza. At first the adjustments were just frantic efforts to protect her secret. Those early months, she was frantic a lot. She'd always had mild asthma; now she needed to do daily meditation to keep her breathing steady. *A twenty-year-*

old dancer with a baby. I'm fucking crazy! But Mary's secret pregnancy tuned her in to her body more intimately than dance ever had. In the dorm room at night, she let the small adjustments evolve into longer phrases of movement; then, when her secret was out and her director was finding ways to work with it, Mary created a series of dances on herself, and this was her birth as a choreographer.

Ross wanted to call the series "Gravità," which in Italian means "seriousness" and "gravity," and brings to mind *gravida,* which means "pregnant," but Mary just called them "The Pregnant Dances." In a rare lucid moment, Dean Greco asked Mary if she'd do a few small performances in the school's theater. Students came from all the different Rome study programs. Mary packed them in. The story had gone around town about the couple who had got knocked up on a dare and now were getting *mucho* credits for nothing but watching the girl's stomach expand. But after the first performance, in November, they came because word got out about how good Mary was.

She wasn't flying as much as she used to, but she was still quick. People watched. There was the thrill of her speed across the stage, and there was the magic act of her transitions from shape to shape. There she'd be, small and pulled into a contraction, and in the next second she'd be huge, arms and legs stretched out so wide they'd be reaching into the wings.

In February, when everyone was back from break, she performed again. It was her sixth month. She wore a white leotard under a white silk slip from the flea market. Ross stood in the back of the audience for this one. In November, he'd sat in the front row, but something about it had been weird for him.

He couldn't figure it out, spent a lot of time doing self-analysis in his journal. Why didn't he like her pregnant performance? In their dorm room, Mary's dancing did nothing but turn him on and on; when she was onstage, though, he could barely watch. Was he jealous that she had all the attention? Or jealous that everyone was getting a look at what her body could do? Yet he also felt an icky pride that his friends were getting a glimpse of what he got every night. Standing in back, leaning up against the wall, he felt the crowd turn liquid. Mary was doing the slowest glide downstage with her head thrown back and the top of her body arched back and up, and even with that white silk draping her full breasts and her wide middle, her sexiness wasn't the thing that caught everyone. The room wasn't turned on, Ross could tell. What they were was alert. Mary was forcing everyone to see there was some way for their bodies to move that they'd forgotten about or never known.

At center stage, Mary lifted up from her arched position, brought her head up to face the audience. Tiny as she was, she had turned grand on the stage. Ross felt he'd never seen a taller person. He knew she was spotting the back wall—maybe his head was her centering spot. He imagined her gaze grazing the top of his height, focusing with such power he felt compressed by it, compressed and made small. For eight slow counts, she just stood there, and the audience seemed not to breathe. Ross noticed people's heads dipped to the side, watching for what she was going to do next. What she did was lift her arms, spread them at her sides. Balanced, still as stone, she began to raise one leg, bent at the knee, and the music crescendoed as the leg straightened and lifted high in front of her. Moving absolutely nothing else, she glided the raised leg to her side.

There was the music and the slow leg and then this thing Ross noticed as it moved across her face. A sadness so stern and forbidding it opened Mary's eyes wider than usual and slackened her mouth, as if she herself were surprised by it. His weight slumped against the wall, his head hit the base of a brass light sconce. Watching Mary dance, Ross was haunted by a premonition: There's danger for me in this.

Before she was pregnant, Mary's dances had been fast, and her hair flew, and only once in a while could you find her face. Before, she could hide. But tonight here she was, dressed in winter white, just like Dean Greco, and, with her hair pulled back and her face exposed, Mary looked as sad as Greco. This, *this* was what got Ross. Mary's face while she danced onstage showed him pain she never told him about, not in talk or in lovemaking. Pain that was the eggplant color of her hair, slippery-surfaced, too hard to puncture, a sadness with depths and depths. Watching her perform, he knew it was beyond him. She would leave him. He knew he was too young to be feeling already the limits of his power to love her, but there it was.

When the pivot of her leg was almost unbearable in its slowness, Mary broke the spell, swung the leg behind her, turned her back to the audience to begin a series of spins. Ross hated that everyone saw the marking on her back—her Mongolian spot, an oblong birthmark floating between her shoulder blades, that small, shallow valley he could fill up with just one of his hands.

IN HER SEVENTH MONTH, she did her last pregnant performance to the happy section of Keith Jarrett's *Köln Concert*. With her body feeling as huge as a continent, her weight stunningly awkward, Mary decided her choreography needed to include Ross. He couldn't believe she'd actually talked him into doing it. She made him dress in black and get onstage, and she held on to his shoulders, arms, and knees while she did arabesques. The music was quick, and her movement was slow. He balanced her while she did extensions. Mary had told him, No matter what happens we keep going to the end of the music. Her stomach was hugely distended but she got her leg right up there, rested it on Ross's chest, held it four counts, turned.

LATE REHEARSAL is always the best, Mary thought. The dance is perfect by then. You're dancing for yourself and the other dancers, no audience yet. Onstage, you had to make so many adjustments—for the space, the sound, costumes, the lights. The makeup made the performance even smell different from rehearsal. Mary never expected much from performances.

That early-June night at the hospital when the baby was born, Mary knew for sure she loved Ross. Just like at the meeting with Dean Greco, his performance was first-rate.

It was past midnight when she went into labor. No taxis. They paid a night guard at the school to drive them to the hospital. The male nurses at the admitting station were sleepy. Mary felt the pains curving upward. She was starting to get scared. At the double doors of the labor room, two nurses tried to make Ross wait outside. Ross blocked the door and wouldn't let them wheel Mary in. By now she was growling. The nurses kept yelling in Italian that Mary had to go in alone, without Ross.

"*Impossibile!*" Ross yelled back. His accent was very good. He wouldn't budge from the doorway until the doctor finally arrived, waving his arms, complaining about the noise. Ross grabbed the doctor's hand. *"Grazie, dottore."* Ross's Italian was sharp enough that he could, quickly, make the doctor understand that Ross must be allowed to stay with Mary throughout the entire delivery. Ross's parents had sent bound galleys of a book on natural childbirth and had told him that he should not, under any circumstances, leave Mary alone in an Italian hospital.

Mary sat in a wheelchair hugging her stomach, her feet raised onto the chipped tile wall to anchor herself against the galloping pains. "Fuck," she howled, "fucking fuck!" while Ross explained to the doctor, "In all the hospitals in Manhattan, this is how it is done, with the father in the delivery room." Picking up on the doctor's hip sideburns and bell-bottoms, Ross had understood how much it would mean to the doctor to do things as they were done in New York.

So, because Ross was very smart, Mary had him next to her for the entire delivery. Neither Mary nor Ross took any drugs. There she was on the table, there they were under the lights. A perfect performance.

THAT NIGHT, Mary came so close to something she hadn't known she wanted—her wish for a partner. Mary had never relied on anyone. Her stepmother had been useless, her half-brothers Mary had just ignored, and her father had had that weak streak that embarrassed her. The only useful lesson had come from the stranger who was her birth mother: Shed burdens, travel light, move ahead alone.

Mary had assumed early on that the journey of her life was hers, and the burdens were hers. Even as a child, she'd understood without anyone's spelling it out for her that dance was her best chance for survival. When she imagined a successful dance career, she never imagined grandeur, just the means to keep body and soul together, a different version of her father going to his warehouse job or her stepmother showing up at the restaurant she managed. So Mary did what she had to do and never talked to anyone about how terrified she was onstage. Nothing was lonelier than performing. Even in an ensemble, she could depend only so much on the other dancers. Her own body and the music were all she had when she performed. No matter how slowly she stepped out of the wings, she felt she was being chased, savage animals coming after her. She wished she could scramble up a steep tree, escape. Music was the firm branch, the counts were tree limbs, and if she could swing herself from count to count, she could save herself.

But the night she was giving birth to Natassia, the pain jagged up all the way into her ears, and she couldn't hear a thing, even though she and Ross had practiced and practiced the breathing. This was it, she was finally going to fuck up. The damn baby was going to turn Mary inside out, show the secret of what was inside her: nothing but panic where other people had heart and lungs and blood. Ross was the calm one; he kept the beat and stayed close-close to her ear, counting, breathing loudly so she could hear him over the racket of her own grunting screams.

THE WEEKEND the baby was born, Ross was supposed to be writing a paper on *War and Peace*, so they chose the name Natassia, the Italian version of "Natasha."

Natassia was huge, two armfuls of buttery flesh, and wanted to eat all the time. After the birth, Mary wrote to Nora, her best and only real friend: "This breastfeeding thing is cool, but it goes really slow. It reminds me of slow-dancing in tenth grade to 'Hey Jude.' Remember that foreign-exchange student from Scotland, how I always ended up dancing with him because he was short? Remember how we could never understand a word he said, even when he was talking English?"

Mary had forgotten the name of the boy from Glasgow, but she could still hear him trying to talk to her about what it was like back where he was from, as if she cared. The way he strangled his words, it sounded like he was sending up messages from the pit of a well. In a few months, her class would start doing drugs, but that fall they were all still pretty straight, dancing in somebody's candlelit rec room. Mary hated the incense, burning for no reason, smothering them with some stink that was supposed to be cool. She just wanted the music to end so they'd be released from the stupor of "Hey Jude."

But also, for as long as the song lasted, she couldn't lift her head off the Scottish guy's shoulder, she couldn't let go of the scent of him. Warm, woody, something like outside but like inside, too, not like food but like wafts off of a wood-burning fire. (It was the homespun wool of his sweater, she found out later; all the other boys she knew back then wore 100-

percent acrylic or army surplus.) So she wrapped her arms around his shoulders, bunched his sweater in her fists. His hands rubbed down to her waist but no farther. Once he realized he didn't have to talk to her, he seemed content to rock in the slow dark. And Mary just wanted to hang on, sluggish and mesmerized, to his unknowable scent.

From the first days the baby was out of her body, Mary treated Natassia like a foreign-exchange student, someone who was purportedly interesting but who, in truth, was merely skirting the edges of the real business of Mary's life. Now that the baby was out, Mary was panicked about losing weight and getting back to dancing seriously again, which was the only way Mary knew how to make a living, which she had better get busy doing now if she was going to keep this baby alive. While pregnant, Mary had lost almost two months of performances. Since the birth, she'd missed five days of classes. Breastfeeding, she felt pulled down, held in a place where she couldn't afford to linger. The hours of sitting with her peasant shirt untied. The baby's sweaty head resting in this elbow or that one. The baby got fussy if Mary stood and did leg lifts or foot flexes while she breastfed. Even if Mary sat somewhere, at attention, the baby didn't want her doing head rolls or rolling her shoulder joints.

"I hate this," Mary said, but the baby wouldn't take a bottle.

"Come on, Mar, it's only for a couple months. It's a couple hours a day."

"I hate *you*," Mary told Ross, and she left their dorm room and carried Natassia up to the roof terrace. Summer now, no breeze anywhere in Rome. Clay-pipe roofs, plastic-enclosed balconies, pigeons on TV antennas, pigeon shit on the carved stone railing. The palazzo rose taller than almost all the surrounding buildings, and the neighborhood kitchens were sending up an overheated olive-oil smell that closed the evening in all around Mary. How stupid to think that Ross could help her carry this off, idiotic to think they could make something like a family.

After a few minutes, he showed up, pushed open the creaking terrace gate. "Want me to write up a proposal so you get extra credit for breastfeeding?"

She wouldn't look at him. "I *don't* hate the baby."

"I know you don't." He sat behind her on the garden table, wrapped his legs and arms around her and Natassia.

"It's too hot, Ross."

"I don't care. I want to hug you two."

Pulled down by the baby's mouth, pressed down by Ross's chest leaning on her back, sluggish and miserable as she was, Mary felt inebriated right then with the baby's scent. Damn baby, didn't she understand how badly things could fall apart if Mary didn't keep dancing? But Natassia kept pulling, and Mary dipped her face into Natassia's neck, couldn't get enough, couldn't understand it, that combination of milk, infant sweat, skin.

"Smell her," she told Ross, "just smell her neck and her head and her skin."

"I know. It's some sweet-smelling part of the inside of you she brought with her when she danced out from between your legs."

"She didn't dance out. She was like a herd of buffalo."

What bothered Ross was his suspicion that the hardest thing for Mary to accept was the possibility that there was something sweet and intoxicating inside herself.

For a long time, quietly, they studied the baby. After a while, Mary said, "She has finger-toes. Did you see that, how long her toes are?"

"My mother's toes are like that."

"She's going to be tall, like five-eleven or something."

"Want to hear a true fact?" Ross asked. "Natassia's eyeballs are the same size right now as they'll be when she's a grown-up woman. Her nose and ears'll keep growing, but not the eyes. Man, can you see her grown-up, what a knockout our girl's going to be?"

"That's good," Mary said, "about the eyeballs." Natassia's eyes were predominantly round, but Mary had been examining them for any slanting tendency that might develop. So far, it wasn't there, nothing Korean in the baby's face, and Mary was relieved.

When the feeding was finally over, Mary leaned back onto Ross and they watched the baby perform. "She's not a buffalo," Ross said. Mary had to admit that there wasn't a false movement in the baby's hands and feet. Infant Natassia moved with a perfect rolling gracefulness. It was beautiful, un-self-conscious movement, Mary could see that, but the fat on Natassia's arms flowed over her wrists. "She looks like a sumo wrestler."

"No! Look at her smile. Look at her lips. She has that same mouth-pout you have. Let me look. I love your gorgeous lips."

"Ross, not now. I'm too tired."

"Sweetie, come on, look at her. Look how she gives that smile away out of the corner of her mouth, just like you. She's just like you."

"She is *not* like me," Mary insisted. Then they just looked at each other. Even Mary could hear that this didn't sound right, but all she could do was quietly add, "She really isn't like me. She's a completely different body type."

FIFTEEN YEARS LATER, Natassia was five-foot-seven, six inches taller than her mother. For the most part, she'd been raised by Ross's parents, Lotte and David Stein, and she still lived with them. Ross and Mary had split up for good when Natassia was five. Ross went to the Northwest to do his residency in family medicine. Mary took off with Tim Dillon Dancers, which at that time was booked in every large city in the world. Natassia's grandparents enrolled Natassia in a Montessori program on the Upper West Side, and she went to live with them in their crammed-with-books apartment on West End Avenue.

Lotte and David were in their mid-fifties then, well established in their careers and in their habits, but they changed their lives for Natassia. And Natassia was an exceptional child, smart and flexible, able to find her place, even as a little girl, in her grandparents' world, which was mostly literary, full of publishing people and writers. By age four, Natassia was reading her own bedtime stories. Though reading was her first passion, she, like her father, had an aptitude for science. By age eight, she could name all the major constellations, even though she lived in Manhattan, where she rarely saw a star. The summer before seventh grade, she memorized much of the Periodic Table, and she and her father, by long-distance telephone, quizzed each other on the abbreviations of the chemical elements and their various properties.

At fifteen, Natassia played the violin well enough to be invited to join her grandfather's Tuesday-night string quartet. She was an honors student who could name most of the major works by the major writers of the nineteenth and twentieth centuries and had read many of them. Natassia's face was not pretty but full of a placid, unostentatious loveliness. Her natural expression was a no-nonsense gaze that made adults think twice about ever talking down to her. She had long legs, excellent coordination, and no desire to dance. At least in this, Mary found some consolation. She never wished on her daughter a dancer's life, or really very much of anything that Mary herself had lived. It seemed that, every time Mary returned from a tour, Natassia was exceptional in some new way. When she considered Natassia's varied talents and accomplishments, Mary knew she could take no credit. Lotte and David were the ones who had shaped Natassia. Mary knew she had no right to feel pride. What she felt for her daughter was awe.

Mary and Nora were at Nora's beach shack in Greenport for the weekend. Sunday night, out on the deck. Even this far from the city, way out on the tip of the North Fork of Long Island, even this close to the water, the night was thick. The bugs were bad. Nora was in her cotton nightgown, Mary in her underwear and a T-shirt, both of them lying back in wooden deck chairs, held in the navy-blue canvas slings. Two bottles of Chardonnay—one empty, one three-quarters gone—stood at the foot of the chairs. It was late enough that one of them could have said, I'm going to bed now. But neither one did. And then Mary dropped her cigarette butt into the empty wine bottle and said, "If you promise to keep your mouth shut, I'll tell you something you're not supposed to know."

"Tell," Nora said.

"You can't breathe a microsyllable of this to anyone, not even Giulia." Their friend Giulia Di Cuore was at the beach with them, but she'd already gone upstairs to bed. "I swear, tell nobody, or you're dead meat."

Nora stretched out her body's long length, showed the pale undersides of her sunburnt arms, wound her white hair into a rope, and twisted it into a chignon; her gestures, as always, were full of unconscious elegance. "Come on," she said, yawning. "What?"

"It's about Natassia." Mary used the tip of a fresh cigarette to go after a mosquito.

"Your sweet baby girl?" Nora asked, yawning again.

"Baby girl, my ass. Out of nowhere, I find out she's got this guy, this boyfriend."

"Natassia's fifteen. Think what we were doing when we were—"

"Let me finish, please. This boyfriend—this schmuck—he's, like, in his twenties. Maybe even thirties. And he's shtupping her. Regularly."

Nora's hands stopped twisting her hair. She turned her full attention to Mary.

"I found condoms in her backpack," Mary said. "A huge box, half empty—"

"But what . . ." Nora interrupted. In addition to being very tall, Nora was, in her work life, Nora Conolly, Ph.D., a therapist, so people always paid attention to her questions. Right now Mary was extra-alert to hear what Nora was going to say next. "What did you say to her?" Nora asked.

"I said, 'What are these for?' "

"And she said?"

"I'm her mother. She told me the bullshit you tell your mother. 'I met this totally great guy, I'm in love.' " Mary had the cigarette up close in her face and was biting down hard on the cuticles around her gnawed thumbnail.

"What do you know about this boy?"

"He's no boy, Nora. He's a man."

Nora's hands let her coiled hair fall. "Who is he?"

"That's where Baby Girl Natassia is being a sneaky little fink, just like me. She won't tell me anything about him, not even his name. She calls him the Boyfriend. Or the BF, for short. All she'll tell me is he's the stars and the moon and so in love with her—"

"And you feel he's older?"

"I don't *feel* it, Nora, I know it. Plus, he's some kind of a foreigner. I found stuff in her drawers, notes he wrote. He has that handwriting they have in Europe. You know? The way Christopher writes—"

"Christopher?"

"I'm sorry, but your husband has weird handwriting. Those extra loops, and the lines through the sevens? I said to her, 'I know he's foreign. Tell me where he's from,' and she says to me, 'Did it ever occur to you that you're a foreigner?' " Mary smashed her cigarette against the lip of the bottle. "Little twit."

"You are half Korean."

"*She's* not. She's Jewish. What she is is a sucker, falling for some green-card slut."

"Describe the notes." Nora's insistence on getting information was offering Mary no comfort.

"I almost puked. It was all this intimate, predatory stuff."

"Like what?"

"Like in one note he's talking about her neck, wanting to take a weekend to do nothing but kiss her neck. Another note's about her breasts. You know she's got those huge breasts, like her grandmother. Then he says—I'm quoting this—'You are not here and my work is hard. I am hard. I think of you. I want you here, naked, on my lap.' "

"He wrote that?" Their chairs had been lined up facing the water; now Nora turned her chair to look at Mary, who noticed that Nora's face had turned as pale as her hair. Mary and Nora's friendship was long and void of bullshit, their bond stronger than sisters'.

Low and rough, Mary asked, "It's bad, isn't it? This shit this guy's writing in these notes, it's bad. Natassia's in trouble, isn't she?"

Nora almost whispered, "You don't need me to tell you that, not if he's as old as you guess he is."

From within a cloud of smoke: "I'm a rotten mother."

"No, you're not." Nora really was whispering now. "You're not a bad mother. You just don't like being a mother."

"I hate being a mother. I love Natassia. I adore Natassia, but I wish I wasn't her mother. I wish she was my mother." Mary reached down for the bottle of wine, emptied it into her glass without offering any to Nora. "She's more reasonable, she's more patient than me. She's so damn responsible. Like even now, with this whole boyfriend thing, her first lover, and she's reading ahead in her chemistry book, for God's sake, and school doesn't start for a week." Nora's smile seemed so sad that Mary's stomach started roiling. "Remember," Mary whispered, "what a knockout little baby she was?" Infant Natassia had had a sheen like the surface of pearls on her cheeks and forehead and chin.

"She still is," Nora whispered back, "very beautiful."

"Who?" Giulia stepped out onto the deck. "I can't sleep, it's so hot. What about Natassia?"

"I was hardly ever around for the kid when she was small."

"Mary, don't do that to yourself." More than anything, these three women tried to be good mothers to one another. Giulia reached for Mary's glass to get a sip of the last of the wine. "You're around now, aren't you? You're doing everything you can. You took the teaching job upstate—"

"Which I hate."

"—so you could be closer to her. You quit the dance company."

"I quit the company because I got tired of performing."

"And because you were injured," Nora added.

"That had nothing to do with it. I performed for twenty years with injuries. I danced with a herniated disk for six whole months. I danced with asthma and bronchial infections and fevers. That injury wasn't why I quit."

"So in the long run this is good," Giulia insisted, "for Natassia and for you. You're being kinder to your body now."

"Less abusive maybe," Mary said.

"Well, whatever, it's good."

"Yeah, whatever." As Giulia handed back the glass, Mary shook her head. "Nah, finish it."

With the wineglass, Giulia headed back inside. "Nora, I'm taking the kitchen fan upstairs into the hallway, okay?"

"Fine." After they heard Giulia's footsteps reach the top of the inside stairs, Nora asked Mary, "Have you talked to Ross?"

"Ross?" Mary lit a new Camel and coughed out smoke. "What can he do? He's across the frigging country. Who the hell even knows where Spokane, Washington, is? He's working in the hospital day and night. All he does when Natassia has a problem is throw a fit over the phone and then he sends money. Besides, he's mad at me."

"How come?" Nora asked.

"It's stupid. Lotte and I have been after him to make his will. Like, you'd think if you were smart enough to be a doctor you'd know that you need a will, especially if you've got money and a kid and a live-in girlfriend. Anyway, he finally made the will. Then we had to decide who we were naming as Natassia's guardians, in case something happens to both of us or to his parents."

"You have a will? That's impressive."

"Lotte shamed me into it. Anyway, Ross is holding us all up because he's trying to decide if he should name Harriet as the guardian instead of you and Christopher. Harriet sounds nice on the phone, but he's only been with her—what?—two years? So I'm—"

"Me and Christopher?" Nora dipped her hand so deeply into her white hair her gold wedding bands disappeared. "Oh, Mary." It was a moan. When Nora lowered her hand, her fingers were trembling. "Mary, you don't want us. Ross is right."

"Nora." Mary leaned toward her and caught that scent that was always on Nora's skin—moisturizer Christopher made for her from olive oil and lanolin and vanilla, a scent constantly connecting Nora to her husband. Nora could be a pain sometime, but Christopher had a wide-open heart, and the two of them together were as solid as they come. Just like Ross's parents. Mary felt reverent before these people's marriages. Of course Nora and Christopher were the right choice to be Natassia's guardians. "You're not telling me you wouldn't do it."

"But, Mary—"

"Nora, relax. If you fucked up, Christopher would know what to do. He's always known what to do with Natassia. He's the one who could talk some sense into her about this boyfriend business."

"Christopher *can't* talk to Natassia about that, Mary."

"No-ra, what's with you tonight?" There'd been a time, ages ago, right after Nora's parents died, when Mary had had to worry about Nora, but Nora had been better now for a good ten years. "Come on, hon, relax."

"Listen," Nora began, tilting her head back into the canvas chair, and Mary, watching her, was thinking, With a neck that long she should have been a ballerina. "Mary, I know you hate it when I say this, but why not find a good therapist?"

Mary leaned her head back, too, but closed her eyes to the night sky. She felt a wash of weariness, that awareness she'd had lately that the words and gestures used to tell the truth almost always hid the truth. She still hadn't told Nora or Giulia or Natassia or anybody about Dr. Cather, the psychologist she'd started therapy with almost three months earlier. "My daughter just turned fifteen," Mary had said at that first session. "It's time for us to start living together, but I don't know how to do it." And Dr. Cather had said, "Can you start by telling me a little of how the two of you have been living until now?" Mary didn't know why she was being so hush-hush about Cather. Probably because every time she had a session she thought about quitting.

Nora reached over and touched the arm of Mary's chair. "Won't you do it? For Natassia?"

Mary sighed. She and Nora never kept secrets from each other, and now, with Nora being so earnest, Mary felt like a fraud. She knew that on the surface her outrage looked convincing. Her daughter was having regular sex with a man who was maybe twice the kid's age, maybe even as old as Mary, thirty-five, and from some godforsaken place where they home-brewed vodka out of potatoes or made their dinner out of dogs. Of course Mary had reason to be worried. Deep inside, though, she was outraged for all the wrong reasons.

"I could give you names, Mary. *Good* people."

"Oh, Nora, *please.*"

And then the friends were silent for a long time (their fourth-grade peevishness), until there was a crack of dry lightning far off in the sky. Then they were silent a while longer, then Nora went inside to return a phone call from Christopher.

AS SOON AS SHE WAS ALONE, Mary stepped off the deck, onto the beach. She could feel little bugs flying up out of the damp sand. This sickened her. Smoking, she walked to the water's edge. Stood there. A soft, warm wave rolled up, wet her bare feet, rolled away. Then a big wave reached her knees and pulled way back, leaving Mary standing on a smooth wet stage of sand. Full moon, pale light all over the place. Mary's limbs felt heavy. Smoke was dense in her lungs. Tossing the half-smoked cigarette, she did a spin, kicked wet sand onto herself. Her shadow was in front of her, behind her; everywhere she looked, she saw her shadow—flat, distorted, scaring her. She started walking.

Natassia was scaring the shit out of Mary with this boyfriend business. If it were the stuff a normal mother would be worried about—AIDS and pregnancy—maybe Mary could talk to Nora about it, but that wasn't what was freaking her out, not at all. The kid was just getting started and she was using condoms. With spermicide. Extra-safe. When Mary was fifteen, it had taken a while for the news to sink in that she really did have to take a pill every single day. There'd been a few crises she could have done without. Still, abortion after abortion, the problem each time had been logistical: when and where and how to get the money. Mary never suffered the doubt that had made Nora so crazy for a couple years after her one and only abortion—sophomore year, college.

And Mary surely never had the parental thing to worry about. By the time she was in high school and having sex, her stepmother, Dorie, had long since given up paying attention to her, and her father, Jerry, paid attention to no one but his wife. When Mary outgrew her clothes, she dressed herself by rummaging through the Lost and Found box at the ballet academy where she spent most of her time. For weeks she'd live with Nora's family, and Jerry and Dorie never even bothered to call the Conollys to find out if Mary was there or not. From fourth grade on, Nora and her parents were Mary's most reliable friends, but dance was and had always been Mary's only mother, the thing that took care of her, body and soul. Every time she got pregnant, Mary knew what to do. She needed to dance. The solutions to the problems of her body had always been within her body, within dance.

"Why did you go ahead and decide to give birth to Natassia?" Dr. Cather had asked at one session. Mary had never managed to figure out why, but it must have been the right thing to do, because she couldn't imagine the universe without Natassia in it. Sometimes Mary wondered if she really had done it for no better reason than to have a child with Ross's long legs.

Another day, Cather asked Mary, "Why do you think you chose never to marry Ross?"

Easy question. Ross was really something—sexy as hell and wicked smart—but basically he just got way too nuts.

Mary turned her back on the water, did a cartwheel that landed her on dry sand. She tried a handstand, faltered, jumped out of it, and landed on both feet. *Oiuu.* Her hip, her sacroiliac joint, was screwed up again, out of alignment. She'd been skimping on warm-ups, telling herself she didn't have time, and now her body was on strike, not doing anything she used to count on it to do. Mary, in her life, had been without money, without apartments, without jobs, but she'd never known deprivation in her body before.

Her friends kept telling her that the teaching job at the private high school upstate was a brave, good choice. Now she was strapped into it, strapped into all those good intentions to be steady for Natassia, to create a home so Natassia could move out of her grandparents' apartment and live with Mary upstate. The teaching job gave Mary medical insurance. She could start saving money for Natassia's college. But Mary suspected—was practically sure—that it was way too late for her mothering to kick in. Besides, she didn't know how to do any of that stuff anyway.

Looking over her shoulder, she saw she was now a long way from the small lights of Nora's cottage. With this guy going after her daughter, Mary was terrified. Not fear for her daughter's safety, not fear of losing her. It was greedier. It was this: If older men, foreign men, exotic men were going after Natassia, then Mary was the *mother*, the taboo. There'd be no one left for her. The truth she had to hide from Nora was that Natassia's guy, in his love notes, sounded like the kind of guy Mary needed for herself.

Nora was swimming and swimming and had been swimming in the Long Island Sound for hours and she still felt no better. Two days had passed since Mary and Giulia had gone back to the city, leaving Nora alone at the beach, but she couldn't get away from herself, and she couldn't get away from Christopher, even in the water, where his phone calls couldn't reach her.

She had swum so far out that when she looked toward the shore the house was a dot in the darkening evening sky. Still, Nora could not escape the word *Natassia*. With each slice of her arm into water, Nora heard Mary's voice: *this guy, this boyfriend, a man, shtupping, some kind of a foreigner. Natassia's in trouble, isn't she?*

With two wet hands, Nora covered her wet face, let her body weight pull her underwater, then spread her arms and floated to the surface. It was happening again, as it hadn't in so long, the torment, which always came to Nora in a cyclone of words. Whereas Christopher was a visual person, and Mary was a body person, Nora knew herself to be a word person. This realization had been one of the hard-earned gifts of the intensive therapy she'd undergone while training to be a psychologist. *You are haunted by language* helped to explain the insomnia she'd suffered for years. Learning that she had mastery over language had helped her gain mastery over her thoughts, then allowed her to repossess sleep, one of the biggest victories of her five years in therapy.

Until a couple of years ago. Then Christopher began pushing—really pushing—to have a baby, even though they had put the baby question permanently on hold, and the old torture began in Nora again, as it had today, anxiety churning out nouns, verbs, adjectives, adverbs—strings of them *(boyfriend, shtupping, trouble)* repeated and repeated, slamming into one another with the fast attraction of magnets, in unpredictable patterns inside her head, inside her chest and heart. What Nora experienced was the sound a word made, or she'd see in her mind's eye the spelling, or sometimes a picture would be summoned up. Usually, during one of her torments, all three manifestations happened at the same time, overstimulating her, making her dizzy, making her sick. Sounds and spellings and images, each one a small, potent representative of the problem within her that refused to be solved. There was no way around it. If Natassia's boyfriend was as old and worldly as Mary had described, the girl was in a relationship that was—as Nora herself might write in a report on one of her patients— inappropriate. *Inappropriate* spun around with *Natassia* and all the other words that wouldn't leave Nora alone.

Why the hell was Mary going around telling her daughter's secrets? When Nora saw *M-A-R-Y* in her mind, it was a tarnished thing with too much light on it, like sun on the fender of a dirty car. Looking at *M-A-R-Y* gave Nora a headache. She shifted the direction of her swimming to be parallel to the beach. All weekend, Mary had worn that mess of brass chains on her ankles, two gold hoops in one earlobe, a stupid feather hanging from her other earlobe. Nora had had to struggle to hold back the thought that Mary always looked dirty, like a kid at camp, a wild child living far away from adult supervision. (Who was the teacher who'd written "wild" and "need for supervision" on one of Mary's report cards? Fifth grade? Sixth?) Mary just refused to be bothered with certain details of adult life. Like raising her daughter, for instance. Thinking it, Nora felt worse. She knew, probably better than anyone else, how much Mary struggled as a mother. But Mary's obstinacy was beginning to annoy Nora. Like the little detail of Mary's insistence that Natassia wasn't part Korean, a statement that was (1) a lie; (2) unfair to Natassia; and (3) racist. *Some greencard slut.* Mary's xenophobia was mean, against everyone, including herself.

Unless it suited her. It wasn't uncommon for Mary, when she needed money, to scour *Backstage*'s audition notices for ASIAN FEMALE. Nora remembered a winter when Mary was badly injured and could rehearse but couldn't teach, and she auditioned for—and landed—a commercial that required her to dress up in a geisha-girl costume. It was a thirty-second spot, late at night, advertising a private midtown men's club. Soft porn, really. Hardly anyone saw it, but still.

This was before most people had VCRs, so Ross had paid some outlandish amount of money to buy a copy of the commercial, which opened with Mary sitting at a makeup mirror having her hair, a black wig, pinned up by another girl in a kimono, whose sleeve was slipping, baring her shoulder. A voice-over said something like "This girl is getting ready for you. Are you ready for her? Don't keep her waiting." Then the camera cut from the mirror scene to a close-up of Mary's made-up face, then cut away to a silhouetted girl with her back exposed, her kimono slipping—it was the other girl, not Mary—then cut to Mary's face, then to the girl's naked shoulders, then a tighter shot of Mary's face staring straight into the camera, then an entire naked back. The last shot was slow-motion: Mary releasing her hairpin and doing a spin, her black-wig hair fanning out.

Residuals from that commercial came in for three years, and Mary heard from the agency that when men came to the club as a result of the commercial, they often asked for "the little Japanese girl at the mirror," even though it was the other girl who showed parts of her body. Mary's face, especially whitened for that TV commercial, had a quality so ancient, a beauty so still, a blankness so unmarred by emotion or personality, that an untraveled Westerner could hardly begin to guess at the soul templed within that girl.

And yet people always tried to figure out who, exactly, Mary was. All kinds of men were always telling her, I'm falling in love with you, simply because they couldn't figure out what to do with the curiosity she aroused in them.

Nora remembered a grad student who liked partying with them, a Ph.D. in international studies, cool guy (Nora had actually been the one to notice him, had her eye on him); he kept following Mary around one night, asking if it bothered her, as a Korean, to be portrayed on TV as Japanese.

"Hell, no," Mary had said.

The guy kept pushing. "Even though the Japanese have been Korea's enemy for most of history?"

"Not my history," Mary said, then, "Hey, somebody's lighting up a bong over there. Let's check it out."

Mary had always played hard against people's assumptions of what to expect from a petite, pretty Korean-faced girl: that she would be polite, respectful, obedient, with a large dose of filial duty, book-smart, with good grades and diligent study habits. So, when Mary answered questions with the same slurry slang all the other kids used, when she belched into a can of soda, when she sat in a classroom with her ankle up on her knee, when she swore on the school bus, when she said, "Go ahead, call my parents, see if I care," when she was caught with boys or cigarettes or beer, the teachers or the bus drivers or the guidance counselors or the friends' parents or even sometimes the other kids were—what?—taken aback?—thrown off?—turned off? Whatever, their hands were tied. What were they going to do, say aloud what they were thinking? *A girl like you shouldn't be bad, you should be grateful you're here. You poor orphan, yanked out of a war zone, no wonder you're wild.* You knew people were thinking it, but no one was going to say it.

And so Mary kept making her point over and over again: *I'm not what you think I am when you look at me.* Talking back. Sassing. Bold, bad-girl behavior Nora never would have risked ("You're only as good as the things gossips tell each other about you," Nora's mother used to say). Maybe it was Mary the American girl attacking the Korean girl within herself. The funky clothes, the sloppiness. It had always annoyed Nora's father that when they took Mary to a nice restaurant she'd tug off her shoes and tuck her legs up onto her chair. "Coarseness," he told his children, "is not the way you want to bring attention to yourself. Of course, you should try never to bring attention to yourself. Just the opposite." Now that she was well into her thirties, Mary was starting to look ridiculous. Needlessly casual. Why did she still have to go around broadcasting to the whole world that she didn't give a damn?

Swimming back up, breaking the surface, shaking her head—*Why am I so focused right now on Mary?*—Nora couldn't help wishing that she'd never invited Mary out for the weekend. *Thank God, Giulia was here to run interference. Really, I should have come out here by myself.*

All Nora wanted these days was to be alone.

Tired in her arms and legs and shoulders, Nora turned onto her back to float. When her body reached this point, whipped into fatigue from the inside out, she felt as if the cyclone had spun its way through her. Now the words were outside of her, nipping at her, like a school of hungry fish.

Limp as her limbs were, Nora tried to keep up the listless paddling of her feet. Her hands pushed small patches of water at her sides. Finally, she just had to stop, lie there in a dead man's float, let what was going to wash over her wash over. Inside, too, she felt so weak she couldn't define the difference between herself and the water, except the water had color and she did not. Her love and her fear had burned each other out. She was ashes, white. Maybe if she floated long enough she'd decompose and sink and meet up with her mother and dad. These were the waters where, eighteen years earlier, Nora and her brother, Kevin, had come with Mary and two carloads of family friends—there was no extended family—to empty out the urns. It was a June afternoon, one month to the day after the middle-of-the-night house fire that had taken their parents. Nora and Mary were seniors in high school; Kevin was two years younger. Family life, as they had known it, was ended.

Nora still remembered the nothingness she'd felt standing on the dock with her fists full of ashes, which were actually bits of bone that felt like large grains of sand. *Right hand, Mommy; left hand, Daddy.* With all that water in front of her, Nora saw only fire. Six years, and much therapy, would pass before she could return to that dock and look at the water without seeing flames, without seeing over and over what had happened that night: She and Kevin, just home from late-night dates, had been sitting in the den watching a TV movie (neither of them was ever able to remember what the movie had been). The spring weekend was warm enough for opened windows. Then she glanced behind her through the screen because she'd heard *whoosh* and sirens. Nora saw flames vining up the side of her house, and the neighbors' garage in the alley lit up, too. She gasped. Kevin, quick, unplugged the TV. They both ran upstairs to wake their sleeping parents. Caught in the stairwell, they watched a room-sized section of the second floor collapse right past them onto the living room. And then a firefighter was pulling them away. *"They're up there! Our parents are up there!"* Nora remembered the onyx air of the kitchen, remembered crawling, then nothing much more.

The whole family was in the same hospital. Daddy died that night, Mommy three days later. The neighbors were unhurt, though it was an ember from their blown-over grill that had started the fire. That summer, Kevin moved in with his best friend's family, and Nora lived in neighbors' houses, since there was no way she could live at Mary's house; Mary could hardly live there. Nora's parents had left some money, lots of insurance, but no will, no designated guardians. For four months, Nora slept on different pillows every few nights, used different showers, ate in different kitchens; everywhere, the smell of smoke. Wherever Nora was staying, Mary visited every evening, slept over if there was room. They cried. And cried. And then it was September.

Nora showed up at the University of Pennsylvania, her dream school, but after two weeks she left. Unlike in high school, where Nora had excelled academically, at Penn she couldn't focus, couldn't sit through class, couldn't talk to strangers or sleep at night. If she was alone, she literally could not put her head down on a pillow and fully recline; she'd get shaky, she felt suffocated, her heart beat ferociously. She transferred to SUNY Purchase, where Mary had a dance scholarship.

Mary's schedule was full, but at least Nora could check in with her daily. Even before the fire, Nora had depended on Mary for a link to the wider world of their high-school universe. "High-achieving," one teacher had written in Nora's college-reference letters, "self-sufficient, mature, confident; somewhat of a loner, by choice."

"Snob" was what some girls in high school had called her, mostly those who had trouble getting boyfriends. Nora had always had a boyfriend, and Mary as her best friend, and her family, and her schoolwork, and she felt she didn't have much to complain about, not the miseries the other girls were hashing over all the time. Sure, there were times Nora's boyfriends weren't acting the way she wanted, weren't saying the things she wanted to hear. And there was Peter Ashley, whom she'd been crazy about since eighth grade, who took her out now and then and treated her badly (she lost her virginity to him in eleventh grade, then he avoided her for months), but *why* would she talk to anyone other than her mother and Mary about that? (Both had consoled Nora with one word: *Bastard!*) "What's to gain," Mommy always said, "by wearing our underwear on top of our clothes? Especially if it's underwear that's not so flattering."

At SUNY Purchase, with no family and unable to study, Nora did what she knew how to do: immediately she got a boyfriend, someone to spend the night with, to eat meals with. When that first guy got too serious, she found another boyfriend. Then another. One guy she dropped when he asked her to transfer to University of Michigan because he'd been accepted there for law school, another when he wanted her to go on a Christmas vacation with his family, another when he asked her to move into an apartment with him. They expected ridiculous things from her. *Tonight how will I get to sleep? How will I get through this afternoon?* Looking into the future, the way some of her boyfriends wanted her to, was not possible, so she moved from one guy to the next with an efficiency much admired by the six other women in the off-campus house she and Mary lived in. Nora's skill with men, together with having survived a recent family tragedy (she and Mary disclosed nothing but "fire" and "both parents dead"), made Nora a favorite in the house.

"Nora Conolly is so gorgeous."

"But nice, *too. No wonder guys are so crazy about her."*

One thing Nora knew about having a boyfriend was that she couldn't be with him *all* the time, so she put in her hours at the house, where, to avoid being alone, she went to whichever room the girls were gathered in. She listened. Mostly it was the same litany of complaints she'd heard in high school—about parents, classes, boyfriends, birth control, part-time jobs—but with nowhere else to go, Nora took more of it in, and over the weeks, she noticed that the girls' problems with their boyfriends were often similar to the problems with their advisers, or with their parents, or between their parents. *God, Nora, you're so smart.* But it was obvious. Everything was there to see; the girls violated every rule of privacy that had been sacred in Nora's family. They'd tell anything.

"My dad is ten thousand dollars in debt." "I never once had an orgasm with my high-school boyfriend—yeah, the guy who visited me last weekend. Cute, I know, but his penis is sort of just not quite right somehow." "My mother's lost a bunch of weight. She started looking great this summer since she's sleeping with the lawyer who's doing her divorce from my dad." "Dad started noticing that Mom smelled sort of funky, but it was a couple months until we found out about her cancer." It wasn't the information that shocked Nora but the girls' insistence—almost a sense of entitlement—that they could and *should* reveal themselves *and their families*!

Nora was appalled, as she knew her mother and father would have been. And yet, anthropologically, it was interesting enough that when her name was yelled up from the kitchen because some guy was on the phone for her, Nora didn't run like the other girls did, dropping a conversation in mid-sentence. "Tell him to call me back later. I'm busy."

"Nora's such a good friend."

"She's really a good listener. I'd tell her anything."

And they did, even though Nora never served up confidences of her own. In those college rooms, dim with lit candles and cigarettes and an occasional joint, Nora's blue-green eyes grabbed all the light, gave nothing back, and no one seemed to mind. The friends just told her more.

In college, Nora came to understand something that as a child she had intuited—that people were drawn to her, as they had been to her whole family, willing to overlook lots, because the Conollys were attractive people (tall, lean, limber, light-haired, turquoise- or jade-eyed, aristocratic bone structure in the face), with a vague air of street smarts and lots of old-money good taste (even though there was no old money, or much of any money). Nora's parents, Ed and Finny, had driven a series of secondhand Saabs. Their house, though mildly dilapidated, had sat on the top of a hill and had been one of the largest in their medium-income part of town, a sprawling Victorian with two landmark features: a master-bedroom fireplace with Italian marble inlay, and a sunken rose garden that Finny pampered. Lots of people were intrigued by the Conollys, and others had no use for them, but everyone knew who the Conollys were and which house was theirs. You knew it whether you liked them or not.

It was generally concluded that the Conollys had "a story," but the truth was known only to Ed and Finny's inner circle, which consisted of Finny's bosses, Dr. Jack and Dr. Rita, a husband-wife team of plastic surgeons who entrusted Finny with every detail of their professional and financial lives; and Dr. Jack's brother and his wife, two lawyers. The three couples had drinks at home and dinner out every Saturday night for twelve years, and over the years, when the mood was right, Ed and Finny, in the offhand manner of a two-part comedy act, revealed their secrets. Eavesdropping during their cocktails, Nora learned most of what she would ever learn about her parents.

Before they met and married, Ed had done time in a Missouri prison for embezzling money from his family's manufacturing business. Finny (née Nora Finn, nicknamed Finny Finn) had been a pregnant California teenager whose mother had sent her to Albany to live in a home for un-wed mothers while telling everyone in Sacramento that Finny had gone east to nursing school. After Finny gave birth, after her newborn son was adopted, she stayed in Albany, became a nurse, and never returned to California. After his prison term, after refusing to have anything more to do with his family, ever, Ed randomly chose a city—Albany—left the Mid-west for good, and drove to New York State in a used Cadillac. "They didn't like Caddies in the Midwest. Too posh."

The Conollys' intimates knew the following series of facts: (1) At some point during his drive east, Ed changed his last name to Conolly; (2) in December 1952, he had a flu so bad he went to the hospital emergency room because he couldn't afford a visit to a doctor. The ER attending physician treated him and recommended that in a week's time he go to a nearby clinic for a follow-up, which Ed did, and there he meet Finny, a graduating nursing student, twenty-two years old. Ed was forty-three. They dated daily for six weeks; then Ed proposed marriage, and Finny ac-cepted, and Conolly became her name, too; (3) within ten months, their first child, Nora, was born, and, two years later, Kevin; (4) the family's in-come, from Finny's job as a nurse, was often compromised by Ed's playing around with stocks.

"When the debt gets out of hand," Ed would tease, "Jack and Rita can fix me up with a new visage, and I'm good to go." He was balding, almost always in a tie, refined, so it was surprising, and sexy, when he winked at his wife. "Don't worry, ma'am. Not without you."

She answered looking right into his eyes. "You're not going anywhere without me, mister."

Not even their children learned which Midwestern town or even which state Ed was from, what his last name had been, if his real first name was Edward, Edwin, or what. He wouldn't say what product his family manufactured. And no one knew how much family—if any—Finny had left in California; she'd stopped communicating with her mother soon af-ter she married Ed. "First she sent me off because I wasn't married," Finny said, with that humor, like Ed's, that made her seem immune from the sad-nesses of her own life. Rolling her eyes, she set up her punch line: "Then, because of Ed's jail time, she disapproved when I *did* marry, so to hell with her." The friends, and even Nora and Kevin, knew about the adopted baby, but no one, not even Finny, knew where he was, and she wouldn't tell his birthdate. The only biographical information Ed and Finny carried forward was (1) her nickname, and (2) the length of Ed's prison time: 1,473 days and nights.

Those were the facts as known by the inner circle.

The general public kept a distance. Nora knew, from hearing things and watching, that lots of people disapproved of the Conollys. Ed was above work, never left his home to go to a job, and he never—not ever—stopped for small talk with anyone, not even the next-door neighbors. The family belonged to no community club, no country club, no church. Mr. and Mrs. didn't seem to care what anyone thought. When you saw them in public, they were always with their hands on each other, so affectionate you'd think they weren't married—as if it wasn't bad enough already that he was so much older than her.

Nora was around ten when her parents told her and Kevin about their father's jail time, saying it was information to be kept in the family but nothing to be ashamed of; the only *shameful* secret, to be kept among the four of them, was how thoroughly Ed's family had screwed him over when they let him go to jail. Even as a little girl, Nora had understood that loyalty in the face of shame was part of the passion between her parents, an erotic charge she noticed in the way they looked at each other. Little Nora shivered to be in the presence of such powerful adult love, and when she was older, she looked for that passion with so many guys—not with the boyfriends who wanted her, but with other guys she couldn't get. Peter Ashley *(Bastard!)*. A grad-student TA too dependent on student evaluations to let his guard down with Nora; a biology professor up for tenure, too nervous to focus when she showed up for all his office hours; her Psychology Department adviser, who never took her seriously when she invited him out to dinner. And then, in late spring of her sophomore year, with the guy headed for law school, Nora got pregnant and after the abortion was so depressed she went to a campus counselor, who kept asking about Nora's family, saying, "I have the sense, Nora, there's much there that needs to be explored."

By then Mary had met Ross. They wanted Nora to go to Rome with them junior year, but instead she went to the Riviera, to a truly bogus study-abroad program (all through college, she never did regain her ability to concentrate), her first radical attempt to rid herself of her phobia of being alone.

In France, within a few days, she hooked up with a married Brit who worked in a tourist office while his wife in London worked on some advanced degree. Mary, in her letters, scolded Nora for messing with a married man ("If his wife doesn't want to be with him, why would you?"), but the Brit let Nora barnacle herself to him, every night, every meal, and he ignored the fact that she clearly had her eye on the manager of a local wine shop. It was while she lingered in the tiny aisles of that shop one day that another customer, stooping down for a bottle on a low shelf, stood up and said, "Those are nice sandals. My sisters would love those."

Nora's feet were large, bony, her least attractive feature, and the man was staring at them. "How many sisters?" she asked.

"Two. And four nieces." His gaze moved from her feet to her face. He was a little older than she was, like the young professors she'd liked, but not as harried. "Hey, I'm a new uncle." He wanted her, Nora could tell, but it was a different wanting than she'd felt with other guys, because she wanted him, too. He was at once dark and light. Auburn hair. Big eyes kaleidoscoping several shades of blue at the same time. She couldn't stop watching him. His smile slipped from eyebrows to cheekbones to chin. "You're American, aren't you? I'm Christopher Sampietro, who're you?"

They didn't get together that first day, but he began courting her, leaving notes for her with her concierge, leaving sketches on her doorstep. They met for coffee once, but he was so shy on a date it was awkward. Then they just ran into each other in the village. In the market, in cafés and shops, he was never alone. "Go ahead without me," he'd tell his friends, sometimes in English, sometimes in French; "I'll catch up with you guys later." Then he'd step in close to talk to Nora, much more easily than he had when he'd asked her out. They were as tall as one another, eye to eye. She loved the scent of his breath, like oranges and fresh bread. With each conversation, Nora entered another story of his family. She began to know their names, the nieces' ages. It was a relief to meet someone who didn't hate his family. Saying goodbye, he'd clasp his big paint-speckled hand around her arm just above her elbow. But he wasn't asking her out again, and Nora, usually not intimidated by men, was afraid to ask him out. She began wearing bright colors—a sweater that was the color of beets, an apricot-paisleyed skirt—hoping to catch his painter's eye in the crowds of the village. Then, one day in the market, he said, "I was wondering, have you ever, you know, like, modeled for a painter? No? I'd love to paint you."

"Paint me?"

"I mean, not with clothes not on." His cool was gone—he became almost inarticulate—and for the first time Nora thought, I have a chance with him. "Really, it's your head that's good. You have a great shape to your head, a strong face. Would you try?"

Those hours when Nora sat in Christopher's studio were edged with the sweetest quiet. Years earlier, Nora had spent one delicious, long Labor Day weekend out at Greenport alone with her mother, closing up the house for the season. Without Daddy around, Mommy was relaxed, not distracted, and she and Nora ended up spending most of the weekend reading on the couch—"silent as stones," Mommy had said. Nora was deep into the Narnia books then. Sometimes, without realizing it, she held Mommy's hand for a whole chapter; sometimes she rested her head on Mommy's lap. Painting, Christopher never spoke, never stopped. Nora's modeling sessions with him were long, slow, felt nice. The space surrounding her was too large and echoey, but, with Christopher nearby, Nora could sit still without fear pumping her heart and dilating her pupils.

"You have good energy," Christopher told her.

"Energy? I'm not doing a thing."

"Yeah, you're perfect for this. You're peaceful," he said, and so she was.

Nora modeled for Christopher three times. Then he took her out for an elaborate dinner, to thank her. He ordered grilled seafood. They couldn't even eat. Nora went home with Christopher that night. She was supposed to meet the married man for lunch the next day, but she didn't show up. That was that. Nora's world stopped.

And then it reorganized itself around Christopher.

Christopher—the name had run through Nora's mind probably once a minute, every minute, for the past fifteen years, played over and over until the word wiped out its own sounds. *Husband* was there but no longer meant anything Nora could understand. *Spouse* had been coming up lately. She hated the word. Too much like *louse, lice,* an insidious plague. Nora's head in the water turned sideways just in time for her to see she was floating through a patch of foamy seaweed. Paddling her feet, she got herself quickly away. What were the things her mother couldn't live with in her own marriage? It really did seem that Nora and Christopher had reached the end of their passion, and now Nora needed to know what, *what,* was the dark side of her parents' marriage, which had always looked *good.* And not just to Nora. *What a special couple, the Conollys.*

The psychotherapist she'd done her training analysis with had warned her—no, had suggested to her—that she had a lot of family-of-origin issues still to be explored. But when Nora terminated that therapy, she was living so much more fully than she'd imagined possible, able to be alone, to ride the subway without panic, even able to concentrate enough to complete her dissertation, "Grief and Post-Traumatic Stress Disorder." How clever, her father-in-law had said, how efficient, to work through her emotional problems and get an education and a career all at the same time. "A real bang for your buck," he'd teased. Working so hard to survive her parents' deaths, Nora hadn't given herself a chance to consider their lives.

But now she needed to know. Why, occasionally, out of nowhere, the closed doors as her mother slept in one of the attic rooms for a few angry nights? How rudderless the house felt then, and little Nora could hardly eat until Mommy got "normal" again. It was impossible for Nora to remember exactly what her parents had argued about (they didn't bicker much, maybe because of the age gap between them), but Nora knew there had been some shadow in the marriage. Some deep trouble that stayed hidden for long stretches of time but then always reappeared. Nora knew there'd been darkness because she could remember feeling afraid of it. But she also knew because, well, she just *knew.*

In her work with patients, Nora had got used to hearing about, and witnessing, the pathology within love, the woes people created for one another, and the chaos they lived within. Occasionally she saw the transcendent moments when people rose above themselves. When two people managed it together, a simultaneous transcendence of two bruised spirits lifting up from the quotidian mess of their lives—God, that was what everyone in therapy lived for.

It hardly ever happened.

Nora dropped her legs, curled in on herself, somersaulted down into a colder depth of water. She dove, as always, with her eyes open, a superstitious action that was really a wish to catch some hint of her parents—ashes, bones, anything. As she rose back up to the surface, a new word was with her—*eternity*.

Lately she'd been working with a patient, a woman who was thirty-nine, almost forty, a few years older than Nora. This woman, a financial adviser, was highly likable, with a cheerful disposition, a fluctuating but basically strong sense of self, and a sad problem. Trying to heal from the breakup of a long-term relationship in which marriage had been planned, she'd joined some friends in renting a summer house in the Hamptons and had a brief affair with the man from whom they'd rented. He was wealthy, narcissistic, married, and careless. Nora's patient was now pregnant, almost two months, and trying to make her decision. She had always wanted a child and was afraid this might be her last chance. Though she hadn't planned to get pregnant, she knew that an unconscious wish had been at work when she'd agreed to sleep with the man. Crying, she told Nora, "This was no mistake. Things went just how my unconscious planned."

Nora made attempts to open discussion of unresolved feelings about the breakup of the previous relationship, but the patient stayed focused on "this pregnancy."

"Have you ever been pregnant before?" Nora asked.

"Are you kidding? We were so careful in my last relationship. You know, we were each other's first lover. I've never been casual about sex. Part of me did *this* on purpose."

Now the woman's consciousness was kicking in hard. When the man found out about the pregnancy, he had shown her what he was really about. Unpredictable. Full of rages. He threatened to hurt her if his wife found out he'd been unfaithful. Then, one week after threatening, he came back and said he'd told his wife, who had forgiven him, and he was seeking legal advice so he could gain shared custody of the child. He and his wife had never had children. He wanted this one. He had money, he had power. Nora's patient was in a panic. What if something happened to her, and her child ended up in the care of this maniac? Was she being fair to the child? Would it be better if this child was not born? Was she just trying to punish herself? She couldn't opt for adoption, because the father said he'd block it. Besides, she doubted she could live knowing she had a child in the world who was being raised by someone else. The woman was haunted by one thought, and she repeated it at every session: "If I have the baby, we'll be eternally linked to that man."

Eternally had been moving through Nora for weeks, trembling within her as her patient got more panicked every Wednesday at three-fifteen. In Nora's mind, *baby* and *eternally* had linked to form a word-picture. It rose up now before her as she began the long diagonal swim back toward the dock. What she saw was a big pink baby sitting on a rustic, ivy-covered swing, swinging and swinging. This motion, Nora knew, was suggested by her patient's indecision about whether or not to abort. But Nora had a strong impression that the woman would go on with her pregnancy, so Nora interpreted the swinging to signify the steady way a child moves into the future, bringing with it mother and father and everything else, which is then passed on through time. The makings of eternity.

It scared Nora, the idea of an endlessly forward-moving energy that gathered and gathered more people, generations of them, accruing mistakes and illnesses, damage on top of damage, as steady and unstoppable as a train wreck.

And swinging into this inevitable accumulation was *baby*. In Nora's mind, the picture of *baby* never varied. There was only one baby, always the same one: the pink, plump infant Natassia.

Natassia. Placid, irresistible, six weeks old, the way she had been in July 1974, arriving in the south of France in the sack-and-frame contraption on Ross's back, while Mary hefted their backpacks. They had hitchhiked all the way from Rome to visit Nora in the south of France. All winter, in her letters, Nora had offered to travel to Rome to visit Mary as soon as the baby was born. Plus, Nora had met Christopher, and she wanted Mary to meet him. "It'd be so easy for us to come to Rome," Nora wrote. But Mary insisted that she and Ross had planned long ago to travel in Europe when classes were out, and having the baby wasn't going to change their plans.

So they arrived. Mary, Ross, and Infant Natassia.

Mary's letters just after the birth had described the baby as "buttery." And she was. Skin soft and a tiny bit damp from the heat. A little melty. She had an itsy-bitsy red mouth puckered like an elbow. Nora had been expecting at least a hint of Mary's Koreanness in Natassia's features, but the baby had huge round dark eyes, crisply etched with long lashes. Tiny, tiny nose, with all the curves and contours of a regular nose but in an impossibly small size. Now and then Natassia would smile, and whoever was near her—Mary, Ross, Christopher, Nora—would call out "Look, look!" and the others would come running from all corners just to see. "Oh my God, that smile!"

At six weeks old, Natassia was a feast of smells and textures and a subtle palette of colors from pink to apricot. Feet as sweet and meaty as slices of a peach. Holding that little baby was like filling your arms with flowers and summer fruits.

And so maybe that was why Christopher did it, gave in to the temptation to fill every one of his senses.

At this point in her reverie, Nora had to stop swimming. There was tightness on the side of her left breast, spiking into her heart. Nearby, on the water, too close, a gang of seagulls were squawking over possession of a dead fish. The cyclone of her thoughts had done it again, overpowered her will, centrifuged all sounds and spellings and meanings away from the words until nothing was left but that tiny town in the south of France, fifteen years ago, Nora pretending to study while Christopher painted, the two of them a couple only a few months but already living together in his warehouse loft, where Mary and Ross came to visit, bringing that poor tiny baby with them. The visit had been going so well that after a week Nora convinced Mary and Ross to go off by themselves for a few days while she and Christopher babysat. What an easy baby Natassia was, and how impressive Christopher was in his care of her, so eager to keep the baby fed and cleaned and entertained. He'd cushioned a dresser drawer to make a crib for her, and the first night he and Nora were tucking Natassia in, he said to Nora, "You and me can make a baby ourselves, you know?" In those days he was endlessly, shamelessly wooing Nora.

It was a Wednesday, late afternoon. Mary and Ross would be back the next day. It was hot, but cooling down a bit, and Nora thought maybe it would be nice to take the baby to the beach; by now she felt confident that she and Christopher could manage a picnic at the beach with the baby. And she was going to ask Christopher what he thought about going to the beach. She stepped into the kitchen, and what she saw—that one moment, that nanosecond powerful enough to obliterate even images of her family's fire—would stay with her forever: Christopher eternally lifting naked Natassia, tiny plump baby. Christopher's one big hand spreading the loaves of the baby's legs. Christopher bringing his mouth to the baby's vagina. To smell her. To taste her.

What would have happened if right then Nora hadn't entered the kitchen? (For years, one of the biggest points in Christopher's defensive self-explanation had been "Honey, if I'd been premeditating this act, would I have done it in the kitchen? What I did was wrong. It was a mistake. It was bad. But it's over. It was just that one time. I'm not a sick person. I'm not pathological. You're not married to a pervert. Please, let's let go of this. I've done my therapy, just like you wanted. I've done my dark nights of penance. It was a one-time aberration thing. It's been so hard for me to forgive myself. Please, why can't you forgive me?" For years he'd showered her with the jargon he'd picked up in therapy, just to show her he was doing it, since counseling was her one condition for staying in the marriage. Lately he'd been infuriating her by telling her, "Sweetie, there's something wrong that you can't let go of this after all these years. Maybe *you* need to talk to someone about this?") That July afternoon in France, if the air hadn't cooled, if Nora hadn't felt ready to go to the beach with Natassia, if she hadn't appeared just as Christopher's tongue trembled there in the air, at the entrance into the baby's body, if Nora hadn't been there to grab the baby from him and hold on to her for the next forty-eight hours, until Mary and Ross finally showed up, what would have happened? What might Christopher have done next?

This was the hell where Nora lived.

What *did* happen before Nora walked in? What happened inside the baby's body? What damage was done to her soul? Any? Maybe nothing. But why did Christopher do it? What was it in him that made him do it?

This event, this eternal moment in time, had shaped Nora's life as much as the fire that had consumed her family. *It* was the reason she and Christopher had stayed in France for five years. *It* had turned her blond hair white, bone white, in the course of one week. *It* was why Nora eventually chose the career she chose. *It* was why she refused to have a child. *It* was why she and Christopher were probably heading toward divorce. The *why* of what happened that July day still hadn't been explained.

Nora knew—had always known—that if she couldn't trust Christopher she should leave him. She couldn't trust, but she didn't dare leave. *What? And float sleepless and crazy and alone through the universe?* So she swallowed her rage (he was supposed to *save* her from disaster, not create more) and made a psychic adjustment, an accommodation: yes, she was protecting a man who had, once, molested a baby; *however*, Nora was deeply committed to the task of trying to find the answer to *why* he had done it. This was Nora's unspoken pact with the universe, a stalling tactic, pathetic, a way to buy time because she didn't have courage. She would not ask for or expect anything more if she could just, please, be spared a return to the abyss she'd lived in before she met Christopher.

In exchange, Nora lived a nimbus life around Natassia, assumed the duty of being vigilant over her—it was the least Nora could do, since she couldn't find the courage to tell Mary what had happened. Nora's therapist, who knew the whole story, had pushed, but, really, how could Nora tell Mary? Nora wasn't sure herself what had happened. A few times, she had brought up with Christopher the idea of telling Mary and Ross, but Christopher said, "What good would it do? Don't meddle." Nora left the secret untold, let the telling became a task still to be done. After that disastrous summer of '74, Nora and Christopher didn't see Natassia again until she was four years old, when they were back from France. By then Ross and Mary were almost splitting up, and the stories were flying: how friends had found Natassia sitting on the stoop outside their walk-up on Thompson Street because no one was home to let her in, how many evenings Natassia slept on dressing-room floors at dance studios until one or two in the morning with nothing but a coat thrown over her, how the fights between Mary and Ross had become bad and loud and vicious. Mary was already a mess of guilt and resentment and dread. Telling her about that moment in Natassia's infancy might make things worse for Mary, and for Natassia.

And for Christopher.

It was in this, her need to protect her husband above all others, that Nora entered the loneliest corner of her marriage. Lately Christopher had begun to accuse *her*: "You're selfish, Nora. Honey. Admit it. The reason you won't let us have a baby of our own is that you're selfish." A baby? He wanted a baby? Couldn't he understand that Nora was just barely getting by? Was he trying to dismantle her completely?

And how could she have a baby with him, create a tie into eternity with a man who—who what? Who *was* he? She was still, after all these years, trying to decide if he was good or bad, worthy or not. *I need to leave. I can't leave.*

By now, the water Nora was swimming in had darkened, the sky around the house was navy blue, more faded than her old bathing suit. She was close to the beach, so she had to tug at the stretched-out straps every few strokes to keep her breasts covered. The tank suit had been her mother's, her last one, nearly new when she died; now the elastic was worn and the foam cups had fallen out. The suit was so loose that Christopher had recently told Nora it was almost sexier on her than her bikini, "if I was turned on by hillbillies wearing hand-me-downs." They had become so mean with each other. A few hundred yards from the dock, Nora had to stop to rest. *I'll sleep out on the dock tonight.* On the dock she'd be far from the phone.

Truly exhausted, she could only float. Another good thing about sleeping on the dock was that it always made Nora feel closer to her mom, who had often slept on the deck when the heat was at its worst. Eighteen years dead, her mother—her mother's voice—still came to her. After the fire, Nora had lost her mother completely, but in her therapy she'd recovered Mommy's voice, and she didn't let a day pass without talking to her, listening. Now, floating slowly toward the shore, Nora tried to hear Mommy listing options for her: "Well, dear, you could leave him." Nora found herself crying into the salt water of Long Island Sound. "Okay," her mother's voice said, "so don't leave him, but give him an ultimatum. Tell him, 'Never talk to me about having a baby ever again or I'll leave.' You could get your tubes tied without telling him. Or, dear, you could decide not to decide now. It's always an option to just go on as you have been."

Terrified, Nora realized that wasn't really an option for her and Christopher anymore.

A FEW HOURS LATER, fixing tuna salad in the kitchen, Nora had just got off the phone with Christopher when the phone rang again and it was her brother, Kevin. She could hear the subway behind him.

"Hi, Nor, it's me."

"Kevin. Where are you, in the subway?"

"Yeah. Seventy-second Street. Listen, I just ran into Giulia buying peaches at Fairway. They're on sale. Real nice. She told me you guys were at the beach this weekend. How's Mary? Still with that guy, that lawyer-for-the-arts guy?"

"The lawyer? Nothing ever happened with that." Nora, tugging her kitchen curtains closed in Greenport, heard train exhaust huffing behind Kevin's voice, and she wished she were back in the city.

Kevin was saying something about some bowling shirts. He made good money as a computer programmer but he had a sideline selling vintage clothes. "These shirts are nice. Something Mary might like. When will she be in town? I can go by her place with these shirts anytime."

"Tell me what colors. I could use something new."

"Not good for you. These are little, Mary's size. I have a robe for you. Quilted silk. Champagne, nice color for you. I'll drop it off. So—Mary must be seeing somebody new, huh? That's good. I didn't like that lawyer." Nora could hear Kevin's train coming into the station, and she imagined him standing on the platform, tall and skinny, his shoulders hunkered over, and his balding, freckled, reddish-haired head bent as if he were a boy apologetic for having grown so much taller than the adults around him. Even now, at thirty-three, he rarely dressed like a grown-up; his hand was always jiggling keys and coins and gum in the pocket of baggy old shorts or work pants. Nora's friends thought he was cute. "Sexy" was what one woman had said. "He's such a boy, but he has that 'I'm ready' look in his eyes, and you just know he's got a constant hard-on." In fact, Kevin was never without a girlfriend, but none of them lasted long. Nora had tried to talk with him about his tendency to sexualize all his relationships, avoiding intimacy, a symptom of someone who'd undergone trauma, but Kevin said he'd made his peace with the past—without the benefit of therapy, and without Nora, and with lots of different girlfriends. And somehow he managed never to make anyone hate him. "He's the biggest sweetheart," said one girlfriend, even after he'd dumped her.

"No, Kevin, Mary's not seeing anybody. But I don't think she's looking. Too much going on with Natassia. Listen, come for dinner tomorrow night. I'll be back in the city, and I have all this frozen pesto I want to get rid of in the freezer."

"I can't tomorrow." The train was squealing to a stop. "So what's new with Mary? I haven't run into her in ages."

"Oh, Kevin." He broke Nora's heart every time he got into one of these Mary binges, which had begun when he was in the sixth grade. Mary had never shown any interest in Kevin, and never would.

"Nor, you sound weird or something, like you were crying. Are you sure you're all right?"

"Yes. Listen to me. Mary, you know—hey, your train—"

"Yeah, I got to go. Can I have dinner Friday night?"

"Sure. I'll be home. Bring that robe, okay?"

"You sure you're all right?"

"I'm fine. Come around seven."

"Bye, Nora."

"Love you, brother. Bye."

When Nora heard Kevin sounding needy the way he just had, when she felt alone the way she did now, when their conversation ached like the one she was hanging up from, two words appeared to her: *We're orphans.*

CHAPTER 4:

AUGUST

1989

Trapped on the train for hours on her way home from Nora's beach house, Mary was not feeling any way she wanted to feel. The B-52s playing on her Walkman matched the buzzed-up, captured beat of her heart. Something like caffeine was fluttering in her pulse. Two stops before her station, Mary was already in the aisle, leaning against the doors under the sign DO NOT LEAN ON DOOR. Her teeth held an unlit cigarette, her AC-chilled fingers spun her Bic lighter. She'd never had patience for travel, that long nothing between one performance city and the next. While others in the company read or played cards, Mary paced the aisles of planes, trains, buses—flexing, stretching, rolling her joints. *I left my kid in New York to do this tour. Let's get there, dance, go.* Up at the Hiliard School, Mary had no real dance life, not much of any life, so the commute to and from the school always felt pointless, and this particular dragged-out trip was killing her.

Three frigging hours on the bus squeezing through traffic on the Long Island Expressway just to get into the city. Then a one-hour wait at Grand Central, then two hours on the train. If she were a good mother, if she had stayed in the city overnight to have dinner with Natassia to try to find out more about this letch she was in love with, Mary would be sitting on her daughter's bed right now, the two of them watching a video and eating cold sesame noodles. Instead, because she was afraid even to try talking to the kid, Mary was locked up in this train, cold as a meat freezer, making her way up the river.

I was stupid to move to Hiliard, Mary said to herself just as the doors opened up at Hiliard, and she got off the train. Three steps onto the platform, she lit her cigarette. In front of the station, four cabs were lined up. Mary walked to the closest one. "Hiliard School," she told the driver. He put her backpack into the backseat for her. She got in, and they drove off.

THE HILIARD SCHOOL wasn't paying Mary much, but they gave her rent-free housing in the old remodeled greenhouse. This was good because the greenhouse was as far away as she could get from the students' dorms and still be on campus. It was bad because the formal flower gardens began right at Mary's front door and spread out in fastidious formations all across the long slope from the greenhouse up to the main buildings. These gardens were where neighborhood people liked to walk their dogs in the evenings. When Mary pulled up in the taxi that night, two matrons in jogging suits were crouched right by Mary's front door sniffing at a bush, and their three bichons frisés were sniffing at the dirt.

Walking toward the greenhouse, Mary turned up her Walkman until it was pulsing bass notes so loud the neighborhood ladies lifted their lapdogs and walked away. Halfway down the pebble path, though, they turned to watch Mary unlock the door. "Beautiful evening," they said to her.

"Yep."

"Do you live here, dear?"

"Yep." Mary slammed the door shut.

Inside, the plants were finally dead. Mary was glad; now she could throw them out. Slowly, systematically, over the past eight months, Mary had been trying to hide or get rid of all the doodads in the place, the stuff that belonged to the family whose home this was—an anthropology teacher and his wife and kids. They were in Peru for his sabbatical year, and everyone on the faculty was saying he'd probably come back divorced.

Mary stepped over the phone machine on the floor. The dusty red light was flashing. Four messages. Mary ignored them because she couldn't deal with Natassia's silliness right now, and there was no one else Mary wanted to hear from. She turned the stereo on to the lousy local jazz station and pulled off her Walkman, then pushed open windows and got the stereo up loud to make sure the nosy women took their dogs far away. After yanking the curtains shut, Mary peeled off her clothes, which smelled from traveling. She took a shower with water cold as she could get it. Afterward, she dried off, wrapped her head in a towel, walked naked into the living room, and filled up her favorite pipe.

A parade of Camels had marched her through the weekend and the long trip home, leading her to this moment when, finally, she could lie back naked on her futon and cup her hand around the warm bowl of this pipe, her meerschaum—white and as smooth as bone, definitely her favorite.

Mary's collection of pipes was extensive and secret. No one knew she was a pipe-smoker. Not Nora, not Natassia. More than ten pipes were hidden around the cottage. A corncob was stuffed between heavy sweaters on a high shelf. She reached for that pipe mostly in winter. When the dry air sapped her skin and left her fingertips numb, the husk rubbing against the palm of her hand was a sharp relief. Mary's most expensive pipe was a Savinelli she'd bought on a whim a few years ago, when the dance company was held over in the Milan airport for a few hours. What a beautiful pipe—black octagonal bowl, an ivory-colored band in the handle. She had lit up that pipe only once, while getting dressed up for a dance-company fund-raising gala, a night that called for something classy, but the pipe was a disappointment. It had a recessed mouthpiece, which brought the smoke up behind her teeth. She must have been badly jet-lagged when she bought it. The Savinelli just got wrapped into its plush little pouch. It was around somewhere, in some corner.

The meerschaum, the pipe she filled up that night when she came out of the shower cooled down and finally soothed, was kept tucked in her underwear drawer so it would always be handy. She liked finding that masculine thing among her underclothes. This was the pipe Mary wanted when she needed comfort, that something she supposed happy couples, people like Nora and Christopher, gave each other.

Mary's futon was skinny, like a pancake, and surrounded by dust kittens, but there really was comfort in this pipe. For one thing, it was beautiful. Carvings swirled into the soft white bowl; the tortoise mouthpiece had a nice curve. And it was a good pipe. A nice, cool smoke. In just a short minute, the tobacco had done its trick, changed from the fruity scent on her fingers into the tasty smoke circling in front of her face and inside her mouth. She tongued the pipe's mouthpiece, the slight slit at the tip. She loved that part of a man's penis, the tiny line you could finger into a little O, vulnerable as an *Oh!,* a small gasp.

It was Barry, she remembered now, the lighting technician, who had got her started smoking a pipe. They were on tour in Scandinavia. Mary couldn't remember which town they were in, or even which country, just that it was as cold as shit, and dark when they went to bed and dark again when they woke up. They had a couple hours in the morning before time to rehearse. It was too early to try calling Natassia, so Mary and Barry stayed in bed. Once, after he lit up, he offered his pipe to Mary.

"I never get high before a performance," she told him.

"This won't make you high. It's just tobacco. Here, taste."

The first puff choked her, but then she liked the burn in her mouth. "How do I do this?"

"Like a cigarette, but hold it in your mouth a while. Give it a chance."

Mary and Barry were lovers all through that run and on into Amsterdam. Then something happened—he got a new job, or the crew changed, or he was forced to take a union break. There was no big breakup, just one nice last morning. Before he left, he gave Mary a present, her own pipe, a brand-new briar. She still had it. Somewhere. Hidden. Once or twice, sharing a pipe in bed with a guy, she'd been asked, "Where'd you learn to do this?" "Ah, I just learned." She'd never tell anyone about Barry and what she and he had done in bed, in the same way she'd never tell any guy about any other guy. Mary was like that, loyal. Never told bed secrets. Ever. All those guys, wherever they were now, gone. In a weird way, though, she felt closer to them than to her best friends or even her own daughter.

Beyond family and blood and the confidences of girlfriends, there was the privacy of secrets shared between bodies together in bed. Mary knew there were those who thought she was a slut, but the secrets men showed her and told her had meant something to her every time it happened. Either you had those secrets in your life or you didn't; and to Mary's mind, if you had them they were a sacred thing. How could she explain this to Natassia? Natassia, who was so full of herself these days she'd actually had

57

the nerve to ask Mary, "Mom, what's the most orgasms you ever had in one night?" Making Mary squirm.

All she had been able to answer was "Natassia, how many orgasms is not the point," and then the next questions had hung between them, unasked and unanswered: What is the point? Why all those other guys after you left Daddy?

Now Mary watched the curtain over the open window puff and collapse in a relaxed adagio. She let her inhale-exhale follow the same slow rhythm. A breeze came through with some kind of pollen in it that made her sneeze, then sneeze twice more. *Where's my asthma inhaler? I better use it tonight. Where's Barry now?* With each guy there'd been some one thing that happened only with that guy, no one else. Rubbing her itchy eyes, she sort of smiled to herself. Weird. Since she'd begun sitting still for fifty minutes each week to talk to Dr. Cather, Mary was remembering things differently. Before, when she thought back, the guys just blurred. It was good now to be able to see that each one had added something to her life before he left. Some token or habit or ritual or game.

Allen, who had managed the company for six months a few years back, had taught her how to use all kinds of work-related expenses as deductions on her income taxes. A musician named Tony had convinced her it was necessary to put out some money if you wanted a good haircut, and she still did that every four months. Mary sneezed again, realized the air was cooling, pulled up her shaggy quilt. Her memory was moving; she let the details bring details.

That guy Yuri, one of their guides in Leningrad, amazing. Something about him, she never figured out what, but she had such orgasms with him that by the end of the week there were black-and-blue marks on his butt from her heels kicking. She remembered a kind of chunky guy in Berlin who said that when she flicked his nipples with her tongue a sadness went all through him, yet he wanted her to do it. So she did, but she rubbed his face real softly at the same time, to comfort him. She forgot names, forgot which of them snored, but she said "Oohh" out loud when she remembered a sweet, skinny, impossibly tall guy whose big feet stuck out through the blankets and hung off the end of the bed. One cold night in a four-star but not great hotel in Paris, she wrapped a towel around his feet to keep him warm. She'd liked him a lot; his gentleness had made her gentle.

Larry. His name was Larry. He hurt his back lifting a scaffold and had to go on disability.

With the round-bowled pipe in her hand, Mary remembered another techie, a kid who worked at the theater in Haifa. He had the plumpest, most rotund testicles she'd ever touched. His face and name were gone, but he'd left her with this one detail: the tender weight of his balls in her hand. Amazed by what she was remembering, Mary sat up, filled her pipe again, lit it, warmed her fingers around the bowl, smiled. She and this Israeli guy had had a game they played in bed. She'd hold one of his balls and ask, "Which do I like best? This one?" Then she'd cup the other and say, "No, wait, I like this one," then cup the first: "But maybe this one." Her hand moved with increasing speed from one side of his sack to the other, touching him, softly, more quickly, doing nothing but stroking him and stroking until he was thick and slick and slipped into her and filled her like a big inhale of smoke.

MARY WAS ASLEEP on the futon for over an hour. When she woke, she'd had a dream she couldn't remember, but some panic made her look quickly around the room, to remind herself which objects belonged to her, to make sure she could still pack everything up in one night if she had to get out. The tobacco in her meerschaum had burned down, and the pipe had tilted over onto her abdomen. "Shit." Someday she was going to burn herself to death. Sitting up, she saw the phone machine flashing at her. "Shit," she said again, and pressed the dusty PLAY button.

The first two messages were hang-ups. The third began with a pause, so Mary sensed immediately that there was trouble. And there was.

"Mary, dear, it's Lotte. Small problem this weekend here in the city with Natassia. Everyone is safe and healthy—no problem that way. But I'm sure she'll want to talk to you as soon as you get in. She was caught—" Lotte's voice was cut off by the machine.

"Fuck! Fucking damn it." Mary stopped screaming so she could hear the machine deliver the last message: "Mary, it's me again. Sorry, long-winded. Here's what happened. Natassia was shoplifting, they say, though the store's evidence is pretty spare. In any case, dear, the police officer wants to talk with you. And Natassia—well, call us when you get in. We love you, dear. I hope you got a rest this weekend. You've needed that, been working too hard. Call. Bye."

It was the sound of people's voices more than the words they said that got to Mary, like music telling her body how to dance. Lotte's voice being kind to her always made Mary go soft, give up some hold on her muscles. "Goddamn it," she moaned slowly, almost weepy, and fell back onto the couch and hugged a pillow to her sweaty naked middle. *Natassia. Shoplifting.* Now Mary was going to have to go back to the damn city. *I need to be in the studio.*

She tossed around the pile of dirty travel clothes on the floor until she found her T-shirt. She pulled it on, yanked open the curtains, stood at the window. The women and the dogs were gone. Mary was looking out on nothing but gardens—darkening grass and shadowed flowers. There was a long rectangle of color in front of her. Sunflowers and long sticks of gladiolus and thick patches of roses and zinnias and other stuff she didn't know the names of, all of it overgrown and too obvious, like some gaudy happiness that was completely foreign to Mary. It even embarrassed Mary to find herself here. In their sessions, Dr. Cather kept harping on the view of this garden, saying it was a beautiful symbol for what Mary was working toward. Cather said that in the act of *choosing* such a place Mary was making progress. As if Mary actually had a choice. *Mothering is about planting and tending. It's about growth. You and Natassia are both growing, together.* This is a joke, Mary thought, this place has nothing to do with our lives.

Here she was, living in a *cottage* where the view from all her low windows was nothing but flowers and the deep green heart of the hedges surrounding the sides of the greenhouse. Everywhere, huge chunks of green. Mary didn't understand a thing. What had got into Natassia? She'd never been in this kind of trouble before. What's wrong with the kid? Why's she doing this to me?

And then the phone right next to her feet rang, and Mary grabbed it.

"Hi. Mom?"

"Nataaa-sia!" Mary whispered the name, because, as soon as she heard the kid's voice, it happened. In Mary's chest the hard rock of her anger loosened and tumbled, and rising up like volcanic froth inside her was all the love she felt for her daughter. Why couldn't she have the rest of it, too? The patience to be a real mother. It always happened like this: that jolt of love, then the regret chasing right after it. The toughness Mary used to talk to the world disappeared. No one but Natassia heard the voice talking now, saying, "Oh, honey."

"I know, Mom. I'm sorry."

Mary and Natassia had begun talking to each other in this gentle whisper when Natassia was a little girl, three or four years old, staying with Lotte and David, or with Ross and one or another of his girlfriends. Mary was always away dancing, but no matter where in the world she was, Mary called Natassia every night, and when she did, Natassia turned her back on everyone she was living with and told Mary her secrets—that Lotte had cooked a dinner that was too creamy, that Ross's girlfriend was wearing stupid clothes, that Ross was acting dumb again (which meant, to Mary, that he was probably getting high too often). These were Natassia's small whispered secrets, and from across oceans, across state lines, across town, Mary would whisper back, "I know, Natassy, none of them are perfect, but you toughen up and be nice to them, and I'll see you soon."

As Natassia got older, there were fewer confidences, the separations became a way of life, but Mary and Natassia held on to their habit of whispering on the phone. In those voices, they could say anything to each other, and now Mary said softly into the receiver, "Natassia, honey. What the fuck's going on, sweetie?"

"They said I was shoplifting."

"Were you?"

Silence. The air was hardening. Lately the whispering never lasted long.

"Natassia, who's they?" Mary stepped up onto the wide, low windowsill and leaned her forehead against the windowpane. "Where were you?"

"At Ralph Lauren, on Madison and Seventy-second."

"So you *were* shoplifting?" Nothing. Mary scratched her knee against the window screen. "Answer me."

"M-o-m-m."

"Answer me."

"It's the BF's birthday this week."

Mary jumped down from the windowsill and landed flat on both feet. The whispers were over. "You stole from a store for your frigging boyfriend? Are you crazy?" she screamed, forgetting everything she'd learned in therapy. Cather was always telling Mary to try not to scream at Natassia, to try expressing her anger with questions and gentle talk. Right now, though, Mary was tired and pissed, and she bagged all the chitchat and took the short-cut straight to her anger. "Natassia, what do you think you're doing?"

"I just want his birthday to be nice, Mom. He hasn't had a nice birthday in, like, years. He told me that. He can't remember his last nice birthday."

"Well, neither can I. Adults never have nice birthdays. This man is ma-nipulating you, Natassia. Can't you see that?"

"Well, at least when it was my birthday he made a bigger deal out of it than you did. And he hardly even knew me then."

"You stop trying to play hardball with me. I want you to tell me the truth right now. How old is this guy? And where did he come from?"

Ready to hear the truth, thinking she really was going to get it, Mary sat down on the edge of the windowsill, but she wasn't wearing under-wear, and a paper clip jabbed her in the butt. She jumped up, strode over to the pile of dirty clothes, pulled on underpants, stepped onto the couch, and sat on one of the arms. "Where's he from, Natassia?"

"I don't know exactly how old, and that's the truth. I'm not lying to you."

"Listen, girl," Mary said, shuffling things around on the coffee table un-til she found a cigarette and matches. Then, because she didn't know what to say next, she said, "You are grounded. For the next two weeks, until we get this mess straightened out, you are grounded. You are home every night."

"Sorry, Mom." Natassia's voice had recently assumed some new, adult tones—deeper, detached, tinged with resolve. Even talking gibberish she sounded grown-up. "His birthday's tomorrow, so I can't stay home this week."

"This is not a dinner invitation. You will do it."

"No, I won't."

"You will."

"Make me. How're you making me from all the way up there?"

Mary sighed, stepped off the couch, kicked open the screen door, and went outside in nothing but her T-shirt and underwear to sit on the stone-step stoop of the greenhouse. The gardens were nothing now but a darker dark in the black of the night. No one was around, and Mary didn't care who saw her. She lit her cigarette, exhaled. For several minutes over the long-distance telephone line, nothing more than this was happening. Not one good thing would come from this call. Lotte would just pay the phone bill.

Mary rolled her neck. Natassia heard it crack. "Gross, what was that? Your neck? You should take care of your bones, Mom. You're going to end up with osteoporosis."

Cather was always telling Mary that anyone could feel love for a kid, that was easy, but if Mary wanted to be a mother she was going to have to follow up. "Mothering," Cather said, "is follow-up." It suddenly seemed to Mary very foolish that she was seeing a shrink to learn how to be a mother. This, Cather would say, is resistance.

Screw Cather and her resistance. From dance, Mary knew one important truth, probably the only important truth: action comes from desire; if you want to move, you will move. The thing that had made Mary step into the studio every day, all those years, was the surety that there were possibilities for her within the space of the dance floor. She just didn't want to step into motherhood. There was nothing there she wanted for herself. All at once, Mary felt that huge tiredness again. This kept happening to her lately. She'd read about diseases that began this way. Maybe she was getting ready to die. Maybe this overpreened garden would be her burial plot. A real joke.

Finally, Natassia asked, "Was Nora's fun this weekend?"

"I just do not like the idea of this guy, Natassia. He's too old for you. He's using you. I don't like any of it."

"Yeah, Mom, but I do."

"Natassia." Mary touched the tip of her cigarette to a patch of dry skin on her foot, held it there until she felt the burn. "What am I supposed to do with you? What am I supposed to do?"

FOR HOURS AFTER THAT PHONE CALL, Mary was awake, lying on her futon on the floor. In the middle of the night, still sleepless, she aimed the remote control at the TV, turned it on. As she tapped her pipe against the edge of the ashtray to empty out the dead tobacco, she clicked through the channels. There was no cable in the greenhouse, no MTV. There was fuzzy NBC and CBS. The PBS station came in clearest. A nature show was on. A mother cheetah named Duma was watching, helpless, as her four cubs were being killed by lions in the jungle. A storm came up. Windy rain whipped the palm trees. When the lions finally went away, Duma tried to drag what was left of her little cub corpses to a safe, dry spot.

"But then," the show's invisible narrator said in his calm PBS voice, so much like the voice of God, all-knowing and unmoved, "Duma has no choice but to leave her cubs to the rain and the predators."

"See," Mary said to the TV, wiping her eyes, "it's not just me. You do what you can. That's all you can do."

In the next scene, filmed a year later, Duma was running with her second litter of cubs. "Slut," Mary said to the TV, but she was happy for Duma's second chance. When the cubs gathered around their mother's teats, she was slit-eyed with pleasure, or with pain. A vulture that looked like George C. Scott flew above them, but it kept its distance. *The mother will do it right this time.* Duma's cubs needed to eat and grow, so she went out into the bush and came back with some lesser, slower jungle-being to feed to her babies. How sorrowful all those beasts looked when they finally had some prey in their mouths.

Mary filled her pipe and lit it again while Duma's new cubs ran wild in the jungle. "And after a year," the cool voice of the narrator said, "one day, as the cubs are playing with their mother"—they were chasing her, she was chasing them, playing tag and hide-and-go-seek, everybody happy—"their mother leaves them. Leaves them to survive on their own."

In mid-game. She just left. The cubs looked around and their mother was gone.

"Jeez," Mary said, "even I wouldn't do that."

CHAPTER 5:

AUGUST

1989

The next morning, Mary got on the case right away. Even before making her coffee, she called Lotte to say she would be down in the city by that afternoon to take care of Natassia's mess.

"No big rush, dear," Lotte said. "David was able to take care of the legalities."

"Already?" Mary was spinning her asthma inhaler on the kitchen counter, Russian-roulette-style. "How? When?"

"Last night. We remembered that one of David's old authors is a detective. The guy made a few phone calls—what's his name?—I can't remember. He wrote a few weak mysteries that never did very well. Anyway, he called the police and—"

"The detective-writer called?"

"Yes, and he found out that the report written up by the store's security guard was badly botched. You know, they hire these kids who aren't trained and who don't care—and why should they care, really, for what they're paid? So now it looks as if the store doesn't have a leg to stand on. They're dropping the charges."

Mary took the inhaler out of her mouth. "Dropping the whole thing?" Her breathing changed, slowed. "The whole mess?"

"Natassia's name and personal information are on file with the manager at Ralph Lauren, and they don't want her shopping there anymore."

"She shouldn't have been in there to begin with."

"Well, I agree with you. Imagine those girls shopping on Madison Avenue like middle-aged matrons. I guess their next stop would have been across the street at Pierre Deux, to look over drapery fabrics."

Mary smiled into the phone. Even in a crisis, Lotte could cheer Mary up.

A FEW HOURS LATER, down in the city, Mary was standing in the dim, tile-floored hallway outside of Lotte and David's Upper West Side apartment, leaning against the door, listening. Her pelvis was doing Kegel exercises, tightening and releasing. Inside the apartment, Natassia was playing the violin—a new piece, some waltzy thing. Mary stared at the Amnesty International sticker stuck on the door, just below the tarnished brass peephole. She gripped her key until it pinched her palm, punishing herself for being so afraid. *What can the kid do to me?* Mary had known enough to come down to the city to talk to Natassia. Now that she was here, though, she had no clue what she was supposed to do next.

Natassia, on the violin, was working her way up the strings to a high note. She almost missed it. Mary winced.

Why wouldn't Natassia be as malleable as a dancer and let Mary choreograph? Lots of dancers let Mary show them what to do. They trusted her judgment. Then they worked together—dancers and choreographer—so nobody looked stupid onstage. Why did Natassia do nothing but blow Mary off?

Mary unlocked the door and yelled "Hello?" so Natassia wouldn't get scared when she heard footsteps. "Hey, Natassia?"

Natassia stopped playing and yelled, "Shit."

"Well, hello to you, too." As Mary walked down the hallway, her sneakers smacked the wood floor. She stopped in the archway of the living room. "Why aren't you dressed yet? It's almost three o'clock."

"You ruined it."

"What?"

"I'm making a violin tape for the BF, for his Walkman, and you ruined it. This is the third time I tried."

The room was a mess—sheets of music, a bowl of cereal milk, shopping bags, a bathrobe, bed pillows, old photo albums, a banana peel, a stack of Blockbuster videos, newspapers—the debris of several different projects all over the chairs and the couch. Natassia, too, was a mess. The scene might have been normal for anybody else's daughter, but Natassia had never been a messy person. Even as a little girl, after just a few weeks of Montessori, she'd been focused enough to finish and put away one game or homework assignment before beginning another, and she'd always been a pain in the butt about wanting her clothes to be clean. Seeing her now, Mary felt embarrassed, as if she had walked in on someone in a state of abandon that should have been private. The thought rose up inside of Mary: My daughter is undone by love. She told Natassia, "You need to wash your hair."

"I know that. And I need to shave my legs and iron the shirt I bought for him. I have a whole list here." And in fact, on the coffee table, there was a legal pad with a long list written in Natassia's slim, upright handwriting. Out of habit, Mary scanned the page for secrets. "Mom, please, would you iron for me? I'm really rushed." While the tape rewound, Natassia held the tape recorder tenderly on her lap, as if it were a kitten.

Mary pulled in her abdominals. "Lotte told you I was coming here to talk to you."

"I'm meeting him at seven o'clock for his birthday dinner, and I still have to get his gifts together and do all this other stuff." The tape recorder clicked. "Okay," Natassia said, and set the machine on the coffee table.

"I told you last night," Mary said, dropping her backpack at her feet and crossing her arms sternly over her middle (like Yul Brynner in *The King and I*), "you're grounded for two weeks."

Natassia swung her long frizzy ponytail over her right shoulder and lifted the violin, which was the same auburn color as her hair. Natassia's hair had the texture of Lotte's—thick and electrified, tight tiny waves all over the place. When it was dirty, like now, it didn't look greasy; it looked stopped, halted. "Okay, quiet now," Natassia said. "This time it has to be perfect."

"Why didn't you think of taping this gift for him before you went into Ralph Lauren with hot little fingers?"

"M-o-m-m, quiet. Please. Will you please switch the tape recorder on when I give you the signal?"

As she sat up straight on the edge of the sofa with her pink cotton nightgown pulled up above her knees, Natassia's long legs stuck out in sharp angles, like Ross's basketball legs. Mary watched Natassia lift her chin to make room for the violin. She raised the bow and nodded her head toward the tape recorder. "Okay, Mom. And this time it has to be perfect. No background noise. Come on, turn it on, please."

Unsure if she was making an idiot's concession or an intelligent negotiation, Mary hit the START button. Natassia's bow bit into the strings.

While Natassia played, Mary sat on the floor, leaning her back against the archway, smoking her cigarette, watching. *The kid really is a mess.* Mary knew that if she got up close, Natassia would smell stale and sweaty. Her lips were red, worried and chapped, licked raw. Mary hated the waltz Natassia was playing, and it embarrassed Mary to see how nervous Natassia was as she picked her way through a tricky fast part. Natassia played the violin like a little girl, keeping the waltz sugary. Mary fought the urge to interrupt and say, "Slow down for the legato. Jazz up the staccato. Vary the rhythm." But if Mary said anything, she'd have to hear the piece again.

She did have to hear it again. To make sure she had the *most* perfect recording, Natassia put in another blank tape and played her piece one more time. Mary lit a second cigarette and bit her cuticles. Natassia had always been thorough and precise preparing her school projects, but it was driving Mary crazy now to see how afraid the kid was to screw up. Sometimes people like this showed up in Mary's dance classes—skilled, capable, but so fucking careful. Nothing oozed out of them but fear and worry, and still they wanted to be professional dancers. *If you want it, you can't be afraid of it.* Mary felt sick to see the relief on Natassia's face when she played the difficult phrase without missing a note. *All for a guy.* Never had Natassia seemed silly to Mary until now, in love. Natassia played the last syrupy section, inching toward the inevitable conclusion.

"Okay," Mary demanded, lighting her third Camel, ready for business, "now tell me what happened at Ralph Lauren."

"It was so stupid." While her recording rewound, Natassia knelt next to the coffee table.

"Uh-uh-uhn," Mary scolded.

"What? Oh." Natassia's thumb had found its way into her mouth. "Sorry."

"Don't apologize to me. Apologize to your teeth. You're not sucking the thumb again, are you? You just got your braces off."

Chagrined as always when caught thumb-sucking, Natassia changed the subject. "I think that last recording was the sharper one, don't you?" In a rushed, businesslike manner, she folded sheets of tissue paper—contrasting shades of deep blue and light blue—and interlaid them in a box that was the perfect size to hold the tape. "Oh, yeah, wait." Natassia jumped up and left the room.

"Don't you ignore me. Come back here." Mary stood and followed Natassia, who was scurrying down the hallway.

"I need scissors," Natassia called over her shoulder. "They're in my room."

"Shit." Mary's cigarette was dripping ash onto the Persian carpet. "I want to know," she called, using her hand as an ashtray and making her way down the dark front hallway, "what you were trying to steal from that store."

"I was not stealing." In the bedroom, Natassia was pawing through a desk drawer. Mary always forgot, until they were both standing, how much her daughter towered over her.

Mary's fingers ringed Natassia's arm tightly. "What did you take? Tell me. What?"

"Ow-w-w-w! You're hurting me. I didn't *take* anything. I was looking, that's all."

"For what? Tell me."

Natassia sighed, as if she were the adult tolerating the kid, and sat down on the edge of her desk so they were eye-level with each other. "He's really been wanting a new leather wallet, like a really, really skinny little one?"

"Natassia." Mary's grip tightened again.

"I wasn't trying to leave with the wallet, I really wasn't. I was just walking around with it in my back pocket, you know? And all we were doing was, like, looking for a mirror to see if it showed through my jeans pocket?" Lately Natassia's voice had started doing that Valley Girl thing of turning everything she knew to be a fact into a question; this happened especially when she talked about her boyfriend. "He's been trying really hard to find a money holder that doesn't show through his pants pocket?" Mary let go of Natassia and felt nauseous. He's vain, Mary thought, can't the kid see how vain?

 69

Natassia turned back to her desk drawer. "Oh, great, here's the scissors," and she rushed out toward the living room.

Mary, quick, turned and grabbed a handful of nightgown and held on tight as she followed Natassia through the hallway to the living room. "Then why did the store people think you were stealing? Did you explain to them what you were doing?"

"Hand me that Scotch tape, please." Natassia was oh-so-carefully trimming the edges of the tissue paper so that her recording was nestled perfectly within the little box. "They simply wouldn't listen to us, Mom. We tried to tell them."

"Who's us? Who were you with?" Mary stubbed out her cigarette, wiped her ash-stained hand on her jeans.

"Carey and Mariah."

"I'm calling their parents." Mary jumped over the back of the sofa and onto the floor.

"Mom! No!" Natassia ran around the coffee table to cut her mother off, but Mary was faster and slipped ahead and was on her way down the back hallway. Natassia followed. Single-file, they had to squeeze between crowded bookshelves and stacks of books to get to the kitchen. Natassia was saying, "You can't do that. Mariah's mother can't find out."

"Why not?" With the phone receiver gripped under her jaw, Mary snapped through the pages of the phone book on the kitchen counter. "What the hell is Mariah's last name, Brown or Greene?"

"No, no, no, no. Please, no. Please, no," Natassia said in a whispery chant as she eased the receiver out from the vise made by Mary's jaw and shoulder. "No, no, please, no. Mariah's mother just got out of the hospital for bad depression. They can't tell her, the doctor said so."

"Why all this consideration for Mariah's mother? Tell me, please. Why do I get all the bullshit and she gets all this consideration?"

Natassia sighed. "Stop being so theatrical." She hung up the receiver and headed back to the living room. "How would you like it if you were in a big depression?"

"Maybe I am." Mary was reaching up into the fuse box for David's bag of potato chips. His cholesterol was through the roof, and he hid his treats so Lotte wouldn't toss them, but everyone else knew where they were. "Come back here. Get that bag of chips for me. Please."

Natassia ran into the kitchen with giddy, fast steps that pissed Mary off. Easily, Natassia lifted the bag out of the fuse box, and handed it to Mary, who was careful to keep the ice in her voice when she said, "Thank you." Natassia bent and kissed her mother on the forehead. Mary slapped Natassia's butt and walked in front of her down the hall to the living room. "I want you to sit in here and talk to me."

"No, Mom, let's go in my bedroom. I've got tons of stuff I need to do in there."

In the bedroom, Natassia turned on her stereo radio. Mary turned the window-unit AC up to high and sat on the radiator with her legs curled under her and the bag of chips in her lap.

"Now," Natassia said, "for the pièce de résistance." She went inside her closet, came back with a shopping bag, and from it pulled a large dark button-down shirt. After yanking her white comforter down, she spread the shirt on the bed, the arms stretched out. "Oh, shoot. Where'd I put the iron? I'm such a ninny. Where's the iron?"

Mary didn't like the look of a man's shirt lying on her daughter's exposed bedsheet. "Where'd you get that? Kevin?"

"Isn't it great? Here, touch this." She scooped up the shirt and tossed it to Mary, but then she said, "No! No! *Don't* touch, you have greasy potato-chip fingers. Here, feel it." Natassia grabbed the shirt back and brushed it against Mary's face.

Soft polished cotton. "What did you pay for this?" Mary wanted to know.

"I got it at the vintage store on Hudson Street."

The color was beautiful, deep maroon. "How did you know what size to buy?"

"The BF wears the same size as Daddy. Isn't that cool?" Natassia had found the iron under her bed. She spread the shirt out on her sheet again, plugged in the iron.

"Since when do you know what size your father wears?"

"One day the BF and I got caught in the rain in the park, and we were, like, totally soaked?" Natassia licked her pinkie and tested the iron's heat. "So we came here and I gave him one of Daddy's old flannel shirts. Dad said he didn't mind. This iron isn't hot enough."

"I don't like you bringing guys here when Lotte and David aren't home."

"Oh, Mom." Natassia rushed to the shaving closet to get a cup of water for the iron. She called out over the running water, "That's completely silly. You know we're at his place all the time alone. You know I'm lovers with him." Natassia came back and Mary stood to face her. Natassia stepped close and ran her hand over her mother's head. Mary felt a gush of relief to have the kid finally looking at her without that withering stare. "Come on, Mom. You had lovers when you were my age, I know you did. Don't tell me you didn't."

Up close, Natassia did smell. She was sweaty, with the scent she used to bring home at the end of a day of playing in the grass. The summer Natassia was four, she, Ross, and Mary had spent a week on somebody's farm in Connecticut, some friend of Lotte's. Now Mary stood as close as she could to Natassia in her dirty nightgown, the pink wilted ruffles, and Mary held the scent for a long minute, afraid she might cry. The green smell of child's play was a gift from somewhere beyond her anger, this chance for a whiff of her small girl again.

"Mom?"

"I had boyfriends when I was your age, Natassia. Not lovers."

"Semantics. What's the dif?" On the bed, the iron tilted over onto its side. "Oops." Natassia ran over to the sink with her glass and filled the iron with water, while on the wall above her, in a row of four framed photographs, Mary spun, lifted a male partner, leaped in a 180-degree split, and took a curtain-call bow. Mary couldn't stand the way she looked in any of the pictures, but they were one of Lotte's efforts to help Mary and Natassia stay connected. A framed poster of Mary's company hung in Natassia's bathroom. Mary had once overheard a little friend of Natassia's saying, "Wow, you have so much dance stuff. I take ballet, too." And Natassia had said, "I hate dance. Those are just my mother." Mary turned away now, looked out the window, over the top of the air conditioner splattered with pigeon shit, down onto West End Avenue. The tedious repetition of New York summers and the effort to survive New York summers seemed almost unbearable. Mary noticed that the air conditioner was sweating, and she thought of all the air conditioners in the city that were churning right now, the efforts of thousands and thousands of people to make life endurable. The windows of Natassia's bedroom still had the baby bars in place. It was impossible to explain to the kid just how much this older, foreign guy knew that Natassia, despite all her precocious intelligence, did not know yet. Could not know. Impossible to make Natassia realize how desperate and unhappy he probably was if he was going after a teenager; and, therefore, how ruthless he could be. "You're too young for lovers, Natassia."

"What, Mom?"

The air conditioner was making a racket. Down on the street, a young man on a bicycle was kissing a man who stood next to him. They'd been alternately talking and kissing for several minutes.

A Michael Jackson song came on the radio, and Natassia screamed so loud, Mary spun and hollered, "What!"

Natassia ran across the room to the stereo and raised the volume.

"Goddamn, lower that stupid song."

"Can't!" The room was full now of Michael Jackson. And in every mirror—the floor-length on the closet door, the three-way dresser mirror, the makeup mirror on the desk—there was Natassia, bouncing. Mary, watching Natassia jerk and spin, was thinking, What a little girl she still is. She was wondering, Can't that man see how young she is? She was noticing, The kid's dancing off the beat.

As soon as the song ended, Natassia, breathless, went back to ironing. "I love that song."

"It's shit. Lower the volume. Please."

"You do it. The knob's lower right." Natassia was poking the shirt cuffs with the hot tip of the iron. Now and then, the thumb of her free hand went to her mouth, where, without realizing it, she bit the tip of it, then sucked it, then bit. "He's going to look so beautiful in this shirt."

Beautiful? He probably had a wretched skinny ponytail full of squiggly gray hairs, tarnished earrings in his sagging earlobes, and a potbelly. "How many gifts does this god need to make his birthday happy enough for him?"

"Mother," Natassia scolded. Now the shirt was spread front-down on the sheet, then folded and tucked perfectly into a gift box, which was stacked with the smaller box of the violin recording. Natassia pulled out from under her bed a roll of Italian watermarked wrapping paper, which she unfurled across her bedsheet. She bent to wrap the gifts. Mary did not like that the wrapping paper looked pricey, and she did not like seeing

Natassia's nightgown hanging open, showing her breasts. Folding up the bag of chips, Mary left the room.

"Where're you going, Mom?"

"Those chips made me thirsty."

"There's iced tea. Will you get me an iced tea? Please? Pretty, pretty please, Mom?"

"Have you even eaten lunch today?" Mary called from the hallway.

"What? I can't hear you."

"I am not going to scream," Mary screamed from the kitchen. "You come in here if you want to talk to me."

She poured two glasses of iced tea, splashed one with gin from the bottle on the counter, and headed back to the bedroom. Rounding the corner out of the too-bright kitchen into the dark hallway, she ran right into Natassia, who was holding scissors. Their arms bumped, iced tea spilled.

"Nice!" Mary scolded.

"I was coming to talk to you."

"Don't run around the house with scissors. Don't *ever* run with scissors."

"Oh, great, you got me an iced tea." Natassia wrapped her hand around her mother's hand on the cold glass Mary offered and stepped close enough to cover Mary's bare toes with her own bare toes. "You're so sweet."

One problem with this visit was that it was off-kilter. They always hugged when they first saw each other, and this time they had not. Natassia knew enough to try to set things right. She wriggled her toes over Mary's toes, and her finger tapped at the feather hanging from Mary's ear. Mary felt the impulse to trace Natassia's jaw, the soft line of blond down that ran from her earlobe, another inheritance from Lotte. Mary felt so much affection for the soft plush on Natassia's and Lotte's arms and jawline, their bushy eyebrows. They both said they envied Mary's hairlessness, her ink-line-thin eyebrows, the invisible silk hair on her arms, but these body differences made Mary feel left out.

It was late afternoon. By now Mary had lost track of all the important points she had come here to make. The kid might end up in jail, but the only thing that made any sense was to hug her. Mary lifted her hand and offered her palm to Natassia, and Natassia pressed her own palm against her mother's. Their fingers locked together, and Mary brought Natassia's big hand up to her lips for a kiss, and she whispered into the kid's knuckles, "I'm going to go home soon, baby."

"Oh no." Like a little girl, Natassia pulled on two of her mother's fingers. "Don't go yet."

They were in their sweetheart whispers, and they sipped from their glasses of tea. "Natassy, I came here to talk." The palms of their hands pressed gently together, back and forth. "And we're not talking."

"Well, the sooner I get all my stuff done, the sooner we can talk."

"Listen, honey. Listen, sweets." Their fingers were intertwined. Mary whispered and Natassia listened. "I'm not trying to be big and mean with you. I'm really not. I'd love it if you met a nice guy. You should have a nice boyfriend. You're gorgeous and terrific and smart." Natassia smiled, but with her head swaying back and forth, as if she were hearing a friendly melody, not real words. "But, Natassy, I want you to be only with men who are wonderful, nothing less than terrific. I don't want you to be with someone who's not good for you."

"M-o-m-m." Natassia still swayed, and Mary lifted their joined hands and made an arch for Natassia to dance under. "The BF is good for me. He's awesome. You don't even know him."

Mary kept hold of Natassia's hand, as if they were partnering, and led the two of them down the hallway to Natassia's room. Feeling sure they would now talk, Mary let go of Natassia and put down her spiked tea, sat on the bed, lay back, and all at once her body realized both the depth of her exhaustion and a delicious release from it. The gift boxes stacked beside her on Natassia's bed didn't seem so lethal anymore. "Natassia, do you know how much I miss you sometimes? Come sit with me."

Natassia plopped down on the other side of the pile of gifts. She really was a precious girl.

"Sweetie, what about our plan? How about you coming to live with me in January? I could get you enrolled now for next semester. I'm pretty sure we get free tuition."

"Ma-ry!" As much as Mary resisted *Mom,* she liked it even less when her daughter used her first name, as she did now: "Mary, Mary, Mary! You must be hallucinating. You really think I'm going to live up there?"

"What's wrong with living up there? I live there."

"My friends don't." Natassia picked up the boxes to inspect her gift-wrapping. "My BF doesn't. Your school's too far away. These gifts are still missing something. They don't look as good as I want them to look."

"Honey, aren't there any good guys in your school?"

"Damn! Ribbon! I forgot to get nice ribbon."

"These gifts are fine without ribbon. You already spent a fortune to wrap them."

"Yes!" Natassia jumped off the bed. "I know what I'll use. I know exactly."

She did a pirouette on her way to her closet and looked back at Mary, who said, "Yes, lovely," then Natassia disappeared. When she stepped out of the closet, she had her Mexican-print cotton skirt and was ripping the seam.

"*What* are you doing?"

"This is so perfect I can't believe it."

Mary sat up straight. "*Stop* that." She tossed a pillow. "*Now!* Stop. That's a good skirt."

"This is what I was wearing the first night we made love." Natassia was holding up the skirt and aiming the scissors for a deep gouge into the cloth.

"Natassia! That skirt cost money."

"Why're you so hung up on money these days? You got a job."

In two long strides Mary was across the room, grabbing the skirt from Natassia and smacking her hand, hard. "This is *not* good. Don't you *ever* tear up anything of yours for a man. Don't do it." She was squeezing Natassia's hand that was holding the scissors, and she squeezed harder and harder, until Natassia yelled "Ow!" and let go of the scissors. They dropped and pierced the skin of Natassia's foot and brought up a drop of blood.

"Mom!" Natassia's voice was full of shock, and Mary's heart was pounding as she bent down to Natassia's foot and wrapped her hands around it to cover the blood. Mary closed her eyes. She felt lightheaded, caught within another of those returned moments: Mary remembered Little Girl Natassia falling while playing, getting her perfect little body cut or bruised or bumped. Afterward, Mary cringed to touch the scabs, the scars. But this time, Mary herself had done the damage, made the cut, brought up the blood. Opening and closing her eyes, Mary sat on the bedroom carpet holding Natassia's foot. A little blood ran through her fingers. Natassia was more scared than injured, Mary could feel that just through the foot in her hand.

"Mom, you're not *crying*, are you? Look. The cut's really small. The blood stopped."

Mary couldn't keep the anger out of her hands. She picked up the scissors and tossed them across the room; the tip dug a point into the floorboards just past the carpet. The scissors stood there, shining and shimmying for a second, then fell over, clattered onto the wood. "Shit."

Natassia slipped her foot out from Mary's hands, gave her the soft voice: "Mom, it's okay."

"I just don't want anything bad to happen to you. I love you."

Sitting there next to Natassia—next to her warm, bloody foot, and her safe, soft voice—Mary was working hard to try to hear Dr. Cather's voice. Every time Cather talked about the good mother caught within Mary's heart, saying shrink-type things like "We have to let that good mother come out," Mary said to herself, Bullshit. But Cather kept coming back to that one fact: through all the years Mary was traveling, every night, every single one, from wherever, she always found a telephone and talked to Natassia, or at least left a message. Dr. Cather acted like she was amazed by this. "You can't think of one night when you didn't call her?"

"Hardly."

"Hold on to that, Mary. That's the core, that's the heart of your mothering. It's good and it's constant."

"Look, Dr. Cather, that and a token will get my kid on the subway. It wasn't enough. I should have been there with her."

"I'm not saying you shouldn't have been, and I'm not saying you should have been. I'm saying there was this one constant act of care that you performed. *You* did it. No one put a gun to your head. You extended yourself, Mary. Whatever made you do that, it's inside of you. It's something to build on."

"Mom?" Natassia asked. "How come you say you just want to love me and then you throw a fit? It's, like, so weird when it happens."

"I don't know, Natassia. All I know is, I don't want you to go to that man's place tonight."

Natassia's eyes widened into her grown-up, stern look. "Mom." Straightening her spine, she looked into Mary's eyes. "I know what's going on here." Natassia ran her hands through her thick hair several times, as if trying to gather her patience. "You're jealous, Mom, aren't you?"

As if a window had fallen shut, Mary couldn't breathe, couldn't talk. She crouched on the carpet a second to get her balance. *Inhaler.* Standing, Mary picked the scissors up off the floor, laid them carefully on the desk, left the room.

"Mom, why're you leaving? Where're you going?"

From the hallway, Mary called, "Where does Lotte keep the train schedule?"

Natassia called back, "But we were talking, Mom."

"Yeah, but you know what you want to do, so go ahead. Just be careful."

"Well . . ."

Mary could tell from Natassia's voice that she was standing at the end of the hallway, watching. "Okay, Mom, if you mean it. Good. Thanks. You know, Mom, all I want is to get along with you."

Walking away, taking air in through her nose, blowing out slowly through her mouth, not looking back, Mary muttered to herself, "Little bitch." In the kitchen she untacked the train schedule from the bulletin board. There was nothing more to do here. She'd been accused of being jealous of her own daughter; now Mary's last option was gone. She couldn't throw herself in front of the door to keep Natassia from going out. She couldn't end up in an asthma attack. She'd look like a fool. The kid had won. Mary walked back into the bedroom. "Where're my cigarettes?"

"Mom, you shouldn't smoke."

And you shouldn't be fucking men old enough to be your father, Mary thought. She said, "Enough advice for one day, Natassia. Where's my smokes?"

"I don't know. Probably where you were sitting, on the window ledge."

The cigarettes were under the radiator. Mary grabbed them and dug into her backpack for matches and her inhaler and enough money to buy a bag of pipe tobacco. "I'm going out."

Still futzing with the strips of torn skirt, Natassia asked, "Where're you going, *Mamita*?"

"I'll be back before you leave."

HALF AN HOUR LATER, Natassia was stepping into a royal-blue leotard when Mary walked into her room, sat on the floor, and spread out the *Daily News*. When Natassia said, "Oh, yippee, you're back!" Mary said, without looking up from her newspaper, "Do you have any subway tokens? I'm getting the six-ten."

"Just one, and I need it to get downtown, but, Mom, you don't want the six-ten. That's peak, it costs more." Natassia's hair was clean and damp and frizzing, hopping long and loose. With her body sleek inside the leotard, she crouched down next to Mary. "Look, can I show you something?" She opened a bottle of moisturizer, rubbed some onto Mary's wrist. "Smell."

The scent was pine—clean and delicious—with musk in it. "Nice." Mary felt Natassia's energy, amped up and consolidated, just the way Mary used to get right before going onstage. When she gathered her focus, entered the zone, no one could mess with Mary, and now, staring at the newspaper, she couldn't think of a damn thing to do to stop, divert, or disrupt Natassia's plan.

"Isn't this lotion great, Mom? He smells like this, you know, like, all the time."

In the moments before curtain, Mary shed the world and got quiet, but some dancers turned chatty, the way Natassia was now. "I bought it for him, but I'm, like, This is so cool I'm keeping it for myself." She dabbed moisturizer onto her wrists and ankles, then dipped into the scoop of her leotard and put the scent between her breasts, then on the tops of her thighs. "We do this thing," she told Mary, "where he has to discover all the places where I have perfume on."

"I'm not one of your girlfriends. You don't tell your mother shit like that."

"Yeah, but you're cool, Mom. Much cooler than Mariah's dysfunctional mother." If Natassia were a different kid, Mary might have suspected drugs. The kid was so airy now, breezy, as if riding some potent whiff of smoke. Pulling on her jeans, Natassia asked, "Who was the best lover you ever had? Daddy?"

"Natassia." Mary snapped over a page of newspaper. "That's none of your business." As she looked down at the newsprint, her eyes blurred.

An electronic watch or clock somewhere in the room beeped five-thirty. The only way Mary could get the early train now was to take a cab, and she didn't have the money. There'd be no time in the studio today. She'd accomplished nothing.

Constancy, follow-up, follow-through.

Leave me alone, Dr. Cather.

You're the mother, you have to be willing to be unpopular now and then. If you think something's important, it probably is important. Stick to your guns. Trust yourself.

"This BS BF of yours, Natassia, is he married? Was he ever married?"

"None of your beeswax."

Natassia's jeans were now belt-buckled; her leotard scooped so low it was riding the curves of her freckled shoulders; her breasts were especially prominent in the leotard—blue, rounded, and held by a seamless bra. She was pulling her red cowboy boots on over her Daffy Duck anklets, an incongruous tease. It occurred to Mary that maybe the guy had no idea how young Natassia was. No, she wasn't on drugs. Natassia was just high on herself, on her own potent young body, and Mary knew there was no way to interrupt that buzz.

"Does Lotte let you take the subway down there by yourself? Are any of your friends going with you?"

"No. He wanted just me."

The BF's gifts were wrapped and ribboned and packed into Natassia's backpack, the backpack slung over her shoulder. Natassia tucked a subway token into the tiny front pocket of her jeans, walked up to Mary, who still sat on the floor, who wouldn't stand up for a hug, so Natassia wrapped her big hands around her mother's head, bent down, and kissed her hair. "I love you, Mom. Thanks for helping me get ready for his birthday. It means a lot."

"I was not helping you." Mary had reached the end of the *News* and was snapping the pages back toward the front.

"Are you okay? Come on, Mom, be okay. Listen, Grammy lets me see him, and I've been riding the subway for years. You know that."

Mary stared at Natassia's boots and caught a whiff of something like dog shit coming off the soles. The stink was strong enough to make Mary feel nauseous. She got up, tossed the newspaper into the wastebasket, sat on the window ledge, breathed. "Natassia, why don't I have any authority with you? That's what I want to know. Why don't I?" The muscles around her sacrum were fisting into pain.

Natassia laughed and turned to leave. "Mom, you're so funny. How'm I supposed to know? You're the adult. What's wrong? Your face looks weird. Is your back hurting again?"

"That's just my fucking point. I'm the adult. I know this thing with this man is not good for you. I'm the mother here." Mary stood too quickly and had to breathe her way through a shot of pain in her lower back. "I know better. I know you should stop it now."

"Why?"

"Any man who has you running around shoplifting, so desperate to see him happy—"

"Who's screaming here?" Natassia, rushing, was dissolving, near tears. "Who's really desperate here?"

She was headed down the hallway, turning the dead bolt on the apartment door, was halfway out, and Mary was yelling behind her, "I want to know where you are going, Natassia. I have no idea where this moron lives. I at least want a phone number."

Natassia stepped back in from the hallway, held the door closed and whispered, "There are people at the elevator listening to you scream. He doesn't have a phone. The frigging phone company disconnected him last month. Oh, Mom, please, let's stop fighting."

"Yes!" Mary hissed back. "Why don't you stop fighting me?" Staring at each other, they stood there. *Damn* it. Mary had always been so sure that Natassia would use her intelligence to keep herself safe. But Natassia wasn't herself anymore. Grown-up and tall and good-looking, sexy now on top of it. As sure of herself as ever, but acting as dumb as a brick, moving toward trouble so huge and inevitable Mary could almost see the shape of it, could feel its ugly heartbeat, and yet she could not think of one way to keep Natassia from craving it. *A real mother would know what to do.* "Just . . .

please." When Mary spoke, her voice was nothing. "Can't you give me an address?" But the door was closing.

Then the door opened again and Natassia's head reappeared. "Mom, why don't you just stay in town tonight? You can sleep in my room, in the AC. I'll be back tomorrow morning."

AFTER NATASSIA WAS GONE, Mary went into the bedroom and looked through the drawers for new notes from the BF, but she didn't find any. She found a black lacy camisole and stringy black underpants, that's all. True, Natassia had been riding the subway without an adult since seventh grade, when Lotte sent her to a self-defense course, quizzed her on the subway map, and said she'd be fine. Lotte always knew when Natassia was ready for the next step, Mary believed that, and Lotte seemed to be letting this BF thing just happen. Mary ate a bowl of cereal, then curled into a ball on Natassia's floor to stretch out her lower back. *I should have followed her, tailed her all the way downtown.* Why was Mary pretending she didn't know what to do? It was like pretending for years that dance wasn't wrecking her body, pretending it was okay to dance through injuries, pretending she could breathe without breath. Her back was so tight she had to ease herself up by leaning first on elbows, then shifting back onto knees. Then she had to hustle to catch the 9:02 Express back upstate.

LATER THAT NIGHT, back in the greenhouse, Mary lay on her futon with an ice pack tucked under her, and the dusty telephone crouched next to her. Smoke from her pipe did sad turns up toward the ceiling, toward the three cedar beams that joined the two sides of the A-frame. All summer, during long, empty evenings lying there and staring up, Mary had visualized herself dancing on those beams. Tonight she imagined a kind of circus act happening within the big tent of the A-frame, saw herself crossing the beams doing spins and flips, the kind of moves that would probably cause injury if she performed them on the floor. In the air, they'd mean certain disaster.

Mary's skin still felt trembly from the aftershocks of the afternoon—Natassia ripping up her clothes, playing hide-and-seek with that lotion all over her body. *You're jealous, Mom, aren't you? Who's really desperate here?* Mary really did feel she was at the end of what she knew how to do with Natassia. Maybe tonight was the night to get up on the ceiling beams and try the dance steps that would finally break all her bones.

"No," Mary said to the urge to pick up the phone and call someone. Turning onto her side, she told the wall, "No fucking point," but still she found herself organizing the events in her head, preparing her defense for the inevitable day when she finally would be called in—to court? to the police station? to a TV talk show?—to account for why she was a lousy mother. *All I wanted to do was find out who this guy is. I go down there, the kid won't talk. She's dressed like a slut. She tells me I'm jealous.* Who would want to hear it?

She rolled onto her back and looked up again, into the ceiling's high arch, built like the cathedrals in Italy, those offerings to God to help get you straight to heaven. Mary remembered that from the art-history course she'd taken in Rome. *Explain that to the lawyer, the judge, the TV audience: The kid was conceived on a dare and was born at the end of spring semester, my junior year in college. While I was dancing professionally, going to classes, rehearsing—*

And why would a dancer make such a selfish choice?

Mary had no idea. Taking a deep inhale on her pipe, she closed her eyes, then exhaled, coughed. Her back pain was easing up, but there really was no way to get this slimy feeling out from inside her. She would not call Cather to set up an extra appointment. It cost too much and couldn't change anything anyway. Mary would not under any circumstances call Ross and let him hear how small she'd become.

"No fucking way," she said out loud. But a little while later, she lifted the receiver and hit the auto-dial button for Ross's phone number in Spokane.

CHAPTER 6:

AUGUST

1989

Ross Stein was sitting alone out on his back deck reading two books—an illustrated volume of ancient Egyptian erotica, and a manual on how to put up cedar siding—going from one book to the other to try to keep himself awake. He wished he could just go to bed, but it wasn't worth it. He had a patient in labor. Sometime soon he'd have to go to the hospital. He held a mouthful of sugared coffee in his mouth and remembered how he used to like to suck on his bourbon before he swallowed it down.

Harriet's calico cat jumped onto Ross's foot, and he kick-tossed the cat deep into the dark yard. The cat hissed. "Die, you beast," Ross muttered. Two years he'd been living with Harriet, and he still went around thinking to himself, Damn that woman and her cat. Something about that wasn't right.

The cat came back. Ross kicked it again, farther. Then he remembered that he'd forgotten to feed it. When Harriet had left for the hospital that afternoon, she'd asked him to feed the cat. Ross went inside, looked in the fridge until he found the fresh turkey pastrami, tore up a few slices, and set out an extra-large portion on the cat's plate. Into the cat's water dish he poured black coffee. He liked to watch the cat jazzed up on caffeine.

Ross had just sat down again, was lifting his feet up onto the wooden railing, when the remote phone rang inside the pocket of his khakis. "Yeah," he answered. "Stein here."

"Hi," Mary said, "it's me."

"Hi, you."

"You busy?"

"Yeah, I'm waiting for the labor room to call."

"Okay, I'll call you later."

"No, it's all right. There's Call Waiting. You're up late—it's two in the morning there."

"You and I have to talk about something," she said.

We haven't had this conversation for a while, he thought. He asked, "What'd I do now?"

"Did you know Natassia's got a boyfriend?"

"Hey, what are you smoking? I hear you sucking on something."

"A Camel, what d'you think I'm smoking?"

"An intern gave me some weed last week. It was terrible shit. He grew it. I threw it out."

"I thought you quit everything."

"I did. That's why I threw out the pot. We tried one joint, took a hit—"

"How's Harriet?"

"She's fine. She's at the hospital."

"On call?"

"Yeah. God, I wish I didn't have to go in tonight. I'm out here on the deck. You know what I still can't get over? There're no bugs out west, not even at night, not even when it's really hot. Imagine Fire Island with no bugs."

"Have you talked to Natassia lately? About this guy?"

"The guy who swiped my shirt from my parents' apartment?" A star shot by over Ross's garage. He should get Natassia out here more often, so she could see stuff.

"You know, Ross, I have totally bad vibes about this guy."

"Yeah? Sounds like he's into art. She told me he takes her to galleries. Is she coming here for Christmas? Tell her I want to see her for Christmas. You want to come?"

"Thanks, I can't. But, yeah, she's coming for her whole winter break."

"So what's wrong with her boyfriend?"

"He turned her into a dimwit."

Ross laughed.

"Don't laugh. He did."

"How dim?"

"Completely. She's lost it. She's not herself. She's slimy, like a cat."

"Slimy?"

"Everything's a secret. Meanwhile, she's lurking around town dressed like a slut, she won't tell me where she's going to meet him. She won't even say his name. Nothing." Ross was pretty sure now that Mary wasn't calling to nail him about anything, but her voice had a panicky edge that wasn't her. After so many years and so much mess between them, he thought he knew her whole repertoire of moods. "She doesn't talk to me, Ross. Does she talk to you? Oh, shit."

"Hey, Mar, you're not crying, are you?" Damn. She never used to cry. Never.

"I'm trying . . ." A full sob. He stood up and walked into the house, wanting to comfort her in some way. "I'm trying so hard, Ross. I've been trying so much to make up to her for everything, but she won't fucking give me a fucking break."

"Hey, make up for what? There's nothing—"

"She's letting this guy—this moron, this asshole, this psychopath per-vert—she's letting him shtup her, Ross."

"Hey, hey, wait a minute." He was turning lamps on in the living room, but the line was getting scratchy on the remote phone. He needed to get closer to the base.

"He's a total letch and a loser. He can't pay his bills. His phone got dis-connected. I was in the city with her all day trying to talk to her, but she was getting ready for this asshole's birthday like it was some kind of a gala performance or something."

"And she's sleeping with him? For sure?" Ross asked.

"Don't you dare tell her I called you about this."

He walked back outside onto the deck and stood looking into the blackness of his yard. There were gnats he hadn't noticed before, flying around in his backyard spotlight. The cat jumped up onto the rail. "Pssh,"

Ross hissed and the cat ran. *Natassia. Sex.* So that was the way it was now. Mary was still talking. "I hate him, Ross. Really hate him."

"Listen, you've got to buy her condoms. Make sure she has plenty of condoms."

"She bought her own."

"Does she know how to use them?"

"Goddamn it, I'm telling you, she knows everything. She's got it all locked up. She treats me like I'm an idiot."

"Mary, come on, calm down. If my parents are okay with it—"

"Don't tell me to calm down. Do you know how old this asshole is? Did you know he's like maybe even in his thirties or something? Maybe as old as we are. And he's some kind of a wetback foreigner."

"What are you talking about?"

"I just know it, okay?"

Silence.

"Honey, she's only fifteen." Ross sat down, crossed one leg over the other, put two fingers on his wrist to count his pulse. "In the next couple years, she's going to fall for men who are older than her, and younger than her, and shorter, and guys who smell bad, and guys who never learned how to drive, and guys so stupid she'll think they're real smart. She's going to fall about ten thousand different times." He couldn't resist: "Just like you did."

Mary said nothing, and Ross heard a train passing through downtown Spokane and wished it would come and smack him. If he lived to be two hundred, he'd never live out the shame he felt for all the ways he'd failed Natassia. Failed Mary, too, but that score was more even.

When Mary's voice came back, she was leading him right into it. "Ross, have we ruined her life?"

"Phfffssshh," he exhaled loud and long. "We've tried to ruin her life," Ross told Mary. "Too early yet to tell how successful we've been."

"Today she told me that the reason I was on her back about this guy is that I'm jealous I don't have a man of my own."

Ross laughed. "Little bitch."

"Does she know we love her?"

He sighed again over the wires. "There's this thing you see out here sometimes on I-90. Hell, even on the back roads you see it. You're driving along and you see a truck with a flatbed, and on the flatbed is half a house. I'm not kidding—somebody's half-a-house is rolling down the interstate. It just weirded me out the first time I saw it."

"Where's the rest of the house?"

"Half-mile down the road. Both halves are there, on the same road, heading in the same direction, just not traveling at the same speed."

"That's how Natassia sees us?"

"Yep."

"Ross, I love you sometimes."

"Yep."

He thought they were almost done for tonight. He'd tucked her in, which was probably all she'd really needed. A few nice good-nights and they'd be done, he'd just be left here feeling worse than he had before. But then Mary said, "I want to tell you something, and I'm telling only you. Never tell your mother I said this, but—"

"But what?"

"Natassia's right. I am jealous. Isn't that pathetic? My own daughter." He could tell by her voice that she was lying down, talking into a pillow. "You know, I quit performing, I took this stupid boarding-school job, I'm trying to do all this stuff right for once in my life, and meanwhile she's . . . God, I'm so mad at her."

"Oh, Mary. Oh, sweetie." This crying, this was all new.

"She's so much smarter than me, she could have so much."

"Mar, you're overtired. We're both tired."

"You know, I went down there today to talk to her, and she's playing the violin—I don't even want to tell you about the violin—but she's play-ing and I'm watching her, and she's, like, so—I don't know—*stiff*. She ac-tually looked afraid, like she was doing what she had to do with this instrument but there wasn't anything inside her that wanted to be doing what she was doing, but she was terrified to stop. I can't explain it. It's like how I felt onstage just before I quit performing." Mary was rambling, and he wasn't hearing words, just voice. He wondered if she was drinking something. He thought about a beer. "I'll never forget that feeling. All of a sudden, Ross, I couldn't even get onstage. Can I tell you something else?"

He waited. A cloud half covered the quarter-moon, then uncovered it. A breeze with a chill in it blew over and left him with goose bumps on his legs. He and Mary had never been any good at knowing what to do with Natassia. It was too late to start now. They could cry if they wanted—he did want to cry—but it was too late.

"Do you know it's almost a year since I was on tour, and since then I haven't slept with anyone—totally no one." He heard her sheepishness, and it was this that finally did get him teary.

He threw back his head, rubbed his eyes. "God, Mar, there've been so many changes in your life this year. Give it time." He realized he was sitting on the pages of the book of Egyptian erotica. He pulled it out from under him, looked down at drawings of people doing it every which way, tossed the book into the yard.

"Taking this school job was a big mistake." By now her voice had turned flat, scary in that way he hadn't heard in so long. "It was a mistake."

Here we go. "Mary, don't *do* that. You made a sound decision. You thought about it every which way."

"I'm really scared, Ross."

"Of what? What, honey?"

"This afternoon I hit her. I didn't hit her, but she was holding these scissors. She wouldn't stop ripping her clothes up to make *ribbons* for this guy's birthday presents, and I was trying to stop her. I was holding her hand really tight, and the scissors dropped onto the top of her foot." So this was where they'd been headed during this whole conversation. Sure, he thought, dump your guilt right here, with me. I can take it. "There was blood," Mary told him.

"A lot?"

"A little."

"She'll live," he said. "Mary." He was conscious of himself alone in the dark now, his voice low, like hers. "I know what you're thinking. Don't think it. Stop. You *are* smart. You're strong. You're talented." At AA meetings, he was always getting reminded that, for every evening he spent on the phone with Mary, he paid with a week of feeling lousy. His sponsor said, "You can choose to tell Mary, clearly, I gotta go now, good-bye. Detach. With love." Yeah, right. Everyone in the world thought Mary was a bitch, but Ross knew she wasn't trying to torture him, she really wasn't. She just had this psychic pain inside her that came and went like an infection, and when it flared up there was nothing but her ugly, smelly behavior, her spewing self-hate. When she got like this, he wanted to grab her, hold her tongue down with a spoon, get her to stop saying the bad stuff she said about herself. "You're remarkable, Mary. Beautiful. Sexy."

"Then why'm I alone, Ross? Why'm I living up here alone like a dog? I swear, if Natassia ever ends up like this, I'll kill myself. I really will. I'm so afraid this'll happen to her."

It was quiet on the phone. "What're you thinking, Ross?"

He was thinking, If you're alone, the only reason you're alone is that you move around so damn much, never stay still. He was thinking that she could be with him now if she hadn't split them up ten years ago. He was also thinking that if he said anything, anything at all about the past, it would start a fight. "I'm alone right now, Mar." His hand was inside his boxer shorts. Years ago this conversation would have gone a different way, but Ross had learned what he and Mary could not do anymore. "I'm alone a lot. It's never easy. Not for anyone."

"Don't give me that every-man-is-an-island bullshit. There's *alone*, Ross, and then there's a-*lone*." He listened as she switched the phone from one ear to another. "Goddamn it, Ross, you keep going silent on me."

"What do you want me to say?" Suddenly he was so lonely for Mary, and even more lonely for his young self, that college boy who fucked and turned over and fucked again. He'd never been like that since, not with anyone. He wasn't sure if it was his youth or Mary's dancer's body that had made him that way. They had fucked in elevators, out on the street at night between cars, on trains, in restaurant bathrooms, on a fire escape in the middle of a dinner party, on park benches pretending they were strangers; sometimes she let him get behind her and pretend she was a guy. Ross remembered all of it. How he had fucking *loved* the way they moved together. For him now, it was gone. He was a fattening, widening middle-aged man with bad habits that would eventually kill him. But Mary still had that *whatever it was* in her body. That's what made him really mad. All that freedom, yet she couldn't even realize it, and his cock in his palm was hard, but if Harriet walked in right now he wouldn't want her.

There was no way over this sadness. Ross had hated Mary, grown away from her, ignored her, betrayed her, but there was no getting around this:

she thrilled him, still. He breathed in and breathed out. His erection, it was going. "Mar, I want to tell you something."

"I'm sorry I yelled at you."

"Forget it. I want to tell you two things."

"Tell me," Mary said.

"Natassia's going to be all right."

"What else?"

"You're going to find somebody. Somebody good."

"You think?"

"I know."

Mary made him listen to her yawn, satisfied like a cat. "You know, Ross, I really am glad for you that you met Harriet."

"I'm glad, too." The cat was back on the deck. He scooped it up, curled it onto his lap, patted it.

"I want to meet her sometime."

"Yeah."

In his garage there were two vintage Mustangs. He had restored the outsides, Harriet had done the insides. She could open up someone's gut and reorganize their intestines, and she could reupholster an old car so that it looked brand-new. He had met Harriet one month to the day after he'd quit all the bad stuff, the coke and the hard booze. Since then, he'd been pretty clean. Not even beers anymore. He had shamed himself into promising himself he would never let Harriet see him completely messed up. She was the kind of person who went around thinking that anything good was possible. When he met her, he knew it was a toss-up: either she was going to become a huge pain-in-the-ass, or he could embrace her, let her try to save him. Sometimes he wanted to ask her, Harriet, since you think anything is possible, do you think Mary and I will ever get back together?

"Ross," Mary was saying, "you're a good friend."

You don't know how good.

"It's amazing, you still take care of me."

You don't know how much.

"When you talk to Natassia, will you tell her how many boyfriends I used to have all the time?" Mary was sounding better now, joking. It made him smile to hear her like that. "So will you—" There was a click on the phone. "Is that your other line?"

"Yeah." Damn. He didn't want to go.

"Go, Ross, you gotta go. Call Natassia when you have a chance."

"Bye, Mar."

AFTER THEY HUNG UP, Mary lay in the dark, pulled the soggy ice pack out from under her, tapped the ash out of her pipe into an ashtray. She couldn't come up with a picture in her mind of what Ross's Spokane life was all about. The last time she'd seen Ross, last Christmas, he'd gained a lot of weight and was deep into AA or NA or some twelve-step thing. Lotte and David nagged Ross to come back to New York. They didn't want him so far away, but he said he needed to hold on to the quiet. He said that out there—wherever the hell he was—the landscape was uncluttered and he felt clear. He made enough money to fly Natassia out a couple times a year. Everybody said he was a great doctor. Only once, a few years ago, had he asked Mary, "Do you think I'm a bad father?"

"You? What, are you kidding? You're a natural. You're a great father."

Sometimes it seemed to Mary that all they ever did was lie to each other.

Chapter 7:

September

1989

Natassia's love affair with the BF lasted ninety-seven days, and she would later chronicle in her journal what she remembered of every one of those days. Even after the guy called everything off, Natassia would not tell anyone anything about him. She wouldn't give his name, age, neighborhood, nationality, citizenship, or profession. Natassia revealed nothing, but the night her grandparents rushed her to a psychiatrist's office, she told her grandmother, "I just want to die."

The BF broke up with her over the phone on a Tuesday night— September 19, 1989. Natassia's third week of eleventh grade. He'd been out of town for a long weekend and had just come back. Every minute of the five days he'd been away, Natassia had been waiting for his return. Over the past three months, they'd never gone so long without seeing each other or at least talking. ("He needs to see old colleagues of his," Natassia told her grandparents. "Colleagues from where?" Lotte asked. Nothing.) Natassia made good use of the weekend: she finished writing a history paper on the Cuban missile crisis that wasn't due for a week, read ahead in chemistry, and wrote a book review for the school paper (a special section on international literature, which had been Natassia's editorial suggestion) with the deadline still two weeks away. Someone had given David tickets to a violin concert at Carnegie Hall for Saturday night, and he asked Natassia to go with him, but she turned him down and stayed home to do homework. She wanted everything done when her boyfriend got back in town.

Tuesday, the day he was due home, Natassia skipped French class, but when she got home there was no message from him yet. Lotte arrived from work around six o'clock with a bag of fresh shrimp and clams from Citarella and asked Natassia, "Paella okay for dinner? I want to use up that sausage Poppy got at Zabar's this weekend," but Natassia said that by dinnertime she'd probably be out.

But he didn't call. Figuring that probably the BF's flight had been delayed, Natassia dialed his apartment and left a message on his machine: "Good, your phone's working again. Call me the very second you get in. I've missed you way too much."

This was the point, Lotte told the others afterward, when she began to feel that things were getting out of hand. That night, though, all she said to Natassia was "Did you ever hear, dear, of playing a little bit hard to get?"

"We don't do that, Grammy. He and I are completely honest with each other."

A few hours passed. By eight-forty-five, there still was no phone call. She sat at the dinner table with Lotte and David, poking a fork at the paella on her plate. She was dressed to go out, in jeans and an antique lace blouse. A cloth napkin was tucked into her neckline, and her ruffled sleeves were pushed above her elbows to make sure she didn't pick up any food stains. She forked a slice of sausage, raised it to her mouth, sniffed, put the fork down. "I really have never cared much for sausage." With her face made up, and her hair pulled back into a French braid, and her silver long-tasseled earrings swinging around her neck, she looked too adult to be sulking about her dinner. She was wearing silver rings on her index fingers and thumbs.

Even Lotte, who never got irritated, was a little irritated. "Eat around it, Natassia. Just pick the sausage out."

"Well, even if you pick it out, the sauce is infused with the taste of it."

"That's the point," David said, and reached over for Natassia's glass and poured her an inch of white wine. "Here, drink this and chill." She pushed the glass away. "Listen, Natassia," David said, "don't you know a deadbeat when you see one? Why hasn't this guy figured out he's supposed to call his girlfriend when he's late?"

"David," Lotte said, "leave it alone. Of course she's upset."

And Natassia said, "I'm not upset. I just don't like sausage. Why's that such a big deal for everybody? God," she sighed, whipped her braid over her shoulder, and left the table.

This time when she dialed his number she got a busy signal; triumphantly, she yelled into the apartment, "He's home!" and ran back to the dinner table. Lotte was clearing away plates. Natassia, in her clogs, clomped behind Lotte across the hallway from the dining room into the kitchen, reached over her grandmother's shoulders to pick shrimp from the serving bowl. Natassia kissed Lotte on the cheek. "I'm sorry about what I said before, Grammy. Don't be mad at me."

"Who's mad?" Lotte handed the bowl and a spoon to Natassia. "Here, eat. And, please, a slice of bread, so I know you've got something solid in your stomach before you go out."

"You know you're the best cook on the Upper West Side. Everybody thinks so. It's not just me. This bread is really, really good. Did you make it?"

"Bought it. Three-forty a loaf."

"Isn't three-forty expensive for bread? Why'd you pay so much?"

As Lotte told everyone later, "Her behavior that night was erratic, snapping at us, then being so, so sweet, trying so hard to control herself."

But Natassia couldn't control herself. Ten minutes after getting the busy signal, she dialed the BF's number again. The line wasn't busy anymore, but he didn't pick up. The machine answered. "Hi, it's me," she said, her voice not as sweet as it had been earlier. "Hi, I know you're there," she said, but he didn't answer. "Pick up!" she finally shouted. "Fucking pick it up!"

And then he got on the phone and broke up with her.

All Lotte heard, all she was able to tell the others about later, when the crisis kicked in, were Natassia's pleas and repeated apologies for having shouted at him. Apparently the guy was trying to say something about having had a chance to think while he was away and deciding that things had got too serious between them.

"That's *your* decision," Natassia told him, crying, sitting on the hallway floor. "That's not my decision. You met somebody in Chicago, didn't you? You met somebody you like better."

For a long time she sat listening to him with her fist in her mouth. Whatever he was saying was making her cry harder. Finally, she whimpered, "I'm boring, aren't I? You think I'm stupid." She told him she didn't want to date other people. "If you want to, you can. But don't break up with me. Please?"

The phone call went on for hours. Stretching the long phone cord, Natassia wandered from the hallway into her bedroom and back, not caring if her grandparents heard her. When she wasn't speaking, her thumb or fingers or fist was in her mouth. It seemed to Lotte that Natassia had to repeat things often, speak slowly. Several times she asked the guy to repeat what he'd said. Lotte began to suspect that maybe he didn't speak English very well. At one point Lotte saw Natassia crumpled on the couch hugging a pillow between her legs, pulling at her hair. "But I love you," she kept crying into the phone. "Please, don't break up with me."

When Mary heard this story a few days later, she wanted to yell at Lotte, Why didn't you get her off the phone? Why'd you let her do that to herself? It was the first time Mary could ever remember feeling that Lotte was wrong, but Mary couldn't say a word. The obvious response would have been, Why weren't you there to take care of your own daughter?

Three times that Tuesday night the guy got off the phone with Natassia, and three times she called him back. It was way past midnight when Lotte found Natassia crying with her head on the kitchen counter.

"THE ENTIRE SCENE WAS PATHETIC," Lotte told them. It was Sunday morning now, and Lotte, Mary, and Ross were sitting at the kitchen table of the apartment on West End Avenue. Ross had arrived on Friday afternoon, because by Thursday they'd had to step up the Valium the psychiatrist had prescribed for Natassia, and she was going in daily for sessions.

"So what happened after the phone call?" Mary asked. She was out of Camels and was shaking a Tareyton from a pack David had left on the table when he went out to buy food.

"Hey, hey," David said from the doorway, and they all turned. He'd just walked in with a hot bag of bagels. "Leave me a few of those smokes."

"I'm just taking one," Mary said. "I'll owe you."

"Ah, you owe me more than a cigarette, my dear."

"Lotte, finish the story," Mary insisted. "After all those phone calls, what?"

"Well, like I told you. Wednesday morning, I got her out of bed. She'd been crying most of the night and only slept a few hours. I asked if she wanted to stay home. She said no. I thought that was a good sign. David made coffee. Oh, by the way, do we need to make more coffee?"

"Yes," Ross and Mary said at the same time.

"David, dear, make more coffee? Half decaf, so we can drink lots. Anyway, on Wednesday morning. We had breakfast. She showered and dressed. I took her to school in a cab."

"How was she then?"

"Oh, I don't know. Quiet. Upset. But not crying. I thought at school her friends would cheer her up. She was still erratic, coming in and out of that terrible dark mood, but when I saw her talking to her girlfriends on the sidewalk I told the cab to go on to the office."

Natassia never went into her school that day. After her grandmother's cab pulled away, Natassia walked to the subway and went downtown to the BF's.

"All I wanted to do was talk to him about it," she told her grandmother later, in Dr. Ralph Silvers' office. "Just talk, that's all." Natassia sat on the psychiatrist's scratched-up leather couch and hugged her legs. "That's really all I wanted, just to talk, but he wouldn't answer his buzzer. Then I tried calling him?" Her voice went up in that query that implied blamelessness. "From the pay phone at the corner? I tried, like, a bunch of times, and he wouldn't answer." She sobbed as the psychiatrist and her grandmother watched, sobbed without bothering to cover her face, which was rubbed raw, and her freckles were scarlet. "I kept thinking about all the times I used to call him from that same pay phone—like if his buzzer wasn't working? or if I went downtown and wanted to surprise him?—and he'd be so happy to see me, and today he wouldn't even pick up. He used to say I made him completely happy. What did I do—" Her chest heaved, and she stuffed her dirty bare feet deeper between the cushions of Dr. Silvers' sofa. She bit the ends of her hair.

Apparently, that Wednesday, Natassia had spent from nine-thirty in the morning until four-fifteen sitting on the stoop of the BF's building, waiting for him to leave his apartment. In late afternoon, when he finally came out to the street, he wouldn't talk to her. That's what Natassia told Lotte.

"Apparently there was a scene," Lotte told the others as she sliced her big white-handled bread knife into a sesame bagel. It had always been Lotte's job at these Sunday breakfasts to slice the bagels. As if no one else could be trusted with the knife. "Here, dear." Lotte handed the halved bagel to Mary and brushed crumbs onto the floor. "Sesame is what you eat, right?"

Pumpernickel was the only kind of bagel Mary allowed herself, but she said, "Yeah, thanks. What do you mean, there was a scene?"

"David, pumpernickel? All I know is, a policewoman brought Natassia to my office. I know it was around five-thirty, because I had an author in for a late meeting. Poor guy had come all the way down from Vermont, but he was gracious when we had to cut it short. Anyway, Natassia—when I went out into the lobby to get her—well, she was hysterical. That's all I can tell you—hysterical, sweaty, dirty, a mess."

"Je-sus," Ross muttered.

David handed Mary the bowl of cream cheese. She put the bowl down. "What was she wearing?"

"Now you want too much from me," Lotte said. "Who remembers what anyone was wearing? I guess the usual jeans. David, why only two onion bagels? Ross needs more than two."

Ross's chubby, clean doctor's fingers kept picking crumbs off the top of the Entenmann's crumb cake. "I guess," he said, "what I don't understand yet is why you took her to Silvers."

Measuring coffee into the glass basket of his Pyrex coffeepot, David counted aloud the last spoonfuls, "Six, seven, eight." He filled the glass pot with water and asked Ross, "What's wrong with Silvers?"

"God, nothing's wrong with Silvers. Silvers is great. No one's been in practice as long as he's been." Ross lifted a slice of lox into his mouth. All morning, Mary had been watching Ross switch from salty foods to sweet, then back to salty. It made her think of years ago, how he used to like to suck on her skin—forearm, thigh, heel, earlobe, anywhere. She didn't particularly like it. Sometimes it hurt. He said that what he liked was having new sensations in his mouth all the time. Done with the salmon, he sliced a big chunk of coffee cake. "Who's got more experience than Silvers? But . . ."

It was clear where Ross was headed. He hated Dr. Silvers, thought he was ancient and senile and nuts, and Ross was coming around to it in that way he had, with that ability to criticize and flatter at the same time. David, too, was crafty with words, and Mary remembered now how David and Ross edged into a fight—agreeing with each other, conceding points, until the two of them eventually strangled each other with cleverness. "I guess I'd just like to see Natassia in therapy with someone younger than Silvers," Ross said, poured himself a huge mug of coffee, and started in with the spoonfuls of sugar. "Maybe a woman therapist. Someone experienced with kids, with crisis intervention."

"Silvers is a brilliant man, the best psychiatrist on—"

"The Upper West Side. I know, Dad, I know."

"And he's been—"

"He's been your ally for over twenty years. But that's another thing." Mary counted eight spoonfuls of sugar. Ross's sugar habit had got much worse since he'd stopped drinking. "Should Silvers really be treating the granddaughter of one of his patients?"

David was crouched down in front of the opened refrigerator, digging around in the vegetable drawer. "You're absolutely right, Ross, to bring that up. For someone else, I'd say no. For someone as good as Silvers is, it's not a problem. In fact, it can only help that he knows her family." David had to grip the counter as he pulled himself up from the refrigerator drawer. For the first time ever, Mary realized, These are old people who are raising my daughter.

"You, Dad. Silvers knows you, not the rest of us."

"Well, he's heard all about you." David came back to the table and put green onions on everyone's plate. Ross bit off the ends of his onions between sips of coffee. Mary gave her onions back, put them on David's plate. David caught Mary's eye. "You, too, he's heard about."

They all looked at Mary. Under the table, Ross tapped his thigh against hers, a sign of support, but she moved her leg away.

Lotte's big hand reached over and covered Mary's hand and greased it up with butter. "What hard days these have been for you, Mary."

"It's not over for her," Mary said, standing to get more coffee. "I mean, shit, we were up with her again all last night. She's still waking up screaming. She cries all the time. She's been fucking crying for four days straight."

"Hey," David said, "you're too short to swear."

"Dad."

"Mary may be right," Lotte said into her coffee mug.

Yeah? If I'm so right, then why won't you tell me what I need to know about my own daughter? For example, what, exactly, did happen in Silvers' office on Wednesday night? And what are we going to do next?

"Sometimes I think the answer is, just bring Natassia to Spokane to live with me out there. And with Harriet."

David looked up from slicing onions and gave Ross that frosted gaze Natassia had mastered. "The answer," David said after a long pause, "is to find the asshole who did this to Natassia and kill him."

"Fuck him," Ross said. "I'm not even going to honor him with discussion. I'd like to beat the living shit out of him."

"Oh, Ross," Lotte said, "the idea of Natassia so far away in Spokane—what would you do with her out there?"

"Hike, ski, canoe. Christ, breathe some fresh air for a change."

"Meaning?" David asked.

"Meaning that life here is fucked. Totally fucked for a kid to be growing up with concrete all around her, and some letch coming on to her, and it was just as fucked up when I—"

"And I take it that life in your Spokane is not fucked?" David said in a flat voice.

All morning it had been cloudy, but as Mary carried her mug back to her place, a shot of sunlight broke through and hit—bull's-eye—right onto the white-painted wooden table. Onto the chipped plates and softening bar of butter and the lox-stained wax paper. Sun on the table brought up the smell of salmon and the green onions on David's plate. There was the sound of traffic, a repetitious static, like a needle caught in the groove of a turntable, coming up from the street and in through the screens, which were rusty and punched in here and there. Mary and Ross and his parents hadn't been together in this kitchen like this in years, but right now it seemed to Mary as if none of them had moved through time. All their lives, it seemed, they had done nothing but sit at this round table covered with this same breakfast, trying to decide what to do about Natassia.

NATASSIA WAS FIVE YEARS OLD when they had sat here with bagels, listening to Lotte finally spell it out—*Here's what David and I would like to do,* meaning, *Here's what we are going to do.* Lotte and David wanted Natassia to live with them, full-time. They wanted to keep her at the Montessori school. They'd pay all the tuition. They'd buy her clothes, feed her, cover her medical care. "She'll be listed as a dependent on our tax returns," David said. Lotte listed all the specifics they wanted to take responsibility for, but the fact was that she and David were already doing everything for Natassia.

At that time, Mary and Ross were supposedly living together. They had a tiny walk-up in the Village, on Thompson Street, but often one or the other of them didn't come home for days at a time. They'd foul up the schedule of whose turn it was to pick up Natassia at her grandparents' or at nursery school, whose turn to feed her or put her to bed. They'd have big fights and forget she was in the room. Or they'd go away and come back and forget where she was.

Ross was in an intensive premed program at Columbia and working as a hospital orderly. He was doing his Dr. Kildare number, working all kinds of crazy hours, but not bringing any money home. Mary was rehearsing full-time for her third tour with Tim Dillon Dancers and still teaching a couple classes and even waiting tables at a coffee shop on Bleecker Street a couple mornings a week. She was having an affair—her first and only infidelity ever, that's how angry she was at Ross—with the accompanist for her classes. Ross knew about the guy and was pretending he didn't know. Mary had picked up some nasty infection that made her itch and burn all the time, and she couldn't shake it, and Ross kept trying to get her into bed. Mary was trying to make sure Ross didn't get the infection, and at the same time she was trying to let him know she wanted out.

Things weren't good.

So, the Sunday of the June weekend when they'd celebrated Natassia's fifth birthday at Lotte and David's, Lotte put it to them. "Please, for everybody's sake, especially Natassia's, let her live here with us. You two, go, go with God's blessing. Live your lives, do what you love to do, but stop making each other crazy. Give yourselves a chance to grow up." Mary watched Lotte's plump-knuckled hand slice a knife through a bagel and felt relief rolling and rolling inside herself.

"Sorry, Mom," Ross said. He was stirring his coffee, acting like this was nothing but chitchat. Mary wanted to say to him, Look at your mother when she talks to you. Listen. "Natassia's ours, Mom. She stays with us."

"Ross." Mary said it clipped, fast, irritated.

David, slurping up a mouthful of cantaloupe, said, "You're both lousy parents. There's been neglect of that child that's bordered on the criminal. Leaving her places, forgetting about her. Things have gone on that could, and *should*, be reported."

"Da-vid," Lotte warned. She handed him a paper towel to wipe the cantaloupe juice caught in the cleft of his chin. As expensively dressed as he always was, David usually had food stains on his clothes—that morning, orange on the front of his white Izod, bagel crumbs caught in the chest hairs peeping out of his open collar.

"You son of a bitch," Ross said to his father, and stood up so fast he sent his chair skidding. His unbrushed long hair was a wild dark bush. "What kind of report have you filed?" But Mary was thinking, It's about time someone turned us in. Ross moved away from the table, as if afraid of what he might do to his father. "What fucking kind of report? She's my daughter, not yours."

"Did you ever hear of grandparents' rights?" David said, smug, not looking at Ross, whose face seemed paralyzed, he was so stunned. "Wise up, boy," David said, spooning up the last scraps of his melon. "Grandparents have the right to petition for custody."

"You stupid jackass," Lotte whispered. She grabbed at his arm. "You and your goddamn grandparents' rights. The right to stick your granddaughter directly into the hands of Social Services, is where she'd end up with your grandparents' rights. A ward of the city, the state, what have you. I'll kill you, David, for sure, before I let you start with that."

But by now Ross had started to cry, saying, "She's mine, not yours," and he slid his back down the surface of the wall until he was sitting in the corner next to the trash can, looking like one of Mary's spoiled brothers throwing a fit.

Jesus, she thought, grow up.

Ross's big feet in his green high-top sneakers were sticking out halfway across the floor. He had a hole in the bottom of one shoe. His wrinkled shirt and pants were from the Goodwill and ragged, yet he was wearing the expensive gold watch his parents had given him when he'd finally finished his college credits. Mary wanted to tell him he was a lie of a human being.

She wanted to tell everything, everything there was to tell. She wanted to inform Ross's parents that just a few weeks earlier she'd walked into the Thompson Street apartment one afternoon and found their brilliant premed son sitting on the futon—jeans on, shirt off—and a nurse dressed in her nurse's clothes was sitting on the floor, and the two of them were shooting up. If Mary hadn't forgotten to pick up Natassia that day, the kid would have seen her father with a needle in his arm.

Ross said he'd done heroin only that one time. The nurse was his friend. She'd offered to share so he could try it just once, with her, and it'd be clean and safe. Ross swore up and down he wasn't sleeping with the nurse, as if Mary cared about that. That Sunday morning, watching him cry on his parents' kitchen floor, Mary wanted to tell Lotte and David to go ahead and file a report with any agency they could think of. She'd help them fill out the papers. Especially when she heard Ross whimpering, "If my baby ended up in Social Services, I'd kill you."

"Hey, Ross," Mary started. She wanted to say, She's my kid, too, and she's not a baby. She's five years old. We missed the baby part completely.

But Lotte was talking now, staring David down. "There will never be a report," Lotte said. "You're our children, and we will never make a report against you." Lotte's chubby face was scalded with indignant love. Mary sat close, right at the edges of Lotte's layers of purple clothing, and she watched Lotte's color rise, highlighting the blond patch of down along her jawline. Lotte's nostrils were tense. Is this what it meant truly to be a mother, to love with such a fierceness it changed the way you looked? How had Mary and her daughter become so lucky, to have this woman on their side? Sitting next to her, Mary could feel Lotte's large, loose body consolidate, her muscles on alert, ready to fight. "We love you," Lotte whispered. "Nothing will ever change that."

David, fed up, shook his big head of black-gray curls, turned away from

Lotte, and said something about how much she pampered Ross, and if she kept it up the boy would never learn how to take care of his own child, and Lotte said something like "Are you threatening me?" And Mary thought, Shit, now Ross and I are even wrecking his parents' marriage.

Lotte began to speak a kind of chant, whispering without pause: "We are *not* reporting you. You kids are just in over your heads. You've tried. You haven't done a great job. You've done the best you could. We love you. We want to help you. And that's all we want. . . ." She couldn't stop herself, and Ross was pleading with her in the same chanting rhythm, "But, Mom . . . But, Mom . . . Mom . . ."

"Please, please, Ross, let Natassia live with your father and me. At least for the next couple of years. She *is* your daughter. You come for her whenever you're ready. Stay here with her whenever you want. But, please, for now, let us take care of her. She needs—"

"Ma–ry," Ross shouted up from the floor, "you're just sitting there. Mar! They're taking our kid away."

"They're trying to help us."

"You can't take our child without our permission."

"We're giving them our permission, Ross. I'll sign a legal document if they want."

Ross called her a coward. Mary asked him why he couldn't see that this was the best thing they could do for Natassia. He called her a coward again, called her a chickenshit slut of a coward, so she finally stood and kicked his leg—right there in front of his parents—yelling back at him, "You're right. I am a coward. And I'm fucked up. And so are you. The only chance we have to not fuck up our kid is to let her live with your mother and father."

But here they were, ten years later, and Natassia was fucked up, and Mary was crawling with anger. She felt cheated. Gypped. Of course David and Lotte had taken a load off her hands, they'd given Mary and Ross ten years of freedom, the chance to work on real careers, but Lotte and David were supposed to have raised Natassia right, not fucked up. That was something Mary could have done herself, even without Ross. Together, she and Ross could have done a superior job of making sure Natassia turned into a mess.

It had sickened Mary when Ross cried at that long-ago breakfast, but now she felt like crying as he had then, *My baby, my baby.* "Look," Mary said, struggling to keep sternness out of her voice. "We need to come up with a real plan here. Before Natassia wakes up again. I'll call her school tomorrow and tell them she'll be out for a while. But what about doctors? Ross? Is there somebody I'm supposed to call or find or what?"

David looked at Lotte. "She's scheduled with Silvers for tomorrow, right?"

Ross was rolling his eyes, trying to get Mary's attention, but, glancing around the table, Mary wasn't able to look any of them in the face. Was it possible, was it actually fucking possible, that even with a very sick kid at stake here—and not just any kid, *Natassia!*—the three of them couldn't stop going at one another? Had it always been so sick at this house?

Lotte reached over and lifted the *New York Times* off the radiator. Soot had come in through the window screen, and she brushed that off the newspaper and then wiped her hand on her robe. As she was disemboweling the stack, section by section, David reached over and snatched Arts & Leisure and Business and the magazine.

"Save some of that for me," Ross said, standing, coming back to the table. "I'm taking it with me tonight. You know what the *Times* costs in Spokane?"

"Don't worry, you won't be out there forever," David said, examining the magazine's table of contents.

"What's that mean?" Ross was taking the real-estate section from his mother's hand.

"You'll get some experience under your belt. Doesn't matter where you get it, just have a good record. In a year or two, the big guys will want a look at you."

"And which big guys are those?"

"The big hospitals, city hospitals, university hospitals. You're going to want to be someplace better later on in your career."

"I don't think so, Dad." Mary watched Ross wipe a swab of jam off his plate and lick his finger. "I'm happy where I am."

"No, you're not," David said, which prompted Ross to say, "And who the hell are you?"

Mary interrupted, "Excuse me, but Natassia? We don't know what we're doing yet."

Ross said, "I already said. I want her seeing someone experienced with kids. A woman, someone younger than Silvers. I can't imagine Natassia's feeling comfortable talking to some old guy. Jesus. That night, when she broke down, she should have gone straight to a hospital."

"A hospital? In New York? Oh, Ross." Lotte was glancing at headlines.

David was looking at his son, shaking his head. "You'd never survive as a doctor in this town. Do you know what city hospitals are like these days? AIDS patients have to sleep in hallways. On stretchers. People are dying in the waiting rooms before Emergency has time to ask them where it hurts. And you think a hospital is going to care about a teenage girl whose boyfriend just broke up with her."

"Hey, Dad, if you haven't noticed, Natassia is having a nervous breakdown. This isn't just a teenager with boy troubles."

"So you would call it a nervous breakdown?" Lotte looked up over the tops of her reading glasses. "I mean, medically, that's what you'd say? Well, then, she probably does need continued care—"

"Of *course* she needs continued care, and it better not be with Silvers. My God."

"Hey, Ross, whose insurance is paying for this?"

"Right, Dad, pull the purse strings. Listen, I'm going to the AMA if she keeps on with Silvers. I'll lodge a complaint."

"And I'll lodge a countercomplaint," David told Ross. "And guess who'll win."

"Me. I'm her father."

"Yeah?" David said. "Think again. Me they've heard of."

"Yeah, you. You they've heard of."

"Pershing Publishers they've heard of. Spokane General Hospital or whatever the hell you call that welfare clinic where you work, filching narcotics is mostly what you're doing there. . . ."

Mary looked over at Ross and hollered, "Ross, *no.* What are we going to do?"

"How . . ." Ross said to his father, "dare . . . you?"

"Ross," Mary insisted.

"How fucking dare—"

"You had to do this?" Lotte asked David. "Now?"

David turned in his chair, crossed his legs. "Somebody finally speaks the truth around here, and everybody—"

"The truth," Mary pleaded, "is, my daughter is in very bad trouble."

And David said, "Oh, listen now to Mrs. Mommy. Excuse me. I mean, Ms. Mommy. You never did get married, did you?" Suddenly David jumped his chair backward, away from the table. "Shit." He swiped a cockroach out from the underside of the table. "Lotte—"

"You're the one who said no to the exterminator."

"Damn exterminators smell up the place with poison."

"Then live with roaches. Are you listening or not? These kids don't want Natassia seeing Silvers. What are they supposed to do?"

"Whatever you want. All of you do whatever the hell you want, which is what you do anyway. I've got business to attend to right now." David stood and grimaced, ready to leave. He had a twin sister retired in Tucson that none of them, not even Lotte, had ever met. He'd stopped talking to his sister in their early twenties. The danger was always there that David would cut you off forever; the list was long of people whose names he would not even say. He leaned down over Lotte's lap and took several more sections of the newspaper.

"Damn you," she told him, "you're going to the bathroom with the best sections of the paper." Lotte looked at Mary and Ross. "I'm left with nothing but the travel section." She yelled into the hallway, "I want that magazine when you're done," but David was gone.

When Mary looked over at Ross, she didn't like the look on his face. "Are you all right?"

Ross's voice was very low as he began to ask his mother, "How come—"

"Ross, ignore. I'm telling you—"

"But, Mom." Ross was staring down at the food on the table. For the first time all morning, he wasn't putting something into his mouth. "Listen, Mom—"

"All I can tell you is what I've always told you, Ross. Your father is a man who knows very well how to be mean. Ignore him. For your own sanity, ignore."

"Mom."

"Doctors pilfering drugs. These days your father has become Mr. Conspiracy Theory. I tell you, he's published too many thrillers."

"Actually, Mom—"

"Ross," Mary said. "About *Natassia*. I'm going to ask Nora for names of therapists. If you don't like this Silvers guy, then—"

"I was trying to say something to my mother here."

"No, Ross," Mary insisted again. "It's not about you right now."

Ross stood and walked to the fridge and opened the door and stared in, then slammed the door. Sitting again at the table, he stretched his neck left, right. "What do you want me to say? Call Nora. Natassia needs to see someone experienced in crisis intervention, not some fat old Freud wannabe. Does Silvers even manage to stay awake when she's in there self-destructing right in front of his eyes?"

"So, I'm calling Nora," Mary said. "Right? Like, today? Now?"

Ross turned to his mother. "How come every time I come home I have to listen to him tell me I work in a lousy hospital?"

"It's your father's way of saying he misses you and wishes you lived closer to us."

"I think it's his way of telling me he thinks I work in a lousy hospital."

"Ross, my son, light of my life, my joy, are you happy doing the work you do?"

"Yeah, Mom, I am. Really happy."

"Good." Lotte leaned over and put a small kiss on his mouth. When she leaned back in her chair, they smiled at each other, and Ross stayed leaning forward with his hands on his lap—Ross had a real belly now that kept him several inches away from the table. "Then why," Lotte asked him, "can't you be happy with the same kind of job in a hospital closer to home? Tell me, why not?"

AS SOON AS ROSS FINISHED his last bagel, he said he had to go out. Earlier, he'd told Mary, privately, that he needed to get to an AA meeting before he boarded his flight or he might flip out in midair. "I'll be back in an hour and a half," he announced, standing up from the kitchen table.

"You're leaving? Where are you going?" Lotte was startled enough to take off her eyeglasses. "We never see you, your plane's in a couple hours, and now you're going where?"

"I won't be long, Mom."

"Stay with us. What if Natassia wakes up and wants you?"

"Ross can go," Mary said. "Natassia'll be asleep for a while."

"Yeah, I won't be long." Leaving, Ross kissed Mary on the ear and whispered, "Thanks."

As Ross slammed out the front door, Lotte looked over at Mary, but Mary found she couldn't meet Lotte's eyes (years ago, how she used to search all over Lotte's face for any hint to what she was thinking). Mary bent her head down to look for her Nikes under the table.

"You're not going out, too, are you?" Lotte asked.

"No, I just need to go read student papers. Do you believe I have to make those kids keep a dance journal? What's to write? You dance or you don't." Mary stood and began piling up dirty plates and glasses.

"Mary, I haven't even had a chance to ask you lately, are you any happier up there at Hiliard? Is it any easier for you this semester than it was last spring?"

"Anything's easier after you've done it a while." Mary heard the rudeness in this. Lotte was still looking at her. Mary sat again but kept busy collecting silverware.

"Just leave it, dear. We'll tidy up later." While Mary went to the fridge with her hands full of food, Lotte said, "You know, Mary, I can imagine this is a nightmare for you, all this with Natassia. I think that for the past few months you've really been trying to—how do I say this?—*reclaim* your daughter, I think you really have. Taking that teaching job so you don't have to be on the road, and you're doing a beautiful job—I don't know if it's my place to say it, because you're not my daughter, but I'm proud of you. I really am. All this that Natassia's going through now, I want you to remember, it's not a reflection on you."

No, it's a reflection on all of us. Mary stayed facing the open fridge, rearranging shelves. In her throat, that terrible thing was happening again that had been happening so much these days.

"I want to make sure you know," Lotte continued, "you're not alone. What's important is that after all these years we're able to come together if there's a crisis, and help one another. We're still a family. Somebody needs help, we come together. Oh, Mary, please, have I made you cry?"

"I'm just tired." Closing the fridge door, Mary grabbed a paper towel and wiped her face. "I'm tired."

"Natassia's going to be all right. She is, dear, I know that. These are growing pains."

"We need to get her help. Really good help."

Lotte was reaching across the table, but Mary stayed where she was, leaning against the counter.

"Everything's going to be fine."

"You think so, Lotte?"

Lotte nodded, and, as always when she was moved by her own conviction, her eyes were shiny and there was that flush across her face, but none of it made Mary feel good the way it used to. Mary was starting to see the truth: Lotte didn't know much more than Mary did.

CHAPTER 8:

SEPTEMBER

1989

Sitting at the Northwest gate at the Minneapolis airport, waiting for his connecting flight to Spokane, Ross felt sick to his stomach.

This airport was a hell to wait in. Ross didn't know what to do with himself. He knew a New York sculptor who now lived in Minneapolis, and he thought of calling him. Very talented guy. Ross had worked with him once, briefly, on a deal to move weed from California along I-80 to New York—sweet deal. But Ross couldn't find the guy listed in the Minneapolis phone book. Another hour to wait. He ate a huge Cinnabon roll, then another. Such a pisser, the serious way his parents were all over Natassia's teenage misery. When Ross was sixteen and a major mess, practically begging for help—*oh, fuck all that, fuck them, too.* He went to the Starbucks counter, had three double espressos in a row. It really pulled his chain, especially with his father, man. Ross tipped the Starbucks girl a couple bucks and went to a pay phone, dialed his parents' number, and hung up, twice. He dialed Harriet and hung up, twice. He called his office, where the receptionist answered and told him they'd had an emergency appendectomy and a couple cases of the flu. Nothing else, besides a teenage-pregnancy scare that was resolved when the girl got her period. Ross didn't bother to ask the receptionist why she was in the office on a Sunday afternoon.

Ross left a message on his New York sponsor's phone machine, another on his Spokane sponsor's machine, and then walked the long stretches of the terminal building, reading to himself the postings at each gate, where planes were taking off for all kinds of places. Detroit, Miami, Amsterdam. Everybody was flying through Amsterdam these days. Ross wanted to worry about Natassia, he really did. He wanted to find a solution and find it fucking *now*, before the kid went completely to pieces. *Jesus. She could end up like me.* Probably, though, he was going to have to kill his father first, really maim him a little, before anything reasonable got done in Ross's life.

I need a drink, he told himself. He walked back to his gate to see how much more time he had before boarding. When he got to the gate, though, it didn't say "Spokane" anymore. He asked the girl at the desk, "What happened to the flight to Spokane?"

"Sir, that flight left twenty minutes ago."

"What the fuck do you mean, twenty minutes ago? Why didn't you announce it?"

"Sir, we did announce it. Are you, by chance, Mr. Stein, sir? We PA-ed your name several times, sir. You weren't here for the boarding call."

"You fucking let them go without me?"

"Sir, I'll have to ask you to refrain from using obscenities. We have children—"

Everything after this happened very quickly. Using both his arms, Ross swiped the ticket agent's computer terminal onto the floor, then he went over to the window just behind her and kicked his foot repeatedly at the glass, screaming curses the whole time.

Months would pass before anyone in Ross's family heard anything about this outburst, about Ross's being restrained and held overnight by airport police and released the next day only after they'd talked on the phone at length with Harriet and with Ross's drug-rehab counselor.

On Sunday, after her father left to go back to Washington State, Natassia sat at the kitchen table and ate a few bites of baked chicken and half a dumpling while her mother and grandparents sat with her. Then she watched a little TV and went back to bed, where she finally got a full night's sleep, waking only once, at dawn. It seemed Dr. Silvers' medications were starting to stabilize her, give her some relief. At breakfast on Monday morning, Lotte said, "Natassia will be her old self in a day or two." Filling Mary's mug with David's good, strong coffee, Lotte asked Mary, "I don't think you need us here today, do you, dear?" Lotte and David were already dressed to go to work.

Mary had called Hiliard and told them she needed to take another personal day. When she had been performing, there'd been no such thing as a personal day. Even if you yourself were having a nervous breakdown, you showed up. But Mary was sure racking up the personal days now. She and Natassia spent most of the day napping on Natassia's big wood-frame bed, Mary huddled under an afghan, Natassia under her comforter, both of them waking, then turning over back into sleep, like two wounded animals, exhausted. Late in the afternoon, they watched the Home Shopping Network for a while. Just before dinner, Natassia actually took a phone call from one of her friends. Mary even heard her laugh for a second.

That night at the dinner table, everyone breathed the calm air of a crisis passed. Natassia agreed to sit at the dining-room table with the others. Filling their plates with slices of herb-encrusted pork roast, complaining about the stack of phone messages from agents and all the work piled up on her desk, Lotte seemed refreshed. Ross had called her in the afternoon, just to say he'd got back okay. "Said he wished he'd stayed longer."

"Hell," David grunted, "I don't know what the hell he thinks he's doing way out there." But, for the most part, David, too, was happy about his day at the office. Slicing his meat into big chunks, he announced he'd taken the first steps toward promoting his youngest editor, Garth. "The kid's just wildly talented, that's all there is to it."

Natassia didn't have it in her to eat more than a few spoonfuls of the garlic mashed potatoes Lotte had prepared specially for her, but Natassia was alert enough to ask her grandfather, "Didn't Wallace tell you a couple months ago there weren't going to be any promotions until the next fiscal year?"

How the hell did Natassia know so much about her grandparents' jobs? "Who's Wallace?"

"Poppy's publisher," Natassia told Mary.

"Wallace can take a proverbial leap into the proverbial lake," David said.

So, Mary thought, this was another of David's tugs-of-war, and this young editor, another pawn. *Whoever Garth is, I feel sorry for him.*

"Hell," David continued, "after Garth brought in that true-crime exposé, how could I not promote him?"

"How nice for Garth," Lotte said.

"Yeah, and Wallace doesn't have a leg to stand on. I've got the entire editorial department lined up to fight him." David forked a large mushroom cap and put the whole thing into his mouth.

After spending a couple days with David for the first time in years, Mary was beginning to feel that thing—that evil—Ross claimed had been in the apartment all the years he was growing up. *Why didn't I ever notice it before?* Since Sunday morning's breakfast, Mary had been thinking it was Lotte who had failed them, but maybe David really was a prick. Besides, Mary found it basically impossible to stay mad at Lotte, so, when Lotte passed around a basket of hot rolls, Mary took the basket, looked Lotte in the eyes for the first time in days, and told her, "You did it again, Lotte. This dinner is really good."

ON TUESDAY, Mary called work, said she needed yet one more personal day. She made Natassia a big bowl of cereal, and Natassia ate a bit, sitting up in her bed. When Mary saw Natassia sliding back down under her comforter, she said, "Come on, honey, let's go out. Put your jeans on. I'll buy you something for twenty-five dollars. That's all I have in my wallet."

"Don't you need to go back to work? Aren't they wondering where you are? Haven't you missed, like, a bunch of your classes?" This was the usual organized Natassia, and Mary was grateful.

"They'll live," Mary told her.

"I don't feel like going back to school yet, Mom."

"You're not going back to school yet. But you have to get out of bed. We've got to go outside for a walk. Come on now, get dressed."

And to Mary's surprise, Natassia pulled off her nightgown and reached for her jeans.

OUT ON THE STREETS, it was the best kind of late-September day. Clear sky. Blue. Sun. Sharp shadows slicing the sidewalks. Warm air, with a little coolness in it. Mary and Natassia walked down West End Avenue a few blocks, then over one block. Everyone on the street was caught in webs of sunlight, and Mary remembered the long-ago September when she, Ross, and Baby Natassia were just back from Rome, staying at David and Lotte's. Lotte had bought a fancy stroller with white mosquito-netting to protect the baby. Just a year before that, when they were students in Rome, Mary and Ross had crawled under the netting over Ross's bed, and when they crawled out—*voilà!*—Natassia! Back in New York, every time they hauled the heavy stroller down the building's front steps and onto West End Avenue, even though Ross was over six feet and Mary knew herself to be as strong as a football player, she looked down at Natassia lying under the white net and wondered how they could ever protect her. Mary thought, The poor little thing looks exactly how I feel: trapped.

Now walking next to Mary was this teenager, this new Natassia, thoroughly exposed, her face uncovered, her expression blank. "Your father and I used to walk you in your stroller on Broadway every day. Just after Rome, when we lived up here."

"Why'd you move downtown? Wouldn't it have been easier to just keep living with Grammy and Poppy? Since Daddy was going to Columbia."

As they walked toward Eighty-sixth Street, Mary caught a glimpse of Nora's friend Candice up ahead, waiting at the corner for the light to change. Candice was pregnant, huge, rubbing her stomach. She had a grim-faced Hispanic woman standing with her, probably her nanny-in-training. They were close enough that Mary could have said hi, but Candice was one of those people who always asked you a bunch of questions about your life, just to hear what a mess it was and to compare it with her own cheery life. Candice was a therapist friend of Nora's who didn't need to work, so she didn't. She was married to some handsome French guy whose family owned a vineyard; they were friends with Meryl Streep and other actors who had houses in Connecticut. *I don't need to hear it, not today.* Mary ignored Candice and answered Natassia's question. "Daddy and I had to move. Lotte and David's apartment got a little tight for the five of us after a while."

"Give me a break. Three bedrooms, three bathrooms, and a maid's room? Downtown, we hardly had any space at all."

Children want to know the truth, Dr. Cather had told Mary, so Mary told Natassia, "We had to move because your grandfather was giving Ross a hard time about wanting to go to medical school. If you can believe it. The only guy on the Upper West Side who could get pissed about his son wanting to be a doctor instead of a writer."

Finally, some expression crossed Natassia's face: a smirk. She let out a cynical, chipped laugh. "Poppy's so funny. Just because he didn't get to be what he wanted to be."

"What d'you mean?"

"He wanted to be a violinist, but his parents made him drop it."

"How come?" It was high noon; the sun was hitting hard. As they raced the yellow light to cross Eighty-sixth Street, Mary put on her sunglasses and pulled out a cigarette so she'd be ready to concentrate on this conversation as soon as they got to the other side of the street. In the apartment, they would never have had this talk. "Why'd they make him not be a violinist?"

Natassia's cynical laugh again. "Poppy doesn't admit it, and he always disses his parents when he talks about them, but I think it's because he's not a very good musician."

"He's not?"

"He sucks. Why do you think he and his friends let me play with them? None of us is very good."

Mary noticed two dancers she knew walking out of a restaurant, but she didn't try to get their attention. "David didn't want to be in publishing?"

"He hates publishing. He only did it because he met Grammy and she was great at it, and she helped him get a job. Grammy understands books and the book business better than anybody. Poppy's smart, but mostly he's a bully."

"Natassia." Mary grabbed the kid's hand, made her stop walking. "Do you know how smart you are?"

Natassia waved away Mary's cigarette smoke. "Mom, it's not *smart*. You can't help seeing stuff when you live with people all the time."

Natassia glanced at the window display at Murray's Sturgeon Shop. Natassia, Lotte, and David always made a big fuss about this place—smoked fish. Mary didn't understand it. "You hungry?"

Natassia shook her head no and asked, "Wasn't that Nora's friend back there, the one with the cute husband and all the money, who knows Meryl Streep? Why didn't you talk to her?"

"She gives me a headache."

They kept walking. "It's weird," Natassia said, "not to be in school in the middle of the day," and Mary realized she had no idea how her daughter usually spent her days.

And there was no way she could ever catch up. All Mary could do was let her shoulder rub against Natassia's arm as they walked side by side through the sidewalk crowds. What a relief. Walking outside, the kid did seem better. When they were in front of a small slice of a store that sold nothing but socks and stockings, Mary asked, "Want some new socks?"

"Nah. I don't need any."

They walked on. At the record shop, she said she didn't want any new tapes. At the Town Shop, Mary offered to buy her some new pajamas or underwear, but Natassia said no. She didn't want to go into Shakespeare & Co. to look for a book. They kept walking. As always, Mary noticed a few people on the street glancing at them, wondering, probably, What's the short Korean woman doing with the tall kid?

When they were almost at Sixty-eighth Street, Mary said she was starving, so they went into a coffee shop, sat in a booth, and ordered grilled-cheese sandwiches and one chocolate milk shake to split. Natassia drank the whole shake but ate none of her sandwich. Mary offered to buy her another shake.

"No, thanks. Let's go to Zabar's and look at coffeepots."

"Sure. Whatever you want."

Out on the street, bumping into each other companionably, they headed back uptown. Mary thought about a friend of hers who had said years ago, about Little Girl Natassia, "When you're with Natassia, you forget she's not an adult. She's such good company."

Natassia was good company, and Mary was enjoying her more than she had in a long time. For one thing, the kid wasn't giddy and silly. Coming out of her crisis, she had developed a cynical little bit of an edge that was actually kind of funny. At lunch, when Mary had mentioned that Nora and Christopher wanted them to go out to the beach house for a weekend, Natassia had said, "Mr. and Mrs. Compulsive? Forget it. I know I'm a neat freak, but all Nora does when I'm out there is tell me not to walk sand into the house. Like, excuse me, are we at the beach or what? She's hawk-eyes about everything I do."

"Natassia! Nora loves you. So does Christopher."

"I don't know how he puts up with her."

"They're the best married people we know, besides your grandparents. And you know Nora and Christopher love you to death. If you ever needed anything, they'd help you in a minute. You know that, don't you?"

"I know, but she's just a dolt sometimes."

And later, when Mary told Natassia, "Your dad really wanted to stay here and be with you longer, but he had to get back to work," Natassia said, "No, he didn't. He has Harriet. He has to punch a time clock with Harriet."

"Why don't you like her?"

"He could do better."

"Well, what does he like about her?"

"She tells him what to do. He doesn't have to think."

"Natassia!" Mary said, laughing.

"Well, you asked."

At Seventy-sixth Street, they had to stop on the curb for a red light. When it turned green, Mary let Natassia walk a few steps ahead so she could watch her. Natassia's jeans were dirty and hanging loose in the rump. In just one week, she'd lost so much weight. One week ago *today*, the asshole had broken up with her. *God, she does look worn out.* Natassia's hair was dirty again, hanging in clumps. It really wasn't funny to have your fifteen-year-old daughter sounding as jaded as your friends who were in their thirties. Natassia had stopped in front of a Korean fruit market and was looking at a display of red pears. Standing in front of the fruit, she sighed. On her face there was a moment of such completely uncovered sadness that Mary felt her own eyes fill up behind her sunglasses. Oh God, how could she ever tell Natassia how much she loved her?

Mary went over to a newsstand outside a stationery shop and pretended to be reading headlines while she lit a cigarette and dried her eyes. Jesus, on the street, crying so hard she had to wipe away the tears with her whole hand. Suddenly a baby boy's blond head popped up right in front of Mary, so close to her she saw the dried snot on the edges of his nostrils. He was hanging in a papoose on his mother's back as she struggled to push a shopping cart through the heavy door, and she had no idea that her baby's face was so close to a stranger's, that he was having this private moment with Mary. The baby boy was pointing at her, so Mary touched his finger with one of her fingers, what she and Little Girl Natassia used to call a finger kiss. Then the baby boy was gone, inside the door. Mary put her finger to her lips and kissed it. When she turned back toward the fruit stand, Natassia was still staring at the pears.

"Honey, ready?"

"Yeah," Natassia said.

"Zabar's, right?"

"No. I'm too tired. Let's just go home."

NATASSIA DID GO right to bed when they got home. Mary kept remind-ing herself that things were better than they'd been a few days earlier, when they'd had to wrap Natassia in a raincoat and get her downstairs for those ridiculous two-hour sessions with Dr. Silvers, who apparently kept asking her, "Did you have any dreams?," even though she wasn't able to sleep.

Right now, with just a little medication, Natassia was sound asleep, hugging two of her pillows, sending up a light snore. Twice, Mary went in to check on her. The kid just needed rest.

But after an hour, Mary's faith in Natassia's quick recovery began to wane. She called Nora, and finally, this time, Nora answered.

"Nor, I need names of shrinks for Natassia."

"Oh no. When you didn't call me yesterday, I hoped that meant she was doing better."

"I think she's better, but not great, and David's still big on this Dr. Silvers."

"I know. Ross called me this morning, really upset. Did you know his flight was so delayed he had to spend the night in the Minneapolis airport? Anyway, he's worried about both of you. This is a lot for you, Mary."

"I just don't know how to do this. Where do you start? Ross said she might need a psychiatrist instead of a psychologist, because she might need medication. Nora, she doesn't need all this medication, does she?"

"Listen, what kind of insurance do they have for her?"

"I'm not sure."

"This needs much discussion, and I have a patient in the waiting room. We're still having dinner tonight, right? I'll make a list of referrals and we'll go over it. We need to spend some time with this. Now I've got to run."

BY NINE O'CLOCK that night, Mary, Nora, and Giulia were sitting in the living room, opening a second bottle of wine, picking around with their chopsticks at what was left of the chicken with cashews, the shrimp with black-bean sauce, and the eggplant with garlic sauce, which Lotte had said wasn't as good as usual, but she'd filled her plate twice and had finally gone into her room to read manuscripts. There was one steamed dumpling left. Mary speared it, lifted it to her mouth, bit into it, then asked, "No one wanted this, did they?"

Giulia and Nora looked at each other and laughed.

"What?" Mary asked.

"Nothing. It's just good to see you being your usual self."

And, in fact, for Mary, the evening did feel almost normal, almost as if Natassia had nothing more serious than the flu. For the first time in days, the situation felt manageable. Mary would get Nora's list, then she'd make a phone call, then a specialist would fix Natassia up.

Weird, but Nora looked like the one who had something bad going on. Mary hadn't seen her in a while, not since the weekend in Greenport. Nora had put on weight, enough that it showed in her face. Mary almost asked, You're not pregnant, are you? But, really, Nora didn't look good. It wasn't just the puffiness in her cheeks (was she taking cortisone for something?), and the tight grip of the buttonholes around the buttons of her silk shirt; Nora also looked pale, washed out, her hair was flat. Someone meeting Nora for the first time tonight wouldn't see she was a knockout. But, then, Mary thought, maybe her nut-case patients really get to her by the end of the day. *At least she's here. She'll know what to do.*

On the coffee table was a box of Mrs. Fields cookies Giulia had brought for Natassia. Nora was finishing her third cookie, and Mary wanted to scream, Stop! "Let's do the list," she said.

"Okay," Nora said, "first there's this woman at the Ackerman Institute."

"What's that?"

"They specialize in work with families." Nora put down her notebook and looked at Mary. "They're going to want you to go to the sessions," Nora said, and then stopped. "And you'll have to talk. Did you realize that?"

"No. But I'll do it."

Nora went on. While she talked about how important it would be for Mary to cooperate with the therapist, to open up, to see this as an opportunity to get a lot off her chest, Mary began to worry about what she would do if Nora's list included Dr. Cather. Nora told Mary about the three women psychologists on the list and gave her the sheet of paper with their names and phone numbers. Cather's name was not on the list. Then

Mary began to worry that maybe Dr. Cather was a bad shrink. Or maybe Nora didn't know the really good ones. How did you ever know whether or not your friends were any good at their jobs?

Nora reached for her fourth cookie, and Giulia got up to bring the box in to Natassia.

"Did you ever hear of somebody named Cather?" Mary asked.

"No. Is it a man?"

"A woman."

"I never heard of her, but that doesn't mean anything."

Giulia came back into the living room. "Mary," she said, "go in and see Natassia. She's kind of weepy again. She asked me to leave, but maybe you should go in."

Mary jumped up, but then the phone rang. Before she reached it, the ringing stopped. Mary stood in the hallway, heard Natassia say "Hi" in a happy way, so Mary went back to the others in the living room. "Well, that's good. Her friends are calling. Last week she didn't want to talk to any of them." Mary sat down and asked Giulia, "What do you mean, she was weepy?"

"She told me the risotto I brought her was salty, and I said I'd make her something else she liked tomorrow. Then she apologized, and I told her she didn't have to, then she got teary."

Mary had just picked up a fortune cookie, but now she tossed it unopened onto her plate. "Erratic." She'd been fooling herself all evening. "That's how Lotte said she was last week. Bitching and then being sweet."

"She didn't bitch at me. She just—"

"Ssh, I don't want her to overhear us talking about her."

"Oh, sorry, you're right," Giulia said. "What a good mother you are."

Mary's face was half hidden inside the wide mouth of her wineglass. She lowered the glass and stared at Giulia. "I'm a shit of a mother. If I were a good mother, my kid wouldn't be racked up like she is."

"Oh, stop."

"No, Giulia. You stop. You're always romanticizing. Did you know that when she was four I left her sitting outside our building for two hours because I forgot to be there when she got home from a playdate? Do you know how many times I fed her Pepsi and peanut-butter crackers for dinner and nothing else? You didn't know that, Giulia."

"Mary, what do you want me to say? That you're a monster? I'm not going to say it."

Mary knew that Giulia had been working overtime in her darkroom so she could spend two full days with Natassia while Mary went back to work. So many people were trying to be helpful. Mary tossed her napkin onto the coffee table. "I don't know."

"So what kind of dinners did you get when you were a kid?" Giulia asked.

"My stepmother didn't know how to cook, and usually she ran out of frozen dinners after she fed the boys and before she got to me. I'd make myself peanut butter and jelly."

"So your kid learned to fend for herself. Just like you did."

They were all silent for a minute.

Mary told Giulia, "I'm sorry I yelled at you."

"That's just what Natassia said. You don't need to apologize. Just don't beat yourself up."

Nora told Mary, "Giulia's right, Mar. There's no way you could ever match Dorie. You've been good to Natassia in ways Dorie could never even dream about."

"Yeah," Giulia said, "and even if you really were Mommie Dearest, this guy Natassia hooked up with—man, bad news."

"Ssh, wait," Mary said. She sat up and raised her voice. "Natassia, are you in the kitchen?"

"Yeah."

"You okay?"

"Yeah."

"Come here, honey, let me see you."

The women all looked at one another, waiting, while Natassia took her time coming down the hallway. When she appeared, she was in her big, long nightgown. The circles under her eyes were purple. "You ready for bed, sweetie? Can I have a kiss?"

Natassia blew one across the room. "That's the best I can do. I'm tired."

"Okay, good night, sweetie."

"Good night, Natassia."

" 'Night."

When she was gone, Nora said, "She's completely worn out by this. She looks like a thirty-year-old woman."

"Why're you telling me that?" Mary said. "Don't tell me that."

The women were quiet. They listened to Natassia's bedroom door close.

"She met him early," Nora said in a low voice.

"Who?" Mary, out of cigarettes, pulled her backpack from under the coffee table and started digging through it, hoping to find a piece of nicotine gum.

"The guy who turns you inside out."

"I was hoping she'd never meet one of those," Mary said.

"You know my friend Candice?" Nora said. "Who married the vineyards after her first husband left her? She has a 'troll at the gate' theory: you don't get the good lover until you get past the bad one who turns you inside out. Mary, remember summer after junior year, high school?"

"Peter Ashley, preppy slime."

"What did he do?" Giulia asked.

"He invited Nora to his summer house on an island. Where?"

"Maine."

"Some island off of Maine, and when she got there with all her brand-new birth-control pills and this halter top we spent forty bucks on—"

"I wanted to die. When I got up there, he had this babe all set up in his cottage behind his parents' big house. He had his own cottage. She was in college; he was a junior in high school, like me. I'll never forget. She had a dark-green Datsun. He was so crazy about her he used to wash her underpants in the stream behind the cottage."

"Oh no. You never told me about the underpants." Mary had found a stale cigarette in the bottom of her bag and was lighting it.

"Do you know how humiliated I was? And then there was a storm and no way off the island for three days, until the ferry came back. I followed the two of them around like a sick dog until his father pulled me aside— his own father—and said, 'My son's a louse. I'm apologizing for him.' Oh, stop. I can't talk about it. It still makes me want to die."

"Did you ever see him again?" Giulia asked.

"Of course. I'm telling you, I was sick over this guy."

"Yeah, but, Nor, you had other guys who were nuts about *you*."

"None of that mattered when it came to Peter Ashley. When school started again, I went out with him. I even slept with him."

"We've all done it," Giulia said.

"Yeah, but I was really hoping Natassia wouldn't. Hey, wait, ssh. . . ." Mary sat up, stiff and alert. "I thought I heard the baby."

Nora and Giulia looked at each other. "The baby?"

Mary stood. "What?"

"You said, 'I thought I heard the baby.' "

"No, I didn't."

"Yeah, Mary, you did."

"Ssh." Mary put her cigarette out in her plate.

There was a faint kittenlike sound of crying, like a kitten caught in wire and crying.

"Natassia?" Mary called.

"M-o-m-m."

Running, followed by the others, Mary screamed, "Natassia! What, honey?"

"Mom!"

Blood on the sheets was the first thing Mary saw. Natassia was sitting on the edge of the bed, her sleeves rolled up. Her face was crumbled. She was poking into her wrists and the crooks of her arms with a Cuisinart blade. "Help me," she whimpered to her mother and her friends. "Help me do this. I can't do this."

In the days following Natassia's attack on herself with the Cuisinart blade, Mary refused to do the thing everybody insisted had to be done. She would not check Natassia into a psychiatric facility. Mary made that decision slowly, during the six hours they spent waiting in the hallway outside of the emergency room.

It was a little past ten-thirty when they got Natassia to the hospital. By midnight, she'd had a shot of penicillin and a tetanus shot, sixteen stitches in her left forearm, six stitches in her right forearm, and the ER resident was just finishing up two stitches on her right wrist. "Why'd you do this to yourself?" the doctor asked her.

Natassia turned her face away from him, into the stiff white pillow. Up until that point, Mary hadn't been sure Natassia was even hearing what was going on around her. Since they'd found her in her bedroom, she'd had a hollow horror in her eyes, a violet emptiness in her irises. The doctor persisted, "Am I hurting you right now? Do you feel this?" When Natassia turned her head back toward him, her eyes were even more hollow, but the horror was out of them. She looked frighteningly as if she didn't care what was being done to her. "Are you cold?" he asked. She was in a hospital gown. Her bloody nightgown and her clogs and the raincoat they'd wrapped her in were rolled into a ball underneath the stretcher.

Earlier, undressing her, a nurse had found three cigarette burns on the inside of Natassia's right thigh; one was oozing pus and needed attention. There was a small moon of a cut on the top of her left thigh, where the Cuisinart blade had dropped while she was gouging herself. "Why'd you do this?"

"Leave her alone," Mary told the doctor, whose name tag said Montrose, and Mary thought, Monster. She had her hands on Natassia's head to keep her still on the stretcher, but Natassia wasn't moving.

"Your daughter's a smart girl," Dr. Monster told Mary. His needle was going in for the last suture. "She doesn't really want to kill herself. She mostly went for flesh. That's a good sign."

Mary moved her hands down over Natassia's ears so she wouldn't hear anything. The way she lay there, with her goose-pimpled, stubbly legs splayed, Natassia looked almost indolent. Or like some animal killed on the side of the road.

"Are *you* okay?" the doctor asked Mary; then she heard him shouting, "Hey, hey! Help over here! The mother's fainting."

Mary felt cold and hot all at once, and she had the taste of metal in her mouth. There was an ammonia smell. She glanced down at two large brown hands supporting her under her arms, but she never did see the person who said, "Whoa, Mama," and lowered her onto the floor.

"I'm okay," Mary said after a few minutes. They helped her up onto a stool, something with wheels, and Mary rolled herself close to Natassia's stretcher. Natassia really did look like roadkill. Somewhere in Mary's gut was the urge to move right on, do a drive-by, leave the mess. *I'm not qualified.* Mary was sure she didn't know the first thing to do to help Natassia.

Lying there on a white sheet, partly covered with a white sheet, Natassia was doing nothing except breathing, deep and slow. Her chest moved, but nothing else. Then, suddenly, riding lightly on one of her shallow exhalations was the question "Mom?"

"I'm here, Natassia." Still so dizzy she couldn't stand, Mary reached her hands up to Natassia's head again.

"Hey, come on, Mom, no need for crying now," the doctor said. "It's a little blood. Natalia's fine. The scare just got to you."

"Her name's Natassia." Mary ran her hands over Natassia's wide forehead. Her skin was cold, but her fuzzy hair was matted with sweat. Mary brushed a wad of loose curlicues away from Natassia's ear. Now that Mary was sitting down, she could whisper right into Natassia's ear. "I love you," Mary whispered. Natassia's eyes were open but didn't even blink. "I love you," Mary insisted. Mary had been waiting for years, afraid but always knowing that eventually they'd get here. *Bottom. We've hit.*

"Okay," Dr. Monster said, tugging off his gloves. "She's done, but I can't release her yet. Things are going to take a while tonight. Get comfortable. You'll be spending a stretch of time here in our wonderful emergency ward."

Finally.

A NURSE and an aide dressed in green lifted Natassia—"One, two, *three!*"—onto a gurney and, because they had no other place for her, wheeled her into the corridor, where Nora and Giulia were waiting. Now, with a blanket over her, Natassia didn't look so much like something left in the street. She lay on her side with her eyes closed.

"Jesus, thank God, she's all right," Giulia gushed. "They kept you guys in there so long, we didn't know what to think."

Nora was standing back a bit, behind Giulia, and Mary got some relief just seeing Nora, her white hair an aura around her silence. Always calm no matter how bad things got. Always practical. "Lotte's been at the pay phone for a while, trying to reach David," Nora told Mary.

They were standing in a too-bright corridor, very noisy, lined with patients on stretchers.

"We're here for a while," Mary told her friends. "That's what the guy said." On the gurney to one side of Natassia's lay an elegantly dressed old woman—attractive but confused—who had had an episode of amnesia at a dinner party. She was being watched over by her silver-bearded boyfriend, who she thought was her husband, who'd been dead twelve years. The guy on the gurney to the other side of Natassia was an HIV patient with two-day head pain so severe he was in a constant moan. He was there by himself, holding an ice pack on his head. When it slipped out of his hands onto the floor, Giulia picked it up for him and held it over his eyes for a while.

At twelve-forty-five, Natassia vomited onto the floor. She couldn't stop vomiting. Mary looked around for a nurse or a doctor, but there was no one. Mary's friends held Natassia to make sure she didn't roll off the stretcher. Mary used the edge of the sheet to wipe Natassia's mouth. Natassia was still vomiting when a nurse came rushing by and yelled at Mary, "You said she didn't take pills. Honey, did you take pills?" Natassia shook her head violently no and looked offended by even the suspicion of an overdose, while the nurse unhinged the brake on the stretcher and started moving Natassia down the hallway.

"I want to go with her," Mary said.

"Yes, you better come with her. We're going to need you in there."

Back in the ER, Natassia was wheeled up against a wall to wait. The nurse gave Mary a bedpan and looked through Natassia's chart. "No pills; then it must be stress. This should teach you, Natalia. Don't ever try this again, you hear me? We can't give you anything yet for pain. You got any pain, Natalia?"

Mary was trying to ask, "But can stress really make her vomit this much?," but the nurse interrupted, "Ah-ah-ah, hold the pan for her, the pan. There she goes again. That's right, just throw it all up. Good girl. You're the mother who got dizzy before, aren't you? You okay now? Need some orange juice or something? I'll check with you in a little while." The nurse rushed away and left the two of them alone.

There were too many stretchers, and not all of them had curtains pulled around them. When Mary looked up from Natassia, she saw, all at once, blood spurt from an obese woman's shoulder, an old man pushing an oxygen mask up against his own face, two male nurses lifting a convulsing teenage boy, another nurse knifing open the inside seam of somebody's jeans and lifting the denim off of a bloody leg.

Mary heard, just beyond the sound of Natassia gagging and the mess plopping into the pink plastic pan, screams in different languages. Sirens were churning outside somewhere. For a disoriented moment, Mary thought about outside. *We're in the city, we're in the hospital.* She didn't know which hospital. Natassia breathed out, "Can't . . . hold . . . this," and Mary realized she'd forgotten to support the pan for Natassia, whose feet were sticking out past the end of the sheet. Her toes, in her black-and-white polka-dot socks, were wiggling at a high speed; her breathing was labored and shallow. She was working hard to catch up with herself between bouts of vomiting. "Relax," Mary told her. "Breathe. Breathe slow."

By two o'clock, Natassia had stopped vomiting, and they wheeled her out into the corridor again, into her place between the amnesic lady and the man with the headache. Lotte and Giulia had been taking turns holding ice bags on his eyes. He kept begging, Someone please turn out the lights. The few chairs in the corridor were already taken. In one of them, a sleeping woman was holding a snoring, congested toddler. In another, an old man sat with his half-full urine bag hanging outside his trousers. Mary stood by Natassia's stretcher with Nora and Giulia. Lotte was back and forth from the pay phone. David was home calling psychiatrists all over the country. Lotte came back once and said, "He'll have something figured out by morning. We're going to take her someplace first-rate. Enough of this . . ." Mary had the sense that people were hugging her a lot; meanwhile, she kept touching Natassia, her shoulder, her back, her feet. Natassia was now sleeping.

After a while, when Lotte went to use the phone again, Nora said, "Lotte and David are kind of forcing your hand, aren't they? Mary, what do you think you want to do?"

"What?"

"Do you want her to go away to get help someplace? That's what they're working on."

Mary leaned against the wall and put her hands into the pouch of her sweatshirt, where she found Natassia's three silver rings and her beaded earrings. Earlier, in the ER, someone had taken off all of Natassia's jewelry and shoved it into Mary's hands. "Do you think she needs to go someplace?" she asked Nora.

They'd now been at the hospital for over four hours. Nora, Giulia, and Lotte had taken turns going to the nurses' station to find out when Natassia would be released, but Mary didn't mind the waiting; within these hours at the hospital she felt safe. She was almost grateful to be held in this sling of time, until she could figure out what to do.

But the wait had hyped up Nora, who was practically crying, insisting, "Mary, I'm the last one who can tell you where Natassia should go and what you need to do. I'm useless, I'm . . ."

"I'm just glad you're here, Nora. Both of you guys. Really."

Nora *was* crying. *Weird.* "The most I can do is call one of those therapists I mentioned. The police are going to get involved, you know. They'll insist on some kind of treatment."

"The police?" Mary said.

"Mary, if you want Natassia to see a specialist in the city," Giulia offered, "the two of you could move into my apartment. There's room."

"Thanks. I don't think so." *Police?*

At three-thirty, Nora convinced Mary to go to the nurses' station. "You're the mother. Maybe they'll tell you something."

Mary wasn't ready yet to be released from the hospital, but she didn't want Nora to cry again. She walked to the desk and told the nurse, "My daughter stopped vomiting a while ago. What happens next?" The employees' time clock was ticking behind the desk. There was a microphone near the nurse's mouth, and on the desk in front of her, a bag of Doritos and a scatter of fat, steel-covered patient files.

"Oh, that vomiting isn't the reason why you're waiting. Your daughter has to see somebody from Psych. She can't leave till somebody from Psych sees her."

"Why?"

With a Dorito halfway into her mouth, the woman looked up at Mary. "You really want me to answer that?"

"When are they coming, these people from Psych?" Mary was hoping they wouldn't come for a while.

"Shortly, honey. They know you're waiting, but things are nutso. We got a circus going tonight. Must be the moon. Here's a blanket. Make her a pillow, so she'll have her head a little up."

At four o'clock, Natassia woke up shivering. Mary took off her sweatshirt and pulled it over Natassia's head. Easing Natassia's arms into the sleeves, she asked, "Does this hurt, sweetie?"

"I don't feel anything," she muttered.

"She doesn't feel anything. She's had tons of Novocain," Nora said, and took off her brushed-silk jacket; they wrapped it around Natassia, who still shivered.

Giulia left and came back with a pair of green surgical pants for Natassia.

"Where'd you get these?" Mary asked.

"Don't ask. I stole them." They pulled the pants onto Natassia, who was still shivering.

No sign yet of anyone from Psych. Mary, Nora, and Giulia sat on the floor. Mary was down to a T-shirt. Nora put her arm around her to warm her. "Hey," Mary said, "you guys should go home now. It's late."

"No. We're waiting with you."

"I don't want to call Ross yet," Mary said. Her friends nodded. "It's really cold, huh?"

"I'm going to find some blankets," Giulia said.

"I'm going to find the damn doctor," Nora said. She and Giulia stood and began to walk away. Then they both stopped and looked back at Mary. "Will you be okay here?"

Mary nodded, so they left.

It was just after five in the morning. All night, Mary's body had followed some instinct learned from dance: When the music is fast, the beat hysterical, the only thing to do is slow your movement. Keep your center of gravity low, hunker down. Keep breathing.

During the hours at the hospital, with panic all around her, Mary had crouched, done nothing, waited until she understood what needed to be done. As soon as she was alone with her daughter, the hospital corridor turned suddenly quiet, and for Mary it was like that hush just before the curtain went up, while the audience quieted and Mary took her place on-stage, in the dark, knowing nothing but her own heartbeat. That night in the hospital corridor, there was *hush* and, within it, Mary's moment of clear sight. Shaking Natassia gently awake, telling her, "Shh," Mary slipped the silk jacket off of Natassia, pulled off the green pants, turned the blood-stained raincoat inside out, wrapped Natassia in it, and slipped the clogs onto her feet. Mary was prepared to tell the other patients, "We're going to the bathroom," but no one was paying attention.

IN THE WEEKS that followed that night, Mary kept going over and over that moment, marveling at how easy it had been to walk her daughter out of the hospital into the predawn damp September morning. There was a taxi by the door. "Grand Central," she told the driver.

An hour later, they were on the train going up the river to Mary's cottage on the Hiliard School campus. They were among just a handful of people in the train car: Four or five sleepy nannies making their way to their jobs in the suburbs. A young drunk in a tux. A crew of construction workers. Mary and Natassia had a wide seat to themselves, and Natassia lay across Mary's lap, letting Mary hold her, as if she were a baby, her head pushed into the crook of Mary's arm, her face turned to hide against Mary's chest. Natassia was awake now and crying, finally crying. Mary said nothing. All Mary knew to do was to hold her. There were no words anymore, so Mary used her arms to tell her daughter, minute by minute, that she was there with her.

When the train shot out of the Grand Central tunnel, it was dawn, light was rising against the train windows, and Natassia spoke—it was really the first time she'd said anything all night. "He called me," she whispered. "That was him on the phone."

"Last night? Your boyfriend called you? Is that what happened?"

Natassia crumbled. "I'm . . . sorry."

"Oh, Natassia. Oh, Natassia."

They were both crying, and Mary rocked Natassia and said into her hair, "Oh no, *I'm* sorry, Natassia, I'm so, so sorry. It's *not* your fault. It's not *your* fault."

Natassia's thumbs were hindered by the bandages, so Mary offered her own pinkie and Natassia took it in her mouth, exactly as she'd done when she was a baby.

For the whole two-hour trip, Mary's arms and legs bore the weight of her big, tall daughter. Staring down at Natassia's face, Mary tried to understand. How could her daughter—this gorgeous, genius girl who was her daughter—be so demolished by love?

WHAT MARY LEARNED in those first days after she brought her daughter upstate was that her love for Natassia was enormous. So huge a thing was Mary's love that it made her wise and able to see a long way inside her daughter's hurt heart.

"Mary," Ross told her over the phone, "I know what you're trying to do. It's beautiful, it's a fine thing, but I don't think you can pull it off. She's too sick. We need to consider one of these places my father's talking about."

And then David would call Mary from his office: "I really should call Social Services on you this time. And Ross, that other imbecile, living up there as dim-witted as an Eskimo. Your daughter needs professional help, she needs to be in a psychiatric facility. They've got a spot for her at one of the best places in the country, and meanwhile you're keeping her hostage up there."

"I'm her mother, David."

"Mother! What do you know about mothering? What," David yelled, "do you think you're doing? What the hell are you *thinking*?"

Mary *wasn't* thinking. She just moved ahead, like an animal. Mary knew that the best and only answer was the simplest one: Natassia needed her mother. Mary had no idea how she had arrived at this conclusion, she just knew she was right.

That first morning when they arrived at the cottage, after bolting from the emergency room and riding the train upstate, Mary helped Natassia lie down on the couch, then Mary went into one of the spare bedrooms, pulled a mattress off the bed, and dragged it into the main room, right next to her own futon. She found clean sheets, made up the bed, put Natassia in it. While Natassia slept, Mary worked with the same focused industriousness that possessed her when she was choreographing under a deadline.

She collected the sharp kitchen knives, razors, scissors, along with all her pipes, into a paper bag to store up in her office. From the closets and drawers, Mary pulled out her largest sweaters and sweatpants so Natassia would have clothes to wear. Every medication in every cabinet and on every shelf was flushed down the toilet. For the first time in years, Mary would be living without Advil close at hand to help her manage the physical pain of her work and her injuries. Within a few hours, she had stripped herself of herself. Mary was ready to become a mother.

Before rumors began circulating, Mary called Natassia's school in the city and told them an abbreviated version of what had happened to Natassia, told them she would be on leave for the rest of the semester, asked them to consider refunding David some of the tuition he'd already paid.

It was past noon by now; Mary had been awake for thirty hours. As Natassia slept, Mary kept working. She called the Hiliard School nurse and got the name of the doctor the school used when students got sick. Dr. Jonson—in his seventies, semi-retired, a general surgeon, gabby—offered to come to campus, and arrived at the cottage wearing yellow golf pants with a matching golf shirt. He had a bristling gray crewcut. "Sorry I couldn't have you come to my office, but there's a young gal, she specialized in that sports medicine, she sees her patients there a few times a week. It's not that I need the rent money, but, hell, the examining rooms are there, and, as my wife said, this gal could use a break to get started. Well, it works out for both of us." He told Mary all this as she was letting him in the door.

"Hey, thanks for coming over," she said.

"No problem. I've helped out around this school for forty-five years. My wife used to teach here, you know. American history." When he saw the mattress set up on the floor and Natassia sleeping, he asked Mary, "Is that where you'll be sleeping, next to her?"

Was everybody always going to question her, doubt her? "Yeah, what's the problem?"

"None at all. Good idea, I'd say. You teach here, do you? What's your area?"

"Dance."

"Good for you. Dance, well. My wife, she's crazy for the ballet. I'm ashamed to say, I fall asleep every time we go down to the city to see that ballet of New York, whatever they call it."

"New York City Ballet."

"I get her the season tickets. She likes that."

His voice was slow, laconic; as he spoke, he unwrapped the bandages around Natassia's wrists.

"They love to use the gauze, don't they? Then they say they need more money from insurance, who charges it all back to the patient. Got you looking like a heavyweight boxer here. You a dancer, too, like your mother?"

Natassia wearily shook her head.

"No? I bet you're a reader, aren't you? You strike me as the intellectual type. My daughter growing up, that's all she did, always lost in some corner of the house reading a book. She's a professor now. Out in Oregon with her husband—Does that hurt you when I do that?" He was dabbing at the stitches with an alcohol rub. Natassia just shrugged. "Doesn't hurt? Okay, that's good." He wrapped her up again with clean gauze. "I want you to come pay me a visit in two days at the office, so I can look at this again."

"Sure," Mary said, "we'll be there." Natassia said nothing.

The doctor held Natassia's fingers in his hand and squeezed them a bit. Her bandages were now minimal; she had much more mobility. "How about you? Are you coming, or you sending your mother alone?"

Natassia finally spoke. "Yeah. I'll be there."

"Good. I'll be glad to see you. Okay, enough of my yakking. You need to sleep, and I need to go kick butt on the golf course." There was even a hint of a smile on Natassia's face as she lay down.

At the cottage door, the doctor motioned with his head for Mary to come outside and join him in the garden. He walked a little ways down the path. "Why'd she do this?" he asked.

"Some guy. A boyfriend." Mary's face wilted as she began to cry. "It's my fault. I—"

"Hey, come on, now. That won't help her. This world today, it's everyone's fault. These kids, they're all fifteen going on forty, their shoulders piled high with all kinds of troubles. She had previous attempts, problems?" Mary shook her head no. "Well, you got to watch her now."

"I know that. That's what I'm going to do. Just keep her with me."

"That's the thing to do. And she needs to talk to somebody. You know that, don't you? We need to call that New York hospital and I'll tell them she's in my care, but only if you get her good help up here. You got someone? A counselor, a minister?"

"I see a therapist in Brooklyn. Well, mostly we talk on the phone. Natassia's grandparents want her down in the city. They have a psychiatrist lined up. Really what they want is to send her away to some place."

"A city psychiatrist? Taking the train down there, in her condition? She's exhausted, and depressed as all hell. Why go down there? Look what she's got here. These gardens, they're looking better every year, aren't they? Up here, she's got you watching her."

"I couldn't let her stay at that hospital. It was so crazy, so—"

"Hey, you don't need to tell me about ERs in those city hospitals." He had pulled a prescription pad out of his bag and was writing. "Here. This is the name and number for a therapist right here in town. She's got a social-work degree, she's starting a small part-time practice. She's my son's wife. They live over the hill, by the railroad station. Heather's her name. Lovely girl. Just had their second baby, presented me with my twelfth grandchild, do you believe it? Anyway, that's why she's part-time now, in their home. I think Natalie—"

"Natassia."

"Sorry. Natassia—pretty name—Natassia might trust her. That's the important thing with these therapists. How can you trust somebody down in the city who's sticking you for one hundred fifty dollars an hour? Bunch of charlatans, if you ask me." He handed Mary the sheet of paper with Heather's name. "Call. Tell her I sent you."

"Okay." Standing out in the sun, Mary felt the exhaustion hit her. Then she remembered, looked in the window of the cottage. Natassia was buried under the comforter; even her head was hidden.

"She allergic to any medications?"

"Well, last night something made her vomit like crazy. They'd given her tetanus and penicillin shots. They tried saying she took pills, but I know she didn't. I never thought about allergies."

"Did she get a rash, trouble breathing? No? That stomach upset wasn't meds, then, it was stress." He was writing and handing Mary sheets from his pad. "Here. This is mild, over-the-counter, for pain. Buy the smallest packet, just five or so, enough for today and tomorrow, and keep them away from her. Just a precaution. You're not using drugs here in this house, or drinking a lot, are you? Parties?"

"Parties? Hardly. All I do is work. I already threw out all my Advil and stuff."

"Smart move, Mother. Is it the adoption Natassia's upset about? Problems with her self-identity and all that?"

"Adoption? No. She's mine. My natural-born daughter."

"Oh, sorry. I just wondered, seeing she's not Oriental and you are."

"Her dad's Jewish."

"I see. And he's—"

"Not around."

"Well, ma'am, can I do anything else for you?"

"No, just thanks. You know, for coming over here. I really wanted her out of the hospital. Hey, I have to pay you."

"My wife will send you a bill. Submit it to your insurance."

"Listen, I got to ask you. Will you please keep this, I mean the details and everything, keep it from anybody you might know around here?"

"I've been a doctor for fifty years this May, and I have never broken a confidence. Listen, Mother, you've got to stop crying. She should be all right. It'll take time. But—"

Mary kicked at a pile of dead leaves.

"Mother, I want you to listen to me." He put a hand on her shoulder. "I believe you know what you're doing here. Any questions or problems, you call me. Another emergency, go straight to the hospital."

"Yes."

"But don't let there be another emergency."

"No."

He was pulling dead leaves off of a rosebush. "Somebody needs to dead-head these plants out here." A plump yellow chrysanthemum in full bloom was hanging bent on its stalk, and he pulled it off. "Here," he said, "put that in water. That should cheer up your Natassia. You'd pay top dollar for a flower like this in the city. Okay, now, got to go."

"Have a good golf game," Mary said.

"Oh, I'm not a very good golfer, you know, but I do enjoy myself. My strategy is to see if I can make the other fellows mess up." She watched him put his black doctor's bag in the trunk of his tan Mercedes. He waved as he got into the car. She waved back.

Well, that was neighborly. As Mary walked into the cottage, she was wondering what world, what fantasy kingdom, that doctor lived in. And how long, how many generations, or how much money did it take before a family could end up living that way.

part
Two

THE MODEL

For five years, Nora lived in the south of France like a woman in a Matisse painting, lying around in a coral-striped robe or bare-breasted, an odalisque reclining on a white-sheeted chaise, on flowered damask pillows, while all around her, like the goldfish in the plump glass bowl, swam the evergreen paisleys and the beet-red blooms, the vines and fringes of the draperies hung beyond the carpet spread before the screen folded neatly as the elbow of Nora's amber arm. Middle of the week, middle of the day, Mediterranean heat, Nora naked after lunch in the center of Christopher's studio or in the studios of the other American painters of their crowd. The French still at table, but the artists tense at the canvas, waiting for the event: sunlight passing over Nora's calm head. Her white long hair up or down, Nora on the cushions, sometimes on a tabletop, sometimes wearing jewelry, seeming to worry about nothing, watching the light fall in from the balcony, through the sun curtains sheer as one of her slips. Light crawls toward her. She allows the painters to pose her, touch her. Why not? No hint that this is recreational nakedness. In the wide space outside the painters' absorption, she wanders freely, there is nothing but safety. What they want is what she wants: the only point of her day is to recline and be still. This is her apprenticeship, but she does not know for what. She thinks, For dinner, eggplant grilled with olive oil. She touches the powder of a flower's center to her nose and wonders what there is in the world beyond the body that she does not know yet.

WHEN THE FRENCH YEARS *were over, and she and Christopher moved back to New York, Nora's friends referred to her as* She Who Has What She Wants.

Nora, shaking, was lying on a rag rug on the bathroom floor of her loft. It was the day after the night at the ER with Natassia. Early afternoon. There wasn't much relief in having found out, fifteen minutes earlier, that Mary and Natassia were safe. Lotte had just called with the news that they were upstate, in the cottage. Mary was insisting that for now the two of them needed to be alone.

"Nora, please," Lotte had begged over the phone, "you're trained in this sort of thing. How do we make Mary be sensible?"

"I don't know, Lotte. I guess we just let her do what she's doing." Nora had had to wrap her arms around herself and hold on tight to the phone.

Now, lying in the bathroom, Nora turned onto her side, and the dusty rag rug curled up beneath her. She had canceled her morning and early-afternoon appointments, which she'd never done before. She had about four hours to pull herself into some kind of shape for her four-fifteen appointment, a guy losing custody of his Downs-syndrome daughter, a guy whose stability was so precarious right now that Nora couldn't risk putting him off for a week. But isn't he going to notice, she wondered, that I'm a bigger mess than he is? She stretched out her arm, rested her head on the inside of her elbow. Her face turned in to her armpit, hip balanced on the floor, leg on leg, trying to make herself thin, a rolled-up wick—light it up and burn away. There was nothing for Nora to do now but disappear.

The bathroom was the only place in the loft where she could close a door, be alone, and keep Christopher's cat away from her. *Mary walked out of the hospital with her suicidal daughter.* Nora was shocked even by the thought of what Mary had done. To play out the possible—probable—disastrous outcomes . . . Nora needed to hide.

All night long at the hospital, like everyone else, Nora had stood around panicked in the hallway outside the ER and stroked Natassia's hair, as if the only thing she cared about was Natassia's recovery. *Like the damn Red Cross.* How she envied the others, even Mary, the clarity of their fear and panic, while Nora had had to mask her impatience: *Did you have to do this? How far are you going to push, until Christopher and I are completely ruined?* Last night Nora had finally admitted to herself that she'd never liked Natassia much. And that she'd always been afraid of her.

If only Nora could be alone for a few minutes, sit still with the truth, unbraid the strands of anger and hate from the strands of fear knotted inside her, but, alone in her own bathroom, Nora kept seeing pictures, last night's events broken down moment by moment. Natassia's thin, parched presence in the hallway of Lotte's apartment when they'd arrived to visit her, not even saying hello. Nora at first thought Natassia was being rude, diffident, but then she noticed that Natassia's breathing was so shallow she could say only a few words at a time. *I should have said something then.* Later, when the Chinese food arrived and the women settled in the living room to eat, Natassia was nothing but a ghost passing through the rooms, making less noise than the old wooden furniture creaking from the radiator heat. There they were, four women assembled because of their shared concern for Natassia; Natassia was the only reason for them to get together last night. And down the cramped hallway, in her bedroom, on the telephone, Natassia was carrying out some drama over a boyfriend that led to her slashing herself with a Cuisinart blade.

Nora covered her face with her hand. When they'd found Natassia, there was blood in a little puddle in the palm of her hand. She'd been calling, "Help me," and when they got to her she said that thing that kept rolling and rolling inside Nora: *Help me do this.* Remembering it made

Nora bite the heel of her hand. There'd been red oblongs of blood on Natassia's nightgown, on the sheets. When they got down to the lobby, the doorman was peeling an apple, and as he ran out to the curb to hail a cab, two cabs, he still had his tiny paring knife in his hand, even as he helped Natassia get into a cab. *"Dios,"* he was saying under his breath, *"Dios."* Nora couldn't remember who had paid for the cab she was in. Giulia? Had anyone paid?

And then the four women and Natassia had entered the eternity of the ER.

At some point in the middle of the night, Nora's period had started, nine days early. A few hours later, Mary asked Nora, "Do you have a Tampax? I got my fucking period." Did Natassia have this power, to force them all to bleed along with her? Lotte and David were going crazy with phone calls back and forth and all over the country. Nora had kept calling the loft, but Christopher wasn't home. She wouldn't embarrass herself by calling their friends to see if anyone had seen him. His new studio in Chelsea didn't have a phone. Wherever he was, he was there all night, never went home. The last time Nora called the loft, it was almost six o'clock in the morning. And then Mary and Natassia had disappeared from the hospital. Not a soul had seen them leave.

Nora didn't for a second believe that Mary could manage what she was trying to do—even with the most informed care, Natassia's recovery would be an iffy business—but Mary deserved some credit for trying.

Also, there was the relief.

Go ahead, Nora challenged herself, say it. *Since Mary took Natassia away, Mary is responsible for her. Christopher and I aren't.*

Her hand was spread out on the cool tile bathroom floor, and when she lifted it, her handprint appeared in the coating of dust and bath powder on the cracked white and black tile hexagons. Originally, this loft had been built as a sewing factory, and this bathroom had been a ladies' room with two toilets. There were now bare spots on the floor where the walls of the stalls had been bolted down. A big potted cactus plant covered the bare patch of concrete where the second toilet used to be. Christmas ornaments and a string of dusty chili-pepper lights clung to the cactus needles. Christopher lit the lights when he and Nora took baths together. That hadn't happened in a long time. Nora sat up to stretch the rug out under her, then curled up again as small as she could.

Eye-level with the floor, she could see how much the surface bubbled, the little tiles roller-coastering across the bathroom to the claw-footed tub. Hundreds of pounds of bathtub. It had taken five guys to get it off the U-Haul truck, into the elevator, off the elevator, and into the bathroom. Such ridiculous efforts to re-create the past. It embarrassed Nora now, the high cost of the worn-out chic she and Christopher and most of their friends (the lucky ones) lived in. How silly they would look to the women who had worked here in the factory and used this bathroom decades ago.

Nora imagined those women rushing in for a pee or a cigarette, quick, so they wouldn't get in trouble with their boss. Nora could see those women, almost feel their presence, as they left their sewing machines and ran into this bathroom to cry. She imagined women relieved to see the blood that assured them there was no baby this month. Praying in Italian, Greek, Polish, Chinese: *Thank you.* Or women panicked to see the blood that meant a baby was leaving them, lost. Suddenly Nora felt so connected to those women, imagined stifled sobs in the bathroom stalls, heartbreak over boyfriends, husbands, lost refugee family members. Monsoons, tidal waves of tears over money, children, the law. "I'm sorry," Nora heard herself say aloud, and she did not feel foolish. She felt weak for how little she was able to do for anyone. *God, please, let her be all right.*

WHEN CHRISTOPHER came home and found her, Nora was asleep. She woke and heard his "Nor? Nor-a!" In the surprise of finding her curled asleep on the bathroom floor, his voice had turned tender, as she hadn't heard it in months. "Sweetie, what are you doing in here like this?"

She looked up at him filling the doorway. "Was I asleep?"

"What's with Natassia? I just listened to your messages from the hospital."

"She's gone." Christopher's eyes got huge, then closed shut, then he grabbed the doorjamb. "No, no," Nora told him, "she didn't die. She and Mary disappeared. A little before six this morning, Mary just left with her, before they were done treating her."

"She just left?" Nora shook her head, wasn't able to answer. "How

145

much did she hurt herself? What the hell happened?" Nora still couldn't speak. Christopher came and sat down on the floor, facing her. He took both her hands, turned them over, rubbed her palms with his thumb. How good it felt, the way he knew where to go to rub the tension out. How he knew her. As she relaxed, Nora felt her face give in to tears, and she leaned her head forward, into his chest. He'd worked all night and then slept in his studio. He hadn't been with some other woman. Nora knew just by the smells on him: turpentine and sleep and paint and coffee. He was still holding her hands. "What, sweetie? Nora, tell me."

They hadn't talked or touched or been close like this in weeks, so many weeks. "It was horrible. So, so bad. We were . . ." Now she was sobbing. "We were all there, eating dinner in the living room, right down the hallway from Natassia's bedroom, and we never knew. We were *there* and couldn't stop her." By now Nora had crawled onto Christopher's lap and they were hugging, hard. He was rocking her. "Christopher, she used the Cuisinart blade. Do you know how bad that is? Do you know?"

"Ssshhh. Oh, baby, ssshhh." Nora was holding on tight. How had she supposed she could manage *Natassia Natassia Natassia* without this hugging, without her husband? "Nora, baby, you poor thing." Her face was against his neck. "Nora, what can I do?"

"I need you to be with me, Christopher. We need to go through this together."

"Yes, yes, yes. That's all I want to do. I want to help you." *He's with me. We're going to talk now. He finally sees how serious our problem with Natassia is. He's finally going to take responsibility.* "I haven't been taking good care of you," he whispered, "I've been bad." His wide hand stroked her back. "All I want to do, Nora, is love you, that's all. I want this all to pass out of your mind. I want it not to be bothering you."

He was still trying to rock her, but Nora stiffened a bit in his arms. Were they talking about the same thing? "We need to talk about Natassia."

But he was holding on harder. "Nora, just let me love you."

She pulled away, looked at his face. It was his eyes more than anything, that surprise of blue under heavy, long, straight dark lashes. His skin never stopped looking tanned. She ran her palm over his auburn buzz cut, the wide curves of his scalp. Except for the light eyes, his coloring was syrupy and matched the warm sounds of *Christopher.* Nora tucked her hands under his stubbly chin, rested her fingers against his broad cheekbones. *Home.* "Christopher, I love you."

"I love *you*, Nora," he insisted, with a hurt twinge in his eyes.

She brushed a loose eyelash off the side of his nose. "I know, I know, and we have this problem, honey. Natassia. We're in this with her. We can't pretend we're not."

"You said she was doing all right."

Nora took her hands off of Christopher's face, pushed back her hair. All of a sudden, she felt sweaty, hot, too close. Just a minute ago, she had seen in his eyes a new acknowledgment of the seriousness of the situation. She couldn't believe he was doing it again. "What I said," she told him, "was that she didn't succeed in killing herself. She's still alive, but she's certainly not all right. There's nothing right about her situation."

With Nora still sitting on his lap, Christopher leaned away from her, took his arms away from her waist, put his hands on the floor behind him, which unbalanced her, and she tipped off of his thighs and onto the tile floor. He sighed a long, tired, irritated sigh. "Why are you doing this?" he asked.

"Doing what?"

"I'm a fool to try with you even anymore."

"What?" she asked again.

"I'm trying to love you, Nora"—his voice was rising away from anything that sounded like love—"and you keep torturing me."

Torture?

"You think I'm a sicko," Christopher said. "You really do think I am."

"I do not think that." Nora knew—she felt strongly—that Christopher was not a sexual deviant. His molestation of Natassia, though hideously wrong, had been a one-time act. She believed that. Pretty much. But there was something she did *not* believe. Something—someone?—she did not believe *in*. Or have faith in. Or trust. *Belief. Faith. Trust. Torture?* Nora had no idea, no idea whatsoever, exactly what it was she wanted from Christopher when she insisted that they still had to deal with Natassia. *I need to be more direct with him. More direct than ever.* "Christopher—"

"Nora, we have *been* through the Natassia business so many—"

"But never satisfactorily. It's all been brushed under the rug. Can't you see? Why can't you see it? What's happening with Natassia now, and the problems you and I are having, it's all connected to what happened when she was a—"

"If you say that this, this suicide try, is connected to some stupid, stupid, *stupid* thing *I* did fifteen years ago—we're talking fifteen years ago. My God, woman, you never let up. You're trying to kill me, aren't you? You're trying to make me go crazy." With his heels, he scooted himself away from her, backed himself against the tile wall.

"Christopher—"

"Shut up. You just shut up. I'm tired of—"

"Don't talk to me that way," Nora said.

He wasn't looking at her, just staring hard out the window, where truck horns were blaring. "I'm your husband," he muttered. "I'll talk to you any way I want." He reached up, grabbed a towel off the towel rack, balled it, threw it hard out the window.

That was a good towel. Nora bit the insides of her lips together.

"Fucking trucks," he muttered. And then Christopher and Nora were silent.

By now, when he got like this, irrational, it had become automatic for Nora to revert to her list of things that needed to be done in order for her to leave him. Pack up her laptop. Get the manila envelope with her important papers, get the checkbook, collect as much clothing as she could stuff into one suitcase. Go straight to the bank and take half their cash and half their savings and go uptown to her office and have the locks changed immediately. Call that lawyer she'd met at the 92nd Street Y gym—Lindsey Lewis, Lucie Lewis? She'd be listed in the phone book under divorce lawyers. Most of last year, this list had existed only in Nora's mind. Over the summer, though, she had once got angry enough to write it out on a sheet of legal paper. The white page was now folded and tucked into her wallet. Along with her driver's license and her American Express card, the list was with her wherever she went. Each time Nora was forced to consider it, the list became more specific. *Once you've given it so much thought, you almost have to do it, don't you?* Was this the occasion when she'd finally begin the process of separating from this long marriage? Nora's heart was pulsing right now with pure white rage. How many times could she feel *this* before she'd hear herself saying aloud to Christopher, *Bye*?

Now, as usual, he took the righteous position, made a beleaguered noise through his lips, the sound of their old radiator spitting fast, hot steam. Once, in a marriage-counseling session, he'd managed to tell her that when he acted exasperated he was feeling attacked, confused, in over his head. But that counseling had been several years earlier. After four months, the therapist had led them into serious discussion of what had happened that day in France between him and Infant Natassia, and Christopher refused to go to any more sessions. Understanding that he'd lose the marriage if he didn't do something, he agreed to individual therapy—with a therapist of his *own choice*. He'd feel less embarrassed, he said, if he was able to talk to someone without Nora in the room. Nora would have been happier if he'd said *less ashamed* rather than *less embarrassed*, which was too mild. He'd gone to therapy for six months with some bozo who made him feel good about himself but never challenged him, and that was it. Nora and Christopher had just gone on, until two years ago, when he'd begun making noises about wanting a child, and Nora had had to tell him flatly, *I don't trust you.*

Christopher's knees were raised. She looked at the paint specks on his ankles, his strong feet stuffed into his cloth espadrilles planted squarely on the bathroom floor. There was sex in the way the bones of his long toes stretched the canvas of his shoes. Sex in the smooth skin of his ankles before the dark hair of his legs began. If she did leave him, what would she do about her desire for him?

After a full ten minutes, when he started in for his next attack, she wasn't surprised. She knew what was coming. He waited until the hour struck—two o'clock—and all twelve of the cuckoo clocks on the bathroom wall went off at the same time. When the clocks were done chiming, he said, "Let me . . . Can I ask you just one question?" He was launching off in his high-and-mighty voice, a false voice he assumed when he was being defensive, warding her off, a voice in which he always made grammatical and idiomatic mistakes and ended up sounding more befuddled than when he'd begun. "Why is it I'm supposed to submit over and over to your cross-examination about something that happened fifteen years ago and you won't grant me the dignity of having what I want to talk about discussed? Namely, why won't you honor my desire to talk about when in the hell you and I are going to fucking get pregnant?"

"Chri—"

"Let me finish," he bellowed, and she asked herself, How can such a fool think he could ever be a father? "All I hear of all the time is about your *fears* and your *needs*"—he mocked the words as he said them. "Meanwhile, you're ruining our life. Don't you understand, Nora, that I can't go on with you, loving you, having my life with you, loving getting older with you, and not have kids? Do you see that at all? It doesn't make sense to me. You and me in twenty years with no kids, I don't see it. I'm forty years old. I've spent over twenty years of day and night doing nothing but painting. I'm used to it that I'll never be a star. I'll never have a show at MoMA. I can live with that. I don't even care about that anymore. I do my work. I show here and there. My work sells sometimes, and sometimes I make money, and sometimes it's good money. The thing I feel most ambitious about is us. Don't you see that? I want a family, Nora. I want a family with you."

The first few times he'd made this speech, he had actually succeeded in getting her to cry. Now, after hearing it so often, she sat and stared just over his head, sickened by the sound of him. Finally, she told him, as she'd told him before, "I can't do it. I don't feel enough trust in our relationship. I can't ignore what I feel."

"You have to make a decision, Nora."

"I have made a decision, honey. I love you and I want us to work through this. I know you feel an emptiness because we haven't had a child yet, and I'm very sorry you feel that. I think I would love to have a baby, but before I can begin to talk about that, I need for us to talk about what happened with Natassia and see you take responsibility for that, and for what's happening now."

Another scornful burst from his tight lips. "You *think* you would like to have a baby. You *think*. Want to mince up your words any more?" For a long minute, his eyes went up and down between her feet and her face. "You made a mess of yourself," he said, "in case you didn't notice."

She looked to where he was looking. Her crotch. Her gray sweatpants were blackened with blood. "I forgot to change my Tampax. I don't have any more, either. I have to go to the drugstore."

"So you're ending the conversation like that? Nail me to the cross and walk away."

"I'll be glad to talk more later, not now. Maybe tonight." She stood and saw that she'd dripped blood onto the rug and the floor. Her periods were never like this, never this heavy.

"I just want to tell you one more thing."

"Christopher, I have to go to the drugstore, unless you'll offer to go for me."

"What you still haven't figured out yet is that your psychoanalysis doesn't explain everything. My God, Nora, have a little forgiveness."

She looked straight at him. Standing, they were eye to eye. "Christopher, I do forgive you. I forgave you thirteen years ago, when I married you. You know that. But we're talking about a young girl who's in trouble, and what I can't forgive is your insistence that it has nothing to do with you. And I can't forgive your insisting that I'm the one keeping us from having a baby. I would love to talk about babies, I'll talk about babies all you want, but not until I can trust you to be a father. I just don't have that faith in you. And why do you force me to spell this out again and again? Why won't—"

"You. You're tired? I'm tired of my sisters' making me an uncle."

"I've asked you to end this right now. I'm tired, and I'm bleeding."

"And I want a kid of my own," he screamed.

So she screamed back, "Just to play baby bingo with your sisters? A nice life to propagate. Contribute to the Kansas City Mafia."

And then he laughed at her, laughed in the most evil way, as if it satisfied him to see her pushed so far into ugliness. He turned to leave the bathroom but stopped and looked back at her from the door. "You're not going to the drugstore like that, are you? In those sweatpants you're big as a cow."

Nora said nothing. And they both knew that during the next days, maybe a week or more, she would continue to say nothing. It was her way of fighting. "WASP artillery," Christopher called it. Another of his inaccuracies. Nora's background was Irish Catholic, not WASP. What Christopher was right about was this: She was a master of angry silence. Absolute, wordless silence.

CHAPTER 12:

SEPTEMBER

1989

AND THE

YEAR BEFORE

Christopher felt that slimy relief as soon as the metal door of their building slammed shut behind him and he walked out into the street. Fucking bitch, he thought. She never lets up. She was going to push and push until he lost it completely. As if he needed this now. Sometimes he thought he should just tell Nora what was going on, but that would be a one-way ticket to divorce court, no turning back from there.

She wasn't even supposed to be home at this time. He'd been planning to spend the afternoon alone at the loft. He needed to use the phone to figure things out with the medical insurance and the bank. He had so much on him these days. He didn't know how much more he could take. He had to hurry up, get stuff done. There wasn't a lot of time.

He turned onto Second Street and headed toward Avenue A. When he reached the avenue, the place was there, just like Denise had said it would be. Christopher walked in.

"Hi there. Help you?" a blonde asked. It was always the girls walking up to him in stores. Why couldn't he get some guy to wait on him, somebody who just wanted to get business done?

"I need a stroller," Christopher said, looking beyond the girl's face. "For a baby."

"Cool. Come on back here with me, this way." Brushing through a narrow aisle of high chairs, she asked, "For a toddler or infant?"

"What?"

"How old is the baby you're buying the stroller for?"

"Not born yet."

"Okay. A newborn."

For fifteen minutes, the blonde showed him strollers. One faced a baby backward. Three faced the baby forward. Some lifted, some detached. Italian strollers, Swiss strollers. The clunky GM-type that Denise had told him to buy was the ugliest, but that's how she did things, based on *Consumer Reports.*

But that wasn't how he did things. "That Italian one, the three-hundred-dollar one, that has the smoothest lines. I like the chrome wheels. I'll take that one."

"Awesome choice." As the blonde led Christopher up to the cash register, her long black skirt clung and showed no underwear lines. Her Doc Martens looked tacky with the skirt. She looked back at him over her shoulder. "You're decisive, aren't you?"

He lifted his eyebrows, didn't answer her.

While he opened his wallet and pulled out cash, she tried to get information from him. "First baby?" He answered again with eyebrows only. "Your wife not interested in seeing this first?"

"It's a gift."

"Oh. Great."

Palming the wad of money, Christopher had felt good, responsible; handing it over, he felt like a fool. He might never even see the baby who'd be riding around in this stroller. Just pay, he told himself, and shut up.

The blonde pushed a big chunk of her hair away from her face. "And we're sending this to where?"

"Nyack. To Denise Wojciekowski. W-O-J— Here, I'll write it." He took the delivery order sheet from her, also the pen from her hand.

"Enclosing a gift card?"

"No, it's my sister. She'll know it's from me."

OUT ON THE STREET, Christopher found a pay phone—it seemed all he did these days was look for pay phones—and dialed the number in Nyack for Denise Wojciekowski, who was not his sister.

"Hey, it's me," he said after her grunted hello. "You okay?"

"Yeah, I'm okay. Nothing great, but okay."

"Okay is good, Denise. Hold on to okay. Listen, I just bought a stroller. I went to that place you said. On Avenue A. It should get to you in a couple of days."

"It'd better not be big. Where'm I supposed to put it?"

"I made room in the garage until I get those bookshelves out of your hallway. *Do not* try to move anything, you hear me? Denise, you hear me?"

"Relax. I'm not moving anything. I can barely move myself."

"He's kicking?" he asked.

"He's nonstop."

"Ten more weeks, he'll be kicking you from the outside."

"I'll kick him back," Denise said. "Listen, you sound tired."

"Yeah. We had a fight. She flipped again."

Silence, then Denise said, "This is all costing you, isn't it?"

"Not your problem, Denise. Nora and I will manage. Listen, Friday I'm coming up there to put that crib together. Do you need anything from down here?"

"I don't think so," she said.

"How's the work? Are you writing?"

"Still on the same chapter."

"Are you eating okay and all?"

"Yeah, yeah, yeah."

"See you Friday, Denise."

She hung up, as always, without a goodbye.

Just my luck, Christopher thought, to be married to one bitch, and having a baby with another.

DENISE'S PLAN had been in place for nearly a year now, and still, sometimes, just walking down the street going about his business, waiting on line to pay for his groceries or to buy subway tokens, Christopher was astonished by the thought: Baby. He could hardly believe he'd had the nerve to try to become part of Denise's plan; he absolutely could not believe that the plan seemed to be working. In the early stages, it had been all exaggerated guy pride, and he'd gone around thinking, *My* baby, *my* baby. Lately, though, since he'd been spending more time in Nyack at Denise's, he'd begun to see the reality of *baby*: day-care interviews, pediatrician interviews, and every day the outpour of money, money, money. Christopher was driven through his days 99 percent by fear.

Thank God that Denise seemed to know exactly what she was doing.

CHRISTOPHER HAD FIRST HEARD about Denise Wojciekowski and her plan a year earlier, October 1988, while he was having a beer with his friend Piper, another painter. They had just been to the New York Film Festival and were sitting at the bar of the Saloon restaurant, across from Lincoln Center. Christopher hadn't even wanted to go out that night, not after the fight he and Nora had had that afternoon, but he wasn't going to let film-festival tickets go to waste. So, when Nora had issued her definitive *I'm not going*, Christopher had called Piper, for no other reason than that the film was French and Piper spoke French. "Nora's sick. Are you free tonight?" Miracle of miracles, Piper had a free night. That was the random beginning of Christopher's involvement in Denise Wojciekowski's plan to have a baby.

The Saloon was crowded, and it took a while for Christopher and Piper to gather two stools together at the far end of the bar. They signaled the bartender to give them whatever he had on tap. The film they had seen was *36 Fillette*. "Good movie," Piper said.

"I didn't like it. Pernicious adolescent girl."

Piper looked at Christopher and asked, "You mean promiscuous?"

"I don't know, just watching her screw around kind of made me sick."

"Paying together or separate?" the bartender asked.

"Together," Piper said. "My treat," he told Christopher.

"Thanks, Piper."

"No problem, my man. Thank *you*." They clicked their glasses together. "Cheers."

"Yeah, cheers." Christopher took a long drink of his beer. He turned on his stool and rested with his back against the bar, facing the crowds filling up the tables. He scowled. "The film tickets were part of an early birthday gift for Nora that I got to surprise her."

"And here you are, stuck with me. You're making me feel guilty."

"You're not guilty. She just— I'm just glad the tickets didn't go to waste." Christopher avoided Piper's eyes and shrugged.

"And she's sick with what? Flu? Lady troubles?" Piper asked.

Christopher, for a moment, considered telling Piper the truth, telling him about the fight, how Nora had flipped that morning when she'd read a review in the paper about the film Christopher had got tickets for. "Christopher, this movie is about an adolescent girl who comes on to an older man. Are you taunting me with this? What's going on?"

"Nora, you said you're homesick for France. I just got tickets because the movie's French. I didn't even look what it's about."

"You won't go to therapy with me to talk about these issues, but you got—"

It was that word "issues" that had made Christopher pop a cork. But when she side-swiped him like that—all he was trying to do was give her a nice surprise, and according to her, he was being bad. Thoughtless, she said, insensitive. *Taunting!* When she sideswiped, he couldn't stop himself, and when he started it was nearly impossible—it was completely impossible—for him to stop. "Fuck you, Nora," he had yelled, "I'm telling you, don't you get started, don't you—"

It went on, got worse; she locked herself into the bedroom. All he wanted to do was explain himself, but he knocked on the glass door too hard, and a small pane shattered, then another one. He cut a finger and got blood on the dhurrie rug.

"Yeah," he now told Piper, "a lady thing. Last-minute. Don't feel guilty."

"Christopher, my man, just for the record, in case you don't know it, we are, all of us, every single one of us, as men, we're guilty of something when it comes to the women. That's just how that particular cookie crumbles, man, no way around that. Maybe you can't figure out what you're doing wrong while you're doing it—or even after you did it, not even when she's trying to spell it all out to you real slow, because of the dummy that you are—but if you're a man and you're dealing with a woman, chances are you are now doing or you just have done or you are just about to do something wrong, quite wrong, which makes you"—Piper held out his hand to present the word—*"guilty."*

Christopher looked at his friend. Even now, ten years into this friendship, Christopher had to pay extra attention to follow Piper in conversation. Smart, funny guy. Piper had a nice dark globe of a head, close-cropped fuzz of hair. What Christopher envied was Piper's style. The guy never had money but always dressed nice, never a painter-slob. Tonight: ironed dark shirt, black trousers, leather belt, suede tie-up shoes. Italians were supposed to have so much fashion sense, but blacks beat Italians on that any day.

"And you know what?" Piper continued. "I think they're right, the women. We're jackasses. All we really want is, we want to play. The girls, they like to play, too, don't get me wrong, but the women, they got this whole inner-body thing going, like a little ocean inside every one of them. Tides coming in and out, with all this erosion going on, and we're like shameless, irresponsible morons trying to ride the waves."

"Men have erosion, too, you know."

"I know we do. I know it." As Piper spoke, there were his hands to watch—fingers and pink palms always moving, shaping the air. "But, basically, what I'm saying to you, Christopher, is that between women and men there exists an unholy alliance. By their thirties, like the age of our wives, man, it's a lie for anybody to think that the woman's main tie is with her man. Hell, no. Her tie is with her body, that's her A-number-one information center."

"Nora used to do the aerobics thing. She was in great shape. But she doesn't even bother anymore."

"No, no, no. You're being too literal. Not the body shape, not the external body, which is the man's preoccupation. The inner body is where the woman lives. Those famous cycles we hear so much about. Those eggs riding in and out every month. Counting days off, taking the temps, trying to be alert for this and that. Meanwhile, all we want to do is shoot our wad. Bless the women, is what I say."

They laughed. A waitress glided by on roller skates. Christopher said, "What I love is, I love a woman's feet."

"The feet, yeah, the feet are good. I had an uncle told me, years ago, I was a little kid, he said to me, 'Pierre, you want to know about a woman, hold her foot. Is it smashed down, rough, showing she got no time to take care of herself? 'Cause, if she not taking care of her own self, she won't be interested in taking any kind of good care of you."

"Micaela? Nice feet?"

"Beautiful, like a young girl's. She's a nurse, you know, and they wear those padded shoes. She works hard, but she knows how to take care of herself, my wife. Speaking of who, I better go call and check in." Piper slid off his bar stool—talking, Piper seemed so much taller than he did standing up—and went to find the pay phone.

Christopher, watching the waitress on roller skates, wished he could call Nora, say something sweet, and hear her say, "Come home, I'm in bed waiting for you, I love you." Would be even nicer to hear, "Sorry I made you upset today." But that wasn't going to happen. She was convinced she had a case against him. He had no clue. He never did.

Piper, back from the phone, spun around on his bar stool and ordered another round. "I'm in good shape. She wants me to stay out late so I'll owe her a full night out."

"You and Micaela," Christopher said, "you really figured out how to get along."

"It's survival. With four kids, we'd be eaten alive if we presented a weak front. They'd demolish us. The problem with you and your wife," Piper said, "because—I hope you'll forgive me for being presumptuous here—I do have the sense there is some kind of a problem in your paradise, the problem is you have too much closeness. Too much intimacy. You need to have kids to create distance between you."

Christopher smirked and reached for his glass of beer. "She says we're not ready for kids."

"I'm not kidding. You need to create obstacles. If you want to save your marriage, man, that's what you have to do."

Christopher asked Piper, "You're totally into your wife, aren't you?"

"I *am*," Piper said, and winced. "Seventeen years and I still haven't reached the point I'm bored or I want someone else."

"You don't lust for other women?"

"What is it, Chris? You lusting? Nora paling on you?"

"Nora? No way, I don't want anyone but Nora, but I keep feeling, like,

I don't know." Then Christopher told Piper what he'd never told anyone: "We fight all the time."

"That happens."

The nearly beautiful waitress roller-skated past them in her tight black pants. When she glanced at Christopher, he looked away.

"Yeah," Christopher said, "it happens. Everybody says that, but Nora and I were never like that. I mean, for a while now, all the time, it's so . . . unpleasant. I feel like . . ."

"Another round here?" the bartender asked.

"Yeah," Christopher said. "I'll get this." He reached for his wallet. "I feel like we're losing each other." The bartender took the money and pretended he'd heard nothing. "And I'm getting old," Christopher continued, "and I just feel my life slipping away."

"Did you tell Nora this?"

"She's not talking to me. You know, I'm forty next year. I mean, we know people who died when they were forty."

"We know people who died before they were forty, but you can't—"

"Who do we know died before forty?"

"A guy had a studio in my building. I think you met him. Don Wojciekowski. Tall guy, big. Quiet. Painted big, big abstract landscapes."

"Landscapes? Did he teach at Art Students League?"

"Yeah."

"I met him, like, two years ago, at Tina's opening. In fact, I was supposed to cover some of his classes for him because he had to go in for treatments, but I was never free at the right time. But he was doing good, he told me. He said he was in, what do you call that, remission?"

Piper shook his head. "No, his remission remitted. He didn't recover. Don died. Don's been dead now over a year."

"Je-sus, you're kidding."

"I kid you not, my friend. And in fact, this is weird talking about it. Just last night, at this opening, somebody was telling me about Don's wife."

"Kids?"

"No. No kids. That's the thing. I guess, when he was dying, he and his wife were trying real hard to have a kid, so now—she's a writer of some kind, name's Denise—she's looking for a painter to be a sperm donor so she can have a baby." Christopher watched Piper pull out his wallet and dig through a clump of business cards.

"She's looking for *painter* sperm?"

"Basically, that's it. As close to her husband as she can get, that's what she wants."

"Why doesn't she just find a new husband?"

"Not interested. Don's not been dead that long, and they were married forever. I mean, really a long time, longer than me and Micaela. Maybe twenty years. This Denise and Don were nuts for each other. I don't know the full story, but apparently, when he died, or maybe before he died, she was pregnant and had a miscarriage, and so now she's all business about— Here." Piper handed Christopher a card. Cheaply made, but the typography was nice, the layout formal and discreet: Denise Wojciekowski, a phone number with a 914 area code, a P.O. box address in Nyack, New York. "Somebody gave me this last night. All Don's old friends are handing these out at openings."

Christopher took the card. "And how does this work?"

"I guess people call her, guys do. Don was solid, had lots of friends. She interviews you and all that. You go to a lab and they test you for HIV and herpes and hep and all that, and then there you are."

"Is she having sex with all these guys she picks?"

"No, cowboy, get with it. You squirt into a tube. Right there in the lab. My brother-in-law had to do it when my sister wasn't getting pregnant. They set you up in a room with a video and magazines and plastic covers on the couch."

"No way. No way you're going to sit around with a bunch of guys . . ." Christopher handed the card back to Piper.

"Ah, man, it's not a circle jerk, it's not the baths. You go in alone, do your business, and come out with it in a little cup."

"And this Denise is actually finding guys who volunteer to do this?"

"Yeah, I guess she just hasn't found the right one, or it hasn't worked or whatnot, because I heard about this a month ago, and then, last night, someone was telling me again. People keep giving around these cards with her name."

"Man," Christopher said. "Man oh man, this is sad. Really sad story."

"But you got to hand it to her, going ahead trying to get what she wants. See? I love that about women, the way they get things *done*."

"She pretty?"

"Denise? No, I can't say she's pretty."

Christopher was aware of feeling relieved. He was already drawn to Denise's story, and if his body were drawn to the woman herself, there'd be trouble.

"No," Piper said, "she's not a looker, this Denise. She's smart. Shrewd, wise, like Old World. She and Don, both of them grew up Hungarian or Polish or something. They met when they were kids, in the old neighborhood. You know, half the time they were growing up, they didn't speak English. Pennsylvania somewhere, I think."

"And what did you say she does?"

"She writes. Some academic subject. You know, she's troubled the way intellectuals get. Neurotic, touchy, impatient. And now that she's bereft, she doesn't take shit from anybody. Don was sick a long time, and she was with him every step. I mean, you say my wife and me, but we communicate over this canyon of all these kids, but Don and Denise were more like with you and Nora. It was just the two of them. Really close."

"Sad. Really, really sad." As Christopher was pulling out his wallet to pay for the last round of beers, Piper handed over Denise's card again. "Here, you take it. I'm supposed to give it to one other person. Now you pass it on to somebody. That's how she's getting this thing done."

Christopher took the card. "Yeah, who knows. Nora's brother is always looking for something weird to do."

The two guys left the Saloon. Christopher was getting his train at Lincoln Center, Piper had to go to Columbus Circle for the train to Brooklyn. On the street, as they parted, Piper said, "Christopher, I'm just going to say this, and maybe I'm totally out of line, but, whatever's going on with you and Nora, figure it out before you have a kid. I'm telling you, it's the best thing you can ever do, being a father, but if you're not both into it, it'll kill you. Take your time."

"Right. Thanks."

"Peace to you, my man. Stay peaceful."

They slapped hands, and each went his way.

WHEN CHRISTOPHER GOT HOME and the bedroom doorknobs were tied inside with a scarf, he stretched out on the couch. Nora had left him a pillow, a blanket. As he was taking off his jeans, the card with Denise's phone number fell out of his pocket. He picked the card up off the rug, slipped it into the pocket of his black T-shirt, went to sleep.

For the next few weeks, the phone number kept traveling all over him, pocket to pocket, wallet to pocket, in a way that Christopher finally understood to mean that sooner or later he would be calling this woman, Denise.

WHEN HE FINALLY CALLED HER, it was from a phone booth. Two and a half weeks had passed since Piper had told Christopher the story of Don and Denise Wojciekowski. During that time, Nora had convinced Christopher for the umpteenth time to go with her to a marriage therapist, but it had been useless, the same thing all over again.

This therapist was chubby, with bad skin, and she'd started the session as most of them did by asking, "How can I help you?" and Christopher had said, "I don't think we need help. I think we just need to have a baby. We have a very good marriage. I think," which was the truth.

And then Chubbo asked Nora, "What are your thoughts?" and Nora ended up saying all her stuff, how for quite a while now she'd been feeling a lack of trust, feeling that Christopher wasn't listening to her when she tried to talk about what was important to her. Nora said she felt "battered" by Christopher's insistence that they have a child. Nora said she was lacking confidence in him and in the marriage—and in herself, too—and that's why she wouldn't have a kid.

And then the therapist asked Nora why she felt all that stuff, and there they were again, back in France, talking about a baby who was now a teenager and about a two-minute mistake Christopher had made fifteen years earlier.

If Christopher could eviscerate those years in France from his life, if he could have those hateful two minutes in France electrocuted out of him, if he could pulverize the entire country of France from the map of Europe, he would do it. He would give anything to be able to do it.

Anything.

"Well," Chubbo said at the end of the session, "there's a lot here that needs to be talked about. There's a lot to work on."

"Can I ask you," Christopher asked her, "based on what you saw here of us and heard today, do you see us as people who should definitely never have a baby?"

"No, of course not." See, Christopher wanted to say to Nora, your therapist herself said it's okay. The therapist continued: "You both worked today to try defining some problems you feel exist in your marriage. Difficult, difficult issues. I see a lot of love. I hear a long shared history between you."

"So we can have a child?"

"Christopher, no one will, or should, ever tell you that you should not have a child. Or that you should. But Nora is saying she does not feel ready, while you say you are ready. There's a lot to discuss. Some crucial past history. A great deal of present emotion. It will take time. And it will be a lot of work."

"Time," Christopher said. "I'm almost forty, you know that? Nora is younger, but I'm almost forty."

"Yes, all this needs to be taken into consideration. But we really do need to stop for today."

Christopher walked out into the hallway while Chubbo and Nora set up a series of six appointments. Nora came to the door and read the dates to him. "Are these times okay with you?"

Christopher nodded yes. But he knew he wouldn't be showing up there again.

When would they leave him alone?

As Christopher and Nora walked single-file down the narrow hallway, Nora close behind him said softly, "Well, that wasn't so bad." They stepped out into the building's European-style courtyard, fountain in the center, walls of elegant old windows reaching up floor by floor. Christopher had always wanted to have a look inside this complex. It took up an entire block on Broadway, between Seventy-ninth and Seventy-eighth streets, and had a gated entrance with a booth for the guard. Christopher took his time looking around before leaving. At least this visit wouldn't be a complete waste.

"I'm glad," Nora said, standing near the gate, waiting for him, "that we're doing this."

Some of the windows looking down into the courtyard were huge. Christopher could only imagine how big the apartments were. *Lucky bastards who bought into this place way back when.*

"How did you feel," Nora asked, "talking to her?"

"She's fine," Christopher said.

"Yeah?"

"Yeah. I felt fine." He actually did feel fine. By now he knew how to manage these sessions. He'd sat through it and had not let himself get upset. Nora got upset. *Let her be the hysterical one.* Man, it happened every damn time. Two minutes into that conversation about France and she was always weeping. *How do women hold on so tight to their misery, and for so long? Why do they do it to themselves?* Christopher was pleased with himself that he had not raised his voice. He had not reacted in any way. He felt proud. His goal had been to show the therapist that he was calm and mature enough to be a parent. Meanwhile, Nora sitting there was a sopping mess.

"Where'd you find her?" Christopher asked when they'd passed the guard.

"A professional recommendation. Why?"

"Just wondering. Nice building."

Out on Broadway, seemingly appeased, maybe a bit amorous, Nora suggested they have lunch at the Cuban-Chinese place a block away, so they did. They got a table by the window, they ordered. They ate, had coffee. *Good fried plantains.* They held hands. Then it was time for Nora to get back to her office. Christopher walked her to the corner. No crosstown bus waiting, so she decided to walk over to the bus stop on Amsterdam. Before leaving him, she said, "It means a lot to me that we're doing this. I love you, you know?"

He kissed her and watched her go.

When Nora was lost in the crowds on Seventy-ninth Street, Christopher went straight to a phone booth, which smelled of piss. He pulled Denise's phone number out of his wallet and used his calling card to place the call. He wasn't going to speak, he just wanted to hear her voice. He wanted to hear the voice of someone else who, like him, had been cheated out of having a baby. Would she sound desperate or sad? Grateful for a call? Excited?

Denise first shocked Christopher by answering her phone on the second ring—he'd been expecting an answering machine. The next shock was that her "Hello" was so annoyed, the impatient voice of someone whose work had been interrupted. "Who is this?" she ordered.

"I'm sorry" was the first thing Christopher said to Denise. "I got your number from my friend Piper. Pierre Trideux? He has a studio over in the Brooklyn boatyards?"

"You're calling about the donor search," she said.

"You're still looking?"

"I'm considering various candidates."

Silence for a beat. Denise wasn't a helper in the conversation. Nora had once explained to Christopher that the way to establish authority quickly in a phone call is to be the person who doesn't rush to fill in the silence. Denise Wojciekowski was that person.

"I mean," Christopher asked, "are you still interviewing?"

"I am."

She was typing on a computer keyboard, and she wasn't stopping. There was nothing easy about this. "Well, if you're still interviewing people and considering people, I wonder if, well, I'd like to talk with you. Maybe we could talk about this a little bit."

"If you know you're interested in being considered, I'll talk to you. But if you're not sure, I can't take the time."

"No. I'm interested. I know that. Yes. I want to talk to you. I just have some questions. I just—"

She said she had work to do now and could not talk. She had answered the phone only because she was in the middle of an argument with an editor, who was supposed to call back any minute. Denise got Christopher's name and told him she'd meet him on Thursday, day after next, at six o'clock at The Diner, at Sixth Avenue and Fifty-third Street. Or was it Fifty-fifth? Denise told him to be on time. She had only an hour's dinner break from her job.

"Can I just ask you a few questions?" he asked.

165

"You're calling from the city, right? It's a toll call. Save your money. We'll talk day after tomorrow."

Knowing he'd cancel by Thursday morning, Christopher hung up and realized he was completely pitted out. His underarms were soaked. The waistband of his khakis was soaked. When he stepped out of the phone booth, there was a breeze. It passed over him and he shivered.

CHAPTER 13:

THE YEAR BEFORE

Two days later, Thursday afternoon, Christopher still hadn't had time to call Denise to cancel. His morning had been busy with errands that *had* to get done. Go to the bank to deposit a check for his motorcycle insurance. Walk to the post office to mail the insurance payment so it wouldn't be overdue. Get the cat out of the vet's by noon or they'd have to pay for an extra day, twenty-five bucks.

It was already one o'clock when he did dial Denise's Nyack number. He got her answering machine, which was no friendlier than her live voice. All business. How stupid not to remember that the reason they were meeting in the city was that she was working in the city today. He didn't have her work number, had no idea what kind of job she had. During a short moment of panic, he thought of tracking down Piper to find out where this Denise Wojciekowski worked. Christopher had to get in touch with her to tell her he'd changed his mind, he wasn't interested. *Jesus.* He'd told her his full name. *Stupid.* Told her he was calling from a phone booth on the Upper West Side, which was a good decoy, since he lived downtown. Denise knew he was a painter and she knew his name, but that was all. If they didn't actually see each other, the fact that he'd considered meeting her wouldn't be real. What if his friends found out? Was he nuts, doing this? In the art world, where people were always tripping over one another? Piper? Piper knew everyone, and sometimes, if he had one too many beers, he talked. *Shit.* What if Nora found out?

No, Christopher told himself, don't cancel. Go there. Make it clear to this woman that the phone call was a huge mistake she should never utter a word about to anyone. *My God.*

Two nights earlier, the night of the day they'd gone to Chubbo, the marriage counselor, Nora had been awake all night. Christopher had turned over and found her sitting cross-legged, trying to meditate. He sat up, too. "Sweetheart, what?" he asked her. "What's wrong?" But he knew immediately, even in the dark, just from the tension in her arm when he put his hand there, and from the stuffy scent on her breath, that she was sinking into her deep sadness again. When she got like this, he felt helpless. It all went back to her parents' dying in the fire, which was something Christopher couldn't do a thing about. At least he hoped the fire was what she was sad about. What if, somehow, she'd found out about the phone call he'd made to this Denise person?

Without any anger in her voice, she told him softly, "I'm so mad at you. The way we've gotten polarized, that you want a child and I'm the one saying no. It doesn't give me a chance to feel how much I want to be a parent. You know I've always wanted a family. Do you know how important it is for me and for Kevin to have children? I mean, after the way we lost our parents. And we have no other family. None."

"I know, Nora, sweetie." He mimicked her soft tone. "I know." Thank God she was sad rather than angry. "I know how much—"

"Chris, you know what I need most from you?"

"What? Anything."

"What I need is for you to *know* me. I wish I had a chance to tell you everything I'm afraid of. I know that if I could just tell you my fears and believe you're on my side—"

"I am on your side. I'm always—"

"But without the yelling, Christopher, without—"

"Nora." Was she really going to do this now, in the middle of the night?

"I never want to leave you, Christopher. I don't want us to be apart. I want us—"

"What?"

"—to *know* each other. To listen."

"We do listen. I'm listening now."

"But even when it's painful to listen, we need to listen. I want us both to have what we want."

"I want that too, sweetie."

Her arms and legs were still stiff, still alert, but his strokes on her back began to have an effect. He could feel her spine collapse a little. Eventually, she kissed him on the top of the head and said, "It'll work out, Christopher. It has to. I love you."

And then they'd had a sweet night of holding on to each other. They even fell asleep and stayed like that for a few hours, before light started spilling into the room. Somewhere in a dream, *It'll work out* passed through Christopher, and within the dream he understood that to Nora *It'll work out* meant they'd stick it out in therapy; meanwhile, to Christopher, the words meant that they would not have to go to therapy anymore. In the dream he told himself, *We'll figure it out.*

What followed was two days of peace between them. Jokes. A shared shower one morning. Their loft became, again, a good place to live. Two nights in a row, they ate dinner together. Together they finished off a nice bottle of Merlot.

No, he had to make it clear to this Denise that his interest in her project was just a mistake. He'd blame it on Kevin, say his brother-in-law was too shy to call. (Yeah, right, shy. Goofy as he was, Kevin managed to have more girlfriends than God.)

By five o'clock Thursday afternoon, Christopher felt he couldn't meet Denise soon enough. He had to impress upon her how important it was that she never, ever mention his name or this appointment, not to anyone. Panicky as he was, he arrived late at The Diner. Back at the loft, the cat had started vomiting again and had to be returned to the vet's.

At ten minutes after six, Christopher walked into the restaurant. Denise was there in a booth, unpretty as Piper had said she would be. She looked like a lot of writers Christopher had met, the serious kind who were always pissed off because nobody had ever heard of their books. "Hi," he said. "Denise? I'm Christopher."

He reached out his hand, but she motioned with her right hand that she was holding a fork and couldn't shake his hand. When she was done chewing, she said, "I went ahead and ordered when I saw you were going to be

169

late. I've got to have my dinner and get back to work. I get cranky if I don't get my dinner." Denise delivered this speech, and then there was a weary relaxation in the lower part of her face. An almost-smile, and though he was still afraid of her, Christopher was so very relieved. A few times before, he'd dealt with people like Denise—someone whose voice on the phone was one thing, but then in person, just because you could see the expression on the face, the voice was something completely different from what you'd heard before. On the phone, her businesslike manner had humiliated him; but here she was, wearing a turtleneck and a plaid flannel shirt, and not scary at all. Just eating, taking care of herself. Christopher was touched by her watch, just an ordinary, utilitarian watch, no flash. Her simple gray wedding ring.

"So," he said, hanging up his jacket at the end of the booth, glad for the way it hid him when he sat down. "Where do you work?"

"Time-Life Building, just down the street. That's why this place is convenient."

"Hey, I know somebody who works there. She copyedits or proofreads or something. For *Time*. Overnight shifts."

"Yeah, that's what I do, too. But I'm not on an every-week shift. I'm not at *Time*. We do two weeks on, two weeks off."

A waitress was suddenly there next to him, asking, "Decided yet?"

"Decided? No. You have a soda fountain here, huh?" He looked over at Denise and smiled, but she was immune to his charms. "Yeah. I'll have a soda. Chocolate."

"Chocolate soda. Very good." She roller-skated away.

"They're all on skates these days," he told Denise.

"How long has your friend worked at *Time*?"

It wasn't really his friend, it was Nora's friend Giulia, but he couldn't tell Denise that. He hadn't counted on their having anything real to talk about, just her ridiculous plan and his even more ridiculous curiosity. He hadn't counted on any overlap in their lives, which was dumb, since they both knew the painting-studio people. He hadn't counted on how thoroughly she'd carry the conversation. "I don't know. A long time, I think."

"What's her name?" Denise asked.

"Listen, I have to ask you something. This is real important." Denise put down her fork and wiped her mouth with her napkin. "This is confidential," he asked, "right?"

"Of course."

"I mean. I'm not really sure why I even called you the other day, except your story. I'm . . . I mean, I'm like you, I know how you feel about really wanting a child, but this has got to be so private that I can't even tell you how private. I don't want—"

"Despite the slightly public nature of my search, all my meetings are completely confidential. I wouldn't do it any other way. You're nervous because you're married."

"How do you know?"

"You're wearing a wedding ring."

"Oh," he said.

She smirked, an almost-laugh. "You weren't going to hide that, were you?"

"No." He heard his own voice—too loud, defensive—and he knew there'd be no raging with this one, or she'd be done with him in less than a second. "I'm not hiding anything, Denise. It's just like this. I can't have my wife find out I'm talking to you. It's not that she'd be mad, my wife. It's just, I need to talk to you. It's for myself. It's—"

"Well, the way I usually conduct these meetings is that I talk first, not to be rude, but it only seems right that I should reveal myself first." Her plain hair, no makeup, no efforts to try making herself better-looking than she was. "And then maybe you'll decide this isn't for you, and you'll have been spared having to reveal any personal information."

Beady eyes, plumpish nose, but he kept having these moments of great relief with this woman. "I appreciate that, Denise."

She asked him, "What's your blood type?"

"I have no idea. Normal, I guess."

"Well, that's important. We'd need to find out. I'm O positive, which is pretty much universally compatible, but for a few exceptions worth looking into. I'm forty-two. I've been pregnant once. With my husband, Don, of course. I miscarried for no reason that the doctors could discern. In any case, it seems there's no medical reason I can't conceive again. Don and I were pregnant when he was diagnosed with the illness that killed him. I lost the baby right after the diagnosis, then I lost Don." For months, that would be the most emotional thing Christopher heard Denise say. "This plan, what I'm doing now, Don and I put in place before he died. When it was clear he wasn't going to make it, we both wanted me to be a mother. At that point, Don's sperm wasn't viable. It was his idea—his wish, really—that the child be fathered by someone connected to the art world he worked in."

"Why . . . It's none of my business, but why don't you try meeting a new guy? You're young, you're—"

"I'm still in love with my husband, that's why. I'm nowhere near ready for a new mate. I don't know if I ever will be. But I know I want a child. I don't want to die without having a child. So I have this option. And I'm grateful. Here's your chocolate soda."

"Can I get either of you anything else?" the waitress asked. "No? Okay, enjoy."

By now Denise had finished eating all her meat loaf, and she started in on her mashed potatoes. Christopher thought how embarrassed he'd be to eat a full dinner like that in front of a stranger, especially considering what they were talking about. But the soda in front of him was so tall, the straw was right under his nose. *Denise Wojciekowski is talking about her husband's deathbed plan to make her a mother, and here's me looking like a kid who wants a summer job mowing lawns.*

"Here's how I proceed," Denise was telling him. "People call me, as you did. We meet, as we are." With her fork she motioned between the two of them. "If you tell me today that you're interested, I'll give you a questionnaire to fill out, questions about your health and family background, that sort of thing. And then I'll want you to explain why you want to do this. I review all the answers with a nurse, then with a lawyer. The applications, of course, are anonymous. So far I've got to this point in the process with three prospective donors."

"How many different guys have you met, interviewed, like me here today?"

"Oh, lots. Fifteen, I think."

"How many guys have filled out questionnaires?"

"Six. After the questionnaire checks out, the man goes to my physician for a physical. I pay for that. I ask for a one-time psychiatric evaluation. I pay for that. Then the man and I sign various preliminary papers. He goes to the lab for the processing of his sperm, which is frozen for six months."

"Then?"

"Well, then the sample is retested, the man is retested. If all's clear, we inseminate. Throughout the process, you're guaranteed no one else can use your sperm sample. Also, you're released of paternity rights. Although I'm not completely closed to considering another arrangement if the man would like some sort of involvement in the child's life."

"You interviewed fifteen guys. Six did the application. Three went to the lab."

"No. Only two have gone to the lab. They're in the six-month wait period. The third applicant dropped out before the psych exam. With the two we're waiting on, both will be up for retest in six weeks. If one of them checks out okay, we'll go on to the insemination. I'm not getting any younger," she said. Another sort-of smile. "Please, keep in mind I may be meeting you too late. I may be able to proceed with an earlier candidate."

Christopher felt dizzy, not sure where or how to plug into all she was telling him. *Candidates.* "What if somebody lies?" he asked. "Like, on the questionnaire."

"Are you considering lying?"

"No. I just—"

"Why would anyone lie? There's nothing in it for the donor. I'm not giving any money. The right person for this will have his own reasons for doing it, reasons that have nothing to do with money or power or any of the reasons that make people lie. I've given this whole project up to the care of my higher power. I know this is the way to go."

She'd lost Christopher completely now. He knew there were questions he should ask—legal, medical, practical questions—but he didn't know where to start. This was the kind of thing Nora would have been much better at. The only thing Christopher could see clearly was how thoroughly Denise was making her way through to what she wanted.

For a few moments, Christopher and Denise sat quietly and he watched her eat. In small squared-off forkfuls she polished off her mashed potatoes. Now she was on to the honey-glazed carrots, stacking one round on top of another before forking them.

"Isn't this kind of weird," he asked, "to be talking about this here? In public?"

Denise smiled her weary smile; already this smile was a power she had over him. She looked around the restaurant. "There isn't a soul in here who would care what you and I are talking about." A while earlier, looking up at the door, Christopher had spotted a teenage girl who was the daughter of someone he knew. She used to show up at studio parties sometimes when she was a little girl. Christopher had envied that family, the way they moved through the weekend in a solid group. Just what he wanted with Nora.

"These guys you're waiting on, for the six-month tests, why're they doing it? What did they tell you?"

Denise had been buttering a roll. She put it down and wiped her mouth. "Let me ask you, Christopher. Why are you interested in doing this?"

"I'm not, I'm not sure."

"Then why are we here?"

The waitress again. "One check or two?"

"Put it on one," Christopher said.

"Two," Denise said. As soon as the waitress was gone, Denise told Christopher, "Sorry, but I'm not going to pay for your soda."

"No! No. I was going to pay for your dinner."

"Why? Why would you pay for my dinner? You don't even know me."

"It was just a thought. A gesture. Sorry."

Denise was impossible to flirt with, impossible to charm.

She asked him, "Are you doing this because you feel sorry for me in some way? Or sorry, just in general, for a woman in my situation? Is it something like that?"

"No. Damn it. You are difficult to talk to, d'you know that? I feel sorry for myself." When he heard it, he knew it was true.

"Did you know Don?" Denise asked.

"Yes. I met him. Once. We talked. Twice." Christopher was aware of having to be precise, accountable for himself and everything he said. He didn't like that. "It was Tina's opening. Piper introduced us. Don needed someone to cover at Art Students League."

"You called and couldn't do it," she said. "I took that call. Now I remember you. Don and I were disappointed, but you at least called back and gave us the name of someone who could cover for him. You've helped us already." It unsettled Christopher to hear that, for her, she and her dead husband were still *us*.

It unsettled him and made him jealous.

"Now I have a question, Christopher. Your wife. Are you going to tell her?"

"My wife. Right now, for various complicated reasons of her own, she's not into it. I've always wanted a child. I'm turning forty soon. I've wanted . . . I don't know, for years I wanted to know, basically, could I make a baby? I know that sounds like messed-up guy stuff, but I have to know. And then there's you, and your story. It just seems—"

"I'm going to stop you there, because I'm pressed for time today, and I should finish the details. I have a lawyer. As I mentioned, I'll assume full parental responsibility, though the father's name would appear on the birth certificate. But this is way ahead of us." She pulled papers out from a canvas bag next to her in the booth. "Here, take the questionnaire if you think you'd like me to consider you as a potential candidate. Think it over. If you'd like to proceed, call me in a week. By then I should know about Candidate Number One, if his six-month review went well. I've got to get back to work."

"Yeah. I'd walk you over, but I don't want to run into my wife's friend."

"Why would you walk me to work? I know where it is."

OUT ON SIXTH AVENUE, Christopher shook hands with Denise Wojciekowski. "So," he said.

"Bye," Denise said, and turned and walked away from him.

CHRISTOPHER WALKED and walked downtown for a long time. At each pay phone, he planned to stop in a few more blocks and leave Denise a message on her answering machine. She could find the message when she got home in the morning. "Sorry," he'd say into the machine, "but this won't work for me. Nice meeting you. Good luck."

ON SATURDAY NIGHT, as Christopher sat at his drafting table filling out Denise's questionnaire, he had to consider aspects of body and soul he'd never thought about before. LIST 5 REASONS YOU WANT TO BE A DONOR. LIST YOUR 5 BEST PERSONALITY TRAITS. LIST YOUR 5 MOST DIFFICULT PER-SONALITY TRAITS. WHAT TRAITS WOULD YOU LIKE A CHILD TO INHERIT?

Nora should be filling this out, these are her kinds of questions. Nora was out somewhere. They'd started fighting again. After a couple weeks of getting along really nicely, this afternoon they'd had a blowup, out of nowhere. Christopher was still spinning. Just this morning, they'd made love for a beautiful long time. It had been great. Then, after lunch, Nora had heard Christopher on the phone with Kevin, making a date to play basketball on Thursday, in the late morning, and she flipped. "Christopher, Thursday morning at eleven is our counseling session."

"Ah, Nora, I hate that Chubbo. We're getting along great. We don't need that."

Her face looking at him was unbelievable. As if he were a criminal, as if he'd just slapped her, or just broken something valuable on purpose, given away her jewelry. "Nora, why are you doing this to me?"

Her voice was low and full of shock. "You're reneging," she said to him. "After everything we've talked about. You promised, and now you're reneging."

Christopher wasn't sure what "renege" meant, but all he knew was that a few hours earlier he'd felt so much in love with his wife he'd been planning to surprise her by making her favorite porcini-mushroom ravioli for dinner. Instead, here he was, eating his fourth frozen waffle, sitting in the loft with a cat that had ulcers, applying for he knew not what.

PLEASE LIST ALL ILLNESSES SINCE CHILDHOOD. PLEASE LIST ALL DRUGS YOU'VE TAKEN, INCLUDING RECREATIONAL DRUGS. WHAT LANGUAGES DO YOU SPEAK? FLUENTLY? PLEASE LIST ALL YOUR EXCEPTIONAL TALENTS, SKILLS, INTERESTS. PLEASE LIST ALL AWARDS, HONORS, CITATIONS. HAVE YOU EVER BEEN ARRESTED?

This was why he never applied for grants. He had a real phobia about forms like this. How the hell do you present yourself with words? And then the writing itself was full of land mines. Commas and spelling. Basically, all people were asking when they gave you a form was for you to make an ass of yourself.

Christopher stood and walked out of the light of his work space and through the unlit archway into the living quarters of the loft. He looked around for something else to do. Whenever he had one big project, he needed a couple other, small ones going at the same time. He already had the potted plants soaking in the bathtub. Wandering into the bedroom, he decided to hang up Nora's tossed-around clothes. *Slob.* She usually appreciated it when he cleaned up after her. He stepped on something, the flowered camisole he'd slipped off of her during that morning's foreplay. He picked it up, held it to his face. Mostly, the scent of her was gone. *Nora, where the fuck are you?*

Christopher tossed the camisole, went back to his drafting table, and in a small brand-new sketchbook began to answer every one of Denise Wojciekowski's questions. He answered the way he knew how—he drew pictures. If she wanted to know everything about him, here he was, in black on white.

THE DRAWING went very fast once he got started. By ten-thirty, he'd completed his answers, filled the sketchbook with precise drawings, labeled clearly, as when he illustrated science journals. YOUR BEST SKILL? A detailed cross-section of an eyeball labeled *Observation.* Then a drawing of his hand holding a pencil. *I draw well.* DRUG USE? He drew an orange tree, *Vitamin C daily.* Then a drawing of a marijuana plant, *1969–1977, occasional use.* REASONS FOR WANTING TO BE CONSIDERED AS A DONOR? He drew the first image that came to mind, a detailed drawing of the barren cliffs of Canyon de Chelly, in Arizona, where he and Nora had driven around a few summers ago; under the drawing of the canyon he wrote *Existential Abyss* (after looking up the spellings in the dictionary).

Nora still wasn't home. No hurry to take the plants out of the tub. He left the loft, went down onto the street. Pay phone, phone card. 1–800–CALL–DENISE. The surprise this time was that she didn't sound angry about getting a call pretty late on Saturday night.

"Hi, this is Christopher. We met last week."

"Yes. Sampietro. I'm glad you called, actually." *Actually. For a change.* "I have information," she said, "that might be of interest to you. I had some bad news this week. One candidate in the six-month wait, it turns out he wasn't as clean as he'd said. There was some pretty serious diabetes in his background. He never told me."

"He lied?" Christopher asked.

"I think he didn't know himself. But it's cost me time and money. The other candidate's sample is up for retest in four weeks, but if you'd like to do an application, I'd consider you." Silence. "Or maybe you were calling to say you aren't interested?"

"I just spent four solid hours filling out your damn application." This made her laugh, so he laughed, too. Then, again, silence. Christopher held it for a long moment, but this time he couldn't get her to talk. "Well, I guess I've got this questionnaire."

"Please, be thorough, or it's wasting my time and yours." *Bitch.* "Hello?"

"Yeah, I'm here," he said. "Okay. I don't want to put this application in the mail. I'll bring it to you at The Diner. Your same break, this coming Thursday."

"I'm off this Thursday. This week I work Wednesday."

"I'll be there on Wednesday, then. Six o'clock." He hung up before Denise had a chance to hang up on him. *What have I done?*

All he knew was that he had to see Denise Wojciekowski again. He could have put his sketchbook of answers in the mail. But he wanted to *see* her. To see her.

I'm falling in love, he told himself. He didn't know what else to call this feeling. He hadn't had it quite like this before, ever. With Nora, it had been all body, the need to touch and be in the room with her, always. This was different. Christopher just wanted to see this person again, whoever she was, and hear what she had to say to him.

I'm in love with an unattractive woman who's in love with her dead husband. Christopher wanted to call up Piper and tell him how weird life was. But Piper would probably be home watching *Saturday Night Live* with his oldest son, Pierre, and waiting for his one and only wife to come home from her nurse job so he could kiss her.

THE NEXT MORNING, when Christopher woke up, he was alone in the bed. He walked out into the living room and found Nora asleep on the couch. He stood over her, watched her pale, deep eyelids flutter. She was awake. "Sweetie," he said, "I'd like to make a nice dinner for you tonight. Okay? Maybe you want to call your brother to join us?"

"You call him." Nora buried her face in the black tweed of the back of the couch.

Fine. Be that way. At least Christopher knew he'd done what he could to make things right between them.

He spent all day cooking and resisting the strong urge to go down to the street to call Denise. What did Denise do on a Sunday afternoon in October? In the city, the weather was cool and sweet, perfect for going out to brunch and walking the streets. What was it like in Nyack? Was the sun shining on Denise? Was she chilly?

"What're you cooking?" Kevin asked when Christopher called to invite him over.

"Simple. Something even you could cook."

"Give me a break, Sampietro. I out-cook you every time."

"This time it's all-American family dinner. Meat loaf, mashed potatoes, carrots." Did Denise make meat loaf for herself at home, or did she just order it when she ate out? Christopher was following a recipe for a veal meat loaf stuffed with red peppers. He spent a long time trying to replicate the eggplant mashed potatoes he and Nora had had one night at Union Square Cafe. Then his favorite carrots, sautéed with vinegar. He had to go out three different times to buy ingredients. Each time, he almost walked up to a pay phone.

Denise's voice, her rudeness, it all did something to him that was maybe a little bit like being turned on. But not really. One thing for sure, Denise Wojciekowski knew how to hold his attention. She made him want to please her. Or was he just afraid of making her mad? Same thing. Whatever, it felt good. It made him ultra-awake.

Christopher knew the eggplant mashed potatoes had had some kind of Asian thing going on in them, so he grated ginger and whisked in a little soy sauce. The mashed potatoes fluffed up perfectly—but why wouldn't they, with a whole stick of sweet butter? Plus, he'd gone out for heavy cream and whipped that in, too. Would Denise like this dinner, or would she be turned off by all the spices? Maybe he should have kept it simpler. Christopher wondered if Denise had high cholesterol.

 179

FOR HIS SECOND MEETING with Denise, Christopher got to The Diner five minutes early, thereby, he believed, capturing the moral high ground. *Good.* A part of him felt smug, but he also hoped that Denise would be pleased with him for not being late this time. Not sure how else to categorize what was happening to him, Christopher decided to believe that maybe he was beginning his first extramarital affair.

A few minutes past six, a waitress skated over to his booth. "Christopher?"

"Yes."

"Phone call for you. Up front."

Holy God. Nora! She found out. He rushed to the phone, hoping that if Nora was calling it was for an emergency, that she wasn't just calling to say she was leaving him. "Hello?" he demanded. "Hello?"

"Yeah," Denise said. "Listen. Christopher?"

"Yes."

"Good. I just wanted to make sure it's you." A pause, and he knew that her weary smile was slipping into place. "You didn't give me a chance to finish talking the other night on the phone, and I didn't have a number to call you back. We're closing the magazine tonight. I have no time to leave the building or take a break."

"Oh." He unzipped his leather jacket. "You didn't tell me."

"You hung up on me," she said.

She was always right. Another woman who could make him feel that, no matter what he did, he was wrong. "What should I do with my questionnaire?" *Shit. It's in my bag, in the booth.* What if someone took it? "I want you to have it. I did all the work."

"Drop it off downstairs. There's a desk in the lobby where they can hold it."

"No. No, Denise, sorry, I can't do that. No." Christopher was standing at the window of the restaurant looking out on Sixth Avenue, watching a police car rushing uptown through webs of traffic. "I can't leave it. I need to put it right into your hands."

"Well, I can't leave this desk. I don't even have time—"

"Yeah, I understand. I just can't come to that building."

"Okay." She sighed, displeased. "Let's see."

I'll do anything, but don't make me come there, to where my wife's friend works. "Hmm, Denise. When you called here, did you happen to give the waitress my name?"

"Just your first name. Relax. Listen. Do this. FedEx it to my house, not the P.O. box. I'll get it in a day or two. Here, write down my address."

"I don't have paper."

"Christopher, you're going to have to help me a little here." She was speaking now to a child, but already the waitress was handing him a piece of paper. She'd been watching him, probably listening, too.

"Okay," he said in a lowered voice. "Where do you live? I got paper."

"My last name is spelled W-O-J-C-I-E-K-O-W-S-K-I."

"What is that anyway, Polish? Czech?"

"Listen." She really was at the end of her rope now. "I don't have time—"

"Come on." He smiled. "I'm writing." She was a tough little number, wasn't she? But it was like sixth grade. The meaner she was to him, the more he knew she liked him.

CHRISTOPHER HUNG up the phone and walked back to their booth. He'd already ordered a bacon cheeseburger. Now he had to eat it. With fries. *Denise.*

This was getting boring, this not seeing her. He needed to see her. No dinner break? If it was true . . . It was probably true. What a drag. Maybe he should have some dinner delivered to her. Not a burger, nothing hot. Maybe a tuna-salad plate?

He was eating more fries than burger. Nora had been making noises lately about wanting to become vegetarian. *Good fries.* He missed Denise. Just about this time almost a week ago, they'd been sitting here together. Now Diana Ross was singing "Baby Love," loud, throughout the restaurant's many speakers, and Christopher felt hidden in the noise.

The waitress came by. "I'll have a Pepsi," he told her.

"Coke?"

"Fine." When she skated away, Christopher noticed a very young European couple at a table across the room. Two beautiful people with shearling jackets draped over their shoulders, good leather shoes, nice jeans. The shopping bags all around their chairs were from 47th St. Photo and Louis Vuitton. They're Italian, Christopher figured. They were eating their hamburgers with knife and fork and studying a subway map. As if, with all the money they obviously had, they couldn't take a cab. The woman looked up from the map with a girlish I've-got-a-great-idea expression on her gorgeous face. The guy was tall and leaned across the table to kiss her forehead. She sent a smooch across the table in his direction. *Honeymoon, probably.* Their four feet were all tangled together under the table. Christopher noticed they were both wearing rings that looked new, fresh.

Finishing his fries, Christopher began to feel really sorry for himself. Imagine beginning married life with all that freedom those Italians had, feeling utterly blameless.

Christopher and Nora had never had such a honeymoon. They did have ten days in Hawaii, his parents' gift, embarrassingly expensive. *Silly.* It was the kind of trip his parents liked to take, starting with two nights in the Sheraton Waikiki. But on day one, Nora had sun-blistered the backs of her knees, falling asleep on a raft at high noon. Day three, they went to Maui, where they blew off his parents' reservations at another chain hotel. Instead, they found a small rental shack, more their style. But the bugs in the room were way too big. So they moved to a condo, where the air conditioning broke down. Maui, where they had basically no sex at all. Because of the sunburn, bugs, heat. And because the two of them were totally weirded out.

Nora was wrapped up all the time in white cotton clothes and wet cloths. She planted herself under a palm tree and read some long Russian novel. Christopher could remember the exact pitch of his loneliness—like when he'd gone to camp with an older cousin, and none of the older boys would include Christopher in their games. A sick-in-the-stomach despair. A call-my-mother-to-come-get-me kind of loneliness. At dinner their first night on the grounds of the condo, they met a couple from San Francisco—two art historians, guys in their fifties, who were interested in asking Christopher all kinds of questions about his art and the New York galleries, and about the time he and Nora had spent in France. For a couple days, Christopher hung out on the beach with them while Nora read. But then the one guy put his hand right on Christopher's leg, his thigh, while the other guy was swimming—it really pissed Christopher off, because he figured it was a competition between the two of them to see who could seduce the straight guy on his honeymoon—so Christopher just stayed under the palm tree with Nora, waiting for her to talk to him. Now, looking back, he realized that during those days both he and Nora had been in shock. They never relaxed until the flights back home. From Waikiki to L.A., on a big double-decker jet. They sat upstairs in the lounge and drank a lot and laughed about how funny it was going to be when they told their friends the story of their honeymoon: sunburn, propositions, broken AC, bugs. God, he could still remember how good it was to see Nora laughing again after so long. But that was just because the mai tais on the plane were free. His parents had popped for first-class tickets.

When they got off the plane in New York that rainy, cold early-December day, with leis around their necks, still laughing drunk, not hung-over yet, a couple of their friends were there to meet them. Somebody had brought copies of the tiny wedding announcement that had made it into the *Times* the weekend before (apparently, Nora's father, that loser, had better investment connections than even she had realized; they had submitted the announcement just as a joke). Christopher remembered overhearing one of Nora's friends teasing her, "If you weren't my friend, I'd hate you! You and your damn perfect life."

SITTING IN THE DINER, running a finger around his plate, then licking salt and ketchup off his finger, Christopher remembered all of this. Sometimes he and Nora managed to have so much loveliness between them, just like those pretty Italians had now.

Nora. Nora.

He was trying to clean the ketchup out from under his fingernail, running it along the edge of a tooth, when it occurred to him in a way it never had before that maybe the damage between Nora and himself was, by now, too bad to be fixed. The waitress had just poured him more ice water, and when he drank it, there was pain in his chest. A hollow that filled up with arrows. "Check, please," he told the waitress.

Denise. He had to talk to Denise. He had to talk to Denise now. At the pay phone, he dialed the phone-card access number, then Denise's Nyack number. By now he knew the tunes by heart, two little ten-note songs. Then the fourteen-note grand march of his card number and his PIN (R-O-A-N, NORA turned inside out). All those digits, memorized. Lifeline. Christopher was going to leave Denise a message, he was going to tell her things. He pretty much knew exactly what he wanted to say.

But he didn't know how to say it. So he listened to Denise's brief, terse message, and then he hung up without saying a word.

CHAPTER 14:

THE YEAR BEFORE
AND SEPTEMBER
1989

By now Christopher was following Denise's instructions in all things. She had told him to mail his completed questionnaire, wait seven business days, and then call her, either first thing in the morning—between seven o'clock and eight-thirty—or at noon, sharp. She would not answer the phone at any other times.

On the seventh business day after the mailing, a Monday, Christopher was wide awake before eight-fifteen, and Nora was out of the loft. He could have called Denise during the early-morning time slot, but he liked the idea of keeping her waiting a bit.

He made coffee. He took out the trash, did a load of laundry. In the freezer, he found a small pork roast, took it out to defrost, and prepared a lime marinade. He pretended it was one of those days a few years back, before all the baby fighting began, and there was no question: his wife would be coming home from work at the end of the day, and they would have a good dinner together, piddle around in the loft, eventually end up sitting together on the big couch to talk and cuddle a while before getting into bed, where they'd roll up against each other, and turn in to each other, and maybe even make love.

That used to be my life. Christopher couldn't remember the last time he and Nora had had a night like that.

By eleven-thirty that Monday morning, he was using the small attachment on the vacuum to get cat hairs out of the sofa cushions. He was watching the clock, could hardly wait to have a real talk with Denise. To sit on his couch and have a conversation. All these sidewalk talks on pay phones, it wasn't working. He needed to know more—like, why was he doing this? If Denise would let him explain it to her, maybe he could explain it to himself.

At noon, sharp, Christopher sat down with the wine-red phone and began punching in Denise's number. Halfway through, he remembered to use his calling card. *Jesus!* What if the call had shown up on the phone bill and Nora had seen it? *What the hell were you doing at home on a Monday morning? Why weren't you at the studio?* He could see how easily people got caught having affairs. Denise answered immediately.

"Hi, Denise. It's Christopher Sampietro."

"Yeah," she said, "I figured."

"Listen—" they both said at the same time. He laughed, she smiled—he just knew she was smiling. Denise began again: "I need to talk with you. I'm going to be completely frank, and I hope you don't mind."

Shit. Was he in trouble? He said, "Well, I was hoping—"

"I got your sketches, Christopher. Your work is, well, you're very good."

"Thanks, Denise. Thank you." He looked out over the shiny wood floors of the just-cleaned loft, and he felt proud. But confused. *Was* he in trouble?

"Yeah, the art here is a nice touch. No one else thought of it, and it's so obvious. I mean, I'm looking for an artist, a visual person. But I'm just going to say this—"

What?

"—I don't understand why you want to do this with me. I mean—"

"Actually, Denise—"

"—let's look at the facts. You're a talented artist with a decent career. You're showing in galleries. You're producing. You've been married a significantly long time. You say here you love your wife and you're committed to your marriage. The portrait you drew here of your wife—Christopher, she's gorgeous. What's more, you're very good-looking yourself. The two of you don't have financial troubles, according to the information you wrote. You own a loft in SoHo, and you have a thousand friends. I'll just be straightforward. You and your wife are in a completely different league than Don and I ever were. Why would you do this, and why would you do this with me?"

"Denise, there's a lot—"

"And I must add, too, I don't need you to boost my confidence. I'm quite happy with who I am and all that. I just need to know who you are, and why you're doing this."

Christopher felt dizzy. She kept making him feel this way. He leaned forward, rested his head on his knees, felt the worn khaki against his unshaven face. She was so quiet, mousy, invisible almost, yet she'd just said bold, unspeakable stuff. That pecking order guided everything among people in New York—though it was never talked about, not as honestly as Denise had just spelled it out. Christopher felt himself sinking and, with no other explanation to cling to, he decided once more that he was falling in love.

"Denise, I need to talk to you. I mean in person. I need to see you. I need to see you today and talk about all this. I'm coming up there."

"Not possible. I don't see donor applicants up here, only in the city. And, besides, today is a writing day for me. At this point in the process—"

"Denise, with all respect, fuck your process. We're talking here about a baby, not a lab experiment. I need to talk to you. Not all of us can put words down on paper. I've gone along with your rules now for weeks." *Don't exaggerate, she's not Nora.* "It's been about two and a half weeks now." He lowered his voice. "I realize your situation here, and I have a lot of respect for how you're going about this. I really do have a lot of respect for you, Denise. I'm trying to follow your rules. But your rules don't account for the other person's needs of their own. I know I don't have as much at stake here as you do, no way like you do, but this is very important and crucial to me in a lot of ways. This is highly personal. And I have to talk to a face. My God, Denise, we're talking about a baby."

There was a long long-distance pause, which by now Christopher knew went against Denise's thriftiness. Something new was happening.

Finally, she said, "I need to work at least three more hours today."

"That would be three o'clock. I'll come by at four. How do I get to your place?"

"No. I won't see you at my house. I don't feel comfortable with that. I'll meet you in a public place in Nyack. In the coffee shop."

"I don't know if I can talk about all this in a coffee shop with people around."

"It's the only arrangement I'll feel comfortable with."

"Tell me where this coffee shop is. Tell me how I get there."

NYACK WAS NO EASY MATTER, even though people had started talking it up as the new perfect place to live. Christopher had to take the subway to Grand Central Station. Then the train to Tarrytown. Denise had told him that if he got the train around four o'clock, there would be a bus at the train station to take him across the bridge to Nyack.

"How about a cab? Can't I just take a cab?"

"Costs too much," she told him.

After getting off the train in Tarrytown, he waited twenty minutes and still no bus, so he took a cab. Denise didn't need to know. In the backseat of the cab, Christopher was about to fall asleep (in the depressurizing zone between leaving the city and arriving somewhere outside the city, he always felt exhausted), but as soon as they drove onto the Tappan Zee Bridge to go over the Hudson River, the dark, serious waters caught his attention. The hugeness of the Hudson. *What the hell am I doing?* As soon as he saw Denise, he'd tell her to forget it. He'd chalk this up to one more lost day when he could have been in his studio. He was going back to his normal life. *Enough of this crazy shit.*

Christopher's disenchantment with Denise Wojciekowski and her plan was confirmed when his taxi got near the Nyack side of the river and Christopher saw the houses and yards of the town tucked into the hills at the foot of the bridge, a small settlement as precious and out-of-date, as kitsch and sweet, as the miniatures in his *nonna*'s Christmas *presepio* display: a couple dozen cardboard cottages glittered with fake snow, tiny chipped ceramic villagers, a forest of bent-bristle trees in unnatural shades of red and blue. And at the center, a manger with glued-on straw. Nonna had bought the whole tacky caboodle, bit by bit as she saved her money, at the five-and-dime store during the 1930s and '40s. Christopher loved his *nonna* very much, but he'd be damned if some stranger, some Denise, was going to drag him back to the aesthetic and cultural wasteland he'd grown up in. "Do you know when's the next train back to Grand Central?" he asked the cabbie.

"You just missed it. But you can pick up a schedule in town. They run in the evening pretty regular." The guy was pulling over to the curb on a tree-lined street of shops in old buildings with bright new awnings.

"This the center of town?" Christopher asked.

"This is it. You get your train schedules and all that over there, in that booth." It was cute and white. "They'll give you even a map."

Christopher paid the guy ten bucks. Denise sure was cheap, acting like a ten-dollar cab fare was a big deal. *Stingy.* Stingy with her time and with her money.

The day had turned on him. When he'd left the city it had been cloudy, nice and cool. Now the sun was hot; the temperature had gone up about ten degrees. Christopher stood under a tree and took off his leather jacket. He was wearing clean black work pants and boots, and a too-hot long-sleeve T-shirt. Itchy. He bunched his jacket under his arm, rolled his sleeves up over his elbows. All those people saying Nyack! Nyack! Arty and crafty, with big houses to rent, much cheaper than the city. They were nuts. *They can have it.* He pulled out his pocket watch, flipped it open. Two hours and twenty minutes to get here from SoHo. Another two hours and twenty minutes to get back.

There was a pay phone not far from the info booth. She answered on the third ring and told him, "Go to the coffee shop across the street."

"Where?"

"Right behind where you're standing. Turn," she directed him. "Look."

Great. So she was in a lousy mood, too.

"Get a booth and wait for me. I'll be there in about ten minutes."

IT TOOK DENISE twenty-five minutes to get to the coffee shop. When she arrived, she was wearing faded old blue jeans that were a little tighter than what he'd seen her in before. A shrunken Penn State sweatshirt with sleeves rolled up. Much more relaxed than she dressed for the city, but she still wasn't attractive. There was this thing Christopher had noticed before but never registered completely: Denise had almost no lips. Her mouth was small and folded in, a hillbilly look that suggested she might be missing front teeth. Of course, she had all her teeth, but there was a low-class quality to her features that Christopher recognized from the old neighborhood his parents had grown up in, the people Nonna called "the white trashy."

Without any hello, she told him, "I don't like interrupting my work."

How could he be in love and not feel any sexual pull to the woman? For the first time, Christopher wondered if Denise was a lesbian. Maybe that was it. He knew he'd been sending some vibe out, but she never responded. *She's gay.* Interesting twist.

They were sitting in a booth in the back, far from the door and cash register and the few other customers. Christopher was facing the entrance. The exit. Denise looked around over her shoulder, then back at Christopher. "What are we here to talk about?" she asked.

Feeling suddenly bored, sleepy, he picked at a patch of dark-blue paint on the outside of his wrist, couldn't look up at her. *God, she's rude.* "You want to know why I'm your guy for this unusual . . . well, this arrangement. I'm going to tell you." Pause. He had no idea what he was going to say.

"Well?" she asked.

"Ever since I was a kid—Did I tell you I was born in Kansas City?"

"Missouri or Kansas?"

"Missouri."

This was a small encouragement. Denise knew, as many New Yorkers did not, that Kansas City was located in two states. He went on to tell Denise what it meant to him that he'd been born in Kansas City, Missouri. It meant that—even though by his teenage years he was considered by the kids in his suburban neighborhood to be someone apart (some said stuck-up) because of all the time he spent in the garage painting, even though he'd been one of the top students in his grad-school class at the Chicago Art Institute—he'd been terrified when he arrived in New York City.

"Terrified of what?" Denise asked him.

"I was afraid everybody would see I was this rube, this idiot dolt from the Midwest who knew nothing." Christopher, just out of grad school, had certainly felt exactly like that when he arrived in New York. And probably he still felt it, even now, after so many years.

"I got here from Chicago," he told Denise, "I didn't even know you had to have correct change for the bus. My first day, I got the bus from LaGuardia to Grand Central. I walked up the street to get the M30, because that's the bus my friend told me to take to his apartment, and I've got my suitcase and portfolio, and it's pouring rain like crazy, and it's noon on Friday, so everybody's running around. The bus shows up, I get on. I try shoving a dollar bill into the coin box, and the driver yells something so fast to me I can't understand him. And these three old ladies—I'll never forget them—they all yell at me, real loud, 'You need correct change! It won't take dollar bills.' And all these people had to pass up coins to me and change my dollar bill."

"That upset you? Those ladies were probably thrilled to have a chance to talk to a good-looking kid. Probably all three of them wanted to take you home," Denise said, but the way she said it, in her flat Denise-voice, she offered no compliment, just fact. "Besides," she continued, "nobody knows you need correct change the first time they get on a bus. You never rode the bus in Chicago?"

"I had a car." Christopher looked away from her, down to his hands on the table. "Can I ask you something? Personal?"

"What?"

"Are you gay?"

"No," she answered.

"Oh," he said.

When he looked up, she was looking at him, waiting for him to go on with his story. He was silent. "Are you gay?" she asked.

"No. No, I'm not."

"Yeah, I didn't think so. But, look, I still don't understand. This Kansas City problem you have. I mean, I came here from Erie. More than twenty years ago. Right out of college. I was a rube then, I'm still a rube. What you sent me in your questionnaire, all those sketches about when you and Nora lived in France—I've gone as far west as Chicago, that's it. I've gone as far over the Atlantic as you can go on the Staten Island Ferry."

"Well, let me explain. Let me tell you. Anyway . . ."

Anyway, it went on for five hours, the rest of the afternoon and into the evening. He told Denise about the good neighborhood ("one-acre lot for each house, no sidewalks, lots of circular driveways") he'd grown up in.

The fancy brand-new Tudor-imitation house his father had built to please his mother.

"Sounds good to me," Denise said. "My sister and my two brothers and I shared a bedroom with two sets of bunk beds. Until one of my brothers went away to school, and then we had more room."

"Where'd he go? Boarding school?"

"Sort of. Detention home for delinquent kids. So—Kansas City, tell me the rest."

There was Christopher's family in their good neighborhood. But also, every Wednesday after school and on Sundays, there was the half-hour drive to visit his father's mother back in the old neighborhood. Westport, where Christopher's grandfather, who never did learn English after immigrating from Italy, began and built up his parking-lot-and-garage business. Westport, where Christopher's father, Juno (some neighborhood version of Junior), and his mother, Grace Giordano, had grown up as next-door neighbors. They lived at home and waited until both had finished college before they got married, but the minute Juno finished law school, he moved his wife and his first baby girl *out* of the old neighborhood. When Juno told the story, you could tell it had been a race to get himself and his family away from Westport. Yet, twice a week, he insisted that Christopher and both his sisters drive back there with him. Their mother never joined them. Christopher's parents bickered as Juno was getting the kids into the car. Then, when they arrived in Westport, neither Christopher nor his sisters were allowed to play with the kids in Nonna's "too rough" neighborhood. The same kids who played in his *nonna's* empty lot, next to her house. Kids his *nonna* sliced up watermelons for on hot summer evenings. Kids she relied on daily to run errands for her, since her own kids didn't live nearby. Kids who, on the rare occasion they caught Christopher alone, called him "snob faggot."

"Your father set you up," Denise told him. "He made you look like a creep."

"No, he just worried." But actually Christopher's mother used to tell Juno pretty much the same thing: "Why take them there if you don't want them leaving the house? Bring your mother here to visit." Grace had no reason to go to the old neighborhood. She tried to move forward, into the new world. She'd taken art-history classes along with her teaching degree, so, as soon as Christopher and his two sisters were in school, Grace volunteered as a docent at the Nelson-Adkins Museum, and she drove the kids downtown for drawing classes once a week. With Christopher, the classes took. He was her talented child. Her boy. When Christopher, in junior high, was selected for special art classes, Juno told him that artwork wasn't a way to live or a way to make a living. When Christopher left for New York, his father told him, "I hope it works out for you, son, but I'm afraid they're going to eat you alive."

"Your father sounds like a jackass," Denise told him. "I don't mean to hurt your feelings, but he does."

"No! That's not it, Denise."

"If you say so, but he sounds scared. For himself. He didn't need to put that on you and your sisters."

"He just loves us a lot. Our family's really close."

Christopher's mother and sisters had encouraged him to go away to art school. But they were the reason it had been almost impossible for Christopher to leave Kansas City. Christopher's mother knew that grad school was right for him, and then that New York was where he needed to be, but he knew that something big would be gone for her when he left. Like Juno, she adored the family, yet in her marriage she was still waiting for Juno to join her, to move on. She was so lonely. And then the sisters. Inexplicably, beautiful as they were, they'd ended up miserable in love. Both were blue-eyed, black-haired beauties, one with extensive piano-training, the other an accomplished ballerina, and they'd dated the worst men in town. "They not only went out with these morons," Christopher told Denise, "they fell in love with them. Gamblers, a lot of gamblers. Christina married one, and now she has five kids, but she calls me crying so hard sometimes."

From the time he was a little boy, Christopher had tried to be good company for his mother and sisters. He tried to cheer them up. The women, all three, adored him. "But then my older sister, Cecilia, spelled it out for me. She said, 'You're here and we're unhappy anyway. You may as well go and do your artwork.'

"I was so lucky when I got to New York. I had this teacher from

193

Chicago who gave me all these names and phone numbers. My first sum-mer I got to house-sit in a nice brownstone on Tenth Street. I met all the right people, immediately."

"See," Denise told him, slapping her hand flat on the table between them. *Her wedding ring. Still.* "That's what I mean. Don and I have never known the right people."

"Let me finish. Please. What I'm saying is that, yeah, I met all these people, but I felt like a total fraud—like, what am I here for? I just felt—"

"You felt 'less than.' "

"What?"

"That's what we call that feeling of inferiority, when you feel 'less than' everyone else."

"Who's this *we*?"

"In AA. I'm an alcoholic. All this you're talking about, all this bad feel-ing you have, I know it very, very well."

"Denise, how can you have a baby if you're alcoholic?" A second after it was out of his mouth, he said, "God, I'm sorry. I shouldn't have said that." But she was smiling at him, a full smile, the first one ever. "Have you been hiding this from me?" he asked her.

"My alcoholism? Ha! Couldn't hide it if I wanted to. It just never came up."

She kept smiling and was transformed in front of him. Not into the beautiful woman he'd hoped for, but into the unveiled person he'd been chasing around for several weeks. *Nora says I have no inner life, but I knew there was some missing piece to Denise. I knew it.* For the first time in months, he didn't feel stupid. If Denise Wojciekowski was letting him come to Ny-ack and hear the truth about her, then maybe he wasn't so bad, maybe he wasn't.

"You're telling me your story," Denise said, "it seemed appropriate to tell mine."

"Well, man, Denise, I really am sorry I said what I said. And I'm sorry you're an alcoholic. I mean, that's a hard one."

"Don't be sorry. If I weren't alcoholic, I never would have found my higher power. It's the best thing in my life. I've been a grateful member of AA for twelve years, and I've been sober—mostly—for eleven years. Don and I, we got sober together. The disease is in both our families. I don't tell most people this, but even before he got sick, we occasionally thought about looking for a sperm donor. To avoid at least some of the drunk genes. Give the kid some odds in her favor. Or his."

"Well, you just heard about my crazy genes."

"Kind of a sad family life, but the genes don't seem so bad. You said in your questionnaire that there's no mental illness? Right?" He nodded. "No addictions. No diabetes. No heart disease." He nodded again. "Your mom sounds unhappy, but she's intelligent. So's your dad. He's just a scaredy-cat control freak."

"Denise, cut it out. I love my family. I take them the way they are."

"You're right, Christopher. I'm sorry. Your loyalty is a fine thing. I will say this: it's unusual to meet someone with your talents and good looks and all that who's also been in a monogamous relationship since before AIDS. You're a sperm bank's dream date. I'll be honest, the monogamy in your personal history really caught my attention."

"I love my wife. I love my wife more than anything. Why would I cheat on her?"

"Is this the point when you tell me why you and Nora haven't had babies yet?"

"Ah, Denise," he said, yawning and stretching. "That's a long story."

"Yeah, and why do I think that's why you came up here, to tell it to me?"

Outside was the clogged traffic of Nyack. How many trains back to the city had he missed? "It's dark." His chin pointed toward the window. "We've been here hours."

She wouldn't turn her head to look. "Am I going to have to give you some gruesome scenes from when I was a drunk? Just to get you to talk?"

"Are you manipulating me?"

"Of course."

They smiled at each other; she gave that nice full smile.

"Let me ask you something," Christopher said. "Does the doctor who's doing this sperm-donor thing, does he know—"

"She."

"Does she know that you're going to be a single mother and you used to drink?"

"She knows everything. We've talked about it for years. She said it's up to me to get to the point where I trust myself."

"And do you?" Christopher asked Denise.

"Yes," she said. Then added, "For the most part, yes. And where I don't trust myself, I trust my higher power. I trust my program. I trust my sponsor."

"I don't know what any of that means, but do you think you can . . . Shit, it's hard, what you're trying to do, Denise. You're going to be a single mother. You're going to have to raise the kid, and make the money, and all of it. Can you do it?"

"That's what I pray for every day. I pray to be able to do it."

I don't care about your prayers, he was thinking, What I want is a guarantee. "If I help you, Denise, don't be offended, but—"

"I understand what you're asking, Christopher, and I think you're right to ask. Yes," she told him. "I do feel ready to have a child and raise it by myself."

"Okay," Christopher said. "Well, then."

"Why do I have a feeling, Christopher, that your reasons for wanting to do this with me have something to do with you and Nora not having a child? What is it? She can't? Or she won't? I can tell how ready you are to be a father. It's all over your work, too."

"It is?"

"Soft shades of color. A general tenderness. If I didn't know, I would have thought some of those watercolors had been done by a woman."

"Maybe I am gay."

They laughed. "No, I don't think so," she said.

"I don't, either," he said.

"So?"

"The book you're writing," he asked, "what's it about? Tell me about your work."

She sighed. "You're avoiding my question. But since we're avoiding— I'm trained as a historian. I got my Ph.D. from City College. I'm writing a scholarly book on famous alcoholics in history."

"The world's great drunks?"

"Basically, that's it."

"Wow." There was a long pause. A few families had come into the coffee shop and left. A few groups of kids talking about homework.

"Christopher," Denise started.

So he just said it: "A long time ago, when Nora and I lived in France, this thing happened." He had never volunteered that information to anyone, not ever.

"Yeah?"

He told Denise about how he'd gone to France just because somebody in New York had offered him use of a huge warehouse studio. Again, when he hesitated, his mother and sisters had urged him to go. He went. After two years of painting like crazy, and feeling, for the first time, that he'd succeeded in doing what his father had insisted he wouldn't be able to do—finding a life in the art world, getting out of Kansas City—he'd met Nora. Just met her in a wine shop one day. My God, she was, really, the most beautiful woman he'd ever talked to. And it turned out she needed him, the way his mother and sisters needed him, only more so, because she'd lost her parents a few years earlier. She was a student in France for the year, she had no one she was really close to. But it was so much easier to give to Nora than it was to give to his sisters and mother. Giving to Nora seemed to be moving him forward into an even fuller life, not dragging him back.

Everything with Nora was great from the start. Four months went by. She'd moved in with him. And then, in June, Nora's friend Mary wrote to say she was coming to visit. The way Nora had talked about Mary, Christopher didn't know what to expect. Some goddess in dance shoes. Mary was already a professional dancer. She'd been Nora's best friend since forever. And Mary was bringing her boyfriend, Ross, who'd grown up in Manhattan and had these Upper West Side parents who were editors, the whole deal. Nora couldn't stop talking about Mary, and about Mary and Ross. And as if Mary and Ross together weren't cool enough, they were coming with their newborn baby.

They showed up in mid-July, having hitchhiked from Rome. Mary was small with a body like iron. And Ross was like somebody on a talk show, just knew everything about everything, and he was such a likable guy. He wanted to go to medical school, he knew all kinds of science stuff. But he knew about literature, too. And then it turned out he was into contemporary art. "They were just," Christopher told Denise, "in a different league."

"See! Again! That's what I said to you this morning on the phone."

"Yeah. Weird. So you know what I'm saying. But it was like I was so

197

afraid before they got there. And then I was so relieved, and, I don't know, they seemed to really, you know, accept me."

"Hey, Christopher. Why wouldn't they?" She shook her head no to the guy behind the counter who was holding up a coffeepot.

"Yeah, but when Mary thought I was a good boyfriend for Nora, that was such a relief to me. I mean, these girlfriends were really tight, like my sisters, except they laughed together all the time. We all got along. It was—the first days they were there—was like the best time in my life. It was like I was taking care of this family, except it was a family I really fit into. For days I kept this party going in my loft. I like to cook, I'm pretty good in the kitchen."

"Your grandmother taught you—that's what you illustrated in your answers." Denise's brown eyes were still not pretty, but Christopher loved the way she locked on to his story.

"Yeah, instant family. Especially with a tiny brand-new baby there." There was no judgment on Denise's face, just avid listening. "Ross was doing some drugs. He was into that. He loved talking about all his acid trips. Nora and Mary wanted to smoke a couple times, and I smoked some weed with them. But I was never that into it, not like Ross. But he's one of these guys who keep pushing the limits, and he's incredibly fun to be with, but there's this, I don't know, a sort of a challenge from him? Like this dare, and if you do keep up with him, he just makes you feel so cool."

"Sure. The opposite of your dad. Must have felt great."

"Now you sound like Nora: she says this stuff all the time, about my dad. But all I knew was that Ross didn't think I was a hick. And he liked my art. Even gave me names of gallery people his parents knew. Mary liked me as Nora's boyfriend. And the baby, man, she was too much. Mary and Ross were spaced out half the time, so I just decided to be the one to keep an eye on the baby. And she loved me. She goo-gooed and smiled at me and stuff. She let me feed her a bottle when even her father couldn't do that yet. Not that he tried so hard.

"After about a week, Nora convinced Mary to go off with Ross for a couple days. They hadn't been alone since the baby, and they were itching to go off by themselves. And so there's me and my new girlfriend, who I'm really in love with. I'm already thinking I'm hoping she'll marry me, and it's like we're playing house. We had this baby to take care of—Denise, I'm telling you, she was an amazing baby, but I didn't know that then, I'd never spent time with a baby before—and I just decided, I'm going to show Nora what a great husband and father I'd be. So I kept getting up early every morning to go to the market and get fresh food. I'd let Nora sleep, and I'd have the baby with me. She'd be on the kitchen counter in this little drawer I fixed up for her. She's on the counter with the vegetables and stuff from the market. Then everything," Christopher said, "went bad."

"What happened?"

In the various therapy sessions with Nora when he'd been asked to talk about what happened next, Christopher had poured on the drama and played for pity ("I felt so responsible for this *infant*"), but he knew that with Denise he would have to tell it straight.

"Well, what happened is, Nora walked in." Christopher leaned forward over the table. He looked up at the door of the coffee shop, stared at the hardware hinging the door to the frame. "She walked into the kitchen, and I was." Pause. "I was. I was kissing the baby. I'd been in the middle of changing her diaper."

"What do you mean, kissing her? On the mouth?" Denise asked.

"No, not on the mouth."

"So you weren't—what? Was she naked?"

"It was all a mistake. Have you ever done something and not known why?"

Denise smiled wide, showed a bunch of teeth. "Christopher. I was a drinking drunk from the time I was seventeen until I turned thirty-one. Have I ever done something and not known why? What do you think?"

"I can't say it. What I did, I can't tell."

They sat still for a long while. Then Denise asked him, "Could you write it?"

It seemed to Christopher that they had agreed silently at some point not to leave the coffee shop until he told his whole story.

"Let me try telling it." He was whispering. "I was changing the baby's diaper. I'd just cleaned her. She was clean." Denise, leaning over, strained to hear. "And she was naked. And when Nora walked in, I was kissing her, the baby."

"Where? Where were you kissing her?" Denise slid a paper napkin over to Christopher. She pulled a pen out of her back pocket, slid it over.

He turned sideways in the booth, away from the napkin and pen; he pulled his legs up onto the bench, stretched them out. Denise wasn't rushing him, but she wasn't going to let him out of this, either. He remembered that there would be a train back to the city around eleven-twenty. Maybe he could tell his secret here, give it to Denise, then go back home and never see Denise again. The city was a long way away. So was Nora. There probably was no safer place than this booth to say it, except maybe a confessional. But Christopher had tried that, and it hadn't worked. Once, he told it in confession, and the priest began to leave his cubicle to come out to find Christopher, to sign him up for a men's rehab group. Another time had been worse: the priest said only, "These things happen to a man."

Such a long silence passed that, when Christopher looked over again at the napkin and pen, they seemed to be there for no reason he could remember. The guy behind the counter came and wiped the table, and asked, again, if they needed anything.

You kissed the baby where, *Christopher?*

So he just picked up the napkin, rested it on his knee, wrote in block letters: *Down there.* He handed the paper to Denise and wrote on a second napkin, *With my tongue.* He passed that paper across the table to her, she had time to glance down, read, and then he grabbed both napkins, tore them into shreds. On a clean napkin, he wrote, *It was more taste than kiss. It never happened before, and I never ever did it again.*

"Down there?" Denise whispered.

"Sssh."

She wrote on a napkin, *You mean her crotch? The baby's vagina?*

His jaw was held so tight his teeth slipped and he bit his tongue. He nodded.

Nora saw you do it? Denise wrote.

His nostrils and his lips and the skin between his nostrils and his top lip— all that was trembling. He had nothing but a small pocket of air to breathe from, a small pocket at the roof of his mouth. His bowels shifted painfully, scarily. He thought he might have to bolt. "We weren't married yet," he said. It seemed important to tell this to Denise. His voice broke the quiet he and Denise had created. Anyone overhearing him wouldn't know what they were talking about, just the story of a regular troubled marriage.

Denise kept her voice low, too. "What did Nora do?"

"My worst fear possible," Christopher said, grabbing a napkin from Denise's hand. "She left me. For two weeks, I didn't know where she was. I was afraid to call her brother, because he might freak. I'm telling you, those two weeks, I went out of my mind."

"She must have been— Well, God."

"Yeah, and I could never make her believe when she got back that it happened just that one time. That one simple act, nothing else happened."

"It wasn't a simple act, Christopher."

"Don't you start, too."

"Christopher." Denise reached over the table and wrapped a big un-fancy hand around his wrist. What was it exactly that made Denise seem of a different generation? Her hand felt like the hands of the old relatives in the nursing homes his family had to visit on holidays when he was a kid. "Christopher, believe me, there is no judgment here. I have done things in my life I would have a hard time telling you about. But I don't need to tell them to you. I've told them to my sponsors, when I've done my Fifth Step. But for you, for *you*, it's really important you believe that what happened that day wasn't a simple act. That should make you feel better. You can't have simple feelings about it. I understand why you're still confused about it all these years later. Nora, too. I understand."

"But it was just one time. One act. Isolating occurrence, they call it—"

"You mean isolated occurrence," Denise said gently.

"Yeah. Two minutes. Less than two minutes."

"Was it premeditated?"

"Nora's asked me that. A couple therapists asked that same question."

"It's a standard question. I used to work on a domestic-abuse hotline."

"Why?"

"That's another story."

"It wasn't premeditated. And if she believed I'm a pervert, why'd she marry me?"

"If she thought you were a pervert, I don't think she would have mar-ried you."

"So why'd she marry me?" If he ended up crying, he'd really have to kill himself.

"Because she was in love with you, I guess. It sounds like you two needed each other, and found each other."

"She said she forgave me. And now she tells me she's afraid to have kids with me. I have never hurt her. Ever. She's thrown things at me. She threw her high-heel boots at me once. But I have never lifted a hand at her."

"I understand now why you want so much to do this with me."

"Why? Why do I want to do it?"

"Oh, Christopher." Denise's face was all different now. Everything was different. Christopher had never felt so peeled to the core, and yet so gently peeled. He loved this woman. He *loved* this Denise. "Well," she said, "if you do this donor deal with me, it gives you a chance to have a child but to stay out of the line of direct fire. My guess is, you're as afraid as Nora is. You want to be a father, but you're afraid to be. You're as worried as Nora is that something's wrong with you."

He felt the tears in his eyes, then on his cheek. "I'm not a monster," he told Denise. "I don't have a monster inside me. Nora thinks I have a monster in me."

"Has she said that to you?"

"I just know that's what she thinks."

Denise was trying to say something like "She couldn't make you feel that if you didn't already feel it yourself," but the guy behind the counter said he really did have to close up the coffee shop now.

CHRISTOPHER AND DENISE went to Denise's house. They sat at her dining-room table and had tea. *So old-fashioned.* As in his *nonna's* house, the dining-room table was where Denise entertained. She brought out a tin of cookies, but, unlike at Nonna's, all the cards were out on the table, no double messages. He told Denise about the legions of therapists he'd agreed to go to with Nora. He told how he always backed out.

"No wonder Nora's mad at you," she said, and he sat still. He heard it.

"Yeah," he said.

They talked until after eleven. When it was time for Denise to drive Christopher to the train, they stood up from the table and hugged. It had been years since Christopher had been hugged like this, devoid of sex or the withholding of sex. A hug with nothing but acceptance in it, not asking for anything. His mother and his sisters, every time they said goodbye to him, they held on a bit longer than he wanted.

"So, do you believe me, what I've told you?" he asked when they let go and she went into the kitchen for her car keys.

"You have no reason to lie to me."

"Exactly." Christopher stood in the threshold of the kitchen and watched her drink a glass of water. Denise made it feel so easy to tell the truth.

"But I have a lot to think about now," she said, rinsing her glass, turning it upside down on the window ledge. "I'm sure you understand. I have to decide what would be best for the baby."

"If you chose me to be the donor, you wouldn't let me near the baby, would you?" Christopher asked, and she turned and leaned against the stove and faced him.

"How close you are to the baby depends on how well you get your stuff together."

"So you're telling me, like Nora, that I have to go to therapy."

"I'm not saying therapy. I'm not saying anything. All I know is, you're a person who really would like to set things right with himself," Denise said, folding up a dish towel, all of it so much like at Nonna's, "about Nora and her friend and that baby, and that guy—Ross? And, God, your father. You have a lot to deal with about your old man."

Nothing to do now but leave. Christopher put on his jacket, zipped up. "Yeah."

"But in the meantime," Denise said, "I'm still tempted to think you might be the best donor candidate."

"I'm not off your list?"

"If you did it, Christopher, donated, what would the repercussions be for you, if you do this and don't tell Nora? Or if you do tell Nora?"

Christopher stood with his hands on the top of a creaking dining-room chair, holding it, not wanting to let go of everything that had happened that afternoon and evening. "I guess we need to go or I'll miss that train."

They went out the kitchen door. Walking through the backyard to the detached garage, they walked across a brick patio with a brick barbecue. "Nice," Christopher said.

"Don could build anything."

As Denise unlocked the passenger-side door for him, Christopher looked up at the sky. Stars, nothing like Manhattan. "I like it here," he told Denise. "It reminds me of the old neighborhood in Kansas City."

"Yeah? Nyack always reminded us of Erie. That's why Don and I moved here. And also because all we could afford in the city was a basement studio on Tenth Avenue."

In the car, they were silent until they got onto the Tappan Zee. The river was under them, and Denise said, "Whatever happens, Christopher, whether we do this together or not, what happened tonight, all you told me, it's really important."

"Yeah. Really important."

Denise drove a 1983 Honda Civic hatchback, very fast. She pulled up to the Tarrytown station just as the train was pulling in on the farthest track. Christopher ran, calling, "Thanks for everything, Denise," up the steps two at a time, across the passageway and down more steps, jumping off the last four, slipping into the sliding door of the Metro-North train car. As the train pulled out, he stood at the door, breathing hard, while other passengers, nodding off in their seats, looked up at him, then looked away.

Christopher had just spent all afternoon and a long evening in Nyack, New York, with a woman who was not his wife. This was the closest he'd ever come to having an affair, but he'd never felt so blameless, so light.

And for three days afterward, Christopher could not stop feeling happy. He woke up early and made buttermilk pancakes for Nora one day. The next day, he made her fresh blueberry muffins. The third day, he saw a red leather purse in a shopwindow and bought it for her, and before he gave it to her, he filled it with chocolates. Nora seemed happy with his gift—not thrilled, but nothing could get in the way of the good feeling Christopher had going on inside.

And then it was the day he was supposed to call Denise to hear her decision. No phone calls from home. He didn't want Denise's decision sitting in the middle of his living room. Not from the street, either. He wanted to be private. He wanted to be sitting down.

Saks Fifth Avenue has good phones. Nora had once told him about a patient who went to Saks to use the phones whenever she needed to talk to Nora between sessions. Nora would never tell him what the patient's problem was, or why she couldn't call from home. Nora never told anything about her patients. But she had, for some reason, let that one detail slip. So, taking a page from Piper's book, Christopher dressed up, wore a black cashmere turtleneck with his jeans. A tweed coat. He was early, so he got a haircut, too, but then he still had half an hour to wait, and he had hairs caught in his collar, itching him, while he walked the first-floor aisles of Saks pretending to shop.

Finally, four o'clock, he could call. The booth was perfect: a stool to sit on, and a noisy fan to cover up the conversation. He dialed. She answered. "I'm rushing," Denise said, "but my sponsor and I talked a long time the other night, and again this morning."

"You talked—"

"Don't worry. I didn't tell her details. But we talked, and I woke up today, and I knew it was the right thing to do. She thinks so, too. Last night, I dreamed about Don. It's always so good to see him. Anyway, since you and I talked, I've had this feeling that, yeah, it's the right thing. And I haven't wavered for four days, so—"

"You're going to let me do it?" Christopher stood up in the tight booth, hit his head. "You trust me? Denise, do you really mean—"

"Yes, if you still want to, yes, but we're on long-distance. You're spending your money. Do you have a piece of paper? I told you to have paper."

"I have paper. I have a pen. I am ready."

"Call this number." And she went on with her instructions. He needed to get in touch with the lab. They'd test him, at his convenience, but he should do it quickly. She told him where to call to set up his physical exam. Then the psychological evaluation. "Just give them your name. The billing is set up. Then, if all the medical stuff checks out—"

"It will check out, Denise, I promise you, so then we freeze my sample"— was he really saying these words?—"for six months, then retest."

"Right. Hey, Christopher?"

"Yeah?"

"Here we go," she said, and he could tell she was smiling like crazy. "I'm glad we're doing this together."

"Yeah, Denise. I'm really happy, too."

A FEW WEEKS LATER, Denise and Christopher met at the lab to sign paperwork. He called her once around Christmas just to say hello. Through all his days, there was some abstraction, some interesting good feeling that he thought of as *Denise*, but he felt no urgency to see her or talk to her. Instead, Christopher and Nora slipped into a blessed time. Since he no longer pressed her about having a baby, she no longer steered clear of him. They were like before. Only better. By Christmas, they were having sex all the time.

In March, things at the loft were going so well Christopher was shocked to get a letter from his Denise life, mailed to his studio, telling him it was time to retest his sample. Of course, the retest was fine. He called Denise a few days after the insemination and she told him it had all gone well, took only a couple of minutes, and now it was just a waiting game. If he wanted, she'd let him know the results of her pregnancy test.

"Of course, you better let me know!" In April, May, he heard nothing from Denise. He figured it hadn't worked and she'd try again in a month or so. He was busy making art, happy with Nora, he let it go.

But then, in June, a letter from Denise arrived at his studio. She wanted him to know that she was pregnant, had been since March. Miraculously—the doctors were thrilled—the first insemination had worked. She hadn't written earlier because she was superstitious. She wanted to let some time pass, but just that morning, she'd seen the sonogram, seen so much of the baby, she was beginning to believe it was true. She was going to have a baby. *And, Christopher,* she wrote, *it's going to be a son. It's a boy!*

SO THE GRAND NEWS of June had turned into the shopping lists of September, and Christopher had just two more months to help Denise get ready, to help her get her house in shape. He simply had not been able to resist having some hand in preparing for this baby. *A son.* One August Sunday, while Nora was in Greenport with her friends, Christopher had gone up to Nyack on his bike. He saw how much work Denise's house needed, how overwhelmed she was trying to finish writing her book before her December due date. He offered to clean out her gutters, which were so bad, small trees were growing in them. Then he offered to help clear junk out of her basement. By now, late September, Christopher was up there weekly. Things with Nora had started to lag during the summer. He'd slipped and mentioned he still wanted Nora to want to have a baby with him. And she'd started again with the Natassia business. Now, to top it all off, Natassia had actually tried last night to kill herself, and Nora had the gall to try tagging it on Christopher. He was tangled and twisted inside, had no idea what it was Nora was wanting from him.

Out on the street now, hanging up the pay phone, coming away from the baby-furniture store where he'd just spent money he didn't have, to buy a stroller for a baby he might never see, he prayed. *God, please, let Denise let me near this baby. God, please, let Natassia stop trying to kill herself. Please, let Nora stop hating me so much.*

After the night at the hospital, Nora was in hell for three days, waiting to
hear something, anything, from Mary. Finally, on Friday afternoon, just as
Nora was walking into the loft, the phone rang.

"Nor." Mary was whispering. "Nor, it's me."

As soon as she heard Mary's voice, the locked-stiff muscles in Nora's
neck loosened. Slowly pacing up and down the kitchen floor as far as the
leash of the black telephone cord allowed her, placing each stocking-
footed step safely within a black or a white floor tile, careful not to step on
any cracks, Nora asked, in a whisper, five or six times, "Are you okay? Is
she all right?"

"She's doing okay," Mary whispered back. "She's going to be all right."
Mary said she could stay on the phone only a minute, because Natassia was
napping and might wake up at any moment.

"But you've got to keep us informed, Mary. You just took off. Lotte
and David were insane with worry. We all were. The police—we didn't
know what to tell them."

"I found a doctor, he's going to talk to them."

"But, Mary, you left us hanging. Call me. At least call me."

"Don't be mad, Nora. That place was a nuthouse."

"I'm not *mad,* but, really, Mary . . ."

"Bye, Nor. I gotta go."

After they hung up, Nora stood in the kitchen. *She's going to be all right.* What did that mean, exactly?

Terror. Nora turned on the faucet to wash the couple dirty dishes she'd left there the night before, but there were sharp knives among the plates. Her hands were trembling. She turned the water off. *Help me do this.* Nora was just beginning to understand how much Natassia terrified her, had always terrified her. No wonder Christopher refused to talk about Natassia. *He said I torture him.* They had not spoken more than five words to each other since that fight in the bathroom on Wednesday afternoon.

But Natassia was *doing okay.* Nora took a damp, clean wineglass out of the dishwasher. As she reached for the dish towel hanging on the refrigerator-door handle, her eyes fell over the potpourri of photos and postcards magnet-held to the fridge door (the one place in the loft where her instincts to hoard had won over Christopher's instinct to clear out) and, within the mess, her eye picked out a photo of Natassia, six years old, smiling wide with no front teeth, rolling with all her might a pumpkin twice as big as her head. She was wearing a red sweater and was surrounded by scads of dead leaves. It was a weekend when Mary was in town (for a change), and Kevin had driven everybody in one of his broken-down vintage cars out to Greenport for the day, one of Nora's first trips back in years. Natassia had run wild through the pumpkin patches, arranging pumpkins into little groups she called "families." In another fridge-door photo, Nora found an older Natassia, Christmas Eve when she was around twelve, already taller than her mother, standing in a smiley hug with Mary and Ross. From this photo, if you didn't know them, you'd never suspect what the three of them had been through, together and apart.

As Nora stared into the pictures at Natassia's intelligent, happy face, Nora's eyes watered and her throat got tight. She had to admit she didn't always like Natassia. But she did love her. There was no way around that. Almost as deep as guilt and fear, there was love, and for the first time since Natassia's crisis had begun, Nora realized that she didn't know what she would do if anything worse happened to Natassia.

Please, God. She'd been saying it under her breath for days. "Please," she said aloud as she pulled open the fridge and reached for the bottle of Pinot Grigio. Then, as she poured herself a glass of wine, two words floated up from far away: *cabana time.*

That's what they had called their Happy Hour in France: Fridays, early evening, the start of the weekend. Christopher and his friends would leave their studios or their jobs and bring a couple bottles of wine down to the beach cabanas. Christopher, always concerned with feeding people, brought the cheese and baguette. Before the Baby Natassia event, Nora had enjoyed herself when she joined the guys at the beach. Afterward, she went just once in a while, to *observe* Christopher among his friends.

After she witnessed Christopher molesting the baby, Nora's dilettantish reading in psychology had become an obsession. She returned to the pages of Erik Erikson, Jung, and Freud every morning, early; and in the afternoons, while she modeled for painters, she thought over what she'd read, tried to eke out some promise of an explanation for the pain she had felt and was feeling in her life.

Now she was thirty-five years old, educated, trained, and professionally licensed. Still wearing her expensive work clothes, Nora walked across her living room to yank the venetian blinds up on this lonely Friday evening that was her life, so far from any cabanas, and she felt sorry for how naïvely she had believed in psychological miracles back then. "Poor you," she muttered as she curled up in the corner of the sofa to look out the big windows. They faced south. It was almost six o'clock now, moving toward dark. Nora was rarely home at this time. Her last appointment for the day had canceled, giving her this chance to see how lucky she and Christopher were: their view was still unimpeded by new buildings. She could see the light saddening into burnt colors all across a long stretch of sky over lower Manhattan. Amber and coral swatches folding out slowly. She watched.

She sipped from her wineglass. "Poor deluded you." Nora pulled up her long skirt and pulled down her gray pantyhose, tossed them across the carpet. Christopher's cat came out from under the couch, purred, and looked at Nora. "Take them," she said, "they have a run in them, they're useless to me." The cat grabbed the stockings in its mouth and trotted them off somewhere. Without the control top, Nora's stomach bulged. What hubris, to think she could help anyone with anything when she herself was nothing but a slob. A fraud, really. *I'm a therapist, and I know of an incident of sexual abuse to an infant, and I continue to keep that secret from the victim and her parents.* Nora pulled the silky turtleneck up over her mouth. *But I'm working on it.*

Through the years, whenever she reached a new level in her education and training, she had used the tools she'd learned as a means for further analyzing her husband. She remembered one July when she and Christopher were out at the house in Greenport, the summer after her second year of grad school. Nora, in possession of her natural work habits again, sat at the dining table for two or three hours every morning and again at night and filled two legal pads. In cases of sexual abuse, she'd learned during the past semester, it was important to evaluate the harm done to the child.

What degree of harm? Was it a case of blurred boundaries on the part of the adult? Was it abuse, exploitation of power, or simply inappropriate behavior, a lapse of judgment? Was physical force used? Was pain suffered by the victim? What degree of pain? If harm was done, how could it be avoided in the future? Never let the offender be with the victim again? Could the harm be reduced by less extreme measures? Was there remedy? Approach the offender with empathy. Was the event of abuse situational? Opportunistic? Chronic, an enduring deviant interest on the part of the offender? Was it a fixated offense, meaning he'd do it again, with premeditation. Had Christopher's act been premeditated? (He insisted no.) Was the child a substitute for an adult sexual partner, or was the child the primary desired object? Or was it a regression during a time of stress? "Yes," Christopher had said in marriage counseling once. "It was stress."

What the hell kind of stress did Christopher have at the age of twenty-five, living cheaply in a huge painting loft in the south of France, not needing to make much money, having endless time to paint, endless space, and a girlfriend living with him who was so crazy about him that just looking at him practically made her come? *Stress, my foot.*

Inevitably, Nora's efforts to understand Christopher collided with her anger at him. No wonder it was unethical for a psychologist to treat a family member.

Natassia's all right. Nora pulled the silver hairpin out of her chignon, and some of the pain in her head abated, but the assault was still there. *Natassia Natassia Natassia.* When she said the name aloud, the *Na* bit her tongue, *ta* blocked her sinuses, *sshhaaa* rolled around behind her face. Since Wednesday, Nora had been taking aspirin every four hours. Yesterday, three different patients had asked, Are you all right?

Natassia Natassia Natassia.

Nora got up and poured herself another half-glass and was putting the wine bottle back into the fridge, but she caught the door before it closed, pulled out the bottle again, and poured herself a little bit more wine, reminding herself what Friday used to be, when she and Christopher were together, a real couple who kept Friday nights for themselves.

Tonight he wouldn't be home for hours, maybe not at all. He was working up in Nyack a lot these days. Some friend of his had a restoration job, and they had to rush to finish it. Big money, supposedly. Some nights Christopher and the guys worked late and slept in sleeping bags at the job site and got up in the morning and kept working. A few months ago, when he told her about the job, Christopher had said he was doing it to help his friend but also because he needed the money for supplies for a new project. God only knew what he was doing with the money. The joint checking and savings accounts weren't any bigger. He kept a separate account for his painting expenses, but in his studio it didn't look as if much was happening. She'd begun, secretly, going over there once in a while to check. Nora wondered if he had developed some kind of habit, some addiction, something.

A girlfriend?

He didn't seem happy enough to be in love. Actually, he looked miserable all the time. When she saw him. Which wasn't often.

Nora knew she shouldn't stay home alone all night. Eventually, she'd get really depressed. *I wonder if Kevin is doing anything good tonight.*

And the phone rang. When Nora heard Christopher's "Hi" she realized she'd been hoping it would be him.

"Sorry to bother you," he said.

"You're not bothering me."

"I'm not feeling so good. I got some kind of a cold."

"The weather's changing. Everybody's sneezing. Are you in Nyack?"

"Yeah. I just wanted to leave you a message that I'm coming home tonight. Later. I need to lie down."

Did he want her to leave the loft? Did he want her to stay home because he wanted to see her? Was it a threat or a plea? Nora had no idea what Christopher wanted from her. "Well," she told him, "I'm going out soon anyway. So you have the place to yourself." That sounded snottier than she'd meant for it to sound.

So now she *had* to go out. Somewhere. Just as well. If she sat at home, even a few more hours, she'd do nothing but get drunk.

"Christopher," she said, "Mary called a little while ago."

"Yeah?" His voice was utterly changed. Interested, hopeful. "Natassia's all right?"

"She didn't say much, just that Natassia's doing okay. She's going to be all right. That's what Mary said."

"See, honey, I told you." Nora was repulsed by the satisfaction in Christopher's voice. "I told you this was just a teenage-girl thing. I hope you can relax a bit now."

"You don't feel a bit of responsibility, do you?"

Silence, a hard, mean silence.

"Do you feel anything?" she asked again.

"I've got to get off, Nora. Someone else needs the phone."

"Christopher."

"I can't now, Nora."

"Fine. Just fine."

"Listen, I love you, you know that. And, um, I don't know—wherever you're going," he said, snotty himself now, "have a good time."

"Yeah. I hope you feel better."

Bye-bye.

TEN MINUTES LATER, having changed out of her work clothes, Nora left the loft, not sure where she was going. Two minutes walking out in the chilly night, she realized she should have brought the movie listings with her. *Stupid.* As she walked up Broadway, then across Prince, then up West Broadway, everyone was rushing, ending the workday or beginning the night, scurrying like kids playing musical chairs, and it shamed Nora to be left standing alone. Anyone seeing her like this on a Friday night might think she was unattached, unloved, single. The shops and restaurants and the traffic were all throwing up light, creating in the streets the artificial, animated atmosphere of a movie set. As she got closer to Washington

Square Park, the Friday-night crowds were more obnoxious, NYU students and couples in from the suburbs, so Nora turned east and headed uptown on Broadway again. The crowds were just as bad. Looking down at her feet, she watched one warm leather laced-up boot step in front of the other. For the first time this year, she had on her long camel-hair overcoat, and when her hands dipped into the pockets they found last winter's Kleenex in one and her mittens in the other. A wind rolled down the avenue. Her ears were getting cold, but she felt so much better than she had sitting at home.

It never failed; alone or not, Nora always felt better out on the streets. Since that first year when she and Christopher had arrived in New York from France, when they were staying in so many different friends' apartments while they renovated the loft, the streets had been a consolation for Nora, a compensation for the claustrophobia she felt in the subway. Passing the Strand, Nora noticed a patient and his girlfriend standing out front going through the discount-book racks; she averted her eyes and quickened her pace to make sure he didn't see her. Walking on Union Square West, she looked up at the studio window of a friend of theirs; her lights were on. A couple years earlier, Nora and Christopher had helped Tina move into the space. She was Brazilian and sexy; for the first time in all the years they'd known Tina, Nora wondered if Christopher had ever slept with her. *What if he's up there with her right now? What if that's where he called me from?* Nora found herself moving toward the buzzers at the door. Tina's name was still there. *Should I buzz?* And then Nora noticed a shadow inside the door moving toward her, and before she could step away, the door was opening and there was Tina, saying "No-ra!," all hugs and kisses.

"Tina, I saw your lights on. . . ."

"Yes, I am in love, No-ra. He is up in studio. Marrr-co. Italian! I am going for snacks for us. We are just now making love. Do you believe it!" Tina's manic energy always made Nora smile, but especially tonight, when Tina was in an amorous froth—and not with Christopher. Tina went on a while about Marco, and Nora smiled, loving the shushiness of the Brazilian accent. It sounded like an Italian speaking Russian, or vice versa. And then Tina was saying, "I must go. Now. Marr-co, poor man, is very hungry." More kisses and hugs, and as they parted, Tina was walking backward, waving, calling out, "Christopher, how is he? Tell him for me a big kiss, eh?"

"I'll tell him."

"*Ciao*, No-ra, *ciao*!"

"*Ciao*, Tina." Nora was still smiling a couple blocks away when she realized that for the first time all week the *Na-ta-sha* sounds weren't battering her head. *Thank God.* The night really was chilly now, and she wished she could go inside ABC Carpet to look around. She turned back up Broadway and pulled on her mittens.

After a few blocks, stopped at a red light, Nora found herself standing beside a pay phone, and the next thing she knew she was fishing a quarter out of her wool trousers pocket. For some reason, one of the few phone numbers she had memorized was Giulia's work number at *Time*. Nora dialed.

"Giulia Di Cuore. Copy Desk."

"Hi. It's me. Are you busy?"

"Hey, where are you?" Giulia asked.

"I'm out walking."

"Come visit. There's nothing much going on yet. Are you all right?"

"No." Nora almost told the truth—*I had another fight with Christopher and I think we're going to get divorced*—but she caught herself in time. "No, I'm not all right. I'm just, you know."

"About the other night? Yeah, come over, we'll talk."

Even before hanging up, Nora felt foolish, hiking to the Time-Life Building to purge herself in person to Giulia. Nora thought of calling back to say she wasn't coming, but she didn't have another quarter, just a ten-dollar bill. At least she hadn't buzzed Tina's studio demanding to know if she was having an affair with Christopher.

I'm not in control of myself.

The *Na-ta-sha* had begun again in Nora's mouth, sinuses, head. She had to keep moving. Maybe she needed to eat something. Going with the green lights, she'd ended up walking crosstown on Twenty-second Street, and then she was looking in the windows of the baking-supply store where she'd bought Christopher's Christmas gift four years ago: a lifetime supply of baking paraphernalia that made Kevin jealous (the guys' competitiveness around cooking was so tedious, that perverse way they'd bonded as brothers). *I'm buying Christopher nothing this year.* They hadn't even talked yet about Thanksgiving, and it wasn't far off.

As she got closer to midtown, the streets were noisier with traffic, and on the sidewalks she was dodging more and more couples. She hated her husband, didn't like being married to him right now, but Nora could barely tolerate the thought of herself as potentially unmarried. Inside her left mitten, Nora was fumbling with her wedding rings, pushing her gold bands down and up and over her knuckle again and again.

At a run-down deli, she bought herself a heated-over knish. Christopher would never have let her buy food from such a place. One block after she finished eating her knish, she stopped at another deli and bought a small bag of potato chips and a medium-sized bag of M&M's. Christopher would have given her grief about this, too. He said if you're going to eat candy you should eat quality chocolate, not junk. She slipped the bag of M&M's into her pocket and tore open the bag of chips. *Right hand, salty. Left, sweet.*

Closer to Fiftieth, the streets got crazier with stalled traffic honking. Something big was going on at Radio City Music Hall. Nora hurried across the street to the Time-Life Building and was glad when she finally slipped into the revolving door.

The lobby was a quiet chamber, just the muted machinery of big furnaces and fans—no people. The sleek chrome planters were full of chrysanthemums. Wide polished floors, marble walls, chrome elevator banks surrounded Nora with a sense of 1950s-era safety. A guard was stationed at the elevators. Nora got off on the twenty-fourth floor and followed her instincts down the hallway—years ago Mary had worked here—until she was at a doorway where new carpeting ended and scraggy carpet began— that had to be where they kept the all-nighters. Nora walked past a short row of inner offices arranged with side-by-side desks. The next-to-last office was Giulia's. She was lying on her stomach across two desks, and a man was bent over her, giving her an enthusiastic back rub.

Nora stood in the threshold. She heard herself say, "Oh," like a shocked and offended parent.

Giulia turned her head. "Hi! I'm getting my back rub."

"Yes, I see."

"This is Abe, my partner. Abe, this is Nora."

Abe didn't say hi, he didn't look up from Giulia's back. He said, "I could never get *my* shrink to make office calls, or even a house call. I've tried. God knows I've tried." There was something Southern in his voice.

"Abe, I told you she's *a* shrink, not *my* shrink; she's my friend. And you're hurting my neck. Over to the right, top of the shoulder."

Why hadn't Giulia ever talked about this guy? He was using his palms, then his fingertips. He was tall, his presence filling the room in a more solid and dark way than Christopher's ever would have. Then Abe glanced over—round glinting eyeglasses—and Nora saw he was sort of ugly, but in a magnificent way. Nora felt duped, feeling sorry for Giulia stuck here on Friday nights, no way to meet anyone. Abe—immediately Nora loved his looks, but he had his knee up on the desk next to Giulia's hip, was pressing everything he had into her shoulder, and he wasn't stopping even though Nora stood in the doorway. She had to do something. "So, Abe, are you a professional masseur?" Nora cringed. She kept sounding like a schoolmarm.

"No, I'm a novelist."

"Massage is just a gift he was born with." Giulia's voice was slack. The room was so tiny, the three of them made a crowd. The lights were low. Nora stuffed her mittens into her coat pockets, pulled a chair out from under a desk, sat down, and realized she had potato-chip crumbs all over the front of herself. She unbuttoned her coat but didn't take it off. Giulia was wearing a torn-up sweatshirt, and Nora didn't want Abe to see the expensive cashmere sweater she herself was wearing.

Slowly, Abe smoothed out Giulia's shoulders where he'd been rubbing. "Okay, contessa." He slapped her butt lightly. "You're done. I'm hungry. I'm going to buy dinner. You want the chicken or the shrimp?"

"You're the best," she told him. "If you get the shrimp, I'll get the chicken and we can share. Nora, do you want anything from the Brazilian place?"

"No. No, thanks. I ate dinner already," Nora lied.

"Okay, then, I'm going." Abe finally turned to Nora. He really was something. Nora felt her attention quicken, the way she'd seen it happen for painters she modeled for in France: gaze and object meet, become vision. Abe's eyes were huge and dark and muddy around the edges with sleepiness, baggy under-eyes extended beyond the rims of his wireless eyeglasses. He looked Eastern European and from a few generations back. In the way

Christopher held on to his boy beauty, this Abe seemed always to have been a man, never a kid. Tall and wide, with long, straight dark hair combed back off his forehead into a leather-string-tied knot at his neck. His head, where it was balding, glistened. He wore a gold earring, a small hoop. His hands were beautiful, his fingers thick as tubes of paint. He was dressed in black jeans and beat-up sneakers. A mud-colored T-shirt. Boys' clothes, like Kevin's, but inappropriate on this man. If Nora had seen Abe on the street, at first glance she might have thought he was homeless, a wandering goon panhandling. On the street, she would have averted her eyes. A dirtiness, a beat-up-ness about him. But in the small room, Nora just looked at his arms, the perfect way the hair grew on his arms, left his wrists smooth. He wore a leather-strapped watch. She couldn't look at his face, afraid of what would show on her own face now that he was finally looking at her.

"So you're a shrink," he said.

"Yes." She usually didn't let people get away with "shrink."

"Psychiatrist, analyst, M.S.W., what?"

"Psychologist. What about your writing?" Nora asked. "What do you write about?"

"The dark, gnarly heart of the South, the Jewish South."

"Time for your break, Abe," Giulia said. "We need dinner."

"I'm out of here. Good evening to you, Nora."

He'd said her name. "Yes, nice meeting you, Abe." Before he could get out the doorway, Nora would have to move her chair. She hesitated. "What do you charge for a massage?" she asked.

"Gratis. You just have to do what Giulia does, spend the night with me."

Then he was gone.

"So," Giulia said, sitting in the chair across from Nora's, "are you okay?" But Nora was listening to Abe's big steps go down the carpeted hallway. Giulia wheeled her chair closer. "Nora?"

"Well, I'm done feeling sorry for *you*. Who *is* that guy?"

"Why'd you feel sorry for me?" Giulia asked.

"You never mentioned him."

"He's been here forever, came with the job, from even before Mary worked here."

"Did Mary go out with him and never tell me?"

"Mary with Abe? Mary knows better."

"He gives you back rubs, he's going to get your dinner."

"Sometimes I go get the dinner," Giulia said. "One of us has to cover the phone."

"But he's kind of great-looking, don't you think?"

"Abe? Yeah, he's—I don't know, he's Abe. He published a novel a couple years ago. Now he's working on another one."

"He must have a girlfriend."

"Abe Shulevitz is *not* an option."

"Shulevitz. Abe."

"Nora, stop. What's wrong? What're you doing wandering around without Christopher on a Friday night?"

Nora sighed. "What can I say? He's working. There's nothing to say. Did Mary call you? She finally called me." They chewed over the little they'd each heard from Mary. Giulia wanted to talk about the ER, but Nora needed to ward off *Natassia Natassia Natassia,* so she dared again: "Where's Abe with your dinner?"

"He's taking his break. He won't be back for an hour."

"Where's he go on his break?" If Nora had known he had an hour, she could have invited him to have a drink with her. She could have followed him. She wanted to know everything about him.

"Never mind. I'm sure it's nothing we'd want to know."

"Tell me," Nora insisted.

The phone rang. "He wanders around Times Square, I guess." Into the receiver, she said, "Hello, Giulia Di Cuore. Yep, I'll be right there." She hung up, pushed out quickly from her desk. "Nora, sorry, I've got to get to work. The cover story's in."

Going down in the elevator, Nora reminded herself to ask Giulia next time they talked, *Tell me, you have to tell me, what does Abe do on his breaks?* Out in the streets, walking home, Nora was carried by her own buoyant energy, thinking, I've lived in New York all these years and I've never come across this man, this Abe.

Nora truly did love the city; it never stopped offering up its gifts.

THE NEXT DAY, Saturday, Giulia called. "Nora, did you lose your wedding ring?"

Nora looked down at her left hand. There was the diamond engagement band, the lapis band from Italy, the tiny white-gold band that was Christopher's *nonna*'s, but the yellow-gold band he'd put on her hand at their wedding, it was gone.

"I found a gold band on the floor of my office last night. Is it yours?"

"Oh. Yeah," Nora said, "it probably is."

Chapter 16:

October

1989

"Excellent," old Dr. Jonson said as he eased the bandages off of Natassia's wrist. "Nicely healed. You've taken good care of yourself." Natassia and Mary, having made it through their first week together upstate, were in the doctor's office for a follow-up.

Dr. Jonson poked a small beam of light into her pupils, pressed her fingernails. "You're anemic," he said, "you need to eat meat."

"Should I take her for a blood test?" Mary asked.

"She doesn't need a blood test. See that?" He lifted Natassia's finger, pressed her nail again. "See how slow the blood's coming in. Nothing a little liver won't take care of."

But that hollow horror was still in Natassia's eyes. Mary caught Dr. Jonson's arm as Natassia walked to the waiting room. "She doesn't seem to be getting any better," Mary told him.

"She's worn out. I told you last time. Same thing today. Way too much emotional excess for a girl her age. She'll probably be fine. But it'll take time."

Out in the waiting room, he told Natassia, "Liver for dinner tonight, young lady. Steak!"

SO MARY BOUGHT MEAT. T-bone steaks and sirloin tip and thick pork chops and lamb chops and ground sirloin for hamburgers. All her life, Mary had only considered foods that would keep her dancer's body thin and in working order. She didn't know much about cooking, and certainly couldn't meet the standards Natassia had got used to while living with Lotte, but Mary remembered that her father sometimes used a grill out on their cracked cement driveway. "You can't really ruin food too much on a grill," he always said. Behind the Hiliard greenhouse apartment was a garden shed, and in there Mary found an old hibachi. She set it up on the stone bench outside her front door, and she made a full dinner every night: grilled meat and a bowl of chopped-up iceberg lettuce, sometimes with a tomato sliced into it, sometimes a cucumber, and every night she boiled a package of frozen peas or beans or spinach (Birds Eye or some other quality brand), and she put out whole-wheat bread. Going against every rule she had for herself, Mary served butter, mashed potatoes, macaroni and cheese, whole milk, ice cream. She bought Häagen-Dazs for Natassia and didn't worry about the fat content or the expense.

To encourage Natassia to eat, Mary sat down to dinner, let herself eat until she actually felt something close to full, and she didn't like it, that stuffed-ness she associated with living at the Steins' and needing to get away. But she stayed at the table; sometimes she tried to light a cigarette, but Natassia complained about the smoke. So Mary just sat. Did head rolls, shoulder rolls, pressed her thumbs into the jutting knobs of her hip bones to make sure they weren't buried yet in fat.

Mary planned her days around the urgent need to get to the grocery store. At first she borrowed the school van and took Natassia with her, but Natassia was so worn down she could hardly drag herself through the aisles. Then Mary's friend Claudia, who taught English, offered Mary the use of her Mazda during her lunch break, and Claudia sat in the cottage to watch Natassia, who slept—or maybe just pretended to sleep—all wrapped up in blankets until Mary came through the door with her arms full, announcing, "Tonight it will be a feast of tenderly grilled chicken breasts with a light lemon seasoning. Chopped tomato on a bed of lettuce. For nourishment, a side dish of green—"

At moments like these, Mary didn't recognize herself anymore. For so many years, she'd been a person who was not only willing but actually relieved to give her child up to someone else's care. That wasn't who Mary was anymore.

THE WISE INSTINCT that propelled her into action also told Mary that her efforts were nothing, just a way to accommodate the beast. No longer waiting at the door but having entered and moved right in, the ferocious truth visited Mary as soon as she woke every morning: *I didn't love my daughter right, and now love is so twisted inside her that she jabbed herself with a Cuisinart blade and burned herself with matches.* These thoughts stabbed Mary a thousand times a day. *She might try to hurt herself again. She is totally dependent on me now for her safety. I'm it.*

Everything else fell away. In some ways this was the easiest time in Mary's life, in that it was the least complicated. She had to teach dance because she got paid to teach dance, so she danced. There were no men, but she didn't care, never thought about sex anymore. Sometimes she forgot to shower. Her thick hair, way overgrown by now, was always slipping out of a rubber-band-held ponytail, a little uneven nub that made the base of her neck itch. Her eyes above her prominent cheekbones were almost swollen-gone. The days passed. The only thing Mary took great care to do was never to let Natassia out of her sight.

Don't let there be another emergency.

Natassia spoke very little, and she wanted her body to be covered all the time. Natassia and Mary had always run around half undressed in front of each other, as oblivious of modesty as dancers in a backstage dressing room. Now Natassia wore sweaters and sweatpants, even in bed. She was always cold. And, worse thing, she couldn't stop hating her body. More than once, Mary saw Natassia look in the full-length mirror on the hall-closet door and, just as Mary had done in front of countless dance-studio mirrors, whisper to herself, "Ugly." Because she wasn't supposed to have heard, Mary couldn't say, No, you're beautiful! Besides, they had passed the point where Mary's words could help. Dr. Cather was always telling Mary, Trust yourself. So Mary did what she knew how to do. *Body.* Mary tried to care for Natassia's body.

In the morning, Mary got up early, ran a hot bath, then coaxed Natassia out of bed. Mary had to rub Natassia's shoulders *(so bony)* and her feet *(two*

pairs of socks?), tug lightly on her hands *(she's so cold!)* until Natassia finally sat up. Mary led her into the bathroom, helped her undress, helped her into the tub, then sat on the blue porcelain edge while Natassia soaked. Mary let her soak a long time, hoping that if Natassia's body could be soothed then her heart would find comfort, too.

Though she let Mary help undress her, Natassia pulled a towel into the water and covered herself, sat with her head falling in front of her, hiding in her wild mess of hair. Her shame and her skinniness seemed to be feeding on each other, the soul cannibalizing the body. Mary, as a dancer, had pushed her own body into all kinds of extreme pain; she had never wanted anything like that for her daughter, but here they were. During the first two weeks upstate, every morning in the bathtub with the warm wrap of the wet towel around her body, Natassia cried.

"Sweetie," Mary said.

Natassia turned away, her face agonized with humiliation.

Mary wanted so much for Natassia to talk to her. Please, she almost pleaded, just let me hear your voice.

Silence.

During this time, Mary came to understand what Ross must have ached for years ago, when they were lovers, every time he pleaded with her, *Mary, talk to me!* and she made it clear she wanted him just to bug off. Maybe now Mary understood a little what he had needed to hear. And if she had been able to open up to him back then, would it have made a difference? Kept them together? Kept Natassia safe? All Mary remembered was a fierce will to protect herself, but, even remembering all that, remembering exactly what it felt like, she could not accept Natassia's silence. *Come on, come on, come on! Talk to me!* Mary wanted to scream it. *Talk to me about what's inside of you, Natassia. I love you so much, I want to know, so I can take care of you, and if I can't take care of it, I want to look out for you.* Is this how Ross had felt? Mary had never experienced love like this, love that wanted to know and know.

Then, one morning, after a night of almost no sleep at all, Natassia lay in the tub and wrapped herself in a heavy green-striped towel and finally she began to talk, and when she did, Mary wished more than anything not to be hearing what she was hearing.

"Why did he . . ." Natassia whispered. She lay so far back that bath-water was lapping the edges of her lips, soap bubbles on her front teeth.

"What, honey? I can't hear you." Mary leaned forward into the water, all the way up to the sleeves of her black T-shirt.

"Why . . ."

"Please, Natassia, talk louder."

"Why did he stop loving me?" Natassia choked it out, then, in one fast move, she dipped her head back until her face was buried under water.

Terrified, Mary pulled Natassia up, but in such a panic that Natassia spun onto her side and her head bumped against the edge of the tub. "Leave me alone," Natassia scolded.

"I'm sorry."

"I hate you," Natassia said, finding her tears again.

"Honey, I need to hear what you're saying."

Natassia lay back again, wrapped in her towel, and stayed that way a long time. With her fingertips wrinkled from the water, Natassia's hands looked like an old lady's, older than Lotte's. Her eyes were closed, so Mary could stare. So much Ross in the kid's face. The plump freckles. That high, wide, intelligent forehead. Mary used to like to stroke Ross there and tell him that was where he stored all the excess information he had about practically everything. He knew so much more than everybody else. Impatience was twitching over Natassia's eyelids. Still, she refused to speak. *I'm the wrong mother for her and she knows it. I'm not smart enough.*

"I don't know how come," Natassia finally said. "Am I really stupid?"

"No!"

"He said it so many times. 'I love you. I love you.' But he was lying. Every night, when we went to sleep, he rubbed my head and said all the reasons he loved me. He said I was so smart."

"You are. You're very smart. Very, very."

"And he said he loved me because I smelled good. And he kept saying he loved my knees and stuff. He made such a big deal out of my knees and my ankles."

And your breasts, Mary thought, remembering the note she'd found in Natassia's drawer. *I should have done something* then. *I should have . . .*

"He said . . ." Natassia's voice was loud and full of attitude, full of you've-been-bugging-me-so-now-you're-going-to-hear-it. "He said we were going to get married." Natassia stopped, let "married" ring in the foggy bathroom. Mary, working hard, did not flinch. "He said he never wanted to marry anybody as much as me. He said that." Natassia's energy was used up; she began to cry again. "How can you say that to somebody and then it goes away?"

"He was wrong to say such things to you. I mean—shit, not because . . . Oh, shit, Natassia, you *are* beautiful and brilliant, and you deserve to be loved. But you're too young for a grown man to be saying shit like that."

"It's not shit. Just because you never got married—"

"Okay, but you're fifteen, it's"—there was a word Cather used a lot—"inappropriate. He was inappropriate. Natassia, do you know he could get arrested for having sex with you? Do you know that? I mean, laws are set up so this kind of thing doesn't happen. It's just plain wrong."

"We didn't have sex. We made love." The dark eyes and their power got lost again under the maze of wet hair. "You're the one who had sex with everybody in the known universe."

Mothers have to take some bad hits sometimes.

Yeah, Dr. Cather, but—

Pick your fights. Let some fights go. Let it go.

Mary's fingernails had been clawing at the nervous itchiness at the back of her neck. "Can you answer a question for me, Natassia? I just—please, can you tell me? Did he ever try to—I don't know—did he get rough or hit or something?"

"Mom."

"Please."

Natassia sat up tall in the tub. Her eyes appeared again. "You don't get it, do you? Everything was great until I wrecked it."

"How did you wreck it?" Mary tried pouring a handful of warm water over Natassia's goose-pimpled shoulder.

"Stop it," Natassia ordered.

"Sorry. But did he," Mary whispered, circling Natassia's ankle, "hurt you? I need to know."

Natassia kicked Mary's hand away. "Mom, nobody hit anybody. If that's what you're looking for, it didn't happen. Do all your stupid boyfriends hit you? Why are you so obsessed with hitting?"

"Because you hurt yourself, Natassia. What made you do that?"

"Oh God, Mom, you're always crying now. Stop it. It's gross."

"Do you have any idea why that happened? With the Cuisinart? Can you tell me?"

"I just can't stand it if I don't see him again." Natassia put her forehead on her raised knees. Down into the water, she said, "The only thing I want is to get back together with him, and I don't want to talk."

Mary waited until Natassia was done soaking, then helped her out of the tub.

THE NIGHTS when she was able to sleep, Mary was having terrible dreams, mostly with babies in them, or dreams of mutilation. A baby with one blue ear, no blood in it, sitting at the mouth of a big sewer. A palace with a dirty-tiled subway station in its basement, a jar of knives at the turnstile. A dream in which Mary was slicing flesh that didn't bleed but turned into meat for a sandwich. Mary's sleep exhausted her. She was desperate for more sleep when the alarm clock went off, but it was always a relief to see daylight. Turning over first thing, Mary usually found Natassia lying on her back, knees bent, arms crossed over her chest, staring at the ceiling. What seemed to be happening was that Natassia fell asleep easily when she got in bed, but woke in the middle of the night and was unable to sleep again. She'd just lie there, not move. She used to be one of those kids who hogged up a bed, spread out diagonally. Now she took up so little room.

BY THE SECOND WEEK of the crisis (the first week, thank God, had coincided with Fall Break), Mary had to get back to her classes. On Monday, after the bathtub routine, Mary held out a leotard for Natassia to step into. "There's no other choice, sweetie," she said when Natassia hesitated.

"I'm not a dancer. I hate dance." But Natassia pulled the leotard on.

"Yeah," Mary said, "dance sucks sometimes." She handed Natassia two sweaters, a pair of tights, and sweatpants. Mary ached while she watched Natassia cover herself up in layers. By quarter to nine, the two of them, wrapped in scarves and sweaters, headed through the meadow up to the studios. Walking, they were always close, bumping into each other.

Mary's first class began at nine-fifteen, ballet. Up at Hiliard, Mary was jack-of-all-trades, teaching multiple levels of ballet and modern, an improv-and-composition class, and a seminar that was supposed to be all reading and writing, though Mary mostly showed dance videos. In addition, Hiliard offered adult ballet and modern classes, quite pricey, for townies. And, by audition, "advanced" training for private students. All day and a couple evenings each week, Mary was in the studio, and she kept Natassia with her.

Natassia didn't put up a fight, which is how Mary knew that Natassia, too, was scared, didn't trust herself to be alone. She sat on the wood floor of the studios, didn't want a cushion; she napped, or read old *New Yorkers* she'd found in the cottage, or wrote in her journal, or stared at the dancers' feet. And, a thousand times a day, Mary walked over to Natassia curled up like a cat following the sunlight around the floor, and Mary patted her daughter's face, massaged her shoulders, held her hand. Mary was almost always touching Natassia. She never, never let her be alone.

"How long can you keep this up?" Dr. Cather asked during one of Mary's weekly phone sessions, which were scheduled during lunchtime so Claudia could sit with Natassia. "I applaud what you're doing, Mary, but, well, you're sure you don't want to bring her into the city, just to be evaluated by a specialist?"

No one had to tell Mary what was wrong with Natassia. Her heart was wrecked, and the only way to make sure someone else—some quack—didn't make things worse was for Mary herself to take care of her daughter. Something somewhere had gone very wrong. Mary remembered a student who had come to her after bad and confusing preparatory training. The kid barely knew one foot position from the next. In situations like that, you have to reteach everything from the beginning. *I'm her mother. She needs her mother.*

"This doctor up here who undid the stitches gave me the name of a therapist," Mary told Dr. Cather. "We're going to try her."

When Mary brought Natassia to Dr. Jonson's for a second follow-up, he had insisted that Mary use the phone right there in his office to call the social worker, Heather Jamison Jonson. "Mary, we had a deal. I did my part, now you do yours." (Mary was fairly sure Nora would say this was wrong, the old doctor forcing Mary to call his daughter-in-law, but so far Dr. Jonson was the only one who had any advice. Plus, Mary sort of liked having the old guy telling her what to do.) When Mary called, the woman answered her own phone. A baby was crying in the background. "Yes," Heather Jamison Jonson said, "I thought you might call." Was this good? Maybe it was bad. Maybe this social worker didn't have any patients, and her father-in-law was just drumming up business for her. "I can see Natassia tomorrow afternoon," Heather said.

"Noon's the only time I have a car to borrow."

"Noon is fine. I'll see you then."

Claudia in the English Department was the only one who knew the whole story of Natassia's breakdown. Mary was so afraid of having Natassia taken away from her, and so afraid of losing her Hiliard job (and cottage and medical insurance), she was working overtime to hide the full situation from the headmaster. When Mary's students began asking about the girl sitting in the studio every day, Mary told them that Natassia was getting over a very serious flu, but it was way past the contagious stage.

"But who is she?" the kids insisted.

"My daughter."

"You're a mother?" the students asked.

"Yeah, I'm a mother."

CHAPTER 17

OCTOBER

1989

It was the week after Nora had met Abe. Even though her dreams were still bad and full of Natassia, Nora's days were a little better. There was not a thing she could do about Natassia, not since Mary had taken it all into her own hands, and Nora was too distracted to bother with Christopher, too busy going over and over in her head Abe's voice; Abe's muscled forearms; the worldly, worn-down leather of Abe Shulevitz's leather watchband. Then, late Saturday afternoon, she was having a cup of soup in Veselka, one of the few places she felt comfortable eating in alone, and she saw Abe.

He was at a table in the middle of the restaurant. He was with a woman. Nora, sitting by the window with her back against the wall, was out of his line of vision, but she had a good view of him and an even better view of his companion, who was dark-haired, tall and skinny, very expensive- and intelligent-looking. Publishing, Nora thought. Maybe a museum administrator. Abe and the woman were having an argument, and, watching them, Nora immediately knew three things: (1) Abe had hurt the woman somehow. (2) The woman's anger probably was not un-founded, for she did not look like a hysteric. And (3) Abe's hand gestures said that he was baffled, clueless, as to what had gone wrong.

Abe and the woman had been sharing a huge cinnamon roll. A waitress had just brought a bowl of borscht for the woman and a plate of breaded cutlet with gravy for Abe. It was four-thirty on a Saturday afternoon. A little late for a postcoital breakfast or lunch, too early for dinner; then Nora remembered that he'd worked until five in the morning. Nora was fighting the evidence that Abe and this woman were having one of those blessed days that organize themselves around a couple's various appetites: food, then sex, then sex, then more food. The shared pastry between them. Their knees interlaced as they sat squished around their tiny table.

Christopher and I haven't had a Saturday like that in—what?—months maybe.

But in the length of time it took to fry up a cutlet, things had fallen apart between Abe and the woman. She was moving her knees away from his; he reached under the table but wasn't able to keep her near him. She turned and sat sideways, literally giving him the cold shoulder. He spoke with affection, as if he really meant everything he was saying, but she was gathering her canvas bags and her leather backpack. The look on her face said she'd probably been through this with him before. Clutching her coat and all her various bags, she moved to the edge of her chair, looked straight at him, and said some goodbye something. He said something apologetic. She stood and walked out of the restaurant without her coat on. Outside, she passed quickly by the front window, still not wearing her coat, and she never looked back. Gone. One more unhappy woman wandering through a weekend alone.

Abe's long ebony hair was loose today, a little damp from the shower. He wasn't wearing eyeglasses, just the earring and watch. Clothes—pretty much the same as when Nora had met him. She gave it ten full minutes, allowed for the possibility that the woman might come back. Abe did, too. He sat there, pushed back his plate. When the waitress came by, he ordered something and she wrote it down. He leaned elbows on the table and rubbed his hands over his eyes and face. The waitress returned with a pot of tea, cup, and saucer, put the bill upside down on the table, and took his plate of food. His lunch was practically untouched. Nora, willfully, forgot the hurt and intelligence she'd noticed in the woman's face, and the possibility that Abe might deserve to be left with a ruined lunch. *Poor guy.*

Nora had finished her soup and ordered an apricot Danish and coffee so she'd have an excuse to stay at her table. It was a rainy Saturday with a lengthening line of people waiting at the door. Within a few minutes, Nora had her Danish, coffee, and bill, and she pulled money out of her pocket, pulled on her coat. If she waited too long he might leave. But then Nora saw the waitress heading for Abe's table with his plate of cutlet, holding it with a towel—she'd zapped it for him; he had never intended to leave his lunch. And he looked up with a flirty smile, any sadness about his girlfriend wiped away. The waitress was a pretty Russian woman. He said something to her, kept her there a few extra minutes. When she left him, the waitress was smiling. Abe dug into his food.

He's a jerk. Nora stood and, with her pastry and coffee, walked to his table. "Can I sit down?"

"Hey. Hi." He was in mid-bite. Swallowing, he ran his napkin over his smiling mouth. "What are you doing here?"

Thinking fast, she said, "Oh, I have a sort of date with myself here every Saturday afternoon." She surprised herself. After fifteen years of monogamy, she still had a knack for quick play with a new man. "My husband paints on Saturday afternoons. He's a painter." She offered this information to help Abe feel safe as she joined him at the table. "He's working on a big project," she said, stirring Sweet 'N Low into her coffee. "I tell him he can have all Saturday to himself, if we have a date for sushi on Sunday night."

Abe put down his fork. "That is a very reasonable marriage. You give him that? That's great."

"What?"

"You don't make him feel the guilt. Jeez—I just had a mess here—"

"I know," Nora said, "I saw."

"You saw that?" He forked a big piece of cutlet and dipped it into his mashed potatoes. "I guess I erred. She says I did, but I have no idea, truly, what I did wrong. I need my time to write, that's all."

"What happened?"

"She's a good woman. An editor at a public-policy journal. Very smart person. Man, she has read all the literature there is to read in a couple different languages." *Ah, so that's what he likes; I'll need to read more novels, maybe poetry.* "She lived in Leningrad and speaks Russian fluently."

Nora looked down into her coffee, stirred it a bit more. *He likes her.* This bothered Nora. She started to put a bit of sugar into her coffee, to hide the aftertaste of the Sweet 'N Low, but Abe said, "Too late to add sugar. Sugar only mixes in when the coffee's hot."

"Excuse me?"

"That's what our friend Giulia says. Her Italian expertise. Anyway, Ava and I—"

Ava, huh?

"—were here having a nice breakfast." Blamelessly, his hands gestured toward the table. "I was telling her just that I needed tonight to write. She wanted me over at her place. I guess she was getting some kind of dinner together with these friends of hers. She says she told me about it last week. I don't know. I mean, we've been together all morning, all afternoon."

"I guess," Nora said, "she was disappointed."

"Yeah, but it's more than that. She seems to have a need—almost a compulsion, I'd call it—to talk about our relationship." Leaning toward Nora a bit over the table, he said, confidentially, "I think she wants to talk about living together. She wants to know if I'm seeing anyone else."

"Are you?" Nora looked up from her coffee, and Abe looked at her, and they both laughed.

"You women. You're all alike."

"I'm kidding you, Abe. But I can understand why she might want to know the answer to that question. She may need to know that information. For herself."

He looked at her and shook his head, his beautiful bony scalp and the black straight hair falling away from it. "You're a shrink, right? Women come to your office all week long to talk about what happened over the weekend with jerks like me, don't they?"

They both laughed again. Nora felt something spin so low in her stomach it was near her groin. *This* she had not felt in years.

"These girls with big careers, man . . ." Nora noted he was talking about girls instead of women, and her conscious mind was offended. But he was looking at her, and she felt what she had felt the first time she met him, in Giulia's office. That skin of sadness she'd been carrying for so long, it shed away when Abe looked at her, as he was now, saying, "They excite me, these girls, with all their busyness . . ."

Up close, she saw that his tired eyes were hazel. ". . . these brilliant, exceedingly beautiful girls, with their unimpeachable professionalism, that unassailable competence. Oh, how it excites me. And they make all that nice money and are so meticulous about saving it up and investing it. And then, invariably"—his language, he's creative with his adjectives and adverbs, Nora thought; Christopher wouldn't know an adjective if it bit him on the shin—"invariably, they slip into that retrograde mentality of charting the progress of a relationship, and each weekend I'm thinking we're just having a nice, enjoyable time, but for them each weekend is a watershed. They want to know, 'Has progress been made? Are we on task?' What am I supposed to do with that?" He was finishing his meal, pushing back his plate so he could lean his arm on the table in front of him. "Noreen—"

"Nora."

"Nora. Sorry. I knew it was something sexy and Irish. And it's Conolly, right? Nora Conolly, you're a woman, you're smart, you talk to these women all the time. You tell me, what do they want?"

Nora told him, "I've never lived the way you're describing, having an agenda for my relations with an intimate. I've never conducted my relationships that way."

He leaned across the table, staring right into her green eyes with his round, tortoisey, big eyes, and with the sternest look on his face. "You're lying," he said, and then dipped his fork into Nora's apricot Danish.

LATER THAT EVENING, sitting by herself in a crowded movie theater waiting for *Mystery Train* to begin, Nora thought about how far along she and Abe had come that day. The miracle of running into him had eliminated the need to figure out a way to track him down. In just one week, she'd met him, and then, among all the people in New York City, she'd found him again. Best of all, she'd found him downtown, in *her* world. She'd been smart enough to mention her marriage a few times, but not too much, just enough to make Abe feel unthreatened. But she'd managed to make him curious, too, and a little envious. "Why can't I meet a woman like you? That's great you give your husband all that freedom," he'd said. For almost two hours that afternoon, Nora and Abe had sat in the restaurant and talked. He told her stories about this girlfriend or that one. Yes, he was using Nora as a sounding board, but she could cut that off quickly if it went too far.

When they'd ordered a second Danish, he said, "I love this place, don't you?"

"Yeah. My husband"—she never once said *Christopher*—"on Thursday nights he teaches late at Cooper Union, so I come here for soup and sit and catch up on my reading for a couple hours, until he's done with his class."

"Every Thursday?"

"Pretty much," Nora said. Christopher didn't teach at Cooper Union anymore, hadn't in a couple of years.

"Great," Abe said, "I'll see you here, this Thursday night. Would that be all right with you, Nora Conolly? What time?"

The theater lights were dimming now, the audience full of couples, but Nora didn't care. With her hand in a carton of buttered popcorn, she snuggled down into the plush seat. Thinking over all that had happened that day, she was proud of herself, tickled.

Within herself, Nora felt herself lifted away from *Na-ta-sha,* saved from the biting torture by *Aaaaabbbbe.*

CHAPTER 18:

OCTOBER

1989

Mary had never in her life given a flying fuck about school or the rules of school. It had always been such a joke to her, like in Rome, when she and Ross managed to hustle the dean into letting them drop most of their classes. Now so much of Mary's well-being, and her daughter's sanity, depended on Mary's ability to please and please the administrators of a private school she would never have been admitted to or been able to afford to attend. The irony wasn't lost on Mary. About the Hiliard School job, she was a nervous wreck all the time, so afraid she wasn't doing it right. It had never been like this with dance jobs.

Her boss, Franklin Fields, the headmaster, wasn't a total idiot, but Mary didn't feel she knew enough about academic life to understand the full extent of his power—or the lack of it. A dance-company director she could figure out immediately, but this headmaster guy, was she supposed to talk to him, ignore him, stay out of his way, or what?

One day, Franklin walked up to Mary in the faculty parking lot as she was taking groceries out of Claudia's car. Franklin, pink-cheeked, mildly lubricated from lunch, had just parked his blue Volvo. "Here, let me help you with those bags," he offered.

Mary calculated quickly. It was embarrassing to have this rich guy carry her groceries, but she couldn't say no to her boss. Could she? "Thanks,"

Mary said, and handed him the lightest bag (as soon as she handed it to him, she realized that toilet-paper rolls were sticking out of the top of the bag—embarrassing). She put on her sunglasses and marched up the path at a clip, so he could see she wasn't wasting time. Franklin kept up close behind her as they cut through the backyards of the dorms. Even though it was cold, some kids' windows were open, spilling out funky Jackson Browne. Ross had explained to her that one way to manage the people who have control over you is to establish a rapport with the people who are above the people who are just above you.

"Hardly see you these days," Franklin said, pausing a moment behind her to catch his breath. "Heard your daughter's with you for a visit."

Who had power over the headmaster? The parents? But the parents weren't around. The kids hardly ever saw them. How could Mary establish a rapport with the Hiliard School parents? She stopped in the path, looked back at Franklin, and just came out with it: "My daughter's having a nervous breakdown, so I need to take care of her."

"Sorry, Mary," he said, "really sorry." She watched his face pinch with the bad news. *Faker.* "I'm sure you're doing a fine job with her. The kids love what you're doing in dance class." Mary and Franklin had reached the path leading to her cottage. She reached over to take her bag of toilet paper from him.

"Let me know," he said, "if I can help in any way with your daughter."

Mary lifted her sunglasses. "So you don't care that she's staying with me? It's not against the rules?"

"You're taking care of your child. If she's having a hard time, I don't know what else you could do. Half the kids in this school are on the edge, several on medication. After a certain point, you don't have a lot of options. Someday I'll tell you about the mess we had in the dorm a couple years ago. If I were you, I wouldn't go out of my way to let the board of trustees know your daughter's in class with you. And, of course, don't advertise it to the parents. They'll say their kids aren't getting attention."

The board members of the dance company had always been in love with Mary. But the Hiliard board of trustees? *Who are they? What do they do?* She'd have to remember to ask Ross.

"Funny. Natassia tells me I give the students too much attention."

Franklin smiled at her—it was sort of a guy's smile, not much of a boss's smile. "Can't win, huh?" Franklin said. "Damned if you do, damned if you don't. Want to have dinner with me Friday night?"

Mary shifted her bags of groceries. "Are you asking me out or something?"

"Yeah. Something."

"I can't. I'm with Natassia all the time."

"You're a good mother." He walked away, tugging at his leather gloves, heading over to his office, but looking back at Mary. "A lousy date, but a good mother."

A GOOD MOTHER. The headmaster of Hiliard School had said it himself. *If I need witnesses in court, maybe I can get Franklin.* Some part of Mary's mind was always preparing to be brought to court by David Stein. He still was giving her a hard time on the phone, really lording it over her that his detective-writer helped get the police to back off of the suicide-attempt follow-up, even though Dr. Jonson's call had been the important one. "You can't just take Natassia like that," David yelled, "out of the hospital, like some kind of hostage."

Lotte got on the extension. "Yes, she can, David. Natassia's her daughter. Mary can do what she wants."

"What about Ross?" David yelled at Lotte. "Natassia's got a father, you know."

"Don't you start on Ross." The arguing continued between David and Lotte, who were in different rooms in the same apartment but yelling at each other via a long-distance phone call. "The way you talk to him," Lotte told David, "how can he bring himself here?"

After listening to a few rounds, not getting a word in, Mary quietly hung up.

Two days later, Lotte and David drove up to Hiliard, without calling ahead, and David asked Natassia what she wanted to do: go back to New York with them, go to stay with her father in Washington State, go to a hospital, or stay where she was?

"I guess I want to stay here," Natassia said. Even Mary was shocked. Of all the adults reaching out to help Natassia, Mary felt her offerings were the most meager. "I mean, since I'm here," Natassia said, "I may as well just stay. For a while."

Lotte and David were standing in the center of the cottage, filling it up with their tallness, their largeness, her expensive flowing purple-and-black clothes, his wrinkled wool overcoat, their bulging leather bags, and a heap of "supplies" for Natassia. Lotte had a suitcase with Natassia's clothes. David had Natassia's violin, which she didn't want. They brought her a MoMA bag full of bound galleys so Natassia would have reading material, and a Zabar's shopping bag full of weird cheeses and pâtés and other stuff Natassia was used to eating, foods that Mary couldn't quite figure out. Lotte made a big deal over a pomegranate. "Cut into this *soon*, girls, I'm telling you, it's *perfect. Now.*"

And then David handed over to Natassia a Zabar's bag with something he said was extra-special. "Here, love, your grandmother almost forgot this, but I know how much you like it. This is from me," he insisted, "and I want you to enjoy it. Every bite. You don't need to give any of this to your mother. She wouldn't appreciate it."

"Da-vid." Lotte sighed. "Jesus Christ, do you have to insult someone, always?"

"It's okay," Mary said. "Honey, what did David bring you?"

Natassia looked into the bag and smiled. "Poppy, great." Mary could hear the effort in her voice. "A David Glass chocolate-mousse cake."

"Mary, here's a pint of delicious chicken soup with good matzoh balls. Heat that up for her tonight," Lotte said. "And that cake, in the freezer it will last till doomsday."

Lotte and David hugged Natassia and Mary goodbye. David was the only one who had tears in his eyes. Mary wanted to slap him. But she didn't.

"We want you back home with us, sweetie," David said to Natassia when he was finally seat-belted into his car. "We want everything back to normal," he warned, "soon."

NATASSIA'S GRANDPARENTS continued calling every night to check in. Lotte sent Mary a one-hundred-dollar check with a note: *For food, whatever. Love to you both.* Ross called every few days. Then, once, he called in the middle of the night, his voice a sort of whimper, and he asked Mary, "Listen, if I moved back to New York, is there any chance you and I could get married? I mean, shit, Mary, it's the only thing we can do here. We have a kid. She's in trouble."

"Ross. Honey, are you drunk?"

"Yes."

Mary turned onto her back, stared up. A fat moon was spilling light in through the tall windows, lighting up cobwebs in the cathedral ceiling. "Oh, Ross. Oh God, Ross."

"I know. I know. It's stupid. It sucks." He screamed a little scream that was caught in his throat. "Shit, Harriet's upstairs sleeping and I'm down here—"

"What time's it there? Is it too late to go to a meeting? Can you call your sponsor?"

"Listen," Ross said solemnly, then he said nothing for a while. "I need to take a break from calling Natassia. It hurts me too much. I know I'm a selfish, bad daddy, and this is really a piece-of-shit thing to do to her, especially now. Tell her to understand. Can she understand? Tell her. Man, I just can't stomach the long-distance from her. I can't stand—" Another caught scream.

"Ross, do whatever you can do, that's enough. Write to her. She'll answer your letters if you write to her. Why'n't you do that?"

"Do you know how much I loved you?" It was a wild whisper, a muffled scream. "Mary, goddamn you, Mary. Do you know I loved you like nothing else?"

Mary closed her eyes, lowered her chin into her neck. When he bullied her like this, his love—or whatever it was he really felt for her—didn't feel like love, just some bad force to get away from, a windstorm carrying lots of sharp, dangerous objects. Lying right next to Mary was Natassia, stirring in her sleep. As soon as Ross stopped ranting to take a breath, Mary whispered to him, "Write to her, Ross. She'll write back. She's writing all the time these days. You should see the stuff. Did you know she's really a good writer?"

"Is she all right?" Ross asked. "Really? Tell me the truth."

"She's great," Mary lied. "She's doing much better."

NATASSIA WAS GETTING WORSE. For almost a month she had progressed safely at Mary's side, eating and sleeping a bit better each day.

Then, the night after her third therapy session with Heather Jamison Jonson, the BF tried to hug Natassia in a dream. It was an early-morning dream, and when she woke up she said she couldn't remember anything specific, just the heat of his hug, and she looked as if she'd been extinguished. Mary's heart slid.

By now, after a solid month of giving constant care, Mary had pretty much depleted her stash of mother energy. *Nothing's changed. She's no better.* After the dream, Natassia wept in the bathtub, wrapped in a towel, as in the first days of the crisis, crying shamelessly, without covering her face. At two years of age, Natassia had once broken down this way on the street at the San Gennaro festival, when her ice cream slipped off her cone and onto the sidewalk. She'd cried so hard Mary had had to walk away, leaving the kid with Ross, as she muttered to herself, "Over a goddamn ice cream." Grown-up Natassia in a tantrum of grief was becoming as distasteful to Mary as Toddler Natassia had been. *Nobody ever sat and watched me throw a fit.* Handing Natassia a warm, wet washcloth, Mary said, "Come on, honey, wipe off your face." The phrase *drama queen* slid through Mary's mind, making Mary hate herself, which exhausted her even more.

"Why'd he just forget about me?" The kid's thumb was near her mouth, tweaking her chin. She was rocking. "He used to say how much he needed me and stuff. What did I do wrong? Why'd he stop loving me?"

"He doesn't love anybody but himself, Natassia." Natassia's hair needed to be washed, but this wasn't the day to push for that. Especially because Natassia had been complaining of an earache. "He's a mean, cruel, sick person," Mary said.

"He's not!" Natassia pulled the grungy shower curtain closed to hide herself from Mary. "You don't even know him, so stop it."

Mary was making mistakes left and right, she knew that. "Natassia, I'm sorry." No answer from the other side of the curtain. *Let her cool.* Mary sat on the toilet to pee, and to collect herself. Don't respond to the words, Cather had said. Listen for the emotion. Respond to that. Validate her feelings. Mary flushed the toilet and sat down on the damp bathmat. "Honey," she said, staring at the shower curtain's plastic spread of Monet water lilies. "I do know how it feels to have a guy break your heart." There was nothing but stillness now on the tub side of the shower curtain. "Natassia?"

"Who broke your heart?" Natassia demanded.

"Antoine."

"Who's that?"

The first guy to get her pregnant. French Canadian. He'd come to the dance academy in Albany to be guest modern-dance choreographer for the summer. The most beautiful male dancer Mary had ever seen, and out of all the students in his master class, Antoine picked Mary. He picked her for a part in a big ensemble piece. He picked her as his regular dinner companion. He picked Mary's attic bedroom window out late at night, tossed pebbles at it, and convinced her to climb down and drive around in the night with him. Mary had assumed he was gay, the dance mistress told her he was gay, but that summer he pursued Mary as if nothing else mattered to him.

Mary told Natassia, "I was a little older than you are. Sixteen. I took my driver's license test in his Karmann Ghia."

"Cool."

"Yeah. All summer, we ran around Albany in that car. He took me to a couple performances at Jacob's Pillow, and I got to go backstage and meet all these dancers."

Natassia opened the curtain a bit. "How old was the guy, Antoine?"

"Somewhere in his twenties. Too old for me."

"But you were in love with him?"

"The asshole said we were going to perform together all over the world. He choreographed a solo for me. He bought me new school clothes. My stepmother hadn't bought me anything new in years. I remember Antoine took me to a doctor to have my knees checked out. I mean, at that time, nobody was doing any of that for me. My parents sure weren't. He was like this gorgeous guardian-angel older-brother love object."

"Then what happened?"

"There was a big high-school party. It was all my friends, and I brought Antoine. After a while I don't see him anywhere, so I go upstairs and he's in bed with this guy."

"M-o-m-m."

"Cute guy, too. He'd asked Nora to go to the prom with him."

"Did you make a scene?" Natassia asked.

"You better believe it. I really was strong then, you know—"

"You're strong now."

"Yeah, well, he didn't know how strong. I lifted the side of the bed and dumped them both onto the floor with the mattress on top of them."

"And then you jumped on top of the mattress."

"You got it. Right on top of them." A few days after that party, as Nora's mother was driving Mary to Planned Parenthood to see about an abortion, Mary began to bleed, miscarry. She'd had to ask Mrs. Conolly to pull over at a Friendly's so she could use the bathroom. Mrs. Conolly sat in a booth and waited, and when Mary came out and told her about the blood, Mrs. Conolly said, "Thank God, Mary, and don't ever do this to me again."

The next year, the next pregnancy, Mary went to Planned Parenthood by herself, since she knew where it was. Now Mary told Natassia, "Antoine almost dislocated his shoulder that night. He was in big pain for a couple weeks."

"No, Mom, *you* dislocated his shoulder for him. He could have sued you."

"Yeah, right, sued his own ass straight into jail, screwing around with an underage girl *and* an underage boy. But you see, honey? I know how it feels, having somebody break your heart."

"It feels terrible," Natassia said softly.

"Like total shit."

And by now Natassia was crying again.

Mary had to help her out of the tub, hold out the leotard for her to step into, then the sweatpants. She had to pull the sweatshirt over Natassia's head. All dressed, still crying, Natassia went back to bed. Mary sat on the windowsill with the window cracked open, lighting her fourth cigarette of the day. Not even nine o'clock yet. From across the living room, she watched Natassia lying in bed in a wash of grief, and Mary began to lose faith.

Just the day before, Natassia had walked out smiling from her first solo appointment with Heather Jamison Jonson. Mary had been included for the first two sessions. Heather seemed okay to her, not as cheery as the father-in-law but just as harmless, and Mary had thought, Great, maybe this shrink can straighten the kid out. Natassia had told Mary she liked Heather and she'd keep seeing her, even when Heather suggested they try two appointments a week; Natassia would be going back in three days. Mary lit a fifth cigarette and wondered if maybe she should cancel Natassia's next appointment. Maybe seeing a shrink was making Natassia worse. Or maybe she needed to go back sooner, like today. *Should I call Heather?* When Natassia, still sniffling, got up to go into the bathroom, Mary yelled out, "Leave that door open."

"I want some aspirin for my earache," Natassia said.

"We don't have aspirin."

Natassia returned from the bathroom with her long hair pulled back into a ponytail and her hand cupping her ear, and began the reel again: "What did I do *wrong*?"

I can't take this.

Natassia was pacing the floor, gripping her head, chewing the ends of her hair.

This was how Lotte said Natassia was acting the night the rotten BF first broke up with her. But then Mary remembered: regression. Cather had taught her this word. When things inside you get too balled up, you go back temporarily to acting the way you did before you knew better. *Temporary.* Mary decided that the thing to do was to hold off for a day, let this regression run itself through Natassia's system. *Don't start calling for help yet.*

Ignoring Natassia's crying, the way they told you to do with a toddler, Mary stood up and said, "Honey, I'm going into the kitchen to make myself more coffee. Do you want some? Do you want some tea?"

Natassia was still gripping her head and whimpering, but she nodded yes.

Mary made Natassia's tea before she made her own coffee, and called for Natassia, who came in and lifted the cup to take a sip and immediately scalded her lip. "Fuck! You burned me," she yelled, and tossed the whole shebang across the kitchen linoleum.

I can't stand this shit another minute. But then Natassia dropped to her knees, crying, apologizing, mopping up the mess with her sweatshirt. "I can't do anything right. No wonder he left me."

If she doesn't stop this, I'm going to kill her.

You have to validate her feelings.

"I understand, Natassia, that you're feeling bad right now. But all these bad things you're saying about yourself, they're not the truth, so that's not why he left." Exhausted and disheartened, Mary sat down on the floor next to Natassia. "Listen, we have to—"

"Sometimes I didn't want to do what he wanted to do. No wonder he got bored." Natassia was cross-legged on the floor, raising her right shoulder up toward her sore ear. "Sometimes he wanted to see me but I said I had homework. I'm such a—"

"Stop." Mary grabbed Natassia's hands, held them tight with one hand; with the other she cupped Natassia's chin and looked into her eyes. "Natassia, you must stop. Now. I'm not letting you say this bad stuff about yourself."

"Now you're sick of me, too, aren't you?" There was no stopping her that day.

THE SECOND DAY after the dream of the BF's hug, after another whimpery bath and no breakfast, Mary said, "I'll cancel classes again if you want me to, but I'd rather we get out of this house and go up to the studio. Which is it?"

Without answering, Natassia put on her shoes.

It was raining and cold, and they walked up the hill quickly, huddled together under one big golf umbrella.

"HEY, HI." Natassia was sitting in her usual corner in the dance studio when a couple of students walked in and asked her, "You feeling better?"

And Natassia told them, normal as could be, "I had a bad earache, but, yeah, I'm better. What's up with you guys?" And then she joined the others for the warm-up.

Mary was thrilled. Here were her "advanced" ballet students, sixteen leotarded, legginged, ballet-slippered, beautiful teenagers of different heights, weights, shapes, skin tones, and hair lengths, with varying degrees of turnout, flexibility, and strength, but all of them now practiced enough to stand at the barre with their vertebrae aligned, their hips tucked under, their abdominals pulled up, their shoulders and hips squared as their feet turned out to find first position. No one's tongue was accidentally hanging out with the effort. Their butts weren't sticking out, their chins weren't tucked in. Gorgeous young bodies ready to learn more about what a body can do. And standing with them in a snaggy old black unitard too short in the legs, with a pair of linty old warm-up tights sagging off her skinny butt, her wild coppery hair reined into a plump braid down her back, was Natassia. All it took was one kid saying, "Hey, Natassia, wanna take class with us?" Without effort, without practice, with those impossibly long legs of hers, Natassia did the warm-up exercises alongside the students who took class every day, and she managed to keep up.

Mary had taught beginners before (which most of these "advanced" students were), but never required classes. About the Hiliard situation, where all 425 students were required to take at least one semester of dance and hand in written evaluations of their teacher at the end of the term, Mary felt both disdain (the only students who interested her were those who came to class voluntarily, not just to fulfill requirements) and intimidation (she needed their good evals more than they needed her experience, so, in essence, the students were her bosses). Today, though, with *Romeo and Juliet* playing on the tape deck, Mary walked up and down the studio observing her dancers at the barre, all of them sneaking glances at themselves in the mirror, but, Mary thought, They're beautiful, and Natassia, she's beautiful with them. "I love you guys," Mary said to the class, "you're getting gorgeous. You're standing taller! You're getting longer and stronger—"

"And hornier!" said Charlie, the class clown, the handsome, long-limbed melding of a Brazilian rock-musician father and a Dutch painter-heiress mother. "And hornier!"

Charlie was cute. Outrageous but cute. By now Mary was getting used to the chatter during class, which she would never have tolerated in a real dance setting; at Hiliard it seemed the kids were allowed to talk all the time. *Money talks.* They did, however, keep one another in line. Gillian, overweight but flexible, a twin daughter of two surgeons, a girl with a crush on Charlie, told him, "Quiet, Charlie, you're disgusting."

"Okay, my beautiful dancers," Mary said, walking to the center of the studio, "line up in groups of three to go across the floor. We start simple today. Mark this with me." They followed her across the wooden floor as she slowly did a series of pirouettes. Mary could see in the mirror that, except for two of the show-offs, Charlie and Gillian, who were overdoing the simple step, everyone looked fine. Jenefer, who was an excellent dancer and not a show-off, was leading one of the groups, and a few of the girls were trying to mimic her simple elegance, a twist of the wrist at the end of her turn that was natural to Jenefer but not to the others. Natassia, in the center of the third line, looked fine.

And just because things were going better than she'd expected, Mary grabbed a Bach tape she hadn't used in class before. With the music, she demonstrated the clean, simple arms she wanted. "Nothing fancy!" Then she turned the music up, called out, "First group, ready? And six and seven and eight, and *one*—" And Group One stepped out and danced. "Second group, get ready!" And then Group Two was pirouetting across the floor.

"Third group!" Mary called out. "Ready?" Natassia lined up between two other girls, in position. *She looks sharp, better than any of them.* When Natassia held out her arms to begin, she bumped hands with the girl next to her, and they both giggled and readied themselves again. It was a delicious moment, so normal normal normal. "And *one*—" And Natassia's group stepped out.

But as soon as they began, the music stopped. The tape had run out. "Keep going!" Mary yelled to Group Three. "You're beautiful. The music will start again." Natassia's first turn was perfect. She was the only one who didn't stumble, because she was the only one to spot the opposite wall. *She just needed to be pulled out of herself.*

Group Three completed two pirouettes without music, then a Sarah Vaughan tape came on, and the kids stayed right on the beat. But with the third chord, Natassia's turn teetered. "Ahh!" She fell onto her knee, toppled over onto the floor, where she lay, holding herself tight, making no sound.

A few of the kids got to Natassia before Mary did. Mary pushed the kids aside. "Are you hurt, Natassia? Can you stand?"

"But don't," Charlie said, "if you can't."

Her breath was all inside of her. "Deep breath, Natassia," Mary commanded. "Come on. Breathe."

And when Natassia exhaled, it was with a scream so loud it made all the other kids step back. "Natassia," Mary commanded, "stop!" But she couldn't control herself. Weeping, she wrapped her arms around her mother's waist. Mary held Natassia's head on her lap. Natassia was wailing. The students just stood there; a few, embarrassed, turned away.

"Want me to get the nurse," Charlie asked, "or call 911 or something?"

Mary shook her head no.

"Maybe we should just leave?" he asked.

Reluctantly, Mary nodded yes.

Slowly, the students gathered their shoes, warm-ups, books, and headed out.

"I'm sorry, you guys," Mary called out to them.

"That's okay," a few said, but none of them turned to look back.

MARY QUICKLY hung up signs canceling the rest of her classes for that day. As she walked Natassia through the rain to the cottage, trying to keep their footsteps out of the puddles, Mary had to admit to herself that she had never imagined Natassia's crisis dragging on for so many weeks. Back in the cottage, Natassia threw herself on the couch and hid her face. Her back trembled with sobs.

"You've got to stop crying, Natassia."

"My ear aches so much it's killing me."

The ugly thoughts were there again: *Drama queen* and *I can't stand this.* Mary was now in the full grip of an old feeling she didn't like, and it scared her so much she went into a back bedroom with the mobile phone, called Dr. Cather, and spoke to her answering machine: "We're not having so much fun up here anymore." Mary knew that Cather would hear the SOS coded in between Mary's flat voice and her sarcastic message.

Within half an hour, Cather returned the call. "Mary? What's going on?"

Natassia was lying on the couch, her back to the room, so Mary left her and went to the bedroom, closed the door but not completely. She whispered to Dr. Cather, "She keeps breaking down."

"Well, Mary, you know, she's grieving. It's a process, with several stages."

"Yeah, but I'm calling about me now." The phone was wedged into her damp neck, her arms were crossed tightly across her chest, her fingers digging into her soaked armpits. "I don't have any patience for it anymore.

I'm losing it. I'm turning into a lousy mother again. Frankly, this is starting to bore the shit out of me," Mary hissed.

And she went on, whispering, confessing to Dr. Cather that she no longer wanted to be mothering this soggy, whimpering blob of flesh that pouted constantly with Ross's thick lips and talked back with Mary's own mean smart-mouth. All the love that had propelled Mary through the difficult weeks since the night in the ER, all that huge love, had suddenly turned to disgust. Mary was tempted again by the wish she'd had when Natassia was small, the wish to say, *Somebody else can take care of her better.* Now Mary started crying. "I never thought I'd resent her again, and I do. I can't stand her."

"Well, of course you're angry with her. She screwed up your class. She's requiring a mammoth amount of attention. Anybody would be mad."

"Really?" The bed in the dusty, unused room was piled with plastic cartons of the sabbatical family's clothes. Mary kicked a space open between two cartons and sat down.

"Of course. The difference this time," Dr. Cather said, "is that while you're feeling it—the anger, the resentment, the exhaustion, all of it— you're continuing to take care of her. You're staying responsible. You're doing what needs to be done."

"But a normal mother wouldn't feel these bad things."

"Who said?" For the first time ever, Mary heard in Cather's voice a genuine human being, not a professional, and Cather kept on: "Any mother in her right mind feels these things a hundred times a day. A thousand times a day. Not acting on these negative feelings is what separates the good mothers from the criminals." Cather slipped back into her therapist's voice: "Mary, I suspect you're expecting too much of yourself."

Mary's hand had been pulling at a yank of hair. Out of nowhere it occurred to her to ask, "Do you have kids?"

"Three sons and a daughter." Silence. Mary could sense Dr. Cather making a decision to tell more. "All my kids are grown now. I love them more than my own life, but I still remember clearly whole days of wanting to kill one or another of them."

"You're kidding."

"I never did it, though, not once."

"What?"

"I never killed any of them," Dr. Cather said.

"How did you manage? I mean, four kids. Shit."

"Sometimes, on really bad days, I'd lock myself in the bathroom and flush the toilet over and over again—our apartment was in a prewar that had those noisy industrial toilets—and I'd scream into the flushing toilet. When I walked out, I felt much better."

There was silence as Mary took this in. Then she said, "I've got to go back out to Natassia. She's being too quiet in there."

"Okay, but before you go in there, punch a pillow a couple times, give it a good fist."

"Yeah. Right." Mary couldn't quite hang up. "Listen. How many times can she break down like this? I mean, how long do these things usually last?"

"There's no usual, Mary. I suppose she'll break down until she actually believes her lover's gone, and whatever else she's grieving along with that. We re-enact separation over and over until we finally believe—and ac-cept—that our loss is real, irrevocable."

"So she still thinks she might get back together with the guy?"

"She might think that if she cries enough he'll hear her and come back. We don't know. She herself doesn't know. It's not logical, it's emotional. In any case, Natassia will cry until her grief runs out, at which point, we hope, she'll be capable of true reflection on the things that have happened to her. That's when her true healing will begin. Much of this, I hate to tell you, is just preliminary."

Thanks a lot, Dr. Cather.

WHEN MARY WENT BACK into the living room, Natassia was asleep on the couch. Mary hadn't punched a pillow, but she knew what Cather was saying: *Feel your feelings.*

I want a good smoke.

She found her corncob pipe hidden in the bottom of her backpack and went into the bathroom, lit up, opened the window, and let the rain come in on her. She still had the mobile phone in her hands, so, when it rang again, she answered in mid-ring, thinking, *Shit, don't wake the baby.*

"Hello, Mary? This is Franklin Fields. Couldn't reach you in the office, glad I found you."

I'm losing my job.

"I've been thinking about your daughter."

Mary wrapped her index finger tight around the bowl of the pipe. With her other index finger, she tapped at the hot ash, seeing how long she could keep her finger on the heat. *I'll call Lotte. Natassia will have to go live with them again. I'll ask Ross for some cash until I find another job, I'll call . . .*

"I don't know what she's up to these days—"

She's trying to save her life, you fucking bastard.

"—but I'm wondering if she'd have any interest in a laptop computer we've got sitting here in the office. Technicians are coming through later today to upgrade our equipment. According to our contract, they're supposed to take what we don't use. I like to keep these laptops available in case faculty want them for traveling or whatever. Anyway, if she wants to keep this computer down in your cottage, she'd be doing me a favor."

"Yeah. That's all, the computer?" Mary said.

"Well, I don't have a printer available, but she's welcome to use the facilities in the computer lab."

"No, no, I mean, is that all you're calling about? I mean, it's really nice of you to think of her. I just . . . Well, I'm sure you know I had to cancel some classes this week because she's been having a hard time. A setback."

"Listen—"

"But I'm calling all the students to set up makeup sessions this weekend."

"I'm not worried about the classes, Mary. Give yourself a break. You've worked hard since you got here."

"Yeah, well, thanks for the computer."

"So let's see if she can use it. Come by my office, pick it up. Sooner the better."

A COUPLE HOURS LATER, leaving Natassia in the cottage with Claudia, Mary headed up the hill to Franklin's office, shaking her head. Just now, as she walked out of the cottage, Natassia had been singing, teasing Mary, "Fra-ank-lin Fi-elds forever." *Is she getting better, or worse? If she can sing now, why'd she pull that shit in the studio?* It was the end of the workday, and up in the Admin Building, the foyer was quiet. Mary dropped her umbrella into the brass umbrella stand, shook off her denim jacket. Franklin's secretary heard her, came out, and told Mary to walk right into Franklin's office. When he saw Mary in his doorway, he came out from behind his wide desk.

Franklin looked a little older in his office than he did wandering around the school, older and more planted. And Mary had an impulse she'd never had before with a man: standing before him, she wished he was her father. Franklin kept being nice to her. He had asked her out, so he was interested in her, but not in any pushy way. Suddenly she wished for something else she'd never wished for before. A nice, polite, respectful guy, a little older than she was, not too needy, not flashy, maybe with a little money. "Have a seat, Mary?" Franklin offered. "Time to visit for a minute?"

As she sat down in his wing-armed chair, hoping her dusty jeans weren't smudging the suede upholstery, she said, "I can't stay long. Natassia—"

"Mary," Franklin said, "you look tired."

"Yeah. Well."

Mary liked the way the curtains were drawn and several small lamps lit in Franklin's office on this rainy late afternoon. On his desk, a bottle of Tums, a bag of candy corn. Mary tried to remember what Claudia had said his deal was—divorced, never married? The smell in his office was good, some accumulation of a man working in a room all day long. Franklin's office was actually two rooms with a big arch between them. His desk and the chairs were in one room. His library was in the other, with a TV, a small couch, and a stack of videos on the floor. There was a bay window behind his desk with piles of paper all over the window seat. *What does he do in this office all day?*

"Mary, I've been wanting to bring you up to speed on some developments that might be of interest to you. We got a donation of a heap of money specifically designated for bringing guest speakers to campus. Since we've got you here, an expert, I thought it might be neat to invite one or two dance companies to perform, maybe give some lectures. 'Master classes' I think is the term, right?"

He's kidding. No one had ever come to her with money to spend on dance. Usually, dancers had to beg. "Great," she said, "how much is a heap?"

"You'd have a budget of about five thousand. Could we attract some good companies with an invitation like that?"

She tried to act calm. "Yeah. There are companies that'd come up here for that."

"We could possibly even better that amount. Put together your wish list. Also, on a different track, we're starting a new program for our first-year minority students. I thought you'd be a good person to be on that committee."

"What would I have to do?"

"At first, just go to meetings, try not to fall asleep."

She liked the way he didn't take himself too seriously, but why was he trying so hard with her? "Once it gets going, this first-year program should be an interesting project. What I'd ask you to do is make phone contact with potential minority students." Ah, so he'd pegged her for this disadvantaged-background thing, that was it. After all these years, Mary thought, my poor-white-trash roots still show. "Let these kids ask you questions. And I'd expect you to answer candidly. I don't want them feeling we're pulling wool over anybody's eyes. When they visit campus, I'd like you to maybe have a meal with them and their parents. You just . . . just seem to have such a gift, Mary, for dealing with these kids. They'll love . . . just love talking to you." He sometimes got a little stutter while talking to Mary. "You'll excite them," he said, and a little embarrassment set in between Franklin and Mary. "Okay, let me show you this computer I dragged you up here to get."

Something extracurricular was definitely in the room. Mary did a quick appraisal. They were still talking about nothing but work; there was the fact that he was her boss, there was the fact that he was cutting her lots of breaks, there was the fact that she might fuck up in some big way that would really disappoint him. And there was something else. *What?* She was pulling away from whatever romance energy might be in the room, but she also was feeling a little sad about that, not wanting to pull away completely. His necktie was loosened—that preppy version of sexiness. He was actually so close to almost being attractive. Not a bad nose at all. He still had lots of hair. But was it the acne scars on his chin? She knew she wasn't attracted to him, but there was *some* pull. Definitely not a body thing. But something.

"Do you think your daughter'll need help setting this up?" Franklin was tucking the computer into its case. "I could come down sometime."

Mary flinched at the thought of Franklin entering the mess of her home. "No, no, we'll be fine. Listen. Thanks. A lot."

The day was darkening by the time Mary walked back down the hill in the rain. Now that she was out of Franklin's office, not looking at him or feeling him looking at her, she *could* imagine some romance thing happening. Almost. But she couldn't help pulling back from his attention, as she had done after performances when people from the audience came backstage and gushed, stepped in too close. Onstage, apparently, she gave something away that made these strangers assume they knew her intimately. But it wasn't *her*; it was some dance-being Mary Mudd, who was not the real Mary Mudd. When people from the audience saw her up close, so many of them would shake their heads and tell her, "But you're so small, so tiny." That's when Mary really wanted to hide, thinking, You don't know how small, and wanting to yell, "Please, don't come any closer." That's how Franklin's attentions were making Mary feel. But for a brief couple of minutes that afternoon, while she walked home, she let herself imagine sex with a bit more seriousness than she was used to. He'd be a little grateful. She'd be grateful, too, but he wouldn't believe it. She imagined them afterward, on really clean white sheets, resting.

Resting. Maybe it wouldn't be Franklin Fields, but, shaking out her umbrella before she opened her front door, Mary began to imagine the presence in her life of a man with whom she could finally lie down and rest.

THAT NIGHT, Mary had a dream. Franklin Fields was handing her a videocassette. As he did, he lightly touched her breast, and she wasn't mad. It felt nice. Good.

Natassia had no interest in the laptop computer the evening Mary brought it home, and not for several days afterward, but Mary's trip to Franklin's office eventually started a new phase in Mary's and Natassia's lives. When she finally did log on to the computer, she wanted to stay in the cottage to write and insisted she could be alone now. "You can't keep canceling your classes, Mom. Just go without me."

At Natassia's next appointment with Dr. Jamison Jonson, Mary asked for a few minutes alone with the therapist. "Can she stay home for a couple hours without me?"

"Yes, she says she's feeling as if she'd like to stay home to work on the computer. She wants to write." They were standing by the closed door of Heather's office. Heather spoke very softly; Mary had to lean toward her, and she was sure she smelled tobacco—and it wasn't hers. *Does Heather smoke?* Mary felt new trust in the woman. "You'll have to start moving toward normalcy sometime," Heather was saying. "Trusting her again."

"I trust her, I'm just afraid that, well, you know."

"Just make sure you check on her every couple hours. She can't do anything irreversible in a couple hours."

Mary's eyes widened.

"But I don't really see her doing anything," Heather said, tugging nervously at her fingers. She really needs a smoke, Mary thought. "Go ahead," Heather said, "try it. But excuse me now. That's all the time we have for today."

BACK IN THE STUDIO, without Natassia in the corner sending a shadow onto the floor, Mary felt good. She felt so good she felt guilty about feeling so good. She was actually glad to be with the Hiliard students. And away from her daughter for a while. "That's okay, Mary," said Dr. Cather's voice, "it's normal."

"I still love her, you know."

"Of course, Mary, that's very clear."

After every class and at mid-class break, Mary called Natassia. Once when she called, Natassia said, out of the blue, "Mom, you know that day when I made a scene in your class and messed everything up?"

"You didn't make a scene. You didn't mess up."

"It was the music that got me. That Sarah Vaughan, when she's singing 'Every Time We Say Goodbye.' He used to listen to that exact same CD all the time. You know, when I was at his place? It really weirded me out when you played that."

"I'm sorry," Mary said. *How the hell could I know that? You never even told me his name.*

"You didn't know, Mom. It's not your fault."

AND THEN, one afternoon, Natassia and Mary were sitting in Claudia's car in the parking lot of the drugstore, waiting for a prescription to be filled (an antibiotic old Dr. Jonson had prescribed for the earache). Since some Hiliard School kids were in the drugstore, Natassia had insisted on waiting in the car, and now, slouching in the passenger seat, she turned to face her mother and said, "Mom? I'm still really embarrassed about what happened that day in your class. I'm so mad—"

"There's no need to—"

"Shush," Natassia insisted, "let me talk. Please. It's like this." Mary turned in her seat and looked at Natassia, whose limbs seemed particularly long when the two of them were packed into the little Mazda. "Before I start crying and stuff, I tell myself, Don't. But then it's like I don't have a choice, it's like it's a physical thing. I don't know how to control what's inside me."

Mary took hold of Natassia's big hands, kneaded them. "Honey, do you want me to call your therapist? Maybe you should tell her all this. Or Nora, should we call Nora?"

Impatient, Natassia turned away. "Thanks a lot."

"No. No." Mary kept hold of Natassia's hands. "It's just . . . I'm scared. Natassia, how can I say this? I want you to tell me anything, anything, but I'm not trained—"

"It all sounds sick and abnormal to you, doesn't it?"

"No! It sounds sad. Here you are, this extraordinary person—"

"And you've never felt this? That's what I need to know." Natassia was looking out at the rain, her face so worried. "How abnormal am I, Mom?"

Mary shook Natassia's shoulder. "You're *better* than normal."

"So, then, you've felt like this? Like you're worthless, like you're stupid, like you're ashamed of yourself, you're unlovable, that no matter what you do—"

"Oh no. No." Mary had to hug Natassia even though the gearshift was poking them both. "Yes, I feel all those things, but I wanted you to never feel them."

"You *do* feel it?"

"I feel it almost all the time."

Natassia gave in to her mother's hug, let herself droop into Mary's arms. "What do you do about it?" Natassia asked softly.

"I don't know." Mary, too, spoke softly. When she opened her eyes, she was staring into the dark, wiggly mass of Natassia's hair, which looked like the exposed roots of plants the campus gardener had dug up from the garden a few days earlier; Natassia even smelled like fresh earth. "I guess I always . . . I don't know." The rain on the hood of the car was loud now. Mary had never felt so vulnerable, so naked. "I know I've never," Mary said, "been able to . . . say it out loud. Like you can."

"But you don't collapse and cry in public and make a fool of yourself. Maybe you feel this bad thing inside you, like you're worthless, but you're still successful."

"Successful?" Mary laughed, pulled away from their hug to see Natassia's face. "Honey, I just keep moving. I don't think I've ever known any-one as brave as you to sit and feel this shit and be able to talk about it."

In a tiny, tiny voice, Natassia said, "That's why I do it, Mom. That's why I tried to hurt myself with the matches, and with the Cuisinart." Mary's heart was beating too fast now. Natassia's eyes looked very scared, and then she slowly turned away from her mother so their eyes couldn't meet. "I never wanted to die, but I just had to punish myself for being such a, such an embarrassing person. Sometimes," Natassia insisted, "I'm so mad at myself for messing up."

"You don't mess up, honey. We're the ones who mess up."

"Who?"

"All of us. Me, your dad, all the adults around you."

"Mom, I know the BF's a jerk. I've known that for a long time. In my—"

Still facing Natassia, who wouldn't look at her, Mary said, "Listen, I have to say this. I'm sorry, Natassia. I'm sorrier than I can ever tell you. I'm just . . . I'm sorry."

"Okay." Natassia rolled her eyes again. "Okay, I know, listen, don't get mad."

"I won't get mad." Mary's tears were dripping off her upper lip, into her mouth.

"Promise? Okay. What happens is that in my head I know he's a jerk, but this thing happens in me, like a switch or something, and I start think-ing this other way, like, okay, he's really smart"—Mary desperately wanted to picture the man, but she didn't have one detail—"and maybe I'm not smart enough to keep his attention, or, like, I'm too boring."

"You are *not* boring." *Big, big bore* was the harshest criticism Lotte and David had for writers they didn't like. "You're not."

"But when I think it, then I am. And I think it so much, I really feel detestable."

"Oh, Natassia." *She's just like me.* Mary pictured the man very tall, very dark, like Ross. "You have every reason to believe—God, Natassia, you are an amazing person. Everyone says so. Nora and Giulia, and now even Claudia, they're always saying it. I don't know how to tell you enough that you're . . . special."

Natassia made an embarrassed face. "I let my hair get really dirty some-times."

She was trying to lighten up, which made Mary feel worse. But she had to follow Natassia's lead. "Sometimes you snore a bit, too. Aside from that, you're perfect."

Natassia shrugged. "If you say so."

Mimicking the words Ross had poured into her ear so often during the years—in bed, over the phone, even sometimes during a fight—Mary said, "You can't give in to all that bad feeling about yourself."

"I know, or I'll end up like Dad. How he keeps stopping drinking, then he starts again. Like now. He's drinking again, isn't he? Maybe he's smoking pot again."

"He called the other night. He wanted to talk to you, but you were asleep."

"I know," Natassia said. "I heard you."

NATASSIA WAS by now spending most of her days on the computer. "What are you writing?" Mary asked.

"Nothing. Is there somewhere at this stupid school where I can print this out?"

Mary took her to the computer lab. Natassia knew what to do. She printed out fifty-three pages. That night, while Natassia slept, Mary snooped. The pages were gathered in a pink manila folder tucked inside Natassia's suitcase, which was in a back bedroom that Natassia now used as her writing room. What Mary found in the folder was a chronicle of Natassia's romance, starting with day one. Mary finally learned everything about the BF.

He was in his early thirties (Natassia didn't know exactly how old); a widower; Soviet; from Tbilisi, Georgia; Jewish. He'd been married to a painter who'd died—he wouldn't tell Natassia the facts, but he implied that it was a bad death. Natassia had met him in the Quad movie theater, on Thirteenth Street, when she'd gone with some friends to see some foreign movie Mary had never heard of. He couldn't believe such young girls were interested in French films, so afterward he'd invited them for coffee. Mariah had to pretend she liked coffee, *which she detests*, Natassia had written. But the guy, apparently, didn't care about Mariah. For a week, he'd telephoned Natassia every night *to practice his English*. They talked for hours. He begged her to go to Brighton Beach with him. She finally said yes. He took her to a Russian restaurant, and they danced on the tables. He drank too much, and she had to get herself to the subway, ride to the Upper West Side alone. *Mom would kill me if she knew.* That one sentence gave Mary some relief but not much.

As she read, Mary kept thinking, Where were Lotte and David? Then, in the entry for day twelve, Natassia answered Mary's question: *My grandparents thought I was spending the night at Mariah's.* The man didn't know how old Natassia was. She made him guess and never told him if he was correct. *Since I live uptown and because I've read so many books, he decided I go to Barnard or Columbia.* How convenient for him, Mary thought.

After the night at Brighton Beach when he got drunk, he wanted to make it up to Natassia. Two nights later, he took her back to Brooklyn, out to dinner and to an art show in a loft in Red Hook. Wasn't there anyone there who recognized her? Mary wondered. Nora, Christopher, Ross—they all had friends in Red Hook. Apparently, in Tbilisi he'd been a sculptor. *He hardly wanted to look at the artwork,* Natassia wrote. *He said he just wanted to look at me.*

He took her back to his apartment in the East Village that night. She went with him willingly. He still didn't know how old she was. That was the night the sex started.

All the details were there. His hands, the hair on his chest, his mouth all over Mary's young daughter. *I felt so much older,* Natassia wrote, *but also like I was a kid rolling around in the ocean when there's waves.* The fifty-three pages covered only the first month of their intimacy. Mary was glad; she couldn't have taken any more.

She put the pink folder back into the suitcase, slipped into bed. Natassia was asleep next to her. Mary lay awake all night. *Everything I did wrong, she's doing. Everything I didn't want her to do. This is my worst nightmare. I never wanted her to be like me.*

OVER THE NEXT DAYS, Natassia kept writing, typing on the laptop, running up to the computer lab to print out her pages. The pink folder got fatter.

"What should I do?" Mary asked Dr. Cather on the phone.

"Let her write. Maybe she's just getting the whole experience out of her system."

By now they had made it to the first week in November. Natassia actually seemed a bit happier. Her appetite improved, and Mary tried to believe this was progress.

Until one Saturday, when the phone bill arrived in the mail. Two calls to Manhattan, a number she didn't recognize. Mary dialed; a man's answering machine, an accented voice. No name, just the gruff command "If you are calling for the lessons of Russian, give me your number. I will call you." Then a grudging "Thank you" and then the beep. Mary hung up and called back. And called again. And again. She heard everything in his message—the ruthlessness, cruelty. She heard approaching middle age, she heard despair. She imagined she heard the need for a green card.

Mary spent an hour choreographing in the studio, lots of combative movement. What the fuck was she supposed to do next? When she got to the cottage, Natassia was lying on the couch reading a big, fat, pretentious book. Mary, unlit cigarette in hand, stood at the foot of the couch. "Natassia, you called him. The calls are on my phone bill."

"I'll pay you back," she said without looking away from her book.

"That's not the problem. Why'd you call him?"

"He called me." Natassia still hid behind the book, as if she and her mother had never talked face-to-face, crying, in the intimacy of that rained-upon Mazda.

"How'd he know where to reach you?" No answer. "You called him first, didn't you? Don't you understand you've been sick, really sick? And this man had something to do with you being sick."

"Mom, he wants to get back together again. You should have heard his voice, how happy he was when he heard me." Natassia rested the book on her chest and smiled at the ceiling. "We love each other. This is real, Mom. I told him I'd be in the city next weekend."

Mary had no idea what to do.

"I guess," Natassia said, turning to her book, "I'll get the train Friday afternoon."

I have to do something. Mary walked away. By the time she reached the kitchen archway, she heard herself saying, "Good, I'm looking forward to meeting him."

Natassia finally sat up. "You're not coming."

"Natassia, if you go, I go. After everything that's gone on, we're all involved with this man. It's time someone else in the family met him. I'll be with you. If you decide to see him." Mary was conscious of giving Natassia an escape hatch. Mary imagined Cather telling her, Well done.

NOBODY SAW HIM, neither Natassia nor Mary. The BF didn't call Natassia on Sunday, as he had said he would, to confirm their plan to get together. On Tuesday, when she tried to call him, there was no answer. On Wednesday, Natassia yelled at Mary because they were out of English muffins, told Mary she hated her. On Thursday morning, Mary had to cancel class to stay in the cottage with Natassia, who was having another crying jag. On Thursday afternoon, Natassia had a double session with Dr. Jamison Jonson.

Friday morning, Natassia was still determined to go to the city, still trying to reach the BF on the phone while she tossed clothes into a canvas bag. Mary pulled out her backpack and started packing, too. Then Natassia dialed the BF once more, and a young man answered and told Natassia that his uncle had gone away on a business trip and that he'd be gone for a while.

"Where did he go? When will he be back? I was supposed to see him today," she said urgently into the phone.

After a few minutes, she hung up. Quietly, in a voice so full of adult bitterness it scared Mary, Natassia cursed, "Bas-tard." She stared at the phone.

"Who'd you talk to?" Mary asked.

"Some guy said he was his nephew."

"What did the nephew say?"

This was the instant everything changed. Natassia looked Mary full in the face a long time, so Mary saw for herself the moment Natassia decided to be sane. "You want to know what the nephew said?" Natassia burst into giggles that crescendoed into huge laughs, and when she spoke again her voice was full of a fake Russian accent. "He said, 'I am not knowing when he is back. Is maybe for big long time.' "

Mary understood the game right away. "Big long time?"

"*Da.* Big long time."

They laughed so hard it was beyond laughter, it was pain in the gut, and they had to walk around the room holding themselves, trying to stop. The rest of Friday and all through the weekend, they spoke in exaggerated Russian accents. Every time they looked at each other, they laughed.

A WEEK PASSED before Mary could bring up with Dr. Cather all the things that Natassia had said in the Mazda that rainy afternoon she spelled out the mess inside herself. "It's so weird," Mary told Cather over the phone. "Everything I ever felt inside that I tried to hide from her, she said it." Sitting in her office with the phone receiver to her ear, Mary found herself weeping. She stood up, turned out the overhead light so no one would knock on her door. Deep-breathing, she sat at her desk.

Cather spoke softly: "Especially with our daughters, Mary. They often bring us to the self we've tried to run from."

"You, too?" Mary asked.

"All of us."

What Mary couldn't understand was this: if she, as Natassia's mother, had been the originator of this bad feeling, why hadn't she, Mary, ever tried to kill herself or hurt herself the way Natassia had? "Why's it more intense in her?"

"I wouldn't say it's more intense in Natassia. Perhaps it's just been more hidden in you. Perhaps you never felt you could vent it, or show it. Maybe what you did instead of self-mutilation was have the abortions. That couldn't have been fun for you."

"It makes me so mad when people say that if you're not anti-abortion you're pro-abortion. Nobody's pro-abortion. It was bad, really bad, every time."

"And also, maybe you didn't act out as Natassia has because you didn't feel anyone would come to help you, the way Natassia knows you will help her."

Mary had to admit that Cather was seeming smarter these days.

Natassia abandoned her chronicle of her love affair with the BF—the last
fifteen days were simply sketched in—and she began to write poetry. She
didn't show any of it to Mary, but she left pages where Mary could find
them. First, Mary found two poems:

ASSHOLE
If I were your
mother I think
I'd have to tell you something
like, it's time to grow up.
I'd say, I'm sorry
I died when you were ten
and your father was so mean
a man and all that, but come on,
it's time to pay your electric bill.
Get a job.

MY BOYFRIEND
The way he kissed me
with his mouth

was like an ocean.
I put my face against
wild wind from
an electric fan the other day
and I remembered his lips
on my eyes.

Mary copied the poems down, word for word, and one afternoon she went to find Claudia in her classroom. "Natassia wrote these. Are they any good?"

Claudia was the kind of no-bullshit person Mary liked. She had a son in the Peace Corps someplace dicey, so the mess with Natassia didn't make her flinch. On her way out the door for the day, Claudia had her poncho on and her book bags hanging around her shoulders, but she squeezed herself into one of the student desks and read the two poems and said, "Hmm."

"What? They're bad?" Mary asked. "They're good? Yeah? Why're they good?"

"They're playful. They're spare. They're full of moments." Claudia lifted her glasses onto the top of her head. "She's good."

"Don't say a thing to her. She doesn't know I look through her stuff."

"So I can't include these in the school literary magazine?" Claudia laughed her huge I-don't-give-a-fuck-who-hears-me laugh.

Mary gritted her teeth and said, "Don't even *think* that thought, don't you dare."

"Don't get too heady," Dr. Cather warned when Mary recited the poems over the phone, "about these early signs of progress. It's definitely progress. It's good. She wants to live, that's what I hear in her poems. But she's still deeply hurt and in need of deep, deep healing. You're sure you feel comfortable with the counseling she's getting up there?"

"HEATHER JAMISON JONSON. Heather Jamison Jonson." Natassia was saying it over and over as Mary drove her to the yellow clapboard house on the hill for her Tuesday appointment. Autumn had become more serious, the heater was up high in Claudia's Mazda. "Heather Jamison Jonson."

"Why do you keep saying her name?" Mary asked.

"It's my mantra. It soothes me."

"It does, does it?" Mary laughed. Since they'd upped Natassia's therapy to two visits each week, Natassia had become almost jolly. For stretches of a couple hours, especially on therapy days, she'd be silly. Now that Mary had learned how to get reimbursed from the insurance company for these expenses, she'd cheered up considerably herself. "What does Heather do that makes you so happy?"

"It's not Heather, Mom. It's Heather Jamison Jonson. You have to say the whole name for the mantra to work. Like this." She closed her eyes, placed her hands palm-upward on her knees. "You say, 'Heather Jamison Jonson, Heather Jamison—' "

From the car, Mary watched Natassia skip up the long stone stairway to Heather Jamison Jonson's house. Ten days had passed since Natassia had turned the corner away from heartbreak. Mary's anxiety was easing up a bit, but her moods were largely defined by what she found in Natassia's journal, the ongoing story of her daughter's secret former life. Mary was relieved that Natassia was no longer addressing her journal to *him*. These days there were poems and lots of talk about HJJ, Natassia's abbreviation for Heather Jamison Jonson. But then, one night, late, Mary turned back a big chunk of pages and landed on one of those early entries that were nothing but a love song to the BF.

> *Oct. 25, 9 p.m.*
>
> *By now you're probably forgetting I ever existed. I don't forget. I think about how you brought me things to eat on that little plastic tray with the picture of Miami Beach on it and you said we'd go there when we got married. After we made love once you brought me small purple grapes and you even popped the pulp into my mouth and then you sucked the skin and you kissed me and we slid the purple skin back and forth between our mouths with our tongues. And by then, whenever I felt your tongue, it was automatic that I needed to touch your penis, too. Your tongue stroked my tongue and then we were making love again. Just because of those pulpy purple grapes, tiny globes. Wine.*

With the pink folder on her lap, Mary forced herself to realize that, together with Lotte, David, and Ross, she had let a fifteen-year-old girl run around New York City at night. They had known—all of them had *known*—that Natassia was out with a *man*, and they'd done nothing to stop her. But when Mary read the October 25, 9 p.m. entry, she saw that even though all four of the adults had failed to protect Natassia—failed to a miserable, possibly criminal, degree—there had been something happening in Natassia that could not have been stopped even if they had tried. Natassia, just like her mother, was ultra-alive in her body. And also there was this: art. Somewhere along the line, the kid really had turned into a writer.

CHAPTER 21:

DECEMBER

1989

One night in early December, as she slept, Nora heard a voice. It was just twenty minutes after she'd turned out her bedside lamp and fallen quickly into her first bout of sleep (blessedly, thoughts of Abe were calming her nights), but then, half awake and shifting her sleep position, she heard a friendly domestic voice calling to her, saying, "No-RA," a male voice with no hint of harm in it but demanding enough that it seemed to expect an answer, and she almost called out, "Yes?"

Nora knew she was alone in the loft. Christopher hadn't slept at home in weeks. Slowly, warily, she reached over to turn the lamp on, then, sitting up, she woke enough to realize that if she did call out and got an answer she'd be in real trouble.

The voice didn't call out again, but *No-RA* echoed in her ear. A little terrified but also curious, she picked up cuticle scissors, small defense, and ventured out into the open space of the loft, switching on overheads to light up the corners ahead of her. Into the living space, into Christopher's studio. In the bathroom the many clocks ticked. Nothing out of place. Nora was relieved but also a little bit sad not to find anyone. *Was it a dream?* That she might have imagined the voice made Nora feel unsure of herself, almost feeble. That she might be wishing so hard for companionship she had begun to hallucinate voices—that was almost scarier than the thought of someone entering while she slept.

WHEN NORA WOKE the next morning, she wasn't rested. Her dreams had been about trying to get to sleep. She pulled open the heavy damask curtain and looked out the filthy window next to the bed. Slushy rain. Unable to decide whether to rain or snow, the day was as full of doubt as she was. It was December 5, and at the end of the workday she was meeting Christopher "to talk." Relying completely on the personal-memo feature of their answering machine, never actually talking to each other, they'd made this date over a week ago. It had become embarrassingly clear that they had to make some plans.

Sometimes Nora wondered what Christopher's secret life was. They hadn't set eyes on each other in over two weeks. Thanksgiving they had ignored until the very last minute, then he'd left a message saying he had to work on the Nyack job, and Nora had spent the day moving office files into a new file cabinet. No turkey.

She knew that on weekdays, while she was at her office, Christopher went to the loft. He'd take his mail, do laundry. Sometimes he left a check to pay for utilities. It seemed that he slept either in his studio or up at the work site in Nyack. That's what he told her. But a friend of theirs had seen him doing a carpentry job in the West Village. He'd never told Nora about that job; she never saw evidence of it in their joint accounts. What was really strange, though, was that over a year ago Christopher had sworn off doing construction work. He used to do a lot of setup construction in galleries, interior work in lofts and brownstones, but it started getting to him that everybody he worked with was about ten years younger than he was and hopeful. Or else they were fifteen years older than Christopher and stuck for good. So he'd decided to make a big push to get more freelance illustration work. And he did get the illustration jobs. He was good. Mostly, he did drawings for medical journals, and those checks were still coming in, but now he was taking construction jobs again. And what was he doing with the extra money?

His gallery in Connecticut had sold two paintings; the gallery owner

had left a message on the answering machine asking him to call back. Nora
had "accidentally" erased the message, then (such a scatterbrain!) forgotten
to leave a note about the call. *Passive-aggressive? Damn right I'm being passive-
aggressive.* The check from the gallery was in a pile of mail she had to bring
for him tonight, but she would ask no questions. If Nora pressed Christopher for details, she might have to reveal something of her own secret life.

By now Nora was getting together with Abe a couple times a week,
and she was scared. Not about losing or damaging her marriage, but about
the way she was flirting with an edge she'd never dared push against so
hard, not wanting to disrupt her pact with the universe and send Christopher's—and her—secret spilling. *I want more, I want more.* More Abe? More
sex? Nora had no idea, just a solid feeling in her gut that Abe was essential.
First of all, there were the particulars of his looks. Whenever an empty
moment was available—riding the subway, walking home from work—
Nora loved saying to herself, *Here's what Abe looks like.*

He had a smashed-in nose that she eventually wanted to ask him about,
but something told her he'd then ask about her white hair, and she didn't
want to tell her usual lie: "Delayed grief, my parents' deaths." Abe was
balding at the forehead. (The only time she'd see him with his hair untied
was that rainy Saturday she'd run into him at the restaurant.) A mustache
and goatee now (he said he changed his facial hair every winter), and his
lips were lost within the darkness of all that busy hair. Small round wire-
framed lenses glinted a purplish bruised light. Nice wide hands. Whenever
Nora was late to meet him, she'd find him writing with a fountain pen in a
small rawhide notebook he carried in his pocket. His right index finger always had a black ink stain.

Eight weeks had passed since their first Thursday-night dinner at
Veselka. That night they'd talked from seven-thirty until ten-thirty, osten-
sibly waiting for Nora's husband to show up after his class at Cooper
Union. By nine-thirty, Abe began to wonder, "Where's your husband?"

"God, yeah, he's late. Sometimes when the students are pushing to finish
a project he stays on with them. I'm guessing that's what happened tonight."

"He sounds like he's a good teacher," Abe said.

A little jealous?

So Abe and Nora continued talking. He had told her all about his novel-in-progress, set in L.A. just before and during the McCarthy era, the story of a young man who comes from a long line of secret Jews and a white woman who discovers that a large portion of her genetic inheritance is African. Blond and pale, she's as much Negro as she is Caucasian, and he's a Southern Baptist who's really a Jew, and both the man and the woman are writers in Hollywood doing studio work and living on the fringes of the Red scare. Abe explained to Nora that, as his characters slowly revealed themselves to each other, their love story would be inter-mingled with sections of their ancestors' stories, which would explain how and why, generation by generation, these families had systematically hid-den who they were.

Nora was intrigued, of course, when Abe talked about his novel, for lots of reasons. And he was fired up by her interest in his work, she could tell. When he was excited, his Southern accent slipped in, and he looked less tired than usual. Outside, in front of the restaurant, saying goodbye, when she shook his hand, he lifted hers and kissed it.

The next Thursday, he was already at their table when Nora arrived. *He* was in pursuit now. Nora remembered from far back in her life, before Christopher, that it was time for her to tone down her interest, be quiet, let *him* draw *her* out. Sunday evening of that week, Nora and Abe went to see *Au Revoir les Enfants.* ("My husband hates foreign films; I'm always looking for somebody to go to them with me"), and during the movie, Abe's elbow found Nora's on the armrest, his black, worn-thin sweater sleeve next to the olive-green sleeve of Nora's Benetton cardigan, and stayed there, touching.

During these early meetings with Abe, Nora believed that her ambition was to move slowly, slowly toward making love with him. Every week, like the girlfriends he'd complained to her about, Nora tried to calculate if progress had been made. And she believed she felt no guilt because she was sure by now that Christopher was betraying her in some way. She could imagine nothing other than that he was having an affair. His secret life? Swindling money, taking drugs, selling drugs, gambling, dressing in women's clothes, joining a cult? She couldn't imagine any of it. Most likely he was having an affair. Nora was just glad that Christopher was occupied, not paying attention. These days, she felt her loyalty was with Abe. She wasn't sure what she and Christopher would have to talk about at dinner tonight.

CHRISTOPHER HAD SUGGESTED that they meet at an Indian place they liked on Sixth Street. "I'm tight on cash," he'd said. *Who're you spending your money on?*

Nora got to the restaurant ten minutes early, probably because she did feel a little guilty. Two nights earlier, Abe had complained about needing a place to live. He'd sublet his Brooklyn apartment so he could ease up on freelance work and have more time to write, but his next apartment-sitting gig wasn't until early January, so Nora had offered Abe the house in Greenport—without consulting Christopher or Kevin. "No one will be there," Nora had told Abe. "The place'll be all yours." And just now, before leaving work to come downtown to meet Christopher, she'd called Abe's machine and left a message, taking a liberty she'd never taken before in their relationship, assuming he'd want to get together with her: "I haven't seen *Babette's Feast* yet, have you? Thursday night?"

When she looked up from her menu and saw Christopher walking out of the crowd at the tight doorway, she thought, Oh yeah, him, my husband. Christopher was scanning the room for her, a frightened look on his face that made her feel sorry for him, almost. By the time he saw her, came to the table, bent to kiss her on the cheek, her sympathy had switched to anger. *What* are *you hiding from me?*

"Jesus," he said as he sat down, bunching his down jacket and stuffing it under his chair. Right away he drank from Nora's glass of water. "What a day."

"Yeah?" He was in work clothes, dusty with sawdust, but, as always, neat. His jeans were belted over his shirt, his sleeves rolled up, the cuffs even and sharply creased.

"Sorry I'm dirty," he said. "I wanted to change, but I didn't want to be late."

"That's okay."

He ordered a Rolling Rock. She ordered a Scotch. She handed him his mail. He leafed through quickly. Just as he saw the envelope from the gallery in Connecticut, she said, "I think there's something there from your gallery."

"Yeah," he said, and opened it up. "Great. A check."

"Big?"

"Big enough. Bigger than nothing. She never called me about this. There was no message from her, was there?" Nora shook her head as she gulped ice water. Christopher said, "That bitch. I made money for her, and she doesn't even call me."

"Which piece did she sell?" Nora asked.

"Actually, she sold two."

"Two? Wow. Well, congratulations." His beer bottle and her glass of Scotch met for a distracted toast over the squat candle at the center of the table. The waiter walked up. As Christopher ordered nan and a hot chicken curry, Nora thought, He's not telling me what the paintings sold for.

"And for you?" the waiter asked.

"I'll have the same curry, but with vegetables, no meat." When the waiter was gone, Nora told Christopher, "The elevator at the building's getting stuck mid-floor again."

"Yeah, I saw that the other day. You want me to call Tomas?"

"Yeah, and we'll have to figure out how much to give him for Christmas. Last year we gave him a hundred dollars and a bottle of vodka, but that year he watched the loft a lot while we were away."

"We can't give him less this year. Another hundred? I'll pick up a bottle?"

"Fair." Each time Nora glanced over at Christopher, she expected him to stop being handsome. But even with sawdust in his hair, he couldn't stop looking good. He was middle-aged, but his blue eyes held so much light they still sparked. Christopher would never escape the trap of his good looks; he'd never be interesting the way Abe was. Nora put her fork down on the edge of her plate of curry. "These vegetables tonight are dead," she said.

"Yeah, I can see. We got here late. Here, have this chicken. I can't eat any more."

They switched plates. He ordered another beer; she, a glass of Chardonnay.

Their Brazilian friend Tina had recently announced her engagement to her Italian boyfriend, and Nora and Christopher talked about that. A film-maker was negotiating to shoot a movie in one of the lofts in the building next door to Christopher and Nora's, so they talked about how much money the loft-owners might end up getting, what a traffic mess the filming would be for everyone else on the street.

Christopher reached across the table and took Nora's hand, wiggled her wedding rings. "You look nice," he said in a soft, hurt voice. "I miss you."

She stroked his hand with her thumb, wanting to be kind but not too reassuring. For a quick, strange moment, she worried, What if Abe were to walk in and see this?

Christopher dared to start: "Things are fucked up, Nor."

"Yeah." It was only in the pause afterward that she understood all that she had just acknowledged.

"What do you want to do?"

"What do *you* want to do?" she repeated, testing. If he said *separation*, would she say okay? If he said *divorce*, maybe even okay to that?

"Me?" Christopher laced his fingers through her fingers. "I want us to be normal again. I want us to be married."

"We are married."

"You know what I mean."

There was desire in his hand, something she had to stave off. "It seems like—"

"What?" he asked.

"Like we're both doing—going in these directions. Different. I mean, you seem to have a lot to do and—"

He jumped way ahead of her. "Do you think this is permanent?" He kept looking bruised, hurt, but Nora also realized he was saying nothing to alleviate her doubts, nothing to explain where he was going off to, what he was doing. All he said was what he'd said before. "I don't want us to not be married." He pushed aside plates and pulled Nora's hand and held it tight to his chest. "I love you. Look at me. I love you. I never stop loving you." When she said nothing, he asked, "Are you okay? Are you—all right these days?" What he meant was, Are you able to sleep, ride the subway, be alone in the loft?

"Yeah, I'm reasonably okay."

"Do you miss me?"

"Chris—"

"Just answer the question." He was squeezing two of her fingers.

"I miss—I don't know. I miss the good part of our marriage. But we both know we can't go back to how it was. There are problems, locked-in problems—"

"Is Natassia getting better?" *He brought it up himself.*

"I think so. She's still upstate with Mary. Mary never seems to have time to talk these days. Giulia's talked to her a few times. She says they're okay."

"Is she still depressed?"

"I think Mary found a therapist for her, but I don't know a lot. Mary never calls."

"Do they know what triggered it? With Natassia? Do they know why—"

He had never before asked so many questions in a row about Natassia. It crossed Nora's mind that maybe he could sense she was feeling cut off from her friends and he was rubbing it in. "If I knew anything about Natassia," Nora told Christopher, "I'd tell you."

"I'm not going to let you go, Nora. I'm not giving up."

He won't talk about Natassia anymore. "Things have to happen before—"

"I know, Nora, I know. Don't start."

How she hated that tone in his voice. "Can I ask, are you in therapy?"

"I'm taking care of things." He released her hand. "I'm doing what I have to do, and I'm doing it my way."

Now she remembered exactly why they were not together. "Well, Frank Sinatra, I guess I'm doing it my way, too."

"Good. Where's the waiter?" Christopher motioned him over and took the check from him. Nora tried to hand Christopher twenty dollars to pay for her dinner and drinks, but he shrugged her money away. "I got it," he said.

"Thanks."

"Listen. I need to stay over tonight. The heat's out at the studio. I'll use the couch."

"Yeah, you'll have to. The bedroom's a total mess with all my—"

"All I need is the couch. I just need to sleep. I'll be gone early."

"Nyack tomorrow?"

He nodded. "Early."

The way he answered, she knew that his secret, whatever it was, was in Nyack.

As they walked out of the restaurant, he held his hand on her back. Anyone watching would think they were a functioning couple.

AS NORA AND CHRISTOPHER WALKED HOME, the sidewalks were wet and slick, their footsteps echoey and loud, and within the noise Nora said, "I found someone who wants to rent Greenport for Christmas, and I told him okay."

Christopher was holding her hand as they walked. "I've been wanting to talk to you about Christmas."

"Yeah?" Afraid of hearing him say something sad, something like he wanted to spend it as they always did, together, with tons of people around, she said, "I'd kind of like to make separate plans this year."

"You do?" he asked, but he seemed more surprised than upset.

Up through a manhole cover, steam rose. "I think I'd like to go away," she said, "by myself."

He paused. Then paused some more. "Well," he finally said. "Okay, if that's what you want."

"We're going to have to let everyone know we're not doing Christmas Eve at the loft this year."

"Or New Year's Eve supper?" he asked.

"Right, or New Year's Eve supper."

"Okay," Christopher agreed.

"What will you do?" Nora asked him.

"I'll find something," he said.

LATER, as she lay sleepless in the bedroom, she heard him on the phone in the living room. Dialing lots of numbers, using his calling card. *Nyack.* She heard him ask, "Everything okay? No change?" She heard, "Early train in the morning." She heard, "Take care. Call me if there's a problem."

An overnight problem for a house-remodeling job?

After a while, Christopher came and stood at the door of the bedroom.

"You're awake. I can tell," he said. And Nora could tell he was standing in the doorway with his hands in the back pockets of his jeans, looking down at the floor. He said, "About Christmas. I wanted to say it myself, but you were the brave one to say it first."

"So you want it separate, too?" Nora asked, and she felt shaky with sadness and had to work to stay very still underneath the comforter.

"Yeah, I do want it separate. This year I do."

He came to the bed, lay down next to her; they turned to each other, and for the first time all night they hugged. Once that familiar world of body, scent, touch was created, Nora's emotions changed course abruptly. "I'm scared, Christopher," she whispered into his salty neck. "I'm so scared."

"Me, too, Nora. Me, too."

The next morning, he left before her alarm went off at seven o'clock. Without waking Nora, he had packed a duffel bag. When he bent to kiss her, she woke slightly. More asleep than awake, she barely saw him leaving the bedroom, wearing his big down jacket, carrying his bag full of clothes.

LATER THAT MORNING, after her ten-fifteen appointment, Nora found a message from Abe on the machine in her office. He was free Thursday night, and, yes, he wanted to go with her to see *Babette's Feast*. Nora and Abe hadn't slept together yet. She hadn't brought him into the loft yet (just the thought still made her squeamish), but the relationship seemed to her to be progressing favorably.

EVERY DAY, Nora dressed thinking of Abe. Shopping or cooking or washing dishes, she thought of him. Thinking of him, she showered. At her office, in between appointments, she replayed his telephone messages.

Wednesday evening, with less than twenty-four hours until she saw Abe again, Nora decided to go through her closet and drawers to finally switch her warm-weather and cold-weather clothes. With Christopher no longer straightening out the bedroom, Nora was having troubles in the morning finding something to wear.

Also, a lot of her clothes no longer fit.

By now Nora understood that her eating was out of control, and that the body she had had—and been envied for—was gone.

She loaded the CD player with a Billie Holiday CD Mary had given them for Christmas the year before, and two Bonnie Raitt albums. She turned the volume up and started clearing out the farthest end of her closet, where she found a half-dozen pairs of rumpled black pants on the floor, including size-two jeans. The only pants on the floor that still fit were polyester, and Nora had no idea how they had arrived in her closet.

Nora forced herself to try on every item hanging there. Anything that no longer fit (hardly anything fit, just a few elastic-waistband silk skirts and the long tunics that went with them) she folded into black plastic garbage bags to give to the cancer thrift shop. In a shopping bag she stacked four long wool skinny skirts and two cropped sweaters to give to Natassia. Then Nora hauled all the bags across the loft and into Christopher's studio.

It was past midnight when she finished her work. Miraculously, she'd worked for hours without eating a thing. She rewarded herself with a very full glass of Chardonnay, an expensive bottle Christopher had stored high on a top shelf of the kitchen, probably saving it for Christmas. Wrapped in the robe Kevin had given her, she sat in the corner of the couch, her perch, her safe spot, and wrote in her journal, *I am eating large quantities of food, and the eating is changing my body.*

Just this afternoon, her pregnant patient, the single woman who had decided to keep her baby, had stood to show Nora the outfit she intended to wear to disguise her pregnancy at her family's annual holiday party. "My parents are getting older. I don't want them worrying any sooner than they have to. My brothers, too." She stood sideways, her long, flowing jacket hanging gently over her flowing pants; a bright-patterned scarf draped over the jacket diverted the eye from the woman's waist. She was six months pregnant now, having successfully distanced herself from the baby's father, who'd lost interest in the baby when his wife began talking about divorce. The mother-to-be was now using her sessions to prepare for single motherhood. "This doesn't look pregnant, does it?"

"It's a very nice outfit," Nora said.

"Yeah, I got the layering idea from you." The woman sat down again, looked at Nora for a long beat of silence, until she finally said, "Would it be okay if I asked you a question about yourself? Yes? Well, I'm wondering, are you, by chance, pregnant?"

Maybe, in gaining so much weight, Nora was testing herself, "trying on" pregnancy—so she could then reject it? Whatever her body was trying to accomplish, it certainly was forcing the question *Are you pregnant?* Perhaps a more useful question was *Are you going to have a baby?* As in *Ever?* Sitting on the couch, Nora asked herself out loud, "Am I ever going to have a child of my own?" Christopher had forced that question for so long, maybe Nora was finally giving herself a chance to—literally—hold the question within her body. Or maybe she was just dissing him: *Here, you want pregnant, I'll give you a pregnant wife, fat and thick and hungry for junk food.*

THE NEXT NIGHT, as Nora and Abe were leaving the theater, there was a lot to say about *Babette's Feast*, but he interrupted himself and said, "You really need to see the view from this place I'm staying in. You can see the river." I'd be a fool, Nora thought, to say no. As they walked from the Village all the way up to Gramercy Park, the blocks passed quickly. Nora was trying to avoid stepping into puddles; Abe walked right through them in his thick-soled boots. Animated, talking all over each other, they listed the scenes they'd liked best, the shots they'd admired. And then they were standing in front of an elegant doorman building and Abe was saying, "This is it. Come on, I'll make some tea."

When they got upstairs, it wasn't just an apartment, it was a penthouse, with a terrace and lots of fancy landscaping. "How do you know these people?" she asked him.

"Don't ask," he told her. He was digging around in a tall walnut bookcase. "Do you really want tea? I just found some nice Scotch here."

"We can't drink their Scotch."

"Yeah, we can. I'll replace it before I leave."

About a week earlier, in a restaurant, Nora had begun to tell Abe a little of the truth of her marriage, that she and her husband were living different lives, and so it only made sense now to fill him in on what she and Christopher had decided on Tuesday night about spending the holidays apart.

"So you're separated?" he asked.

"Not in any official way," Nora said, "but, well—"

"But if he knew you were here with me now, it wouldn't be completely cool, would it?" They were sitting on the floor in front of a gas fireplace. Abe was fingering the bands on the fourth finger of Nora's left hand. "Is something here a wedding ring?"

"One is. Lots of them aren't," Nora said. "The wedding ring is the smallest one."

Abe gently left Nora's hand in her lap and, leaning against the far end of the couch, began to talk about his Ava. They were still seeing each other, though she wasn't very happy with him. Next, Abe brought up another woman, a political scientist who was in Prague on a Fulbright. *All his romances involve women with high-profile careers.* Out in this new world, away from Christopher, Nora was being forced to deal with a lot of successful women. She didn't like that.

But Nora put in her time, listened, because, as he talked, Abe was doing things all over her with his eyes. When Nora yawned and stretched out on the rug just under a skylight, Abe followed her. He lay on his side next to her, leaning on his elbow, looking at her, not touching, but it was like being touched. She ached.

And, eventually, Abe got to the unhappy part of the story about his romance with the woman in Prague: she had begun to feel he was using her and her life to provide details for the characters of his novel. "She understood zilch about the creative process, nothing about intuition. It was all empirical knowledge with her. I hate it when you come up against the limits of an intelligent woman's intelligence."

How about an intelligent man's limits? But by now Abe was leaning over her, saying, "At least with you, you get it about people. You're willing to host the chaos."

Yeah?

Abe continued, "You're not reductive, you're not simplistic. You got the stomach for contradiction." He brushed his lips against hers. "Ambivalence." And there was a kiss, and then deeper kisses, then Nora's shirt unbuttoned, and then Abe was pulling away, saying, "But you're married," and he stopped.

No! Come back!

By now it was close to midnight. Nora was lying on the rug, watching Abe sit up, grimace with an ache in his back. She loved the cigarette taste Abe's kisses had left in her mouth. He was sitting a bit away now, but she could reach him with her foot. As he yawned and stretched, she ran her toes up his side and under his arm.

"Don't," he said, grabbing her wool-socked foot.

"Why?"

He tried to tell her it was a guy thing, he didn't believe in poaching on another guy's wife. She listened. And then they were kissing again, his big left hand cupping her breast, enjoying the size of it. He didn't mind her new thickness, she could tell. To him, it wasn't new. It was her—Nora now. *I'm not the Nora that Christopher fell in love with.* With this thought, she felt very free. Abe was fingering her nipple. "Then what do you call this," Nora whispered, smiling, "what you're doing? This isn't poaching?" Abe liked that. He growled and squeezed her breast and kissed her neck. She remembered, from her teenage dating life, that if she intended to go home, now would be a good time to quit.

Abe took Nora downstairs to get a cab. They stood out in front of his building, kissing and groping as taxi after taxi passed them.

A FEW DAYS LATER, Abe wanted to go to the movies again. *Cinema Paradiso.* His body and his tongue and his mouth—Nora had thought about nothing else since the evening at Gramercy Park. But when she greeted him in front of the theater with a quick kiss, Abe was withdrawn, unresponsive.

The movie alternately enthralled him and repulsed him ("sentimental nonsense"), and he held Nora's hand limply. Finally, they were back at the penthouse, under the skylight, Scotch in hand. Nora hadn't worn a bra, and she'd worn new lace underpants, but Abe discovered none of that. He lay beside her, not looking at her, not doing what he was able to do to her with his eyes. He treated her like a friend, talking about the movie, talking, talking. He was rereading *The Unbearable Lightness of Being,* and he talked about how sexy the book was. He was thinking of having a character in his novel be a therapist, and he asked all about her training. The evening was going nowhere, and eventually Nora feel asleep.

AT SOME POINT he had covered her with a blanket, put a pillow under her head; the next morning, that's how she found herself. And walking toward her with a mug of coffee was Abe, his hair already tied back and his eyeglasses on.

"Good," she said, sipping from some stranger's mug.

"There's nothing to eat," he told her.

"That's okay," she said, and, oddly, the thought came to her that he still hadn't asked her why her hair was all white.

Abe sat in the low chair close to where Nora lay on the floor. She could look up the loose legs of his boxers. She saw his leg hair thicken. The plaid cotton bulge of his groin—and she had an erotic jolt so potent she reached out and wrapped her hand around his ankle, pulled herself up. Then she did what she would have done with her husband. By the time she thought about it, she was already doing it, running her hands up Abe's legs. She felt unbearable desire for Abe's newness, and also for the familiar touch of male skin. She hadn't made love in two and a half months. Nora knew herself well enough to know she wasn't going to stop what she was feeling and doing.

She was rubbing up his legs. Her face went to his lap, and she breathed lightly on the inside of his thigh. Breathed lightly, then brushed there with her lips, a lick. His thigh. Licked his knee, the other knee. He wouldn't let her linger long there, he pulled her up and kissed her face. Her hand went inside his shorts; everything was loose, and both her hands held him, rubbing him up and down. Abe was lifting off Nora's sweater, but she wasn't paying attention. He lifted her, but now she was urgent, she climbed onto his lap.

Still in her jeans, she straddled him, felt him through the jeans. Her breasts were in his mouth, his face in her chest, his hands rubbing her back. She arched; her eyes, when they opened, looked up at a skylight. "Too much," she murmured, but she was already coming, pushing and pushing against him. While her back arched, his big hands cupped her armpits. "Come on, baby," he whispered. Big bouquets of orgasm were rising up and breaking into shouts, and he rubbed his hands into the backside of her jeans. He was still hard and she was still rubbing, and the second orgasm surprised them both. She was calling out again. He leaned her down onto the carpet and let her slide him out of his underwear, off with his T-shirt. "Your body," she whispered. He was so much of everything Christopher was not. Kind of sloppy, a bit of a hairy paunch, a deeper scent, firmer hands. Calmer. Not so eager, a bit detached. Christopher's immersion in Nora when they made love was complete, deep; but this, with Abe—

Abe never came. When he was naked, Nora touched him, wrapped her hand around him, but he began to fade from her, and she was aware of how thick her waist was, how heavy her thighs. "That was great," she told him, "what you did to me."

"You needed that," he told her gently.

"I needed that," she echoed in a whisper. He had let her have her utter pleasure, without taking any for himself. It wasn't until later in the day, when she was sitting in a session struggling to listen to a patient, that the thought crossed Nora's mind that maybe Abe wasn't all that attracted to her.

TWO DAYS LATER, at home, while she was emptying the dishwasher from a week's worth of dishes, another thought occurred to Nora. If she'd been with Christopher and fallen asleep on the floor, he never would have let her spend the whole night down there, the way Abe did. Christopher would have done something—lifted her and carried her if he had to—to make sure she spent the night in a comfortable bed.

But then she forgot about all that. She had to get ready quickly to get to the restaurant on time to meet Abe.

What if I hadn't made it on time? Christopher was standing in the operating room watching Denise, who was lying on the operating table. The attending physician was the one doctor Denise had hoped would not deliver the baby, but that's who was on call, Dr. Baerent, who had just announced, "I'm doing a cesarean."

It was five o'clock in the afternoon, Wednesday, December 6, ten days before Denise's due date. Earlier, when Christopher had arrived in Nyack, Denise was in excruciating pain, back-to-back contractions that lasted a long time. Then she began to bleed. Christopher immediately called the doctor's office and rushed Denise to the hospital, and there was Dr. Baerent, waiting. She examined Denise and said it seemed the baby had somehow turned and put his little hand through the amniotic sac. On the external heart monitors, both the baby's and Denise's heart rates were lowering. And the next thing Christopher knew, a nurse was shaving Denise's pubic hair to prepare her for surgery. A couple weeks earlier, Denise had told Christopher she'd read that the shaving wasn't necessary for delivery and she didn't want it done, but when they started shaving, Denise said nothing.

"Okay, Denise," the nurse said, "now I'm inserting a catheter into the urethra to empty your bladder."

"Can't she just . . ." Christopher heard his voice sounding as afraid as a boy's. Calm down, he told himself. "Couldn't she make it into the bath-room? Or get a bedpan?"

"Too late, honey," another nurse told him. "From now on, we'll need her as still as possible. Hear me, Denise?" This nurse was inserting an IV needle into the top of Denise's right hand. Christopher watched the nurse tape the tube down and then cover Denise's hand with a white fishnet glove, which looked like a Michael Jackson accessory and gave Christo-pher the creeps.

He had studied photographs of these procedures. He'd even done drawings for an article in a paramedics' newsletter on how to insert an IV needle, but now, watching, Christopher felt a humming shock.

For the past two months, Denise had been practicing her breathing with Christopher and with friends of hers who had planned to be in the birthing room during the delivery. Now no one was focusing on Denise's breathing; they were all busy with tubes. None of Denise's support group was here, just him.

A tiny red alarm buzzed on the IV pole. "What?" Christopher de-manded, too loudly, and Denise echoed, "What?"

"Hey, calm down, you two. What, you never had a baby before? My little IV soldier here isn't cooperating." The nurse pushed buttons, patted Denise's arm. "Not to worry."

It got worse. Christopher was watching them begin to attach the inter-nal fetal monitor. "How will that monitor find the baby's heartbeat?"

"Tiny screw," whispered a nurse next to Christopher, "screws into the baby's head." Christopher had to sit down. "Don't worry, Dad, really. They do it all the time."

When he looked up, someone was adjusting an elastic strap around Denise's thigh to gather up and hold the wires from the fetal monitor. A blood-pressure cuff was attached to Denise's arm. They were conducting a perverse bondage ritual. *She's in a sci-fi movie.*

Watching Denise, Christopher saw it in her face, the disappointment. Denise hadn't wanted any of this—the IV, the nurses, the drugs. In *The New Our Bodies, Ourselves*, another of Denise's bibles, the childbirth chapter said that, without the interference of an IV, the mother in labor is free to drink fruit juice and tea with honey. Since the lying-down position works against gravity, the mother should walk around, squat, take a shower, ask people to hold her, rub her, massage her. Christopher had been apprehensive about the holding, rubbing, massaging; he had counted on the neighborhood friends to do that. But, in general, he'd understood the kind of delivery Denise had had in mind.

Now this. A screen was put up below Denise's shoulders so she couldn't watch what was happening, but Christopher could see in the mirror as they shifted her onto her side. It turned out that one of the guys standing around the table was an anesthesiologist. He inserted a catheter at the base of Denise's spine and started the drugs for the epidural. Denise was now facing Christopher; her hospital gown had slipped, revealing her shoulder. Careful not to touch skin, Christopher covered her, raised the blanket. It was so cold in this damn operating room, and there was so little comfort he could offer.

Through the past weeks, Christopher had begun to feel great affection for Denise. As the due date got closer, his allegiance to her and the baby had grown so much, he'd left the city and spent most of his time in Nyack, in a frenzy of fixing Denise's house for the baby's arrival. But at no point had Christopher felt a sexual draw to Denise, a corporal tug. What he felt was something like his attachment to his sisters, but without the guilt he felt with his sisters. Watching Denise being prepared for surgery, as each new element of technology was introduced, he felt really bad for her. She was so alone in this, even with him standing there. How much Denise must miss her husband right now. *Don. Hey, man, I'm doing the best I can.* But Christopher knew he couldn't do enough. Again, he felt like a boy, miserable and shy. Even standing here watching felt a little obscene. If there'd been time, he could have run out into the hallway to call one of Denise's girlfriends from the neighborhood, her AA sponsor, her brother and sister-in-law in Erie, Pennsylvania. All those people were supposed to have been here if things had gone normally. None of this was normal.

"You're completely numb, aren't you?" the doctor asked. "Denise, feel nothing?"

"No."

"Go-od. Good girl. Now"—Dr. Baerent threw her voice toward Christopher—"I'm making the incision. Nice cut." She knew he did medical illustrations and assumed he wanted all the details. He forced himself to watch in the mirror a small horizontal cut appearing low on Denise's abdomen.

"It's so small," Christopher whispered to a nurse, "the baby can't fit."

"What?" Denise said very loudly, in a blur. "What's too small?"

The nurse touched Christopher's arm, and the doctor told Denise, "It's fine. It's a beautiful incision. You're doing great, Denise."

Mute but palpable shame hung over the whole procedure, and the doctor and nurses and all the technicians were drawing Christopher into collusion with them.

The doctor's eyes were almost invisible between mask and cap. She was short and bent very low over the incision. Denise's feet in the stirrups were in flannelette socks. Christopher had never noticed before how wide her feet were. He'd never seen her so close to being naked. *She's got big bones.* Christopher was still worried that the baby would be too big for the doctor's small incision. "You okay?" he whispered to Denise. At least he was holding her hand, her cold fingers.

"Listen, don't let me sleep," she ordered him. Her voice was blurry but strong, and full of trust in him, but a reluctant trust, trust that understood there was no choice.

"I won't let you sleep. You'll see everything."

"I have to hold the baby as soon as—"

"Relax, honey," a nurse told her. "It's better for Baby if you're still."

"Shut up," Denise said to the nurse, then added, "please."

In the mirror, Christopher saw layers pulled away, the baby lifted out, saw his son a second before his first cry, which panicked Denise. "He's okay? Tell me what's wrong."

"Nothing's wrong! A boy," the doctor announced. "Healthy, a perfect baby boy."

"Don," Denise demanded in a tired, pained voice. "Do-on," she said, her arms out.

"Just a minute," Christopher told her. He was holding her shoulders, because she was trying to lift up.

"Do not make quick moves," a nurse ordered. "Doctor's not done yet."

"Give me my baby!"

Christopher was watching a nurse suction the baby's nose and mouth, and Christopher watched as his son was placed on Denise's chest.

The baby, the baby.

Baby Don was crying like crazy and seemed to be really angry, and

Christopher was afraid of him. Every picture Christopher had imagined of the baby-to-be was obliterated by the reality in Denise's hands: a long, writhing, red animal body. Her hands were wrapped around something that looked like a rib cage, but the limbs were floppy, the head was lolling. Christopher was sure there was no skeleton beneath the flesh. The baby was nothing but a swollen red scream.

"Christopher, is Don okay? You have to check if he's okay."

"He's healthy, Denise. He's perfect." But Christopher could see the mark on the infant's head where the monitor had screwed in. Nothing about any of this looked good.

The doctor was still busy inside Denise's abdomen. Christopher looked up at the mirror and saw the doctor lift up a mass, a mess, drop it into a basin. "I just took out the placenta. Denise, just a little longer, then you can—"

"Is that epidural still holding for you, Denise?" a nurse asked as she checked the blood pressure for the millionth time.

Everything happening at Denise's abdomen had nothing to do with the expressions on Denise's face, or with the emergency-alarm cries coming from the baby. The blood-pressure and oxygen and heartbeat monitors were getting lots of attention from the nurses. Christopher was crying soundlessly while the baby cried loudly.

"Thank God," Denise was whispering over and over, which made Christopher whisper, "Thank God."

"Hold still for me, Denise," the doctor said. "We're not quite through here yet."

"When can I feed Baby Don?" Denise muttered.

"Relax, Denise," the doctor said firmly. "There's two layers of stitching here to do. You want this done right."

The nurse: "You don't want to be rupturing a week from now."

"That's for sure," another nurse said. "You don't want any infection setting in."

"Or hemorrhage."

Next to Christopher, a nurse whispered, "Everything's fine, Daddy. Perfect. Why're you crying so hard?"

"I don't know."

But he did know, he just couldn't say. *I miss Nora so much. I miss my wife.*

THE MORNING after the day of the birth, though, as soon as he was awake, Christopher remembered—he loved remembering it again and again—*The baby is here, the baby is healthy and he's here.*

Christopher's bed was the daybed in Denise's study, and before he got up he reached for the phone on her desk and dialed the hospital. Waiting to be connected to Denise's room, he stared at the rows of ultrasounds pinned to the bulletin board above her computer: the first dark dot that was the yolk sac, then the larger yolk sac, then the picture of the heartbeat, then the head and digits and limbs and body that were now Baby Don.

And then, over the phone, there was Don's full, hardy cry. And Denise's uncharacteristically welcoming "Hello!" Before he said anything, Christopher savored the deep relief of knowing that the two of them had made it through the night.

Without coffee, without breakfast, as soon as he pulled on his T-shirt and work pants, Christopher turned to the first job of the day. The baby's early arrival meant ten fewer days for preparation, but Christopher was still determined to put shelves up in Don's nursery so Denise could display his books and stuffed animals. The cut shelves were in the garage (where Christopher had painted them, so the smell wouldn't irritate the baby), but now, due to the recent rain, the wood was swollen, so Christopher had to make several trips back and forth, from baby's room to garage, to measure and trim and trim and measure, until the shelves fit perfectly. There were nine shelves to put up on three different walls, so he had to find studs in the walls to drill in the braces to hold up the shelves. Then the vacuuming and dusting when the job was finished.

The room had to be immaculate.

One of Denise's friends had, two days before, brought over a wooden rocker from a garage sale. Christopher insisted that, before the chair made its way into the baby's room, the padding had to be torn off, the chair scrubbed with Lysol and then reupholstered. He did the job quickly, gluing in new padding, covering it with clean, soft cotton and thumbtacking it down. The chair looked nice, not great, but at least he knew it was clean.

There was more to do.

Christopher still had to go to the Grand Union to buy a long list of groceries. He also wanted to do laundry and make up all the beds with clean sheets. He wanted to vacuum all of Denise's upholstered furniture. As he changed the Brita filter, he remembered that Denise had no extra furnace filters, so he went downstairs to check the size, then added *furnace filters* to his grocery list. He wanted to scrub the bathtub and the shower tile (a little filmy). But then, standing in the hot shower, he asked himself, Why am I doing this? It would be years before Baby Don would be taking a shower. And that's when Christopher knew it was time to go to the hospital.

WAITING IN THE HOSPITAL LOBBY for the elevator, he jiggled his key ring; the hole in his jeans pocket was much larger than it had been three days earlier. When he got upstairs and down the hallway and was finally standing in the threshold of Denise's room, there was Baby Don lying on her chest, and there was Denise smiling and smiling and smiling.

"Hey, Daddyo's here! Look at Baby Don, Christopher, look!"

"Yeah, yeah, let me look."

The baby was warm and surprisingly squirmy in Christopher's arms, and Christopher knew instinctively to keep his hold light but secure. *This is easier than I thought it'd be.* He just kept thinking about the baby's reality—*He's so tiny, and he just got out of his mother's stomach*—and then Christopher felt he knew exactly what to do.

Baby Don still had that beleaguered old-man look on his face. Denise said, "It's weird, but he really looks like my husband."

To Christopher, the baby looked like no one. Maybe, if anyone, he looked like Mary Mudd: his not fully opened eyes gave Don a slightly Asian appearance. Then, looking at Baby Don and thinking about Mary, Christopher remembered. *Baby Natassia.*

The memory of France hollowed him out like a bolt of nausea—he probably squeezed a bit, because the baby grimaced *(Oh, baby)* until Christopher's hold softened again—but he resisted the urge to hand the boy back to his mother. Holding his son and remembering rosy, plump Natassia and what he had done to her, Christopher knew he was now a different man. He felt it in his arms first, in his hand full of the baby's head, his other hand full of baby feet. Then he felt it in his heart, the deep conviction that his purpose on earth from now on was to help keep this boy safe. Though new, this emotion within Christopher was profound, as powerful as the surety of death, and it far outweighed any fear of himself that might make him want to run.

He wouldn't have been able to verbalize it yet, but inside himself Christopher knew he had done the right thing in helping Denise have a baby, *this* baby. He knew why he had done it, and he prayed that Nora would eventually understand.

CHRISTOPHER STAYED at the hospital all day and into the evening. Five or six of Denise's neighbors and her sponsor, Carole, visited. Then the announcement came over the PA system that visiting hours were over. "Okay, Denise," he said, rolling her bedside table back into her reach. "Water pitcher's full. TV remote handy. Call if you or Baby Don need me before tomorrow morning."

As he leaned over to peck her cheek and to kiss the baby's head, Denise told him, "Well, buddy, we did it."

"Okay, Papa, let's go." A nurse was at the door. "Mama and Baby need their rest."

Christopher's own exhaustion never hit him until he was back at the house, brushing his teeth and taking off his clothes. As he closed the venetian blinds, he saw how dusty they were. "Shit." He wouldn't have time to take them all down and scrub them. The baby was coming home tomorrow morning.

CHAPTER 23:

DECEMBER

1989

The first thing Denise saw when she entered the house with her new baby was the framed photo of Don that always greeted her from the front-hall table as soon as she walked in the door. *Husband.* That's what she used to call him, and now she said to herself, *Husband, where are you when I need you?* Just the short drive from the hospital had sapped her completely of all her good-will. She'd been such a good citizen since she and the baby had come out of the surgery alive. Now, as Christopher was steadying her, walking her toward her living-room couch, she scolded him, "Don't let go."

"No, no, I'm not."

For two days, as a new mommy on morphine, Denise had been happy, happy, happy, but since this morning, when she'd taken off the hospital gown, showered, put on underwear for the first time in days, and dressed in her own clothes, she'd begun to feel like a sick person. Within the regime of hospital life—with bars on each side of her bed, painkillers dripping into her arm, forbidden even to take a pee without help from some-one—in the hospital, where so little was expected of her, she'd done fine. It had been a shock this morning when she realized they really expected her to go home within a few hours. And they were sending her home with the baby.

They're nuts.

Christopher was doing more for her and her baby than anyone could have expected. But it scared Denise. He could leave at any moment. She had to be prepared for that. She had to believe that if he left—when he left—she and the baby would be okay.

She didn't believe that at all.

Baby Don was in his bassinet in the living room. Christopher had just helped Denise take off her coat, helped her sit down. She couldn't even do that alone. Pain was stitched tight across her abdomen. As a drunk, she'd been clumsy. Stitches in her skull once. Broken bones in her shoulder. Nothing, though, had hurt as much as this cesarean.

Now here was Christopher again, his arms full of her suitcase and her junk, his face as excited as a boy's. "How's it feel to be back in your house?" he asked.

"It's so clean in here," she complained. She'd never be able to keep up the good order he'd established.

When he had put everything away and checked on the baby, he came and stood in front of her. "So, Mama, how do you feel?"

"Like shit."

"Lie down, Denise. You really should be lying down." Again, he had to help her, lift her feet onto the couch. She couldn't lower her body without gripping his arm. Across the lower part of her abdomen, the incision burned, made her catch her breath.

"Hey, hey, hey," Christopher said, "we forgot your belly pillow." When he handed it to her, she grabbed it, the rolled-up-sheet cushion she'd fallen in love with at the hospital. She wanted that wad of flannel close to her right now more than she wanted her own child, who had begun to cry with a shrillness that seemed to be focused directly at her, something he'd never done at the hospital.

Christopher lifted Prince Charming. "You hungry? Hey, little bruiser, what's up?"

"Here," Denise said, "give me." Thank God that when the baby was in her arms her love locked back into place. "My baby guy, my tiny boy." She covered his forehead with kisses, ashamed of the lapse of affection that had just shuddered through her.

Christopher hustled around getting pillows, cracking jokes. It broke Denise's heart the way he always smelled so good. Even after emergency

293

surgery, three days' hospital duty, and getting her house ready, his voice was still kind. Christopher hadn't slacked yet, not once. She felt jealous of his consistent goodwill. She knew he had it in him to be moody, but he'd learned how to tackle that impulse. She didn't feel worthy.

Husband, I found us the right father. She'd found him, but she doubted her ability to keep Christopher from running away from her and the baby very soon.

AFTER BREASTFEEDING for fifteen minutes, Baby Don still cried.

"It's not working, Christopher," Denise said; then she tried to take the blame out of her voice. "I wonder if I'm doing something wrong." *Lord, grant me the serenity.*

"Well, the baby—it's a big change for him, too, being home and all. No, you're doing it all perfect. He'll just need time. Listen, you need to eat. I'm going to make you lunch. There're all kinds of casseroles and stuff in the freezer from your friends."

"Get me anything. I just realized I'm starving."

Half an hour later, with the baby still crying, still hungry, and not nursing well, Denise reminded Christopher about the casserole in the oven. When he lifted it out, he found that the dish had cracked.

"Oh, shoot." They had promised each other not to swear in front of the baby.

"You didn't put that casserole straight into the hot oven from the freezer, did you?"

"I guess I did," he said. "Really stupid. I'm sorry, Denise. I'll buy you a new—"

"It's not mine. It's somebody else's. We'll have to replace it. Just make me a peanut-butter-and-jelly sandwich. Make it quick. Please. I'm starving."

Eighth Step: think of those you have harmed and become willing to make amends to them all.

"Christopher?" No answer. "Chris?" He walked into the living room. She was surprised, a bit disappointed, to find him still smiling at her. "I'm sorry I snapped at you. Everybody cracks a Pyrex now and then."

"Me? I've never done it before. Now the boy thinks his dad's a dud."

"You're not a dud."

"Yeah, I am. Sometimes." He was walking back to the kitchen.

"You're not a dud, and I don't want to bug you, but I'm starving and I really need to eat something soon."

A LITTLE WHILE LATER, the baby cried himself to sleep (he wasn't feeding half as well as he had been in the hospital), and Denise decided this was her opportunity to try going to the bathroom. Christopher, with his endlessly patient hands, helped her sit up, then stand up, then walk across the living room.

"You dizzy?" he asked.

"A little bit."

Holding her arm, he walked into the bathroom with her, lifted the toilet lid. "You can leave me now," she told him.

"No, I want to wait until you're sitting down. I don't want you falling."

What the hell. By now he'd seen everything. So had doctors, nurses, student nurses, interns, lab technicians. Her pubic area had become a public area, a badly repaired crossroads. As soon as she was sitting, Christopher left and closed the door. With her pants lowered, her upper thighs rubbed against the rough scrape of her growing-back-in pubic hair, which felt like a crop of nail heads. There was a quick trill of pain with the first drops of urine, then a dull burn in the bladder, a meanness. Still, three days after surgery, the odor of anesthesia wafted up from her hot urine. A reminder of the foreign substances that had been run through her. Metal, industrial. Her groin reminded her of Newark.

And then, at the end of a long rush of urine—*This can't be happening! Not now!*—a rope of pain pulled down inside her from just behind her navel, tugging so hard and fast, wringing her insides out, reminding her of everything she'd ever done wrong.

Bladder infection.

Denise knew what would happen next. As soon as her urine flow stopped, she'd feel a cruel pressure of needing to pee some more but there'd be nothing there, just burning pain. She could picture the pain, a thin, sharp wrinkle folding down slowly from the bottom of her gut, then the next roll of pain would increase, big heavy sheets and blankets slapped and folding in a big spill from abdomen to the edge of her vaginal lips,

295

where the fear of the burn would precede the burn, which, when it came, felt like asphalt assaulted by sun.

CHRISTOPHER KNOCKED on the door. "You okay? You've been in there a long time."

"No." She was crying, which made Christopher open the door a crack. "Denise, what?"

Still sitting on the toilet, her elbows on her knees, she was weeping into her hands. "I have a bladder infection. How did this happen? I'm going to kill myself."

"No, Denise, no."

"What did I do wrong? Why is this happening?"

He helped her stand so she could pull up her sweatpants. He waited, steadying her, while she tied the tie around her sore waist. Walking her back to the couch, he said, "Bladder infection. Isn't there that medicine that turns the urine orange and takes the pain away really fast?"

"Yes," Denise said, grudgingly. If he knew all this, probably his gorgeous babe of a wife had had it once. Probably, Denise thought, I should just give them the baby, let them raise him. Probably that's what he'd had in mind all along. That's why he's being so nice to me. "But you keep forgetting that I'm breastfeeding a baby. How can I take the medicine if I'm breastfeeding?"

"Oh, man, that's right, you don't want meds if you're—"

"No, I *do* want them. I want the meds. But they'd never give me a prescription. Even though I'll probably never manage to nurse this baby again."

"Let's take this one step at a time. Let's get you lying down."

One day at a time. Lord, grant me the serenity . . .

Christopher's hands lifting her feet were like God's immediate answer to her prayer. "Okay. Now," he said, "do you have any cranberry juice?"

He really did know about this infection. "No, of course not. I just—"

"Okay. I'll get juice when I go to Target to get the medicine. Let's call the doctor."

"She won't give you the prescriptions."

"Let's try. Where's the number?"

"Christopher! I need an antibiotic and the orange-pee medicine, and they won't let me take them, I'm telling you. Just bring me the phone. I need the phone to call Carole. I need to go to a meeting."

"First things first. I'm dialing the doctor."

"Stop! Just stop. I just remembered. I have spare prescriptions for Bactrim and Pyridium. My friend who's a PA gave them to me."

"A production assistant?"

"Physician's assistant. If you're really going to Target, try to get a new Pyrex. I don't like owing people things."

"Yeah, I'll go, but what about taking this stuff while you're breastfeeding? I really would like to talk to the doctor first."

"If you don't go, I'll drive to Target myself. If I can take morphine, I can take a little orange-pee medicine."

"But what about the antibiotic? Can't we just call—"

"Are you going?"

"All right. All right."

Lord, grant me the serenity. If you can, grant it now.

Christopher was at Target, sitting in a plastic chair at the pharmacy waiting for the Bactrim and the Pyridium for Denise's bladder infection. He didn't like this one bit. She wouldn't take the painkillers the doctor had told her it was okay to take, but she was going to take this other shit without asking anyone. Holding a shopping basket on his lap, Christopher went over his list to make sure he had everything: three giant-sized bottles of cranberry juice, paper towels (Bounty, Denise's one splurge), an eight-by-twelve Pyrex, three bottles of antibacterial soap.

He wasn't feeling as happy as he would have liked, and the truth was that, after the first-day high, he'd been . . . troubled. Maybe because of the cesarean?

Shit, he had so much to be glad about, he'd been so lucky. Denise had picked him, in spite of his bad history, to be the father. Then he'd been lucky again when she called him last summer and let him get involved in the pregnancy. Then—more—the baby was born healthy, everything had gone pretty well. Nora still hadn't found out; they were still married. Everything was going great. Pretty smooth.

Not enough. If only he could call someone to talk, but he had told no one. Not even Piper, who had started this whole baby caper.

It was too hot inside Target, and they were taking too long with the damn prescriptions. There were people everywhere—tired, nervous young mothers like his sisters—making desperate, ugly purchases just because Christmas was a few weeks away.

In part, Christopher blamed himself for the cesarean. Maybe if he'd arrived in Nyack sooner, if he hadn't spent the night in Manhattan, if he'd got Denise to the hospital sooner. Denise kept saying she didn't mind that she'd had to have the surgery. She never for a minute showed any regret. She was so healthy, so unequivocally grateful. *She's an alcoholic widow single mother, and here's me, feeling sorry for myself.* Why was this pharmacist taking so long? Why wasn't Christopher happier? For months now, it had been so easy to be good to Denise. He still had no problem helping her out, but he couldn't stop thinking, What's in this for me?

What an asshole. What a greedy, selfish asshole I am.

If he didn't lose his greediness, Nora would never have a baby with him. If they didn't have a baby, probably their marriage would be over. A few days had passed since he'd seen Nora, but it seemed like so much longer.

"Denise Woj . . . Woji . . . ?"

"Here. Here I am."

"You're Denise?" the pharmacist asked.

"I'm picking them up for her."

"How do you pronounce this name?"

"Never mind." Christopher heard his own rudeness, smelled his own stale breath. "It's an impossible name."

The pharmacist was a woman, young. African American, tall, a looker actually, and she was smiling at him. "Your wife?" Why did they always do that? Her question was full of suggestion. Christopher ignored her, didn't look up. She's rude, he told himself, which made it easier not to ask the question he knew he should ask, about whether or not it was all right for a breastfeeding woman to take these medications. He said nothing for a second, so then the pharmacist got back on track. "Anyway, she needs to take these a full seven days. Don't let her stop before she's been through the whole prescription."

"Got it," Christopher said. "Thanks for your help."

"Merry Christmas!" the woman said.

"Yeah," he answered.

On his way out of Target, Christopher saw a refrigerator magnet shaped like a cappuccino machine, the kind of thing he'd normally tuck into Nora's Christmas stocking. He picked it up, ready to go back and buy it, but then he saw the long checkout lines. Denise was desperate for this orange-pee medicine and cranberry juice. Besides, how would he get the magnet to Nora? Who knew where Nora was? It was unimaginable but true: Christopher had no idea where his wife would be this Christmas.

"IT'S A MIRACLE," Denise said. "It worked."

Her pee was now orange and painless, and the baby was nursing, feeding better than he had at the hospital.

"See," Christopher told Denise, who was set up on the couch with pillows, burping Baby Don, "I told you you were a natural."

She was dressed in a big old nightgown and a horrible brown polyester robe, as she had been since her return from the hospital the day before yesterday, and she looked up from the baby and smiled at Christopher, big. Sometimes the slightest bit of nice talk made her feel so good. With some people it took so little. "You done burping on me, boy?" Denise said softly, then lay back on the couch and rested the baby on her chest.

The past two days and nights had been exhausting, but in the little house in Nyack they were making all kinds of progress. Diapers, feeding, sleep, food. They had their systems down, and now here they were. "I'm glad you feel better," Christopher said. He was lying on the floor, next to the couch, so he could watch the baby's face and listen to the purring contentment in his sleepy breathing. "Lady, you got yourself one happy boy. That's a baby who l-o-o-ves his mama. You should see his face right now."

"I feel better, and so does my little peeper. Don't you, my little pumpkin-eater? My little boyo and his mommy are so much happier now than that first day home, when Mommy was the Wicked Stitch of the West. My poor little rabbit."

Denise was shameless when she cooed at the baby. The goings-on between Denise and Baby Don opened a bit of a door into how her marriage with Big Don might have been. *Nice.* Maybe even nicer than what Christopher and Nora had, maybe steadier. Denise had the terrible grief of having lost Don, but at least she could live the rest of her life knowing that the person she loved had loved her back completely, and that if he hadn't died he'd be with her this Christmas.

Christopher, his head heavy on a pillow on the floor, looked at the baby and couldn't help thinking it was some cruel joke that he and Denise should get along so well and have this dynamite baby, and not be in love with each other. But it was more than sex that was missing. If he could feel for Denise the kind of love he felt for Nora . . . but he couldn't. He was in love with Nora.

The day was turning dark, sending in shadows. An electric timer turned on a living-room lamp.

Out of the quiet, Denise said, "What's wrong, Daddy? You're not looking happy."

He yawned, reached back, flipped the pillow under his head. Maybe he was getting a headache. Maybe he should take a nap. He kind of wanted a cup of good coffee. He kind of wanted a beer. "I don't know. Nothing."

"Yeah, but what's wrong?" Denise insisted.

"I don't want to make you feel bad."

"You can't, not now. I'm as content as a pig."

"It's just that, well, all along I felt so bad for you, even at the birth, because you have to do all this alone, without your husband."

"And now here I am with my beautiful baby, and I'm so happy, and you feel completely left out, right? And on top of it, you're worried about what this says about you. If you're feeling this, does that mean you're a terrible egotist?"

They both laughed.

"What on earth," he teased, "would make you say that?"

"Imagine. What could possibly make me think such a thing, because, of course, *I* never felt that way myself."

Now, with the ice broken, he confided, "I feel weird."

"Don't you think that's pretty normal? Postpartum depression. I expected you'd feel weird. Didn't you? I mean, here you are, taking care of a strange woman who's breastfeeding your son, who you won't be living with full-time because you're married to a woman you're deeply in love with, whom you're separated from, and on top of it all, it's Christmastime."

"You're smart," he told Denise. He had decided long ago not to unload on her about his marriage. Denise, either respecting his reticence or not wanting to hear it, never pressed for details. But she sure had summed it up right: he and his wife were separated.

And it was his own fault.

"Why don't we go out for a while?" Denise suggested. "I need to get out of the house, and so does Baby Don."

"You can't take him outside. It's winter."

"Ah! You think we're staying in here all winter? Not my boy, not my tough boy. Right, sweetie?" Denise and the baby were face to face and she was smooching him. "Besides, we have to get Daddy's Christmas gift."

"No, Denise. Save your money. You don't need to get me a gift."

"Not from me. Baby Don wants to get a gift for his dad. He told me." She waved the baby's hand at Christopher and said in a Tweety Bird voice, "Let's go out, Daddy! The mall! The mall!"

WALKING OUT OF THE HOUSE, Denise needed to hold her belly blanket to support her middle. Christopher first helped her into the car, then went in to get Don, whose face was a pin dot surrounded by a cap and scarf and the white furry trim of his snowsuit hood. At almost one week old, Don was starting to look more like a baby than he had right after birth.

Denise's Honda was small and beat-up, and when Christopher saw how ridiculously tiny Don looked in the car seat, he almost said, We can't do this. But Denise really was needing to get out.

"Okay, buster," Christopher said to the baby. "I'm strapping you in for your maiden voyage into the twentieth century. Your first outing, Nanuet Mall. If you behave, we'll buy you a hot dog and a Cherry Coke." Christopher pulled the straps of the infant car seat tight but not too tight, snapped the buckle, unsnapped it and snapped it again, checked the seat belt that held the car seat in place. He checked everything twice. When he finally was in the driver's seat, he turned and looked. He locked his door, leaned back and locked the back doors, and asked Denise, please, to lock her door, too. "Okay, here we go."

Denise was looking at him. "What?" he asked.

"Nothing, just— You're good at being a parent."

"Thank you, Denise."

"No problem. It's the truth." Down the road, at a red light, she said,

"Listen, how would you feel about staying home alone sometime with Don for about an hour and a half? Carole said she'd pick me up to go to a meeting in a couple days. I could take the baby with me, but I'd rather not. There'd be people smoking and breathing on him and everything."

"You trust me to stay with him?"

"You're his father. Why wouldn't I?"

For the next several days, Christopher wanted more than anything to call Nora and tell her the big news, that there was a woman in Nyack—an intelligent woman—who trusted him with her newborn baby. Then, late one night less than a week before Christmas, after Denise and Baby Don were in bed, Christopher dialed the loft, and he was surprised when Nora answered. "Hey," he said, "hi, it's me."

"Yeah. Hi," Nora said. "How are you? I'm glad you called."

"Yeah?"

"Your parents called the other night to thank us for the Christmas gifts I sent, and I realized you didn't know I'd sent gifts, and I wanted to fill you in before you talk to them."

Christopher got up out of bed and smiled at the bookcase in Denise's crowded study. "You're kidding? You sent them stuff?" That seemed a good sign. "What'd you send? I sent them stuff, too, but just a couple things from the Williams-Sonoma catalogue."

"Christopher." Nora was laughing. "I sent from Williams-Sonoma, too. What if we sent the same thing?"

He was beaming, pacing, clutching a handful of hair, pulling it a bit to make sure this phone call was real. "Tell me," he urged her, "tell me what you sent."

"I sent carved wooden candlesticks to your parents. And a dried-sage wreath and a set of hand towels to each of your sisters, and a wooden birdhouse to each of the kids."

Christopher laughed and laughed, and forgot to worry that he might be waking the baby down the hall.

Nora was laughing, too, laughing with him. She was *with* him. "What's so funny? Christopher, tell me what you sent."

"The candlesticks to my parents, and just the wreath to my sisters. No hand towels. You were more generous."

"They're going to have duplicates of all this stuff."

My. God. Nora. Please. Don't stop laughing.

Christopher picked up a small framed photograph of Baby Don from Denise's desk. He had to catch his breath before he could talk. "Well, we'll just tell them that Williams-Sonoma made a mistake."

"Yeah, okay." Nora's voice was still happy, but calming down. "We'll blame Williams-Sonoma." There was a pause, a shift, then Nora asked, "Have you told your parents and your sisters that you and I won't be together for Christmas?"

"Of course not." *Calm down.* "No. I didn't, I just told them we were doing something different this year. I told them just you and me were going away to have a quiet time, and we weren't having all the usual parties and dinners and stuff."

"Okay," she said softly, "just so I know what to say if they call again."

"Nora," Christopher said, "I love you. Do you still love me?"

Pause. "This is a difficult time for us, Christopher."

"Yeah. You're right. It's weird." Christopher was using his thumbnail on the photo frame to try rubbing off the glue mark from the price tag. "How's the loft? Everything okay?"

"Yeah, fine. By the way, why did you call? You okay?"

"Just to say hi."

"Well," she said, "I should go."

"Just remember that, Nora, that I love you."

CHAPTER 25:

DECEMBER

1989

Nora and Abe were sitting in the Beekman Theater on the Upper East Side waiting for *Sweetie* to begin. "How will you get all your writing materials out to Greenport?" she asked him.

Abe wasn't touching her yet in any way, no hand-holding—he usually did nothing until after the lights went out—but she noticed him glance over his shoulder to make sure no one was sitting in the few rows behind them.

"Train," Abe said. "I don't need much stuff."

"And you'll be there three or four weeks?"

"Yeah, I was counting on it. I need to get this half a manuscript done to show this agent. The place is still available, isn't it?"

"Yeah, I told my husband and brother it's rented. Nobody will bother you."

Abe knocked Nora's knee with his knee, which thrilled her more than it should have. She'd gone to a holiday party before coming to meet him and was a little buzzed. That extra glass of Merlot she could have done without. She rarely drank red and wasn't good at gauging it. "How about you?" Abe asked. "Are you going out for a couple days?"

"Sure," she said, "I'll visit. Unless it'll be a distraction to your work."

"Don't worry, you won't be a distraction to my work."

She elbowed him. "Well, thank you. Thank you very much." But she was not really angry. She couldn't be. There was nothing in their relationship that entitled either of them entry into the other's life beyond the limits of their once- or twice-a-week meetings (never on a Friday, Saturday, or Sunday) for dinner and a movie and fooling around afterward in whatever apartment Abe was house-sitting. Nora comforted herself with the thought that maybe things between them would become clearer during their time together out at the beach house. She was renting it to him for a pittance, just enough to cover the utilities, enough to keep up the pretense.

The movie-house lights dimmed into darkness.

"CAN I ASK YOU SOMETHING?" Nora said to Abe after the movie. They were eating a not very good dinner in a coffee shop near Lexington Avenue, the kind of predictably mediocre place Christopher never would have set foot in. "At *Time*, when you take your break, where do you go?"

"Wherever. Whatever the contessa feels like eating that night."

Usually when Abe mentioned Giulia, he called her the contessa. This bothered Nora more than it should have. She hadn't told Giulia anything about all the time she was spending with Abe. Nora hadn't talked to Giulia in weeks, actually.

"So you just go get dinner? Then bring it back to work?"

"I walk," Abe said.

"But where do you go?"

"Around." He signaled the waiter for another beer.

Nora was pretty sure her hunch was right. Something about the hit-and-run nature of their relationship. Her guess was that during his hour-long break Abe went to Times Square, into those adults-only places where girls danced behind glass for men who stood in curtained booths and jerked off.

Franklin Fields stopped Mary on the stairs after a faculty meeting and told her, "Hey, I'm hearing all kinds . . . just all sorts of super things from your dance students. The performance coming up, they're *excited*," and as he said *"excited,"* his own eyes gleamed.

Mary had decided by now that Franklin was okay. She enjoyed the minor sexiness of his rolled-up sleeves and always loosened Brooks Brothers tie. But, no, there was no way you'd take this man to bed. Today he had a little shaving nick on his jaw. *He needs somebody to tell him this stuff.* "So—what are you up to down in that dance studio?"

She made her voice all-business. "I think the kids will impress you. They've worked—they're working quite hard." *Shit, now he's got me stuttering.*

"I'm sure they are," he said and looked deflated.

"Yes. They're quite focused." At least she was learning the lingo.

THE STUDENTS' PERFORMANCE was scheduled for just before the holiday break, a Friday night. In the afternoon there would be an opening in the campus art gallery, a group show of Hudson Valley painters, then a buffet dinner (seventy-five dollars per person) and a silent auction. Most of the parents would be there, people from the community (the rich and arty), along with members of the board of trustees, who were having their annual luncheon that day, then staying on for the festivities of Hiliard Winter Weekend.

Ross had tried to explain to Mary how a board's power to decide policy affected all of a school's dealings, including the teachers' jobs and the conditions of their jobs. "For example, your budget for the dance department," Ross said.

"I don't care about my budget. Just so they pay me."

"Mary." He was exasperated. "You have to care about your budget. Think long-term. Think beyond survival. Think."

Mary, who had never had the luxury of thinking beyond survival, did understand that whenever the board showed up the stakes were high. The upcoming student performance had the welt on the back of her neck itching constantly. Why did this job feel scarier than preparing a solo for a world premiere? Why weren't these kids better dancers? Mary knew she could perform. Mary knew she could choreograph. It seemed, though, that she knew very little about how to teach nonprofessionals how to perform.

"TWO WEEKS! We have only two weeks until you're onstage." On the studio floor in front of Mary, sixteen teenagers were collapsed and breathing hard. But not hard enough. "What you just showed me is absolutely not ready." The kids pinched their eyebrows together and nodded agreement.

The students adored Mary, and they embraced the idea of being worked hard, like professionals, but part of Mary's drill had nothing to do with serious dance business, part of it was her personal anxiety and dread.

Franklin was expecting a performance, and these just were not performance-ready dancers. The class met three times a week. The students got there on time. Charlie and Jenefer showed up early. After class, most of them lingered. They couldn't get enough. Still, their progress was pathetic.

The piece they were preparing was the one Mary had begun to choreograph that morning in late August after she'd spent the night staring up at the beams that crossed the cottage ceiling, wondering if maybe it was time for her finally to check out. She'd titled the dance simply "Pas de Deux."

There were eight couples—in all kinds of combinations of height and gender, just as she had planned—and the couples were always intersecting with one another. The dance had changed a lot from when she'd first conceived it. There was less chasing involved; it was more close-close. The two people within each couple were always touching, one partnering the other for a turn or a lift, one leading the other in a waltz step. The partners pirouetted in and out of each other's arms. They climbed onto each other and made shapes, they lay next to each other on the floor and coordinated the movement of their legs and arms. Mary overheard the students on the staircase one day:

"This dance is getting pretty touchy-feely. It's turning into a romance thing."

"Yeah, she must have gotten laid or something."

"Franklin Fields, you think?"

"In. His. Dreams."

ONE MORNING, ten days before the performance, the advanced students were in the studio stretching out before class, and Charlie told Mary, suggestively, "Mr. Fields keeps asking us about you and your class and your dance that we're working on."

"*My* dance?" Mary said. "It's not mine."

"You choreographed it," Charlie said. "Isn't it yours?"

"No. By now it should be yours. Every dance you perform is *your* dance."

They stopped stretching. Mary wanted to hug Charlie. He had just helped her figure out her teaching problem. "The dancer's job is to take the choreographer's steps and"—and what? thirty-two eyes staring at her—"and *breathe* into them." Mary paused, half expecting one of Charlie's irreverent asides, like *Breathe into your own steps!* But the kids continued to stare at her. Apparently the idea she had just presented was, in fact, news.

"So, in other words," Charlie volunteered, "you're not Balanchine?"

"Who's Balanchine?" someone asked.

A few people moaned. Charlie condescended to answer, "He's a great Russian ballet choreographer who made the ballerinas all look exactly alike."

"No, I don't want you exactly alike. A dancer . . ." What? How to put it into words? She had never needed to explain this before. "Well, a dancer says everything they have to say, all the important stuff—not just like 'Excuse me, where's the bathroom?' or 'Can I have a Diet Coke, please?'—Hey, wait, let's, why don't we try this. Charlie, center stage."

"Me? Now?"

"Hurry. Yes, you. Say this with your body: Can I please have a Diet Coke?"

Clownishly, embarrassed, he mimed praying hands, then gripped his throat to show thirst. "Oh, you!" Mary said, laughing. "Enough. You're playing charades. Jenefer, center stage. You try."

" 'Can I please have a Diet Coke?' "

"Yup. Ask the question using your body."

Jenefer was the right choice. An experienced acting student, she threw her arms up over her head, made her body a skinny long tube of energy. Jenefer, usually shy and modest, was meticulous about the details of every step; the whole room was rapt as she transformed her body into a slow, slinky stretch of sexiness, then, with an abdominal contraction, collapsed her torso down over her legs, drooped her head to the floor, rolled up to a flat-back position, extended her arms, *slow-slow-slow,* kept her palms facing downward, and then, finally, with a clipped gesture, turned one palm over in a supplication. She held the shape, breathed into it, and kept it alive. The students exploded into applause. When they quieted down, Mary asked, "So, what do you think of that?"

"She's Coke. The real thing," Charlie said, forlornly. "I'm generic-brand cola."

They laughed. There was energy now in the room. Bridgit, a slightly overweight, stocky girl, raised her hand, "I want to try 'Excuse me, where's the bathroom?' "

"Sure, give it a try."

Bridgit, usually self-consciously imitative of Jenefer, surprised Mary by doing movements Jenefer's body would never have discovered. In a staccato version of her usual between-class frenzy, Bridgit spun all over the floor, using the space more fully than Jenefer had, circling shapes suggested by her round, squat body. Now and then, with her chunky legs solid, she stopped in a quick, surprising halt, her hands flexed in Egyptian-style early-modern-dance shapes that demanded, Stop!

Mary whistled when Bridgit was done. As Bridgit bowed and everyone clapped and whooped for her, her confident dance-self morphed back into her day-to-day self, and Mary saw Bridgit change from the woman she would eventually become, back into the girl she was stuck being for now. *Have faith.*

"Great," Mary said. "Who can tell us what happened? What did Bridgit do that was so exciting?"

"She . . . Well . . ." Charlie, of course, was the first to try. "She . . . I don't know what she did, but it was deeply satisfying to watch."

"Yes!" Mary was thrilled; "satisfying" was the perfect word. "Who can say *why* Bridgit's dance was satisfying to watch?"

Stefan—a handsome, tall boy who rarely spoke, just followed everything with an intelligent watchfulness, a boy Mary had seen Natassia talking to once or twice, a boy who loved to read and who just happened to have a dancer's body—Stefan offered this: "Bridgit's movement was an extension of the shapes of her body, that's why it was satisfying to watch. The movement was organic to her body." Mary was holding her breath; she couldn't believe how smart these kids were. Was it growing up in rich families that taught them how to talk like this? Stefan went on: "The question, about where's the bathroom, that was there in the urgency of the quick steps."

"Yeah," another guy interrupted Stefan, "and in the kind of awkwardness of those poses she made."

"Right," Stefan continued, "it's usually an artificial politeness when someone asks where's the bathroom. They call it the gents' or the powder room or something stupid like that, so those sort of artificial shapes said that."

"Holy shit," Mary said, "you guys are so smart. How, *how* did you learn to talk like that?"

They laughed at her, and she laughed with them. The kids' energy was overheating the room. "Okay, let's keep going here."

Mary next asked them to get with their partners for a new eight-count combination. It was easy; they got the steps quickly. "Do it again!" Mary said. "And five and six and—"

Six, ten, fifteen times over, Mary had them do the combination, and they did it until it wasn't dance anymore, it wasn't steps, it was the body's imperative, and after the sixteenth time, the kids' minds were numb, their bodies nothing but that eight-count phrase of movement, and by the twentieth time, their personalities began to move into the steps. Each body was the dance, and each dance was slightly different. And perfect.

"Something happened here today," Mary said at the end of class. "You were in here with your *bodies* today. Today you danced. How did it feel?"

"Great!"

"How was it different from our last class?" she asked.

"More free. More fun."

"Less boring."

"Okay, in the dorm tonight, for twenty minutes, do it again. Put on any music you like, your favorite music, and just be in your body. Move. Like animals. Yeah. Hey, listen. At eight-thirty or nine, something like that, on PBS, there's this great animal show on TV. That's the second part of your homework. Watch that animal show. Watch how the animals move. That's our goal here. Not just to learn the steps but to get you moving naturally, the way animals do. They don't think. Our goal is to get you to stop thinking and start moving." She bowed to them. "Thank you, class."

They applauded and bowed, and she applauded them.

Mary had just learned lesson number one in how to teach raw beginners to dance. Now maybe she wouldn't lose her job.

THE DAYS PASSED, and then there was only a week left. "Okay," Mary said to the class at rehearsal. "It really is starting to look like something." They were hanging on to every word. "Now that you know I love you, we're going to *work*. Today's Friday. For the next seven days, forget about the rest of your life. Besides our regular classes, all of you need to be here every night after dinner. Seven-thirty sharp. Monday, we set lights. Tuesday, costume fittings. Wednesday and Thursday, dress rehearsals. You'll be here at least until ten o'clock every night. Probably longer. I'll be giving lots of notes."

The students cheered.

"MOVE LIKE THE ANIMALS," she shouted at the eight couples spilling across the floor, into and out of the narrow aisles between groupings.

"Eat up the space, use *all* the space." Their arabesques were now perfectly timed. "Bridgit, leg a little higher! Yes! Get it *there* every time." The couples glided forward for their eight counts of lifts. "That's it! You're slinking, slinky, you're leopards. Stefan, looser arms. You're thinking too much. This isn't algebra or chemistry. This is physics. Action, reaction. Animals know how to do this. You're animals. Forget your brains."

That night, after about an hour of rehearsal, the students asked for a ten-minute break. But after fifteen minutes, no one was coming back into the studio. Mary thought she'd finally pushed them too far. Probably they'd gone to Franklin Fields to complain. Maybe they were on the phone with their parents or the board of trustees. Mary was going to lose her job; she and Natassia would be out on the street for Christmas. Mary went to the studio door and looked up and down the hallways. No one. No sounds. "Where are you?" she screamed. Even Natassia was gone. Mary stepped back into the studio, closed the door to keep the heat in. She started to pack up her CDs and tapes. She pulled out her asthma inhaler.

And then the door burst open and the lights went out just at the moment she was inhaling, and in the darkness she almost choked. It was so dark she saw nothing, heard only a rush at the door as all the kids leaped into the studio. They were growling. And then the lights slowly came up but stayed dim, and Mary saw that all sixteen students were painted with animal stripes, their arms and legs and faces. Somebody turned on Bruce Springsteen singing "Jungleland." "What," Mary screamed, "are you doing? What is this?"

They growled and surrounded her, made a circle. They danced around her with animal leaps, rolling on the floor, arching up, lifting Mary off her feet. "Oh God!" She was laughing very hard. "Put me down!" When they were done with "Jungleland" and breathing hard, Mary yelled, "Do it again!" And, hardly able to stay still herself, she watched them slink through the song a second time and right into "Thunder Road." Mary applauded wildly. They whistled and hooted for themselves. And then Natassia came in with a lit-up birthday cake, and they all sang "Happy Birthday" to Mary. As someone turned the lights way up, Charlie leaped out of the crowd—under his animal markings, he was completely naked. All the girls yelled at him, "Oh God, put on your clothes."

"I was improvising," Charlie said, smiling.

ON MONDAY, Franklin Fields came to Mary's studio and, without any stuttering, with his tie knotted tightly and his sleeves buttoned at his wrists, told her that one of the board members had called because she had heard there'd been nudity in the dance studio. None of Mary's students had told; somebody's roommate had.

"Who is this board lady? Tell her to come to the performance. The kids are dancing so good now. She'll love it."

"Mary," Franklin said, "this is serious. If they want to, the trustees can go to town with this kind of thing."

"What's this woman's name?"

"Paine-Pinkney. Mrs. Paine-Pinkney."

"Give me her number. I'll call her. I can explain."

IT WAS THURSDAY, a few hours before dress rehearsal. The lights the night before had been a disaster, but the theater teacher said he'd fix things up. Mary had no confidence in him or his techies. Costumes had been downgraded to black leotards and tights. The student "seamstresses" had quit on the job. Mary and her students were just finishing class. As they toweled themselves off and caught their breath so they could go through the whole dance one more time, Mary said, "This performance tomorrow night is going to have to be perfect. There are people we have to impress. Got it?"

"What if we make a mistake?" Bridgit asked.

"You will *not* make a mistake. Don't even think that. If something's off, you just keep dancing. Everybody knows that, right?"

"Yeah, but—"

"No 'yeah but's. Did I ever tell you about the performance I saw in Italy where the ballerina had to go offstage to throw up?"

"No!"

"Years ago. This company in Florence was doing *Giselle*. On the second night, a top-billed ballerina—I don't know, she must have been sick with the flu—during Act One she just danced off, vomited, danced back on. Meanwhile, her partner, he improvised a solo for three whole minutes. Do you know how long three minutes is when you're onstage? He got ballerinas in the corps de ballet to come downstage with him and dance. They all just kept going. And you know why they could do it?"

"Why?"

"Because they were all plugged in. They were pros. Everybody was alert. There you had a vomiting prima ballerina, pretty much the worst possible situation, short of somebody dropping dead. But probably most people in the audience never noticed."

"How'd you know that she was vomiting backstage? Could you hear?"

"Of course not. I knew one of the dancers. He told me."

"Maybe she was just bulimic, the prima ballerina."

"Whatever. The point is, never *ever* anticipate a mistake. That messes with your head. Just know that, whatever happens, you'll pull it off."

They stared at Mary, wide-eyed, probably because she was speaking with such uncharacteristic seriousness—she had spittle in the corners of her mouth—trying so hard to convince them and herself that nothing would happen that couldn't be handled.

WHEN MARY got back to the cottage at the end of rehearsal, a car was parked in front. She didn't recognize it until she saw the piled-up clothes in the backseat. "Kevin? What's he doing here?"

She rushed inside. He was sitting at the table doing something to Natassia's computer. "Kevin," Mary said, "did something happen?" It was over two months since the night at the hospital with Natassia, but still, every time the phone rang, Mary expected disaster. The sight of Kevin's unexpected car had her heart beating too fast. "Is Nora all right?"

"No. She's turned into a total bitch. She's standing us all up for Christmas, did you know that? I came to tell you, in case you hadn't heard."

He had a beard now, reddish rough stuff all over his face. Mary hadn't seen him in a year. It always surprised her at first that he was as tall as he was, that he wasn't still twelve years old. Kevin was wearing a dark-blue flannel shirt, and a tie (loosened, like Franklin Fields). Nora and Christopher always teased Kevin about how he never traveled without wearing a tie. Kevin was always kind of cartoony. "You drove all the way up from the city," she asked him, "to tell us Nora's not having Christmas?"

"There was an estate sale in Tarrytown," Kevin said.

"Still, that's an hour south of here."

"Once I'm out of the city, I like to keep going. Nice computer you guys've got."

Mary's eyes met Natassia's over Kevin's head. They both shrugged.

His eyes didn't leave the computer screen. "Nice computer. Nice cottage. Pretty place. Quiet. Beautiful deal. You did good, Mar. Natassia said you wouldn't mind if I went through the fridge and cooked something up. Lasagne'll be ready in about half an hour. Why don't you take a shower, relax. I brought some nice wine."

THE NEXT NIGHT, the night of the performance, Kevin was still at Mary's cottage when she rushed home to change. Having him there gave Mary a chance to vent. "I fucking can't believe I fucking had to explain to these kids how to explain to their parents why they can't go out for a nice fancy dinner tonight even though the parents made reservations a week ago. They didn't know that for a seven-thirty curtain they had to be backstage by five-thirty. And these are the people who are judging *me* and deciding if I'm good enough for this lousy job."

"They're lucky to have you," Kevin said.

"They're firing me. Tonight's it. For sure."

When Mary walked into the living room dressed in jeans, boots, and a black turtleneck, he told her, "No. Wrong look. Too casual."

Mary went back into the bathroom and changed into a short black spaghetti-strap dress, black sheers, suede pumps, an outfit she'd worn to lots of first-night parties.

Both Kevin and Natassia nixed that. "Way too sexy," Kevin told her.

"Mom, why're you acting like you've never done this before? What do you normally wear?"

"There's nothing normal about this place. I don't understand these people. They have too much money, and I don't know what they want from me."

"For starters," Kevin explained, "you don't want to be threatening in any way. You can't look better than they do, but you've got to look like you belong to their club. I have something in the car. Just a sec."

He was already dressed for the event, wearing a nice blue-striped shirt, a tie, a wool blazer. Natassia looked elegant but understated in a long black skirt and a bulky black sweater, with a long silk scarf wrapped around her neck. *How does she know how to do that? Where'd she learn?*

Kevin walked back in from his car with a black sweater. "Here, try this."

Mary sniffed it. "Is this clean?"

"Clean enough."

The sweater was cashmere, a pullover, short-sleeved, round neck, with a yoke of tiny black beads. Mary held it out in front of her.

"It's perfect," Natassia told her.

Kevin was dealing out a hand of gin rummy to play with Natassia. In many ways, he was still a kid, always needing to be occupied. "I got it at that estate sale. They had a huge box of beaded sweaters, but that black one's the best. It was going to be your Christmas gift."

"Yeah, well, ho-ho-ho."

A FEW DAYS EARLIER, during their phone session, Dr. Cather had asked Mary, "Do you think you're fully aware of the depth of your anger?" Now— on Friday night, walking into the Hiliard School theater—Mary was aware that her anger had never been so deep. Or so wide or so big. *I've worked so friggin hard and still they want more from me.* Leading Natassia and Kevin to their seats, Mary looked over the packed auditorium. The chatter-hum was full of those upper-class tones Mary couldn't imitate or decode. She didn't know which one was Mrs. Paine-Pinkney, so Mary hated them all.

Mary glanced back at Natassia and Kevin—Natassia looked a little too young to be his date, he looked a little too young to be her dad, but they both had that ability to look the crowd over as if they owned the place. Mary took off her coat and tossed it onto a seat. "I better get backstage."

As soon as she saw the students in the wings, she was pretty sure the night was going to be a disaster. Jenefer, close to hyperventilating, was breathing into a paper bag.

"Oh Christ," Mary muttered to herself, and stuck an unlit cigarette between her teeth.

Bridgit chose that moment to confide in Mary: "I just feel I have to tell

317

someone—I've been bingeing and throwing up all day. My mother's come up to see this show, and I feel so much anger at her. Her and her stupid boyf—"

"You're onstage in ten minutes. What are you thinking about your mother for?"

"I just don't think"—Bridgit broke into tears—"I don't think I can do it."

"You have to do it. You don't have a choice." Mary walked away. "Charlie, who did your makeup?"

"I did."

He looked like a transvestite. "Too much. Wipe some off."

Three kids were sharing a big bag of barbecue potato chips. "Jesus," Mary yelled, "you don't eat when you're in costume."

"We were nervous."

Mary grabbed the bag of chips and went out the stage door into the cold, foggy night air. She lit her cigarette. It's going to be bad, she thought, but if it's really bad I'll leave before the curtain call. I'll disappear. She blew smoke into the frosted night and thought of Baryshnikov, July 1974, running away from his KGB escorts after a performance in Toronto. Mary thought of Natalia Makarova, 1970, London, ditching the Kirov and the Soviet Union, running right into a whole new life. Freedom. Mary thought about how, just a year earlier, she herself had been standing, in costume, in the warm air outside a theater in Phoenix, having a cigarette before the curtain went up for what turned out to be her own last performance. That night, at the reception afterward, the money people were looking for her—not to find fault, the way Mrs. Paine-Pinkney was doing, but just because they wanted to shake Mary's hand. They told her how much they'd loved her solo. They'd read about her in the papers. Two different critics had singled out and praised her performance. But by then none of it meant anything to Mary. She swapped it all for this Hiliard deal.

Mary tossed the bag of potato chips behind a shrub. Several weeks had passed since the day Natassia had insisted on describing, in detail, how she'd felt with the BF, wanting to know, Am I normal? Is this normal? Since that day, Mary had felt more trapped inside herself than ever. Before, the bad feelings had permeated Mary, but invisibly, like weather. After Natassia had named every bad feeling—worthless, stupid, ashamed, useless—Mary knew exactly what had always bricked her in. When the student stage manager stuck her head out the door, Mary was scratching fiercely at the base of her neck. "Hey, Ms. Mudd, five minutes to curtain."

Mary stamped out the butt of her cigarette. When she walked back inside, she motioned the students over to her with her arms. They hurried, making a circle around her. "I just yelled at a bunch of you," Mary told them. "I'm sorry. I shouldn't have done that. I get nervous before a performance."

"You do?"

"Everybody does."

"We thought you were angry at us about the other night. You know, the animal dancing. We heard you got in trouble."

"Yeah, maybe. But you guys aren't in trouble. You did great. And you're going to dance great again tonight."

"Like the animals," Charlie whispered.

"Yeah, just like animals. Come on," she said, grabbing two kids' hands, "circle." Pulled in together, gripping hands, they did look like wild hunted-down animals. *I have to do something.* "Listen," Mary told them, "you *are* dancers, you're good dancers." And she felt their hands squeeze all around the circle, and in that moment Mary wanted for the Hiliard School kids exactly what she wanted for Natassia—just for them to be okay. "You go out there and let them see what you can do."

"One minute to curtain."

"Please," one of the kids whispered, "stay backstage with us."

"I'll be back here. I'm with you. You're great."

And the house lights went down and the stage lights came up and music started and the kids didn't need Mary anymore: they *danced*. Mary stood backstage and loved what she saw. Yes, each arabesque was solid and deep, each turn stopped clean with no trembling, but greater than technique were their faces—beautiful, smiling, utterly lost within what they now knew how to do. The most Mary had hoped for was that they would remember all the steps and not make her look bad. Onstage, they went beyond. Each movement was clean and made sense. Part of that was her choreography, but the students really had made the dance their own. They no longer looked like floundering kids with too much money and show-off vocabulary. In the wings they stayed focused, and no one missed a cue.

They're beautiful. The kids reminded her why, for years, she'd chased all over the world, chasing *this*, a couple minutes onstage when you feel and look and are wiser than yourself.

Jenefer's solo made the audience whistle and clap.

Mary had prepared the kids to do an encore. It was a fairly simple dance that began with their warm-up isolations and then a few easy combinations, but they danced it to Joe Cocker singing "Bye Bye Blackbird," and all their forty-something parents, mostly trust-fund-hippies-turned-yuppies, ate it up. Standing ovations, a few affected *Bravi, bravi.* Mary was escorted onto the stage by Charlie and given a bouquet of yellow and white roses from Jenefer. Bowing, Mary scanned the crowd. She located Franklin, but she couldn't read his face. Where was that troublesome bitch, Mrs. Paine-Pinkney? All Mary could see clearly was Natassia and Kevin up on their feet, clapping and smiling and clapping for her.

"NOW FOR THE REAL PERFORMANCE," Mary muttered to Natassia as they walked into the party in the Admin Building Commons Room.

"You'll be fine," Natassia whispered back. "Just mingle."

As soon as he saw her, Franklin led Mary to the center of the room, got everyone's attention, handed her a glass of champagne—in a real glass, not plastic—and toasted her. *What the fuck is he trying to prove?* Everyone was applauding. Then a too-tan couple, blonds dressed in sporty imported wool, were tapping her elbow. "Ms. Mudd, we're Jenefer's parents."

And the show began.

For the next hour, Mary shook hands and smiled and listened to people say ridiculous things about how much Mary had added to the community of the school, how lucky the school was to have her. They asked her about her plans for the holiday break, then told her about their vacations. In Aspen, Switzerland, St. Thomas, St. Croix, Hawaii. She heard about grandparents who owned Vermont ski lodges and grandparents who rented chalets in western Canada for the whole family to come together for Christmas. Someone had inherited a small castle in France. Someone else owned an island. She heard about New Year's plans in Nepal, in New Mexico, in New Orleans, in the White House, the Governor's Mansion, and

Gracie Mansion in New York. She heard about plans to see the *Nutcracker* in Vienna, Mark Morris at BAM, and the Kirov in Russia.

Out of the corner of her eye, Mary spotted Natassia and Kevin roaming the room separately, always engaged in conversation. Once she overheard Natassia say, "No, my father was never a dancer. He's a physician. He lives in the Pacific Northwest."

Kevin was saying, "We all grew up together—Mary, my sister, and I. I can't remember a time when Mary wasn't part of our family," giving Mary's scattered life a veneer of solidity that was a complete joke. But Kevin was a salesman. "I own an antiques business. My sister is a psychotherapist in practice in Manhattan."

"Oh my, how interesting."

Even from a distance, unseen, Nora had the power to intimidate.

Toward the end of the evening, Mary felt a hand on her arm. She turned and it was old Dr. Jonson. Since he'd taken out Natassia's stitches and set her up for therapy with his daughter-in-law, Mary had seen him only once, for Natassia's earache. "Congratulations, dear. You've done a fine job."

Mary repeated what she'd been saying all night. "It was the kids. They worked hard."

"I don't mean the dance." Dr. Jonson kept on social-smiling, but his gray eyes turned serious, showed the smarts he usually hid behind chatter. "I mean your daughter. She's a different girl. Healthy, smiling. I see her over there." He nodded toward the buffet table, where Natassia was balancing a plate and laughing with some adults. "I see a happy teenage girl. Big change in a few months. Mother, you made excellent decisions."

He smelled of Old Spice and looked tan. Expensive, but nice, too. Franklin walked up. "Doctor, good to see you. Have you met Ms. Mudd?"

"I was just telling her that her hard work at Hiliard has paid off." Dr. Jonson was still holding Mary's hand in his. "You need to give this woman a salary increase, Mr. Fields, or she's going to get away, go teach in one of those fancy schools in the big city." Dr. Jonson winked a little wink. "Best of luck to you, dear."

Alone with Fields, Mary asked, "Okay, which one is Mrs. Paine-Pinkney?"

"Oh, she never comes to evening events," he said. "Her family won't let her. She drinks too much and says all the wrong things."

"I OWE YOU GUYS," Mary said to Natassia and Kevin as they walked and skidded down the frozen pavement back to the cottage. "You two really worked that room."

"Natassia takes the prize," Kevin said. "I think she talked to everybody and his brother." Natassia, grinning, breathed frosty breath up into the sky.

Mary laughed. "Yeah, and she made sure everybody knew that her dad's a *physician*."

"I knew they'd like that, to think that at some point in her life the unconventional Ms. Mudd had done something as conventional as marry a doctor. I didn't mention that you never did marry him. Or that he's also an alcoholic-pothead."

"Natassia, don't talk about your father that way."

"But it's true."

"Then especially don't talk about him that way."

"Okay. You're right."

Mary put one arm through Natassia's, her other through Kevin's. "Who wants dinner at Friendly's? My treat."

BECAUSE MARY hadn't had time to give a thought to the Christmas break, she accepted Kevin's invitation to drive down to the city with him. She and Natassia had nowhere else to go. Some writer had invited Lotte and David to London for Christmas; Lotte had accepted, she told Mary, in order to keep David out of Mary's hair. Nora had called and left a message that Mary and Natassia were welcome to stay in the loft during the holidays, but Nora and Christopher would not be there. "Just call Kevin first and arrange your times with him," Nora had said, "because I offered him the loft, too." It wasn't until Mary, Natassia, and Kevin were in New York, in the loft, that the oddness of the situation finally sunk in. Nora and Christopher weren't home. No one, not even Kevin, knew exactly where they were.

The place was dusty. The mailbox was crammed full with Christmas cards. There were a dozen UPS and FedEx delivery receipts. A pile of boxes had been left for them at the laundry next door. The cat was gone.

Standing in the kitchen loosening his tie, Kevin said, "Things are worse than I thought. The Brita filter is more than a month overdue. Under normal circumstances, Christopher would never let that happen."

CHAPTER 27:

DECEMBER

1989

It fell on a Sunday, but the day felt like a Saturday, as Christmas Eve always does. Christopher was hauling Denise's artificial tree down from her attic. What he wanted was to talk her into letting him buy a real evergreen. She refused. Waste of money. He unpacked her boxes labeled CHRISTMAS so she could decorate as she and Don always had: rolls of cotton for the mantel, tinsel for the fake tree, and a hundred other tacky touches Christopher couldn't believe were part of the house where he was spending Christmas.

As he changed Baby Don's diaper and bathed him in the sink, Christopher sang "Little Drummer Boy." As he gift-wrapped a package of high-quality computer paper and a nice brass letter-opener for Denise, and wrapped a set of hand-painted German-made wooden blocks for Baby Don, along with a set of four handmade puppets, and filled stockings for them with candy and trinkets, and shoveled the walkway and driveway so he could drive to the grocery store, he sang "O Tannenbaum" and "Come, All Ye Faithful." And the whole time, Christopher couldn't stop thinking about what he and Nora would be doing if this were a normal Christmas Eve.

By now they would have come home from Jefferson Market, where they always went together to buy the fresh seafood for Christmas Eve dinner. By two o'clock, Christopher would have cleaned the squid, shrimp, and scallops. He'd have some squid steaming to make into a salad, more squid ready to fry for the antipasto, and the majority of the squid ready to sauté with shrimp and scallops for the pasta sauce. By now he'd be kneading the dough to fry the *zeppole*, with the pan full of honey right by the stove so he could dip the fried dough while it was still hot; and then he'd call Nonna in Kansas City and tell her that his *zeppole* weren't as good as hers, and she'd make a big fuss, again, about how it was her grandson, and none of her granddaughters, who cared enough to keep up the family's traditions. By now he would already have made the angel-hair pasta and hung it to dry. He'd be stuffing the lobster tails. He'd be trying to talk Nora into doing something to help him, at least slice the mozzarella and the tomatoes, wash the basil leaves! His coconut cake would be baking. The biscotti would already be baked. He'd have the pancetta and the Arborio rice for the Christmas Day risotto. Nora, eventually, would fill vases with fresh-cut flowers. She would wrap gifts with ribbon so expensive that if Denise ever heard about it she'd choke. Nora would be answering the buzzer and taking in boxes sent by his parents, flower deliveries from their friends. She'd be futzing with the stockings, all embroidered with names, which she lined up in alphabetical order along the fake-fireplace mantel: Christopher, David, Giulia, Lotte, Kevin, Mary, Natassia, Nora, Ross. And there would be a couple extra stockings for any unexpected visitors who happened to show up at the last minute for Christmas in Christopher and Nora's loft.

Nora would have candles set in candlesticks everywhere. She would be wearing some new sexy underwear, because that was one of the ways she surprised Christopher every Christmas Eve night. They'd be listening to Italian Christmas music on the CD player. Somehow, during their years together, Christmas had become Italian: the stacks of cookies, the rolls of dried figs, the baskets of fruits.

And, always, Christopher's festival of food. At the end of his dinners, people scraped their plates with their forks. Every year—it was tradition by now—Ross picked up his plate and licked it.

All of this should be going on. All of this was Christmas. None of it was happening this year.

A few days earlier, Christopher had stopped in a market in Nyack and found a big panettone. When he brought the cake home, Denise had said,

"Why'd you spend the money? We have all those cookies my sister-in-law sent."

"I like the smell of panettone when you slice it open."

"I bet you spent ten bucks on that, and just to smell it? We'll never eat all this."

He had to cut down his enthusiasms. He had to cut down his spending, which was difficult. Christopher had never felt as generous and full-hearted as he did these days every time he held Baby Don.

But away from the baby, Christopher had never felt sadder in all his life.

Or more scared.

JUST A FEW HOURS EARLIER, late morning on Christmas Eve, he'd come home with groceries and found that things at Denise's had turned a little strange. When he walked in the front door, there was a votive candle lit in front of Don's photograph in the hallway. A four-foot-by-three-foot painting Christopher recognized as one of Don's had been hauled up into the living room from the basement. The canvas had cobwebs in its corners; the surface of the painting had been dusted off in streaks.

Christopher stood in the living room with his boots off and his jacket on, holding four grocery bags. "Denise," he called. "You didn't carry that up here yourself, did you?"

Her voice came from the kitchen. "I dragged it, I didn't carry it."

When Christopher entered the kitchen, Denise didn't turn to look at him. She was sponging off the counter. The kitchen was a mess in some way he'd never seen it before.

"Denise?"

"Would you check on the big guy? I put him down for his nap, but I think I just heard him fussing." She started opening cabinets, closing cabinets.

"What are you looking for?" he asked.

"Stuff I need. I'm baking Don's sister's turkey stuffing. And we need salt for the driveway; you probably didn't get any, did you? That's okay. Maybe next door those people have some extra next door."

She was still in her robe. Her bare feet, Christopher noticed, were dirty.

"Denise?" He walked up to her, and she moved away, but as she did, there was a scent around her. Something gingery but not quite innocent. Something stuffy, like a closed-in closet.

And then her foot shuffling over the floor caught on the leg of a chair, and she screamed, "Fuck shit fuck," curses completely unheard from her before, and Christopher felt the first clutch of fear in his stomach. As she grabbed at her foot, she stumbled and then lowered herself onto the step stool, almost missing it. When she looked up at the ceiling, Christopher saw that her face was red, very red. Ruddy, overheated, not right.

"Denise, have you been drinking?"

She burst out laughing. She was hugging her foot; her bathrobe opened, showing her thighs. "I'm not sure," she said in a voice detached from her, not speaking to him, "what you mean by that question."

LATER, AFTER SHE finally agreed to go lie down in her bed, after he diapered the baby and put him down again to nap, Christopher found an uncorked bottle of port in the basement. It was a souvenir bottle, shaped like a painter in a beret holding a paintbrush, and it was sitting on a shelf next to Don's tools. The bottle was half empty.

Christopher was still in the basement, trying to figure out what to do, when the phone rang, and it was Carole, Denise's sponsor. He heard Denise on the phone with Carole for a long time. And then he heard nothing, so he figured Denise had fallen asleep. Her bedroom door was closed. When he peeked in, she was in bed, all covered up. Christopher cleaned the kitchen. Egg yolks were floating on the counter, and eggshells were spread all over the window ledge. Bread crumbs were underfoot. On the cutting board were stalks of half-chopped celery, and a knife with a dash of blood on it. Two big bowls were greasy all over with oil or butter. A dish towel had slipped halfway down into the garbage disposal. Christopher had been gone less than two hours.

The baby was happy that day, easily satisfied with the bottle Christopher made up from Denise's expressed milk stored in the freezer. But as Christopher held and fed him, Baby Don looked smaller than he had the week before. "Ah, baby, what's going to happen? What'll I do for you, boy?" All afternoon Christopher whispered, kept the noise down, tiptoed. When the phone rang late in the afternoon, he jumped, grabbed it on the first ring. "Yes, hello."

"Hey there, this is Melany, Denise's sister-in-law. In Erie?"

"Yeah, Melany. I heard about you."

"You did, huh? Well, you, too. Hey, how's your Christmas up there? Got snow coming? It's coming down here like buckets."

"Yeah, a little snow. A little."

"So, how's the mommy? How's our sister doing, that nutty girl?"

"Well, she's . . ."

"She's not drinking yet, is she?"

"What?"

The woman laughed. "I shouldn't say it, but I guess we worry. The reason I'm asking before you put her on is because sometimes at Christmas, since Don's sickness and all, she's had a little return of her problem. It doesn't happen every year, but—"

"Well, it happened this year." Christopher had the phone receiver tucked into his neck and was burping the baby. "I came home this morning and she was . . . I don't know. She's sleeping it off. She's been in bed all afternoon."

"Ah, shit. Ah, shit and shit. Reg," the woman said to someone in the room with her, "looks like she had another slip."

The man's voice came near the phone. "That guy's there? She's not alone?"

"Is the baby all right?" the woman asked, a little testy.

Already Christopher felt defensive. "Yeah, he's fine. I'm holding him."

"Bless his heart, that little thing. If my brother Don could—"

"So this happened before?" Christopher asked.

"I told you," the woman said, again with that tone of irritation, "at Christmas, once in a while, we've had a little problem with her. It just gets so she can't handle it some Christmases and she ties on a good one. Those are her only slips."

Christopher heard the man's voice again, testier than the woman's. Christopher did need help from these people, but he was glad they were in Erie, in snow.

"Well, right. Reg just reminded me there was that once on Don's birthday, too."

The baby was turning his face in to Christopher's chest, yawning, and Christopher imagined himself and Baby Don, Christmas after Christmas, holding on to each other, waiting for Denise to sleep it off, not able to call Nora.

"When's Don's birthday?" Christopher asked, testy himself now.

"May. Why?"

"I just wish I'd known. So I could be prepared or something."

"Are you needing to leave there?" Melany asked. "Is there somebody can come by watch the baby till Denise pulls herself together?"

"I'm not going anywhere. I'm here. I'm staying till after the holidays, till Don and Denise get settled in together. I'm not leaving them. She just had surgery."

There was a silence. "I'm glad you're there with her. You sound like a nice guy. I have to tell you, we was worried."

Christopher didn't like this world he and his baby were living in, and he felt a huge rush of anger at Nora. If it weren't for her stubborn, high-and-mighty refusal to have a baby in their marriage . . .

But if it weren't for Nora's stubbornness, *this* baby wouldn't be here. Christopher hated that thought. He kissed Baby Don's forehead. "Okay," he said to Melany, "what do I need to know about Denise and Christmas, and what's going to happen here? The baby and I need to be prepared."

"Nothing. She'll sleep it off. I'd say, if you can, don't leave her alone. It's the loneliness for Don, the depression, that gets her. She likes to go to her meetings. That gal she's got, that Carole, she'll help you out. I'd say it's better if you're not drinking in the house. I know it's Christmas—"

"I never drink in front of Denise. There's no liquor in this house. She found some souvenir bottle of port downstairs."

"Port," the woman told Reg, "that souvenir bottle we brought Don from Vegas, remember? I told you we shouldn't never brought it. That's what she was drinking.

"Yeah," Melany said to Christopher, "you probably seen the worse. She's never did it twice. Just once, usually late on Christmas Day. This is early. She's going to wake up hating herself and feeling like crapola. Just

329

feed her coffee and let her be while she pulls together. And listen, I'm real sorry we won't be there with you guys. Reg and I are working things to be up there with her by New Year's, so you can make your plans, too." Melany broke off to talk to Reg. "What?" she asked him. "Can't you see I'm on the phone? No, Reg, he's not calling Social Services. He's not leaving the baby with her when she's drinking. She's not drinking now. She's sleeping." Back to Christopher: "I'm sorry. He gets nuts sometimes, too."

"Well, I'm not leaving here until Denise feels good enough to take care of the baby." Or until he's old enough to take care of himself, Christopher thought as he hung up the phone. It was dark outside, time to turn on the blinking lights on the artificial tree. The baby was falling asleep in Christopher's arms, so he spread a blanket on the floor and laid the baby down right next to him. It was hard enough to resist the urge to keep the baby in his arms; no way could Christopher sit in this sad living room by himself on Christmas Eve with Baby Don in another room. Lying on his back, the baby automatically lifted his arms over his head—a sign of surrender, defeat? The seriousness on his face during sleep made Christopher sad. Already Don seemed to understand the precariousness of his life.

Christopher knew the 800 number for TWA by heart. He picked up the phone, dialed. By some Christmas miracle, he got a real voice instead of a recorded message. He asked about flights from LaGuardia to Kansas City. "Let me check that for you, sir. Two adults with an infant, right? One moment, please." The TWA attendant put Christopher on hold, and then Christopher hung up. The despair had passed through him, and he'd come to his senses. As soon as he hung up the phone, his hands stopped trembling.

There was nothing to do but sit it out—Denise's drunk, the holidays, Baby Don's childhood and adolescence and early adulthood. Christopher put pillows all around the baby's blanket and walked across the living room to the front door. He looked back at the baby—he was safe—and then Christopher opened the front door, stepped onto the porch, went to a branch of evergreen hanging over the stoop, bent his face into the cold needles, and breathed. He rubbed his face into the snow on the branch, then broke it off and brought it into the house, stomped his shoes, and locked up the door for the night. He laid the branch under the tree, next to Denise's fake-wood manger, then stretched out nearby so he could catch the evergreen scent.

Christopher remembered a morning in late August, after he'd started traveling up to Nyack to help Denise get the house ready. It was very early, and he'd sat out on the front porch drinking a cup of coffee, noticing how quiet Denise's street was compared with his street in New York. And then, within the quiet, sounds rose up and were all over him. The incessant chatter of birds, the 1960s sound of whirring lawn-sprinklers. There was the cranking of the neighbor's garage door being lifted—one car started, one guy going off to work, instead of the hundreds of people who daily rushed by below the loft's windows.

In his life before Denise, Christopher would have felt sorry for any guy living in a house like Denise's or the one next door to hers. Aluminum siding. Crooked porch with a cheap, rusty railing. A plastic eagle on the plastic mailbox. A year earlier, Christopher would have thought, *Can't these people do better? Where's their taste?* He would have told Nora, *Let's get out of here, let's get back to the city. Fast.*

The guy driving off to work that morning had waved at Christopher. A bird landed on the overhung branch of the evergreen, not far from where Christopher sat on Denise's aluminum lawn chair. *It's not a pigeon.* It was a little smaller than a pigeon and had the muted colors of a female, some kind of dove, with a sweet bluish head, a sharp beak, a longish tail. Christopher would have liked to sketch the bird, but it was almost September, and he hadn't finished emptying Don's painting studio so it could be turned into a nursery—strip wallpaper, plaster, maybe even drywall. *I could trim the shrubs for Denise. I should plant some hostas down the walkway.* First, though, he'd have to go up into the attic and repair the rafters, then probably up onto the roof. Denise had had to buy a new furnace unexpectedly, so she didn't have the extra money in her budget to hire people to do the work she'd planned to hire out. She'd have to dip into the money saved for the first year of day care. Christopher couldn't let her do that.

Until that summer, he'd never had a close-up look at such a careful life, a life lived with no financial net. He began to realize what advantages he had, starting with the deep foundation of his father's money. Top that with the good taste acquired from his mother and her art education. Also, thanks to his mother, some halfway-good looks. All just luck.

The bird in the evergreen sat.

And sat there, forcing Christopher to know something new.

To keep up her mediocre bad-taste house, Denise had to exert more effort, take more risk, and use more caution than Christopher had ever applied to anything. On top of it all, at the end of the day, Denise couldn't even sit down with the comfort of a glass of wine or a beer. Not without paying for it, in spades.

It was his own pampered life that was the mediocrity. And as he sat there that summer morning, it occurred to him that Nora's struggle was harder than his, too. She, too, had always had some backup—the money left to her and Kevin when they lost their parents. But, man, the way they'd lost their parents. Two kids in high school. *Shit.* Their house burned down. Insurance money, yeah, but a lot of it went to paying their dad's debts. *That loser.* Ed Conolly. The way Kevin and Nora talked about him, you'd have thought he was some kind of Irish saint sent to Albany by God himself. Christopher didn't get it. In every story they told about Ed Conolly, he was acting superior to everybody else, making his wife and kids cover up for him about having been in jail and all that. And lazy, too. Maybe Nora and Kevin just couldn't see it. Nora's mother must have been like Nora, always working, always pulling her own load, plus extra to cover the father's debts and his bad manners. Nora and Kevin still had the house at the beach, but it really was a shack, not worth the time and work Nora and Kevin had put into it through the years. And the time and work they'd got Christopher to put into it.

He and Nora had had one of the big fights of their marriage several years back, when Christopher's father had suggested they raze the Greenport house, fix up the property, and he, Juno Sampietro, would pay for a decent house to be built. "My investment, your pleasure," his father had said. Christopher understood now, as he hadn't then, why Nora had flipped. But, boy, what a drag that had been, his father insulted to have his offer turned away, Nora furious at Christopher for even considering it. "Hey, where are my grandchildren?" Christopher's father used to say on the phone each week. Nora finally had said, "Juno, I know you care about us, but it's not appropriate to ask us that question." Which, of course, got Juno pissed off. "What's with your wife?" And then an earful from Nora about not "taking responsibility," not "setting boundaries."

Responsibility. Lying on the floor in front of Denise's ugly tree, Christopher stretched out on his stomach on Denise's worn-down wall-to-wall carpeting and watched the muted TV, all about the Berlin Wall falling. He stacked Baby Don's new wooden blocks into a long curved wall. Then, with a flick of fingers, he knocked the stack down.

The baby cried. Christopher sat up, settled him with a hand on his stomach. "Hey, guy, okay, it's okay." It was a fake cry; Don fell back to sleep. He was starting to look like something. Objectively, Christopher was looking at one good-looking baby.

Every good feature of Denise's, the baby had. She did have nice, smooth, really young-looking skin. Baby had a nice line of eyebrows that Christopher recognized as Denise's. If Christopher had to force himself really to be objective, he would admit that Baby Don had only one feature that wasn't aesthetically pleasing—his little ears stuck out quite a bit. Noticeably. This was the only immediate feature of his own that Christopher could find in the baby. Denise had even mentioned it: "Now, where do you think he got these ears?" Eventually, Christopher would have to tell Denise the truth—Christopher's mother had had him go through the surgery to have his ears pinned back when he was a kid. In his earliest photos, Christopher had huge stick-out ears.

Nora was the only one who knew it. Sometimes, teasing, if she really wanted to get to Christopher, she'd call him Dumbo. But she only did that when Christopher teased Kevin about being such a hopeless fanatic about collecting junk, or whenever Christopher teased Nora about her all-white hair.

Don and Christopher lay together on the floor, Christopher leaning his arm on a faded denim Santa Claus pillow.

Four days after Christmas, Franklin Fields called Mary at the loft in New York. It was Friday morning, not even noon yet. Mary and Natassia were still asleep in the bedroom, Kevin asleep on the couch, and none of them heard the phone ring. Franklin left a message asking Mary to call him back. His voice had that friendliness it always had, but he wasn't stuttering, and Mary was convinced she heard an urgency, something like *Call me as soon as possible because your ass is in trouble.*

"They're firing me," she concluded after listening to the message for the third time. She, Natassia, and Kevin, holding their coffee mugs, stood in a circle around the answering machine, staring at it.

"That was your boss?" Kevin asked. "He sounds friendly, like he likes you or something."

"He has a major crush on her," Natassia said. "He tried asking her out."

"Is that kosher, the headmaster asking a teacher out?"

"Kevin's right, Mom. If Franklin's firing you, you can sue his ass for sexual harassment."

"He never harassed me. If the board told him to fire me, he has to fire me."

"I'm sorry," Kevin said, "to disagree with you, but there is nothing in this message that sounds like your boss is going to fire you. He said, 'I need to talk to you. Soon, if possible.' He sounds like he's the one in trouble, like he needs you to help him. Maybe he just wants to ask you out again. Maybe they're firing *him*."

"They should," Natassia mumbled, "fucking asshole."

"He's not married, huh?" Kevin said. "I wonder what's up with that."

"Natassia, hand me the telephone. I'm calling Ross."

ROSS TOLD MARY what she already knew. She had to return Franklin's call. Soon. When she did return the call, she got Franklin's answering machine. Mary left a message, and then she and Natassia and Kevin ate waffles.

After their late breakfast, Natassia vacuumed. Kevin folded up his blankets. Mary changed the sheets on the bed and did a load of everyone's laundry. Without any discussion, they all participated in the housecleaning, which convinced Mary that Kevin and Natassia were as worried as she was and were making this offering to the gods. Kevin had just poured a bag of split peas into a bowl of cold water to soak, announcing he would make a healthy pea soup, and Natassia was plucking Mary's eyebrows, when the phone rang, finally.

"Mary, Franklin here. I'm just sorry as hell to bother you during the holidays, but I thought it best to reach you sooner than later. You're in the city. Having a good time?"

"I was. What's up?"

"Well." Mary was fishing her asthma inhaler out of her backpack. "There's a letter I got here from the board of trustees that we need to deal with." *The naked dancing. Damn Charlie.* "It looks like they're going after two programs I've been trying to develop, and I'll be damned if they're getting them. It's black studies and the dance program."

Why won't he say right out it's the naked dancing? "So they want to cancel the dance classes?" Mary signaled to Natassia to bring her a cigarette.

"No, no, no. They can't cancel classes that easily, certainly not classes already in the curriculum. What we're talking about here is the extended program in dance I discussed with you when you came on board last spring."

Mary remembered, vaguely, something about how he wanted, eventually, a whole Dance Department, and how Mary would be first in line to

335

be director, which would mean a pay increase, but at the time she hadn't paid attention. *If he'd just say it's the naked dancing, I could explain.*

"I'm real peeved," Franklin said, "about how the board's going about this, slipping this request in during the holidays, adding this to the agenda for their January meeting. But if they're asking for this information now, we've got to get it to them. I'll need your help in writing up the report. And, remember, Mary, you're first in line to direct this program when it comes about, should you be interested in that."

"Sure, Franklin. What'd you need me to do?" *If he won't say naked dancing, neither will I.*

A few minutes later, the board's letter came through the fax machine. When Mary read down the list of requested information, she wished Franklin had just fired her and been done with it.

Here was what the board of trustees wanted:

1. A detailed description of the dance program as it currently exists.
2. A detailed rationale for a continued dance program, with explicit explanation of how such a program will augment/benefit the general curriculum.
3. A detailed five-year plan for the projected dance program.
4. A summation description of six other existing programs at six other schools. The six schools must be comparable to the Hiliard School, citing establishment date, endowment, total enrollment, enrollment in dance classes, number of dance classes, background of the faculty, and summary of dance curriculum. With comments from alumni if possible.
5. Detailed course plans from last semester and for the forthcoming semester.
6. A reading list.
7. Copies of all exams given to date.
8. Current instructor's CV.
9. Bibliography.
10. Detailed description of current instructor's training, including pedagogical training.
11. A brief (no more than five pages) statement of instructor's teaching philosophy.

12. Reference letters in support of instructor.

13. Standards for safety in the current dance studios.

Mary faxed the list to Ross, who called her back immediately. "Jesus, Mary, they're treating this thing seriously. They're not kidding around. Somebody wants blood. How much time do you have left on that contract you signed?"

"The rest of this year, and then another full year."

"With medical benefits that whole time?"

"Yeah."

"Okay, I see. It's because Natassia's on your medical plan," Ross said. "They're trying to get you to quit so they don't have to fire you and pay you severance and risk your suing their sorry asses for breach of contract, but clearly they want you gone. They don't like it that your daughter's living with you and she has mental-health problems."

"Ross! Don't say that about her."

"Hey, she had a nervous breakdown serious enough to miss a whole semester of eleventh grade. The label here is 'mental-health problems'— that's what'll be on the record and that's what they'll call it. How's she doing anyway? You guys hardly ever call me anymore. She want to talk to me?"

"Not now. I need you to help me. What'm I going to do?"

"You're going to give them everything they want. Start writing. Don't waste time with the stuff that's impossible. There's no way you're going to come up with all that academic stuff they're asking for. You're no academic."

"Goddamn it, Ross."

"Stop it. Mary, you're not going to get through this if you make it personal. This has nothing to do with you, and—and—don't interrupt me or swear at me again—I didn't say you don't know how to teach. This isn't about abilities. This is about background. Do you have a Ph.D.? No, so you're not an academic. That's a fact. And for the record, most academics don't know how to teach. You're a professional dancer. You're an artist. You've got experience up the wazoo. Plus, there's stuff you can do for that lousy school that your board of trustees hasn't even thought of. That's what you've got to show them."

"Like what, what can I do?"

"You're a world-class performer, you've got connections that can bring guest teachers up there who could get major press for the school, which can attract major money from alumni and the community and everybody else."

"Slow," Mary told him, "I'm writing this."

"Then, if they happen to have even one or two students who actually are any good, you could help get the kid into a dance company or a college with a big dance program or something. Your connections, Mary, are more valuable to that school than a long list of academic papers, but they can't ask you for connections, so you've just got to offer the information. Make a case for yourself. Wow them with what you've got, and show them why they need what you've got."

"So how—"

"Get on the horn. Call in all your favors. All those people you worked with at Jacob's Pillow. People in the company. Who else've you got? Then get together all your reviews and performance programs so they can see where you've performed."

"I don't have reviews. I never save that stuff."

"The company has files. And the major reviews from foreign countries, you'll need to get them translated."

Silence. Mary was drawing on the top of a bakery box, little stick figures doing karate kicks at one another. "The company's on tour. They're in Japan and Europe and stuff." She covered her face with her hands. "All this for a lousy high-school job?"

"Don't think *job*, Mary, think *career*."

"But my résumé lists—"

"Not good enough. You got to take them by the hand, educate them. Spell it all out. Tell them what it means to have danced solos at the Joyce. Tell them what it means to—"

"How low do I have to go in spelling it out? I mean, shit."

"*That's* the idea. Just go lower than you ever imagined possible. And lots of paper. Just bury them in documentation. Tons of support letters. Make charts. Natassia can show you how to do that on the computer."

"Charts of what?"

"I don't know. Muscle tone. Numbers of injuries. Charts are good. By the way, did they ask for your medical records or tax forms? How much do they know about Natassia?"

Ross's voice was beginning to make Mary feel very alone. "You're scaring me. You're acting like I'm in serious shit."

"Don't get mad but, hey, I've got my own questions here. *Are* you losing your job? Is Natassia going to have a place to live or what?"

So there it was. Ross. During Christmas, Mary and Natassia had felt a little guilty that they weren't with Ross or that he wasn't with them. But he *wasn't* with them, he hadn't been *with* them during the whole crisis, all fall.

Mary tried to make her voice flat. "It's bad enough already. You don't have to hurt my feelings."

A long, hot sigh somewhere in Spokane, Washington. It could go either way now, depending on how far gone he was.

"Honey," Ross said, then paused. "They're the assholes, Mar. I'm just mad at them for jerking you around. I don't want you losing that job. I know how you love having that job."

"I hate the job. I like the kids. They turned out to be not too bad, but the job—"

"What would you do if you lost it? Where would you go? Perform again? On the road? Would the company even take you back? I mean, Natassia's at risk here, too."

"Okay, Ross. I better go."

"Do you want help with this thing or what?"

"I'll call you," Mary told him, and hung up. Then she took the phone off the hook to keep the line busy, because Ross would be trying to call back, hitting REDIAL for the next half-hour or so, and then he'd stop trying and go on to something else. The next time he and Mary spoke, things would be better. Or they'd be worse.

HOW LOW CAN YOU GO? *How low can you go?* Mary read the list of questions for the umpteenth time. Her life was now a take-home exam. Ross had said, Just pick one and start. *A brief statement of instructor's teaching philosophy.* A good place to begin, since they wanted it brief.

It was Friday night. Kevin and Natassia had gone out to a sushi place that had a TV so they could watch the coverage of the opening of the Brandenburg Gate. Mary had stayed home to begin writing her philosophy. Also because she thought sushi was gross. As soon as she was alone in the loft, Mary pulled a chair up to the head of the long dining table and set down a fresh legal pad she'd found in Nora's bedroom, a pen, a glass of ice water. Kevin had said that if she wrote longhand he'd type everything up for her on the laptop. Mary sat down.

Suddenly Mary pushed back her chair and stood up.

This was the first time since the BF breakup in September that Natassia was out without her mother. *Jesus.* Natassia and Kevin were already gone. Mary walked to the window, opened the blinds. *Natassia's with Kevin.* It felt okay to trust Kevin, but was he alert enough? What if Natassia gave him the slip, got on a bus or a train or a plane, and went off to find the BF?

Mary forced the window open, and a tiny wall of snow fell in onto the sill. Maybe Natassia and her BF had been communicating all along by secret code. Leaning her whole upper body out into the cold, Mary knew it was ridiculous to try finding Natassia and Kevin in the crowds down on the sidewalks, but she was looking. *I should've at least warned Kevin first.* The air was damp, a heavy Friday night. Scanning the crowds below, Mary felt inside her body that provocative tug that's inevitable when leaning out into a high height. She was five stories up. The feeling scared her, mostly because it thrilled her body. *How easy it would be. If you wanted to, how easy.* She imagined the headline: WOMAN ON FIRST NIGHT HOME ALONE WITHOUT DAUGHTER JUMPS. After a few minutes, the combination of cold air and anxiety made Mary want a cigarette, but she'd been quitting since Christmas Day. She pulled in her head and let the window slam shut.

On her way back to the table, Mary got her cigarettes out of her backpack, tossed them way down onto the middle of the table, far from the notepad and pen. She sat again to write. It was shocking to think that she used to spend her nights alone while Natassia wandered around the city, "using her own good judgment," as Lotte liked to say.

What complete horseshit.

During a Dr. Cather session on the phone about a month earlier, Mary had broken down, whispering, "Dr. Cather, I did terrible things. I left her with other people, and they let her run around. We all did. We let her *go.*"

"But *now*, Mary," Dr. Cather had said, "you are holding your daughter in a way that you yourself were never held. You're holding her physically, emotionally."

"But when she was little . . ."

"Some people never in their lifetime receive what Natassia is receiving from you now. Some never manage to do for another what you are doing for your daughter now. *Now*, Mary, look at now."

Right now Natassia was out for sushi with Kevin. *If they're not home in two hours, I'll call the police. I won't let her out all night the way we used to.*

Now Mary needed to keep her job. She pulled her legs up and settled herself Indian-style on the straight-back chair. *Instructor's teaching philosophy. Five pages.*

The silence in the loft was a whisper of noises: the ice-cube machine in the fancy fridge, radiator pipes hiccupping, traffic. Mary looked at the word "philosophy." It made her think of Ross. She hated being in a fight with him. Her feet were cold. On her way into the bedroom for socks, she picked up the mobile phone and dialed Ross's number. She hung up. Then she hit REDIAL. Harriet answered. Ross wasn't home, so Mary and Harriet talked a while about the letter from Franklin. Harriet was sympathetic, said she hated writing that kind of stuff, too, when she applied for grants or whatever. She said the only thing to do was sit down and get it over with. She said, "Sometimes a mug of green tea settles me."

Harriet and Mary had never met, but they'd been having phone conversations for over two years now, arranging Natassia's visits to Spokane, and, recently, discussing her recovery. Mary decided to go for it. "So— Ross sounds, I don't know, jumpy lately."

There was a pause, and Mary thought, I should have kept my mouth shut.

"*Jumpy's* not even the word. Mary, things aren't great around here. I've thought of calling you. I'm glad, for Natassia's sake, that she didn't come visit this New Year's. She wouldn't enjoy her dad much these days."

"What?"

"Oh, Mary"—a new Harriet slipped through—"he's not in good shape."

"He's using?" *Why'm I acting like I don't know?*

"After that trip to New York for Natassia, he plummeted. But you know, it's not just her breakdown. It's—it's Ross. What can I say? It was very bad for a while. I had to tell his supervisor."

"At the hospital? You told?"

"He's a doctor, Mary. He could kill somebody if he made a mistake. I could lose my own license for protecting him." Mary could hear in Harriet's voice traces of an argument, hints of a battle that had gone on, maybe was still going on. "It's not just cocaine now. He's starting in with fentanyl."

"What's that? Is it bad?"

"Bad? It's like morphine, only about eighty times more potent. It's used by the anesthesiologists, who happened to notice their supplies were down. One thing led to another. Anyway, they've got him on probation now. They love him at the hospital, they really do. He's an excellent doctor. Even when he's high, he does the work better than most. He's in a rehab program, doing daily check-ins with a counselor. Random urine tests." Making her way down this treatment list, Harriet eased back into her doctor's voice. "He's in private therapy and in a group."

"Urine tests? Isn't that what they do with addicts?"

"Mary. He *is* an addict. He was injecting this stuff."

"Oh, man, Harriet, I just—"

"I know, Mary, I know. And he refused to tell you any of this, because, well, as you know, he lies a lot. But, really, he didn't want to worry you, on top of everything else you've got with Natassia. And he certainly doesn't want his parents to know. Mary, who are these people? I mean, good Lord, how destructive they've been to him. How . . ."

Lotte and David? Were they really that bad? Were they?

"Anyway," Harriet said, "it really is better for Natassia not to be here this year. We miss her, but her dad's sleeping down in Natassia's little room." And the next thing Mary knew, Harriet was confiding that she and Ross were in couples counseling, too, but it was that doctor's voice offering this information. Composed, Harriet went on: "I've just had to draw some boundaries. Things seem a little better now, with this rehab program."

"Is he going to lose his job?" Mary asked.

"No." Harriet's voice was clipped, firm. "As I said, he's a brilliant physician, Mary, and well liked. He won't lose his job." Pause, then Harriet let herself sound like a woman again. "He might lose me, but not the job." Harriet laughed that low, wry hurt-woman's laugh Mary had heard from Natassia after the BF left her. Then, from somewhere close to Harriet, came unpleasant cat noises. "Oh no, kitten! My little kitty here just got sick on my shoe. Oh, poor cat. Mary, I should get off."

"Oh yeah, listen, let me know. And if you guys need anything. Really, anything."

"Well, just, please, wait for him to tell you himself. We're clear on this, right?"

"Sure. Bye." *Wow.* Mary had to walk around the loft. None of it was news, it just felt bad to have it spelled out. *Rehab. Probation. Urine tests. Injecting.*

Mary pushed open the window again, just a crack, and squatted there smoking a cigarette, letting the smoke out into the night. (Nothing made a cigarette taste better than quitting for a few days.) No wonder he'd been such a jackass to her on the phone, he was worried about his own job. If they both fucked up, where *would* Natassia live? *How destructive. . . .* Lotte and David probably weren't a possibility anymore. "I've got to write this job thing," Mary said out loud. "Now. Tonight."

She smashed her cigarette on the sill and tossed the butt down into the street, let the window slam. Her feet were freezing. She went into the bedroom and dug around in the laundry basket of clean clothes. Ross had been in some kind of rehab once before. It had helped, for a while. He'd been clean for over three years, since he'd first met Harriet. Putting on her socks, Mary noticed someone's toenail clipper on the dresser, and she stopped to clip her toenails. There was a nail file, too, so she filed her fingernails. *How could Lotte and David* not *know about Ross? And they went to London for Christmas?* Mary noticed her toenail clippings on the wooden floor, and with her foot she swept them under the bed.

On the way back from the bedroom, with socks on, Mary stopped on the bare wood floor between two dhurrie rugs and squared her feet in a parallel second position. Her body was full of antsiness that wasn't letting her sit down to write. She did an abdominal contraction and rolled her head down to her feet, hands to the floor, felt her spine loosen, then rolled herself back up slowly, vertebra by vertebra. She'd been working out at a gym down the street in the mornings. She'd taken a dance class that after-noon. Her joints were nice and loose; inside, in her guts, though, she was knots. *Ross. Ross.* It would have been good to call Dr. Cather. But four days after Christmas, on a Friday night at eight-thirty? Lying on her side, Mary V-ed open her legs and used one arm to raise herself off the floor, hinged herself up to a standing position. *That felt nice.* She got down on the floor again, V-ed her legs, hinged up, then did four counts of shoulder iso-lations and four counts of hip isolations.

Kevin and Natassia had been playing an Edith Piaf CD, and there was one song . . . Mary found the song on the CD and improvised, starting on the floor with her legs V-ed open. The CD player was on REPEAT, and Piaf's singing sounded like the howling inside Mary's chest as she let herself dance the album through three times. Mary liked what she'd just improvised, so she danced it through again. And then she couldn't hold herself back.

Turning off the music, she walked straight into the bedroom, opened Natassia's backpack, and dug around until she found Natassia's journal.

For a terrible, sick moment while she'd been dancing, she'd let herself wonder, Is Natassia using? What if Ross is supplying her? Messed-up father, sick daughter? As a doctor, Ross could get anything. *Reading this journal feels much worse than giving in to a smoke.* There was a powerful body sensation every time Mary held the pink folder. Touching the tips of the pages, Mary's fingers trembled and felt hot; but inside, Mary felt oddly at one with herself: her impulses and her actions were aligned. *This is probably how it feels to Ross every time he starts using.*

She wasn't looking just for the dreaded initials BF now, she was looking for anything. An early-December entry relieved Mary's most immediate worry: *Daddy's messed up again. She won't tell me but I can tell from their phone conversations. Poor sick Daddy. I never could stand it when he's like that.*

So they weren't in cahoots, father and daughter. Mary put the pink folder away, tucking it under the same white T-shirt where she'd found it. By now Mary was perspiring and dusty and decided she could use a hot bath before sitting down again to write.

The bathroom was cluttered. Kevin's guy stuff was everywhere: a slopped-up shaving-soap dish, a wood-handled shaving brush. His boxers were crumpled on the floor by the toilet. It had been a long time since

Mary had been around so much guyness. After she cleared his stuff from the tub, she started to run the bathwater, and then Mary noticed a red hair, bright, a single pubic curl. It had to be Kevin's, because it wasn't hers and it wasn't Natassia's. Mary filled the tub with hot water. Nora's Annick Goutal bath oil was in the shower caddie, so Mary poured in a generous amount. Stepping into the bath, Mary was not aware of watching Kevin's red pubic hair whirl in the water, then float. But she was watching. Mary's bubble bath was hot and deep, and she soaked.

Paging through Nora's Tweeds catalogue, Mary tried to figure out which items on the dog-eared pages Nora was interested in. *How much does she spend on her clothes? Where is she? What's up with those two? I need to talk to her.* Soaking, Mary knew the evening was wasting. No progress whatsoever on the job stuff. *If Natassia and Kevin aren't back soon . . .* But something in her gut, not just laziness, told Mary it was okay to trust Kevin to watch the kid—at least for a little while.

When the water was losing its heat, Mary got up out of the tub and toweled off. Wearing Nora's bathrobe, Mary went into the kitchen and poured herself a big glass of ice water. She drank it, lay down on the couch. Her left foot was aching. She got up and found a bag of peas in the freezer and lay down again with the bag of peas on her warmly socked foot. Five minutes, she told herself.

WHEN KEVIN AND NATASSIA came home, Mary was sound asleep on the couch, snoring a little; her Nicorette gum had slipped out of her mouth onto a pillow.

Natassia and Kevin looked at the skimpy bit of writing on the legal pad on the dining-room table. "I'm going to have to help her," Natassia said to Kevin.

"That might be a good idea."

CHAPTER 29:

DECEMBER

1989

It is a cold, clear glass of a day. Saturday, December 30. Kevin is walking cross-town bouncing a basketball. A little past noon, the day is fresh and just started. Standing at the corner of Houston and Broadway, waiting for the light to change, he's smiling to himself, and can't stop bouncing. He's got on fingerless gloves, and he scratches under his beard. Kevin still can't believe the way his luck has turned—day after day of living with Mary Mudd. In the proximity of, in the same air space with Mary Mudd. *God, she smells good.* And there's at least a couple more days to go. *Best Christmas ever. Thank you, Santa.* Entertaining Mary's daughter is a small price to pay for the miracle of living so close to Mary. Now and then, Kevin has to step outside, just to look at it—his current life.

This is probably the first time since he was twelve years old that he hasn't been wondering about how long until he'll get to see Mary again. Now he sees her first thing in the morning, last thing at night. They go to the gym together every few days. Yesterday he watched her climb and climb the Stairmaster. She totally out-climbed him and everybody else in the place. Oblivious, wearing her Walkman, she had her eyes on CNN: the Berlin Wall falling, the big gate opening. *Just like me, man, that's me!* When he was tuckered from his workout, Mary was still going strong, halfway up Mount Everest. Before he left the machines to go to a mat, he shifted a floor fan so the breeze would cool her off. She didn't notice, but he likes doing nice things for her.

All around in the gym were the garish girls in spandex—blue, pink, green stripes on black. Mary, in faded gray sweats, radiated beyond them. She hadn't worn socks; her chains and baubles shimmered on her ankles above her old Reeboks, which she'd laced loosely so she could slip her shoes easily on and off. Her shoelaces were broken, tied together. As long as he's known her, since she was a kid, she's been dressed in worn-out, secondhand clothes. Probably his whole deal with vintage clothes started with Mary; all the years Kevin has been scavenging, he's been shopping for clothes for Mary Mudd.

When he crosses Thompson Street, the street he lives on, he realizes it's been over a week since he's been to his own apartment, which actually is Mary's apartment from way back when. He's been subletting from her for years. This makes him feel good, too; together, they've managed to hold on to rent control for almost fifteen years. If that Hiliard School jerk ends up firing her, maybe Mary will need to move back into the walk-up— with Kevin. Man, he'd treat her well. Cook for her all the time, like Christopher does for Nora.

Anything could happen. Kevin is wide open to this particular day. At the corner, some teenage girls are watching him, so he finger-spins the basketball. The girls giggle. The light changes. He moves on. Last night, they were watching *It's a Wonderful Life* and he got to spend two hours sitting on the couch, with Mary's smallness curled not far from him, at the other end of the couch, her feet tucked into the crack between the sofa cushions. It was all there: The slope from her hip down to her feet. The tumble of shoulder and arms. The clean, strong lines of her. The rumbly way she laughed. Then she fell asleep. Her ankle chains. Her ankles, her bones, her wrists. Ear. Feather.

He wanted to stare, but he couldn't stare. He took her in in bits, little glances, and it was like glimpsing beautiful stuff on a beach—rocks and shells and stones and chunks of weathered wood you want to scoop up and take home. His heartbeat was a fast dance all through the movie, while he pushed the pillow against his hard-on, which hasn't subsided for a minute during the eight days he's been lucky enough to live in the loft with Mary.

Heading over to the basketball courts on Sixth Avenue, hearing the bouncing, the running, he looks up at a sky so blue; it's solid and matte, like an unchipped piece of original Fiesta stoneware. He wants to wrap his legs and arms round the whole wide world and just fuck and fuck.

Nora's first miscalculation (she didn't like the word "mistake") was, probably, her decision to surprise Abe by going out to Greenport a day earlier
than they had planned. If a patient in a session had made this decision,
Nora would have asked, What are your intentions with this surprise? How
do you imagine it will be received? And she would have thought to herself, This person is trying to extract information. Is there a lack of trust
here? In other words, Are you spying? But all Nora allowed herself to
consider was this: If nine days and nights with Abe will be great, won't ten
be better?

When she arrived at the house that evening, she had to let herself in
with Christopher's key (which she'd taken to make sure he couldn't just
show up). Abe wasn't there. Two lamps were lit in the living room. The
bathroom light and fan were going. Very tall piles of paper lay all over
the kitchen table, which was in the living room, where it did not belong.
The bed in the biggest bedroom was unmade. The toilet seat was up. She
dumped her bags in the smallest bedroom and opened the bottle of good
Scotch she'd brought with her and sat down and waited.

It was after midnight, and she was in the den watching the news, when
Abe got home. "Hey! Nora Conolly," he said, and smiled. He took his
boots off at the door and, still in his overcoat, walked over to Nora. When

he shrugged out of his coat, his sweater smelled like a good dinner party—wine, spiced-up food, cigarettes. He carefully lowered a plate of leftovers onto the coffee table. Nora asked, "Where've you been?" *Schoolmarm.*

"Met that couple down the road, the retired advertising people?" He leaned back on the couch and took Nora's legs across his lap. *Maybe it's okay about the toilet seat. He didn't know I was coming.* "Nice folks. They invited me to chow."

"They invited you?" She knew who he meant. Two women who had an extensive garden of hybrid roses and a greenhouse built onto their two-story garage. "They never talk to us." *Keep Christopher out of this.* "My lawn's too shabby for them. They ignore me."

Abe laced his fingers through Nora's. "They felt sorry for me out here alone."

"How'd you meet them?"

"Outside, smoking. They walk by all the time with their dogs. You got lots of nice neighbors, Nora Conolly, out here in Greenport, Long Island."

"I hope you're not smoking out in the cold for my benefit."

"Don't want to stink up the Nora Conolly beach house with smoke."

His eyes were on her. He was a little drunker than she'd noticed at first—his eyelids were heavy—but that gaze of his was almost too much. "It's nice of you not to smoke in the house," Nora said, and leaned forward, rested her forehead on Abe's cold cheek. She closed her eyes, breathed. "You didn't make your bed," she whispered.

"Yeah," he whispered back. "Let's go check that out." He stood and pulled her up by both hands, and, whispering, led her across the room. "This is pretty," he said. "This is a Nora Conolly bathrobe, huh? Is that what this is? Let's take this off."

They had never been together on an actual bed before. He put a pillow under her legs and Nora stretched her arms out on the sheets, really stretched, tried to relax, but she was working hard to remember the moment even as it was happening. *First his hand was on my breast, now my belly, my leg.* Finally, she was here with him. *Abe.* She'd planted condoms in the drawer of the bedside table. There was no question. They would make love. There was nothing to stop them, no reason to stop. Finally, tonight, he'd be inside her. Then they'd sleep together, and wake together, and that would be only the first night, with so many more ahead of them. *Merry Christmas.*

Before she got Abe out of his jeans, he fell asleep. "Abe?" Nothing. And then he actually began to snore. Lightly, but still. *It's okay. He didn't expect me. Of course the first night would be awkward.* She tried curling up against him. She tried turning away. Finally, after almost two hours, she got out of the bed, picked up her robe from the floor, went into the little room, to the single bed covered with all her stuff.

That night was the closest Nora ever got to spending a night in bed with Abe.

NORA'S GREENPORT CHRISTMAS HOLIDAY was a disaster. All Abe did was work. Every morning, Nora woke early to call her answering service, dreading the possibility that a patient might want to talk to her. *Thank God, nothing.* Then she checked the morning TV shows to see what was going on with the opening of the Brandenburg Gate. Then she went back to bed. Her day sleep was her best sleep. At night she was awake trying to think of ways to get Abe into bed with her. But he worked and worked, waking at six to get started. First thing, he went straight into the kitchen. While his coffee brewed, he did a twenty-minute meditation, sitting cross-legged in front of a lit candle, ringing chimes and reciting Hebrew phrases. One morning she got up early, on purpose, and asked if she could join him. "Suit yourself," he said. She sat and crossed her legs inside her long nightgown, keeping her knee close but not touching his, sitting as still as she had learned to sit when she was a painters' model. But Abe had no interest in looking at her.

By seven o'clock, he was on his laptop or dealing with the piles of papers spread from the table to the floor. He had lists Scotch-taped to the living-room wall. He made phone calls (remembering every time to use his phone card) to the New York Public Library to check facts. He had manila folders stuffed with biographical information he'd photocopied from files in the *Time* library. He had one fat folder on 1950s cars because in one paragraph the main character bought a new car. Abe was obsessed with making sure his story was accurate in every way. But when Nora stuck her head into the living room to try to get Abe to come into the den to watch TV with her, he wasn't interested. "Abe, you need to see this. This is one of the biggest events of our lifetime."

"The fact of it is big. The news coverage is soap opera trying to sell soap suds."

A few times, including Christmas Day, Nora tried to make a lunch-brunch thing happen, tried to scramble eggs and have toast ready all at the same time, but Abe wasn't interested. Around one-thirty every afternoon, he collapsed for a nap, no more than an hour. Waking, he'd come find her and ease her into the big bedroom and they'd mess around on the bed a bit (Nora always ended up shirtless, but he never even got unzipped), no longer than fifteen minutes, then back to work. Saturday, Sunday, Monday passed, and he didn't stop to shave. His kisses began to scratch. Did it make sense for Nora to be intimate with someone she didn't know well enough to tell, "You need to shave"? He had not yet asked about her hair, why it was white. Maybe he simply wasn't interested in her.

When she wasn't napping or watching CNN, Nora tried to read the professional journals she'd brought with her, but her focus slipped every few sentences. She began writing out Christmas cards but got no farther than the "F"s in her address book, and she included no newsy notes this year, just a sloppy signature: *N & Chr.* Wherever Christopher was, Nora was sure he was having a more successful infidelity than she was.

On Friday, Abe woke from his nap, joined her on the couch in the den, and said, "You're not having much fun. I'm lousy company. I tried to warn you, Nora Conolly."

"Abe Shulevitz," Nora said, "it's all right." Not only was the guy talented and sexy, he was observant and intuitive, too. Nora had let herself become another of his women, smart *girls* who knew that romance with Abe wasn't going anywhere but who couldn't just write him off.

"Let's talk," Abe said. Nora stood, ready to head for the bedroom with the big bed, but he tugged her back down onto the couch. "No," he said, "let's talk." *Embarrassing.* "First, though, I'm making tea. You want tea, Nora Conolly? A beer?"

"Tea's good."

As he brought her a hot mug, she tried to pretend that he'd been offering these small attentions all week.

"I'm thinking," he said, setting his tea mug on a coaster (Kevin never did that), scrunching up next to her again, "that I'm some way that you didn't expect. You're not happy with me." He lifted her legs up onto his lap, his favorite talking position.

"Abe, you told me you'd be working. The reason we're here is so you can work. It's not your responsibility to keep me entertained."

"Being around a writer with a deadline is a lousy way to spend your holiday. Nora Conolly, if you want to head back to the city—"

"Do you want me to—"

"I knew that's what you'd hear. No, I don't want you to go, but if there are things you could be doing for New Year's that would be more fun for you . . ."

He really did have very beautifully shaped hands. She was staring at them resting on her leg. "I haven't had time off like this in . . . I don't know. I really needed this time to just, you know, relax."

"But you don't seem too relaxed. I don't think you're sleeping at night. Missing your husband for Christmas? Your brother?"

"My brother, yeah. I feel bad about my brother." God, Abe was even offering her a face-saver. "It's always hard to come here. Holidays are hard."

"Had nice Christmases here when you were a little girl? I bet you did. How'd you all do for Christmas, the Nora Conolly family?"

"We didn't do holidays."

"What? You Conollys are heathen Jews or something?"

"If only. When I was a kid, I envied my two Jewish friends. Their families got together on Christmas Day and went to the movies and out for Chinese, and at night the parents played bridge and the kids got to stay up late. But our family didn't do Christmas, and we didn't do the alternative thing. We didn't have relatives, and my parents weren't going to hang out with other people's relatives. Mom and Daddy were both estranged from their families."

"No aunties and uncles and gramps around? No Conolly cousins? Hell, I pictured you people like the Kennedys, out there all dressed up and tossing the pigskin."

"Kevin and Mom and I always tried to see who could sleep in latest on Christmas Day. Daddy always got up early, to check the market in Asia."

"No church?"

353

"Church? My father was no joiner of anything, especially not something like a church, where some other guy would be in charge and telling him what to do. Never."

"Rotten parents. They gave you nothing to reject and rebel against."

"Well, I mean, they didn't totally ignore it. Mom always gave us some books for Christmas, or a new game or something. And, you know, now that you mention it, I remember one year going to Mass with her. I was probably eight or nine, that age when girls are so tied up with their mothers. Maybe she was feeling nostalgic, or maybe she was just bored, but all of a sudden, on Christmas Eve, she says, 'Who's going to Midnight Mass with me?' So I went. Oh, and I remember I didn't want to stop reading the new book she'd bought me, so we sat in the little room for people with crying babies. Since it was so late, it was just the two of us in there, along with this young mother from out of town with her baby, and we started talking to her, and she ended up crying to us about her in-law problems, and Mommy spent the whole time giving her advice."

"You call your mama Mommy. That's nice," Abe said.

"Kevin does it, too. We can't seem to call her anything else." It drove Christopher crazy, but Nora didn't mention that to Abe.

"Tell me about her, your mommy. Tall, I bet, huh?"

"Oh, tall, yes. Very, very. Lots of authority."

"Like you," Abe said.

"Me? Ha!"

"No *ha*! Nora Conolly, you walk in and the place takes notice. You know that, ma'am, you can't pretend you don't."

"Yeah, we're tall. . . ." She loved this opportunity Abe was giving her to talk about Mommy in the present tense, and he was giving her all the time in the world.

"Daddy?" Abe asked.

"Oh yes. Six-three. Like Kevin."

"Mommy, Daddy, Nora, Kevin Conolly," Abe chanted.

Abe's eyes were smiling, covering her not with sex but with affection. A few days earlier, for one crazy moment, Nora had considered telling Abe about Natassia—about France—just as a way to maybe spark something intimate between them, but instead, now, Abe was making it happen, and she heard herself say, "Did I ever tell you my father spent time in jail? For embezzling."

Abe's eyes behind the glinty glasses widened. "I'd have remembered that."

"Yeah. Mommy met him right when he got out. I guess that's why she was always protective of him."

"A convicted embezzler and he needed *her* protection?"

"Oh, Daddy was harmless, but I think jail made him kind of, I don't know, a hermit. Maybe even a little crotchety. And Mommy just sort of, well, kept things running. So he could stay private. People thought—Well, he *was* a snob."

"And who was it your daddy stole from?"

"A company." After the fire, Nora had never told anyone but a few therapists this story. Of the people who knew Nora now, Mary and Christopher were the only ones who knew about Daddy's jail time. "Actually, he stole from his family's company."

"From his own people? I can see why he needed protection." He aimed a finger-gun at his head.

They both laughed. Nora had never been able to amuse anyone before with stories about her family. She started laughing harder.

"What?" Abe asked.

"I just remembered this one Christmas, a new neighbor came over with a tray of cookies. My father answered the door because she kept ringing it—usually he never answered the doorbell, never. And she handed him this big tray of homemade cookies, and he didn't know what to do with it. He said, 'Why are you bringing these here?' And she said, 'I figured you had the Christmas songs on so loud you didn't hear the bell, and I didn't want the squirrels getting these goodies if I left them on the porch.' For years we laughed about that word, 'goodies.' He must have made her so nervous—Daddy was extremely handsome, even when he was older—she kept saying, 'Enjoy the goodies.' Daddy just left the tray on the bench in the hallway, and no one moved it. It's not like we had company over or anything. All during Christmas break, Kevin ate cookies off the tray in the hallway. Kevin. I remember him buying his own Girl Scout cookies from his friend's sister, because Daddy wouldn't let anybody answer the door for the neighborhood girls." Nora kept laughing.

"Nora Conolly, that story makes me sadder than anything else you've told me about your family, including that fire."

In a few months' time, Nora would come to feel the sadness of the apart way her family lived, the shared shame that held them hostage, but that afternoon in Greenport with Abe she laughed. "Abe Shulevitz, if you dare use my family in your fiction . . ."

"I'm using it all. 'The Tales of the Conolly Clan.' " Abe tickled her, and Nora wrestled him to the floor, where they rolled and played—just *played*—for a good long time. Until Abe said, "Time for your commentary on the news. Don't miss it. I've got to get back to work."

"You don't want a sandwich or something?"

That tickle fest was pretty much the high point of Nora's holiday.

On New Year's Eve, close to noon, Mary and Natassia were at a crowded coffeehouse on the Upper West Side. They'd managed to nab a sofa way in back, where Mary could smoke, with a coffee table where they could spread out all their papers and their mugs. "Okay, Mom. Once again, what is the most important thing to tell your students when you're teaching them how to dance? Be clear."

"*Move.* I tell them to move."

Natassia was biting into her second éclair, licking cream off of her fingers. Mary was thinking it probably would have been better to hire somebody to write the job papers rather than submit to this drawn-out, humiliating collaboration with Natassia, who, seemingly freed of her BF yearnings, was brattier each day they spent in New York. With sticky fingers, the kid typed into the laptop, *My teaching philosophy is based, first of all, on kinetic principles.* Mary read over Natassia's shoulder. "I didn't say that."

"Yes, you did. What's the second-biggest thing you tell them?"

For the past week, Mary, Natassia, and Kevin had talked continually about beginning the work—after the next meal, after the next coffee, after the next nap. Mary had called Japan, then Thailand, to track down her company, and she'd had some success. Everyone she'd reached was happy to fax a letter. The company, however, had no way of coming up with old reviews. Natassia told Mary, "Lincoln Center's dance library will have all of it." So they'd gone to the Upper West Side, where they found the library not open; then they had landed in this coffeehouse with the expensive pastries, which, Mary understood now, had been Natassia's destination all along. The hot chocolates were almost three bucks each; Natassia was sipping her second.

"Okay, Mom, what else do you tell your students?"

"I tell them, Dance big. Fill the space. Make yourself big."

Natassia wrote: *I introduce, early on, the principle of spatial challenge, so that my students are, from the start, involved in dual problem-solving, movement intersecting with space, a challenge which increases in complexity as their abilities augment.*

"You're amazing," Mary said. "You could quit school and get paid to write this kind of stuff."

Natassia was not flattered. "Name the exercises." Mary was digging into the bottom of her backpack. "Mom, it's really, really bad to chew nicotine gum if you're smoking."

"Not now, Natassia. Don't even think about starting in with the lectures until this thing is done and written."

"The job won't do you any good if you're dead from lung cancer."

"I'll need the medical insurance for my chemo. Come on, write."

THAT EVENING in the loft, Mary and Natassia continued on the job papers while Kevin was in the kitchen cleaning, stuffing, and trussing six squabs according to the directions in one of Christopher's cookbooks. "Sorry this is taking a while," he called out to Mary and Natassia, who had the laptop set up at one end of the dining table; the other end was set with Christopher and Nora's good linens and heavy Italian ceramic plates.

"No problem," Mary called back. Natassia typed while Mary described her usual warm-up. "I start *dégagés*. Right foot front, and side, and back, and side. Left foot . . ." Mary glanced up at the kitchen counter, where Kevin was holding a tiny squab, moving its tiny legs, and mouthing, "Front and side and back . . ."

Mary burst out laughing.

Natassia looked up.

Kevin jumped the squab into the air, calling out, "And *changement*! And now left! And front and side and . . ."

THE LITTLE SQUABS tasted okay, but they weren't anything great. That's what Mary thought. Of course she told Kevin it was all delicious, but she couldn't help thinking that if he'd made one big fat regular chicken they'd have leftovers. Collapsed into a dining-room chair, Kevin was still wearing his big wraparound apron slopped up with food. He was overheated and sweating, and he pulled a dish towel out of his back pocket and wiped his moist freckled head. He looked more like a mechanic who'd come out from under a car than someone who'd been cooking tiny birds. Kevin didn't seem like a kid anymore, but his body was sure in better shape than the bodies of a lot of guys Mary's age.

About the squab, Natassia made a fuss—in French: *"C'est formidable!"*

"Sampietro would've never pulled it off."

For dessert, Kevin had made chocolate crème brûlée, which, he and Natassia decided, they would torch at the stroke of midnight. Already it was ten o'clock. Mary stood up from the table and said she'd clean the kitchen. Kevin and Natassia went to the sofa to resume their Scrabble game. They'd been playing back-to-back Scrabble games since Christmas Eve.

"Hey, we're starting a new game pretty soon," Kevin called into the kitchen. "Come play with us. It's better with three."

"I'd rather scrub dirty pots," Mary said.

She heard Natassia tell Kevin, in a low voice, "She's not much of a word person." And then Kevin must have said something in Mary's defense, because Mary heard Natassia say, "I'm *not* dissing my mother, I'm just saying . . ."

Kevin just did not let Natassia get away with being a brat. Probably he was the person they should write into their wills to be Natassia's guardian. The guardian issue had never got resolved. How easy it had seemed to Mary a few months ago, just last summer. Now the thought of Natassia in anyone's care but Mary's was—not acceptable, as Cather would say. Not even Ross was acceptable anymore. In an emergency? Especially in an emergency. Maybe Mary should think about asking Kevin to step in if she and Ross croaked. Kevin really did seem to know what he was doing.

In the kitchen, though, he was a slob. "Jesus," Mary whispered. She didn't know a lot about kitchens, but she knew Kevin had done a number of stupid things. A grease-filled pan sat on the still-turned-on burner, bubbling, smoking, ready to set off the smoke alarm. Another pan, full of good wineglasses, tilted on the top of the trash can. Linen napkins were clumped here and there on the counter, sopping up gunk. "Jesus," she whispered again.

But who was she to complain? The guy was in the next room teaching Natassia how to act like a civilized human being. They were now into their second week of sharing a living space, and it was getting harder to think of Kevin as a little brother. As Mary scooped up all the goop caught in the drain, it occurred to her that having Kevin around made it even nicer than when Mary and Natassia were alone together. Since Natassia's breakdown, Mary hadn't wanted—hadn't trusted—anyone else to be with them. But this time with Kevin was . . . *something*.

There was brown caked-up stuff stuck in a big pan. Mary went at it with steel wool, even though she had a hunch she wasn't supposed to. Nora yelled every Christmas, while guests were helping to clean up her kitchen, that the good pots should *not* be scoured. Tough shit. Nora wasn't here. She hadn't even bothered calling Kevin on Christmas. How lost they'd all felt at first—Mary, Natassia, and Kevin—together just because everyone else had somewhere to go and the three of them didn't. But it had shifted into a sweet slow-motion, a dance of inertia. Incubating, hibernating, blissful inertia.

By eleven-thirty, the kitchen was clean, and Natassia and Kevin were tied at Scrabble. They put in a video, *The Last Emperor.* Close to midnight, they switched to TV and counted down until the ball dropped in Times Square. "Goodbye, 1989," Mary mumbled. She was half asleep, curled up in a nest of cushions on the carpet. "Good riddance."

Kevin opened a small bottle of champagne, which he and Mary split. Kevin asked Mary if it was all right to offer a small glass of champagne to Natassia. Mary said okay, but Natassia didn't want any. *"Je déteste le champagne!* We should go to the roof to watch fireworks," Natassia said. "The view'd be great up there."

Kevin yawned.

Which made Natassia yawn and say, "But we'd have to walk up the steps."

Mary said, "We don't have to go up there."

They ate the chocolate crème brûlée without torching it. Mary didn't finish hers, so Kevin and Natassia split it. Everyone was in bed by twelve-thirty.

"I'M NOT READY to go upstate yet," Natassia announced on the morning of January 2, when Mary said they'd be leaving the next day. "I'll stay in the city at Grammy's."

"Absolutely not," Mary told her. "I want you with me."

"M-o-m-m," she said, like a toddler. "I hate it up there."

"Natassia." Kevin's tone of voice meant, *Stop it.* He was tired and pissed. He'd said only once, "I can't believe Nora hasn't even called," but Mary could tell that Kevin was disappointed that Nora and Christopher had never shown up.

"You guys—"

"Natassia, you're acting like a two-year-old who doesn't understand English," Mary told her.

"You're treating me like a two-year-old."

Kevin intervened. "If you get yourself packed and ready in twenty minutes, I'll drive you and your mother upstate. And I'll take you skiing tomorrow."

"Cool. I've never been skiing," Natassia said. "Thanks."

Mary wanted to kiss him.

CHAPTER 32:
JANUARY
1990

Kevin's Rambler held up until they reached Hiliard, and when they arrived, the car died. A local garage said they would need two days to get the car going again. Mary was relieved on two counts: they wouldn't be able to go skiing (Mary couldn't afford an injury right now), and she wouldn't be left alone yet with Natassia.

During the process of getting the car towed, Kevin had became friendly with Mr. Tommy, the school's groundskeeper, and now, Wednesday afternoon, Kevin and Natassia were helping him shovel walkways. Since early morning, Mary had been at the computer, one-finger-typing additional information into the pages Natassia and Kevin had typed for her in the city. When Kevin came into the cottage to get a Pepsi, he said, "While I'm up here, Mary, let me know if there's anything I can help you with."

"What you can do for me is keep that kid away from me."

"Right-o."

"You probably think I'm a rotten mother."

"Yeah," Kevin said, grunting a little as he unbuckled his black old-man overshoes. "You really are. Especially since she's a completely charming, undemanding, self-sufficient, gracious, and sweet-tempered kid."

Mary turned away from the computer and faced him. "You're fed up with her, too? It's not just me? You think she's been difficult?"

"She's been"—he was bending over, sopping up chunks of muddy snow off the slate floor with a bathroom towel—"a ridiculous brat."

"Kevin! I didn't think you noticed. You treat her so nice. How can you stand to be with her?"

"She's not my kid, that's how."

"What would you do if she was?"

"Slap her silly."

Mary, delighted, laughed out loud. "So it's not just me."

MR. TOMMY was a silent Japanese man. His work brought him close to the cottage almost every day, but he never spoke to Mary or Natassia. He'd only nod at them, sternly. Mary had taken offense at Mr. Tommy's manner. "I don't know what's bugging him. He's always pissed off when he sees us."

"How would you like it," Natassia had asked Mary, "if you were a grown man who's like in his fifties and a master gardener, and you had all these rich kids calling you Mr. Tommy? And rich garden ladies bugging you for clippings and manure all the time."

"Well, he could say hello. He's not the only one who hates working here."

Over those couple winter days, though, Kevin got Mr. Tommy talking. First about where to find a mechanic for the decrepit Rambler. Then about the old vehicles in Mr. Tommy's storage barn. Kevin and Natassia found a broken sled, and Mr. Tommy let them use his tool shop to fix it up. Natassia and Kevin sledded all afternoon while Mary sat in the cottage working on her papers. When Natassia and Kevin came back in, Kevin told her, "Tomio said to ask him if you ever need help around the cottage."

"You're supposed to call him Mr. Tommy."

"His name's Tomio, and, Mom, like right away he knew your dad was a U.S. serviceman during the Korean War. He said he recognized your mixed looks."

"You should talk to him, Mar," Kevin said. "He was in Korea during the war. Interesting guy. He knows all kinds of stuff. I think I've got some engine belts down in the city that I'm going to bring up here to see if he can do something with them."

Later, as they sat around the coffee table eating Kevin's beef stew, Natassia started again: "Mom, Tomio said that after the war, in Korea, there were thousands and thousands of servicemen's babies who were, like, totally rejected by society. He said it was really sad. All these kids wandering around the cities and in the countryside and everywhere, trying to find food or someplace to live. Nobody would take them in, because they didn't have fathers, and without a father's family name, you're basically considered like nobody in Korea."

Kevin stood to gather up plates. "If you need help with anything, Mary, you should ask him. He really did say to tell you that."

"And, Mom, Tomio said—"

"Natassia, your mom can talk to him herself about all that if she feels like."

"I just wanted to tell her how he said she was really lucky. Mom, he couldn't believe when I told him the story of how your father went back to Korea to find you and bring you home. He said he never heard a story like that."

"Yeah," Mary said, "lucky."

"I'm just glad we broke the ice with him," Natassia said. "It was so weird, we're like the only Asian people on this campus, and we weren't even talking to each other."

Mary looked at Natassia. "Why do you do that? You don't even look Asian."

"But I am."

"You're Jewish," Mary told her.

"Just half."

Mary had never thought of Natassia as anything but Jewish, and, by association, Mary actually thought of herself as being a little Jewish—more Jewish than anything else. "Do you tell people you're Asian? When they ask, is that what you say? When you're filling out those forms and you have to check off if you're white or African American or Asian or whatever—"

"I check off 'white' and I check off 'Asian.' Usually. When people ask me, I say I'm half Jewish and part Korean. What do you say?"

"I say I'm nothing. American. A mutt. I say my father went to the Korean War and screwed around. Then he felt guilty and went back and pulled me out of an orphanage."

Natassia pushed back from the coffee table and rose up onto her knees.

"*You* were in an *orphanage?* I can't believe you lived in an orphanage and you never told me."

"After he found me, he had to put me there for a couple months while paperwork cleared. I was six or seven months old when he got me. I don't remember any of it."

"Like, was it a really bad orphanage or what?" Natassia asked.

"I'm telling you, I missed the whole thing." Mary was watching Kevin stack logs in the fireplace for a fire, something Mary had never thought of doing. She had actually never really noticed the fireplace—it was just where she kept her suitcases and empty boxes.

ON THURSDAY, Kevin's car was ready, and he headed back to the city. As soon as Natassia and Mary were alone, Natassia said, "Now what am I supposed to do up here for two weeks until classes start? I don't even know why we're here."

"Because it's our home."

"It's your pathetic home, not mine."

"Natassia, it's going to be a long couple of weeks for both of us if—"

The phone rang. They let it ring four times until the machine picked up. They listened. "Mary, it's me. If you're there, pick up. I think you're there, so—"

Mary grabbed the receiver. "Nora. Hi."

"Mary, when you stayed in the loft, did you call Japan? And Thailand and Germany?"

"Oh yeah, I forgot—"

"You forgot? How'm I supposed to pay for this? I'm not Lotte, Mary."

"Nora—"

"What do you think I am?"

"Nora, *stop.* Don't say another thing. How much do I owe you for the phone calls? I'll send cash, tomorrow, FedEx Overnight."

"Look, Overnight isn't necessary. And, sorry, I'm a little—"

"Just tell me how much."

"It comes to twenty-eight dollars and seventy-nine cents."

"You'll have it—but Nora, are you okay? Something's wrong. You're being totally weird," Mary said, and Nora hung up on her.

"Bitch," Mary said to the phone as she slammed down the receiver.

"What'd she want?"

"Put your coat on, Natassia. I have to walk down into town to get money out of a cash machine."

"It's cold. There's no way I'm walking all the way out there."

"You were outside for hours sledding with Kevin, and it was colder than today."

"Don't stare at me like that, Mom. You're hallucinating. Go by yourself."

There were a thousand angry things Mary wanted to say to Natassia. All of them would have started a fight, and this mess with Nora was already bad enough. Mary stepped into her boots, grabbed her coat, pulled on her cap, forgot her gloves, left.

The walk across the campus was white and deep, and Mary cried as she walked. She cried because she so much wanted to kill something, someone, anything. But she couldn't kill—she still hadn't finished writing the papers for the board of trustees.

Everything was snowed over. The campus was pretty, and then the neighborhood she had to walk through was pretty; Mary hated all of it. She felt better when she finally got out of the pristine streets and was walking along the side of the main road, in the gravel and debris. Step by angry step, she thought of a TV show she'd watched late the night before. It was about crocodiles, the relationship between crocodiles and lions. The show was filmed during the dry season, all the lakes and ponds were parched, and a crocodile was stuck in a mud bath—the croc indistinguishable from the mud until you noticed its eyeballs moving. The big deal for the animals, obviously, was hunger and thirst. Cut to close-up of a dead buffalo, torn open, and a hippo eating the buffalo's innards, munching the undigested grassy stuff in its stomach. Crocs smelled the food from four miles away. They, too, came slinking up to the carcass. All the animals were out to get what they could, like looting during a blackout in the city. When the crocs arrived at the buffalo, lions came up and started nipping at the crocs, which were soon circled by lions. It looked really bad for the crocodiles, but, unbelievably, they still had the advantage. Why? Their digestive system, being less delicate than the lions', less delicate than most other animals' digestive systems, made it possible for the crocs to eat anything, everything. Meat, skin, bone, horns, the whole shebang. Those crocs weren't going to die.

It's just like this business with the school and the board of trustees, and with Nora, and with Natassia, too. Everybody's a scavenger. Whoever had the strongest stomach would eat.

BY THE TIME Mary got back home from the cash machine, Natassia had moved all of her belongings—books and blankets and clothes—into the small bedroom at the far end of the cottage. She'd pulled her mattress from the living room. She did not want to sleep next to her mother anymore.

"Listen," Mary said, "I called Heather from a pay phone. You have an appointment with her tomorrow at three, and another one the next day at three."

"I won't be able to go. I called Daddy and told him I want to fly out to Spokane to visit him and Harriet until classes start."

"Oh, you did?" Mary stood holding her dripping hat and coat.

"Daddy's working on getting me a ticket. He said he'll call back tonight with the flight schedule. We're trying to get me something for tomorrow."

"Oh. Tomorrow?" *But your father's an addict.* Natassia, defiant, was standing tall next to the wall phone. Mary had no idea what to do. "Where'd you take the TV to?"

"My room. You can have it all to yourself when I'm gone, but I want to watch a movie by myself now, before I kill myself from boredom."

"Natassia!"

"I just mean it's deadly boring up here, that's all. Is that news to anybody?"

BY TEN THAT NIGHT, Ross hadn't called. When Natassia called him, Harriet answered. She knew nothing about the plane tickets or Natassia's plans. Mary understood everything, just from watching Natassia's face. "Yeah," Natassia said, "I'll wait here for him to call."

Forty minutes later, Ross called. Again, Mary could read between the lines. Ross had never got around to calling the travel agent. He was trying to convince Natassia that it might be better if she stayed put for now and kept her appointments with Heather. He was trying to promise that he'd plan something spectacular for Spring Break. They'd drive to Jasper, go skiing. He'd take Natassia to see a glacier.

"I'm not really into glaciers," she told him.

That night, in her new room, Natassia cried. In the living room, lying on her futon, aching, Mary listened. *She wants her father, she wants him to be a better father than he is.* Hell, that's what Ross wanted, too. There wasn't a thing Mary could do about that. Ross and Natassia would have to figure it out. Mary had to stay out of the way.

Natassia's weeping quieted around midnight, and Mary went in to check on her. She was asleep, her face striped with red tearstains. Mary covered her up to her chin with blankets. The cottage was getting cold tonight. She tucked a pillow up against Natassia's side, where she knew Natassia liked it. Mary turned on a night light. As she was turning off the reading light by the bed, she glanced at the notebook opened on the floor: a poem.

GET OUT OF MY LIFE
Go on,
goon.
No! Go.

Mary stared at sleeping Natassia and felt the deep relief of not having the kid's angry face staring at her. Mary kissed Natassia's head. Without opening her eyes, Natassia made a kissing sound. "I love you," Mary said. Another too-sleepy kiss from Natassia.

A few hours later, Mary woke and went into Natassia's room to check on her. She was asleep, hadn't moved. On the way back to her futon, Mary needed a blanket for herself, and she stepped into the room where Kevin had slept. The wind whipping around the cottage was making everything icy. Confused, sleepy, Mary stood a moment in the dark bedroom. Suddenly she wanted very much to lie down in the sheets where Kevin had slept.

IT ICED during the night. The next morning, when Mary headed up to the Admin Building, Mr. Tommy was tossing salt onto the walkways. He nodded but said nothing, just like always. This time, though, Mary spoke. "Hey, hi. Cold morning, huh?"

"Hello," he said. He pointed to the walkways and warned Mary, "Dangerous. You must be careful."

"Yeah," she said, "thanks," but he was already bowing his head and looking away.

Up at the building, Mary stood just inside the lobby doors, waiting for the FedEx truck to come pick up her envelope of cash for Nora. Fifty bucks: $28.79 for the phone calls, plus some extra to help Nora get rid of the bug up her butt, whatever it was. Mary was nervous. She hadn't done this FedEx business much before, not Overnight Priority, so when a brown UPS truck drove up and the driver walked into the building with a box, she said, "Oh no. Did I call the wrong place? I need this to go overnight delivery."

"Sorry, I'm not here for a pickup. I'm here to deliver." He kept walking toward Franklin's secretary's office.

A moment later, Tracey, the secretary, stuck her head out into the hallway. "Mary Mudd. I thought I heard your voice." Anytime Tracey spoke to her, Mary felt reprimanded, but Tracey treated most of the faculty, particularly the women, as if they were troublemakers, bad kids. "Mary, this UPS is for you. Want to sign for it, so this gentleman can be on his way? I'm sure he's busy."

THE UPS PACKAGE had been sent from Lotte's office. Curious, Mary tore the box open right there in the lobby. Inside, she found a note in Lotte's handwriting: *Use this to help document your training, career, etc. Whatever that board of trustees wants, you've got it. Hugging you with love, Lotte.*

Dance memorabilia—the box was full of it. And Lotte had even organized everything into piles secured with rubber bands. The first pile, with a Post-it note saying *Use these to chart your early influences,* was programs from dance performances Lotte and Mary had gone to together, including Baryshnikov's first New York City performance. Twyla Tharp performances. Natalia Makarova on Broadway. On the program for the Alvin

369

Ailey company at City Center, the margins were filled with David's notes and numbers about a manuscript he was thinking of buying. The next pile—this really got Mary—was programs and reviews from a bunch of Mary's performances. Mary had never realized how many times Lotte had come to see Mary dance. Right on top was a program for a performance Mary had done at St. Mark's Church. Mary's solo came right after the intermission. Lotte had drawn little stars all around Mary's name. In a separate pile were three programs for performances Mary hadn't danced in but students of hers had, and in the program notes they had included a special thank-you to Mary; Lotte had yellow-highlighted those thanks. Her Post-it note said, *Use these to substantiate your teaching experience.*

Walking down the path from Admin to the cottage, carrying the square, awkward box in a tight hug, Mary was walking so fast she slipped on ice three times, but she managed to keep the box out of the snow. She was still dumbfounded and stunned to realize that someone—particularly Lotte, who had so much else to do—had kept track of her dance life in this minutely detailed way, like no one else would do.

LIKE A MOTHER. Lotte and the package she'd sent were still on Mary's mind days later as she stood at the photocopy machine in Franklin Fields's office on Martin Luther King Day. After Lotte's package, other things had arrived: two editors from big publishing houses, friends of Lotte's, had sent letters saying how Mary had been an important consultant to them on dance books they had published. Mary called Lotte and said, "But all I did with both of those people was just talk to them at a party. I gave them a couple names."

"Do you have any idea," Lotte said, "how important it is, when you're trying to create buzz for a book, to get the right blurbs? It's everything."

What was it to be a mother? As Mary watched the photocopy pages shoot out into the collating trays—*Please, God, let this machine not fuck up on me again*—Mary realized that motherhood was all different in her head now from what it had been before.

She used to think that a good mother, a real mother, *did* certain things. Now Mary had begun to understand that it had more to do with how you felt inside, the way you felt about your kid without even trying, the way love so big inside you could choke you even before you got out of bed in the morning, before you put a foot on the floor. In writing about her early influences, Mary had talked about Merce Cunningham, who said dance could be about anything—everything the body can do—even just walking. And dance didn't need costumes or a story or even a stage and music. None of that external stuff was necessary to create dance, because dance just *happened* wherever there was movement.

There was your body, and there was the way your body naturally moved, and out of that came dance.

There was your kid, and there was the way you felt about your kid—how you felt way inside, the deep below, under the guilt and fear, the love in your bones and in your blood, even when you were furious at the kid and at yourself. And that deep stuff made you do certain things for your kid, things no one else would think of, maybe uncharacteristic things that no one would expect from you. Like collecting seventeen years' worth of dance memorabilia, like drawing stars all around a name on a dance program.

"Fucking machine." It was stuck again; a little button of red light blinked at her. "More paper. More paper. All right, I'll give you more paper, just quit flashing me."

TWO WEEKS PASSED. No word from Franklin Fields about the board of trustees' decision. Finally, Mary asked him.

"They haven't, haven't, got back to me about it yet," he told her, "but you did a top-notch job outlining the program. Terrifically detailed. Guest artists. Mary, terrific stuff. Very, very exciting."

"So you haven't heard anything from them yet, huh?"

"I'll tell you as soon as I do. But we should get together for coffee sometime. I'd love to hear more about your time with Tim Dillon Dancers."

In. Your. Dreams.

NATASSIA HAD begun taking a full load of classes, which she said were kindergarten compared with her city school. She insisted she had no friends at Hiliard, no *real* friends, but she did have a group to eat lunch

371

with every day. Some evenings, she went up to the dorms to do home-work with a study group. Mary was doing what Lotte had advised her to do: Teach your classes as if there had never been a problem, teach as if you intend to stay.

Another week passed. Franklin Fields finally called Mary into his office. "I'm sorry, Mary—"

They have to pay me through the spring term. I'll get word out in the city that I need to teach a bunch of classes. David won't like it, but Lotte'll let me and Natassia move back into the apartment. I could commute down to Atlantic City and dance in a casino if worse comes to worst.

"—I got word from the trustees," Franklin was saying, leaning back in his desk chair, rocking. "They voted to table the discussion of the dance program for at least six months." He was talking to the window, not look-ing at her, David Stein–style. "Apparently, there's some sort of alumni money available for a dormitory-expansion plan."

"But, Franklin . . ." He looked at Mary, surprised by her interruption. "Listen, I'm sorry to cut you off, Franklin, but what about my contract? Am I fired or what? I've got to know now. I have a daughter. I need to know if I've got a job."

"Mary." Franklin turned, put his hands flat on his desk, leaned forward toward her. "Of *course* you have a job. You're signed on for another—what?—two years. I'm trying to figure out how we can keep you here be-yond that, permanently, before one of the colleges with a good tenure-track offer snatches you away. I promised you when you inter-viewed that we were working on getting a full dance program, and we *will* get a program. I just need you to be patient for now. Don't worry about Natassia's tuition, of course. Of course, you'll have to move out of the cot-tage next year, but one of the other faculty-housing units will be available to you and Natassia. For now, Mary, just . . . patience, please. Rest assured that within the next few years—I'd say five, max—we will have a full pro-gram for you, and it will be *your* program."

MARY CALLED ROSS immediately. "Can you translate, please? What's he telling me?"

"What you need to do now is go back to him and ask for a letter, get it in writing."

"Why?"

"Because you've got the upper hand right now."

"I do?"

"Mary! He asked you to do a bunch of work for *his* plan. It's part of *his* agenda, which may just be to get inside your pants—who knows?—but, for whatever reason, he wants you around. Right now he's got to apologize to you for not coming through with something he wants you to think he's promising you, so here's your chance to get stuff. Go for it. Ask for a raise, maybe."

"What about the naked dancing? Did they decide they're letting that go?"

"Forget the naked dancing, for God's sake. That was half a dozen moves back on the game board. In this current round, you're queen bee, so, quick, get what you can. Get a written something from the man."

"Then what'll I do with it?"

"If this job does end up blowing up in your face, you've got a good recommendation letter. Mary, with just a year in that job, you've set yourself up to go places."

"To where?"

"A better school. Maybe a college program. For one thing, you've got a whole dance program written up to take with you. You got all kinds of possibilities now."

"Ross, I don't understand this. It's been over a year since I performed. I haven't done any choreography that means anything. Why would anybody even look at me for a job at this point?"

"You got a paper trail now, Mary. *Now* you've got a career; all of it's on paper."

CHAPTER 33:

WINTER

1990

In the days after she got back from her Christmas vacation in Greenport, Nora was completely alone in the loft. Abe didn't call and she didn't call him, and she knew that if they did get together again for dinner or a movie it wouldn't make much difference. He had opened that one nice conversation but then left her alone, and she was sleepless again, arcane flashes of her family running through her insomnia, and there was no one for her to talk to.

No sign Christopher had been at the loft during the holidays. Nora had no idea where he was. Kevin's leftovers were in the fridge and freezer (his chili really wasn't as good as Christopher's), and he'd left a note on the counter: "Nora, I don't know what's going on, but it was lousy of you to take off for Christmas without even letting me know where you are." Nora called his apartment, left messages, but Kevin wasn't calling back. Under her bed, Nora found dirty socks and a T-shirt, clueing her that Mary and Natassia had been there at some point, but they'd left no note.

In the early days of January, not able to manage being in the loft alone, Nora spent as much time as possible outside, walking the streets. After work, all the way from Eighty-seventh and Lex, she walked home to SoHo. She tried taking the subway once, but as soon as she slipped her token into the turnstile, she knew she couldn't do it. She pushed through the exit gate and rushed up into the street, grateful for the blocks and blocks and blocks of sidewalks, and for the way she was hemmed in on one side by slushy traffic and on the other side by storefronts and buildings. Nora walked. *Mommy, is Christopher ever coming back? Will Natassia ever be all right? Will Kevin talk to me again? I made a fool of myself with Abe.* Nora stopped only when a bakery window caught her eye. She let herself eat whatever she wanted. Sugar cookies, sour-cream muffins, glazed petits fours. When she reached home, hours after leaving her office, she was so worn out she pulled off her clothes and almost immediately fell into bed.

And then, on the evening of Monday, January 15, Nora unlocked the door and walked into the loft, and Christopher was in the kitchen. "*No-ra!*" He was making chicken soup. He came to her and hesitated. Christopher wanted, she could tell, to hug her. She had missed him so much and was so relieved to see how happy he was to see her, she asked no questions. Neither did he.

Nora and Christopher made love immediately, without wariness, without a pause, with total agreement between them. There simply were no questions. There was the black-and-white kitchen floor as they lay down, there were the dust balls skittering under the counters as their clothes came off, there was Christopher's skin, and his stewy scent when his sweater was lifted off, then their voices echoing each other, saying nothing but *I missed you, I missed* you, *I missed*—and then, afterward, still on the kitchen linoleum, they held each other for an hour.

NORA AND CHRISTOPHER began living in the loft again together, more or less. They were even back to sleeping in the same bed. Occasionally, they made love, and when they did, it was an orgy of *touch touch touch,* none of the fast, hot rubbing Nora had known with Abe. It moved her deeply now, the slow reverence Christopher's hands had for her skin. After more than fifteen years, his eyes still stared with a kind of wonderment at whichever part of her body he was stroking. She appreciated it now, Christopher's way of touching her. And the firm curve of his shoulders, and the velvet plush of his skin.

But this lovemaking didn't happen often, just enough to keep them both grateful, to make it possible for them to live in the loft together while still avoiding any serious discussion of what, exactly, had gone on during the holidays. *Where were you? What were you doing? Who were you with?* Neither one asked.

Their days were productive. Christopher began, again, to check in with Nora by phone every afternoon before her three-o'clock appointment. Three or four nights a week, they had dinner together, at home or in a neighborhood restaurant. This all felt congenial enough to convince Nora—and Christopher, too? she couldn't quite tell—that their marriage was reinstated. One weekend at the end of January they made a quick trip to Kansas City to visit Christopher's family, and they presented themselves as if the marriage had never missed a beat.

Back home after Kansas City, they carried on. They didn't have the energy to put together one of their usual winter dinner parties, but they went to an opening together in Brooklyn one Saturday night. Life was pretty smooth.

Except that, occasionally, Nora felt a strain, a small tugging between them, a boredom maybe. Something should have been happening that wasn't happening; she couldn't shake that feeling, it was all over her life. After the holidays, Nora's pregnant patient had come back wearing maternity clothes. She'd told her boss about the baby and had set up maternity leave and was interviewing nannies. She cried a lot, in fear, but was moving ahead. When Nora had asked, "You've told your family?" the woman said, "No. No need yet." Clearly, there was something important that needed to happen.

THEN, ONE SUNDAY morning in mid-February, Nora and Christopher woke to a day of white wind. More snow falling on top of snow already piled up. Everything, including the cold, had gone on too long (and showed no sign of changing). There was nothing interesting or cozy in this bleak, cold Sunday. White swirls whipped the streets and the buildings. On the windowsills across the street, the snow was catching in small drifts.

Around noon, while Christopher hogged up the couch with the *Times*, Nora made herself French toast with hot syrup and offered him some. He said, "No, thank you," which was, she was sure, his way of being superior.

He'd been hinting that she needed to watch her weight. *Nice rump*, he'd said a few nights earlier. *Doughy*, he'd said while kneading her waist. Wrapped in her robe, feeling that bulge at her middle as she held her plate in front of her, Nora sat in the rocker across from the couch, her feet on the coffee table. The hot syrup on the French toast made the heaviness— of her flesh, of the day—worse. She licked syrup off of her fingers. And then Christopher looked up from the sports pages and said, "You know what we need to do, don't you?"

"Yeah, I know," Nora said.

They sat a moment longer. Then they stood up—first Christopher, and, a few seconds later, Nora. After going to their respective file cabinets and desk drawers, they returned to the big table with W-4s, plump files of re- ceipts and bills. Christopher set himself up at one end of the table, his back to the long windows; Nora set up at the other end, facing the windows and the snow. All afternoon, they slid the calculator back and forth be- tween them and went through the bits and pieces of the previous financial year.

Just as they had prepared their taxes every winter for the past thirteen years.

Look at us, it's like we're normal, it's like we love each other and have a mar- riage.

The CD player ran through three Miles Davis albums and a Thelonious Monk, and then Christopher hit the REPLAY button. Clean jazz. Neither of them had ever been able to work with lyrics in the background.

Hours passed.

When Nora looked up, she saw that on the building across the street, on the roof, architectural landmarks of snow had shaped themselves around the water tanks. The sky, which had been the color of skim milk all day, was now deepening into blue ink, a color the soul could reach out to a bit. "I'm almost done here," Nora said.

"Yeah. Me, too. Almost done."

"Will you look at this," Nora asked, handing him a FedEx receipt, "and tell me if you remember what it's for?"

"Yeah, and then I've got something I need to go over with you."

We're sharing. That clichéd phrase, which she hated, rolled through her consciousness just as she looked up again and noticed that the windows of their own loft were getting glittery with the formation of ice flecks, and Nora chose to see hope in this.

Christopher stood up. "I've got this stack of receipts," he said, and walked to a chair closer to her, about mid-table.

"Yeah?" She was paper-clipping her piles of receipts.

Leaning back in his chair, Christopher crossed his legs. Nora pushed her chair away from the head of the table so she could face him more directly. He looked troubled, and she smiled to herself. Every year, there was some small situation that he got paranoid about. If he deducted too much for supplies, would that be a red flag? Wasn't it a red flag to deduct their Thanksgiving and Christmas Eve dinners as business expenses, even though everybody they invited worked in the arts in some way? Then Nora would have to reassure him that the IRS didn't care too much about who was invited to their parties.

"Nora," he said now, "there's something."

"Yeah?" She leaned into the table and hit the OFF button on the calculator.

"I have to tell you about something."

And then his face got funny, with a sheen of fear that turned him an ugly ocher color, and Nora finally got scared. *He is in love with somebody. He's leaving me.*

"I don't know how to even start, goddamn it." He shuddered as if with a chill, then stood up fast. He shoved the chair into the table. "Shit." The way he said it, the word was a bullet. Then, softer, but still angry: "I'm sorry, Nora, I'm not mad at you."

I should think not.

"God—" Christopher was fisting his pile of receipts. He walked away from the table and came back, still looking afraid and ugly, and Nora was aware of feeling almost giddy with how far over the cliff they were dangling now. Their marriage was much more in the vicinity of danger than of safety. She pulled her socked feet up onto her chair, hugged her knees, felt that roll of flesh around her middle. Though the air within her was too thin for her to form any clear thought—for example, *No violence*—she knew she had to make a choice not to hit him, not to hurt him physically, no matter what he told her.

"I don't know how to tell you all this." He was whining now.

"You met a woman."

"Yes." He tossed down the receipts. Put his foot on the chair, put his elbow on his knee, grabbed his hair. "Yes, about a year ago I met this woman."

"And you're in love."

"No!" He spit that out. "No, no, no, no." He came to Nora, knelt in front of her chair. She pulled her feet in closer to her body, squeezed her belly flesh tighter. He tried to touch her sock, but she covered her foot with her hand. Looking down, she noticed bits of gunk in his hair.

"I'm starting at the start," he told her. "This is long. More than a year ago. October, all right? Not this one, the one before. You and I weren't, you know. We'd already been having a hard time with each other for a long time."

Go ahead, try blaming it on me. Just try.

"We were—you and me. I just felt like I couldn't do anything right. I mean, of course, you were right. You've always been right, your having your doubts about getting pregnant with me and having a baby. I was just—I just wanted to have a baby so much." He sat in the chair. "Nora, I was afraid you were leaving me."

She lifted her eyebrows. "I'm still here."

"Yeah, but it's a fucking miracle. I really thought you were leaving and you'd had enough of me, and then I'd have nothing. Remember that night, it was a Sunday, you wouldn't come to the film festival with me?"

"You're in love with some other woman because I wouldn't go to the New York Film Festival?"

"I'm not in love with anyone, sweetie. There's no one else. I promise. It's just that that night I had a drink with Piper and I found out about this woman."

"What's her name?"

"Let me tell this my own way. Please? Can I do that? Does it always have to be your way?" he yelled, then leaned down to kiss her hand.

She kicked a fast kick at his leg. "Get away from me. Tell me the rest. Hurry."

"This woman. I heard about her from Piper that night because she was a widow of this guy, this painter everybody knew, who had died of something really bad."

"AIDS. You're telling me this woman gave you AIDS."

"No! Nobody has AIDS. I don't have AIDS. The husband died of cancer. Some cancer. And that's it, it's just basically this really, really sad story. They were married a really, really long time. Longer than us. The woman, this widow, after he was gone she wanted a baby a lot. She was pregnant when he died, then she had a miscarriage."

Nora was very confused by now.

Christopher was starting to look exasperated. He tried to explain. "She lost her husband, Nora, then she lost her baby."

"I lost my father, then my mother, all in the same week."

"You really— Okay, you be however you want to be, but I'm finishing this story. This widow—"

"If you say 'widow' one more time I'm going to—"

"She was looking," he insisted, "looking in a very formal and organized way, she was having a search, for a donor to donate sperm so she could finish the plan she and her husband planned before he died."

"What plan?"

"For her to have a baby. Aren't you listening? I just called her after drinks with Piper. The first time I called her was because I just wanted to talk to somebody who wanted a baby as much as me. Then I filled out the questionnaire and got the tests. And I went to this lab after she picked me to be the donor. I never thought she'd pick me. I never touched her, not once. I swear that to you. This all happened with tubes and doctors."

"You let yourself be an anonymous sperm donor for this person?"

"Yeah. But, no, it's not anonymous. I had to be an artist, because of her husband. She wanted to pick very specifically, so she'd have the right person, like her and her husband had planned. I told you. The questionnaire was really long. She liked my drawings."

"She liked your drawings. You were the right person because you're an artist."

"Yes. A painter. I had to be a painter."

"So now this woman is going to try to get pregnant with your sperm."

"Nora!"

"I'm just trying to understand here. I'm trying—"

"It's done, Nora. Sweetie, the baby's born." Christopher's face cracked into tears, like a boy's face. He went to the far end of the table and got his wallet from the piles of papers and brought the wallet back to Nora. He opened it. "I have a son. I have this baby son, Nora. His name is Don, like his mother's husband's name, the one who died."

He pulled out a photo and tossed it onto the table in front of her, and she saw nothing but the closed-eye animal look of an infant, then its purply skin. And within the confusion that Christopher had already created, Nora thought, when she saw the picture, that Christopher was telling her that something monstrous was wrong with this child. The news and the photograph fused together into something monstrous and ugly, and Nora screamed. She tossed a New York State tax form on top of the photo to hide it. She screamed again, screamed big, her words sloppy: "What's wrong? Tell me what's wrong with that baby, what happened?"

"Nothing, nothing, nothing, Nora. He's fine. He's healthy."

"*Don't* you touch me."

"No-ra, are you? Okay, Nora? You're white. Don't you, don't you faint on me."

Her head was full of moths, fluttering light, and as soon as he said *faint*, she knew what was happening to her, and knew, from the two times before in her life when she'd fainted (once, right off the toilet seat in her college house, when she realized she was pregnant; the second time, right after the abortion, when she realized she no longer was), she knew the downward spin wouldn't stop now, it was already happening. There was a subway-collision boom in the apartment.

And then Nora was rising up out of a cotton-ball darkness into cold, a cold calm; she realized she was lying on the floor, and Christopher was holding ice cubes to her wrists and her forehead.

"Nora, sweetie." His whisper smelled like coffee, and her stomach folded close to a gag. Then she remembered what had happened.

"What happened?" she said.

"You fainted. I caught you just before you hit the floor."

"How long?" What had he done to her in between the time she slumped over and when she came to? He could have done anything. She had to call the police.

"You were out just about one minute."

"Give me the phone."

"Who're you calling?"

"*Where* is the phone? Bring it to me."

She noticed the digital clock. He wasn't lying. It was just six-eighteen, and she remembered that it had been only six-ten when they'd started to talk, when he'd come down to her end of the table with the receipts. Still, though, when he brought her the phone she took it and dialed 911, and when she got an answer, she said, Sorry, and hung up.

"Did you just call 911?" Christopher asked.

"Yes. And I'll call again if you come near me."

He sighed. She saw him decide not to get angry. "You've got to get off the floor. I have to help you up off the floor."

"Get out of this house."

"Sorry, I'll take you to the hospital if you want to spend the night there, but I'm not leaving you alone tonight. Uh-uh."

"Why did you show me that picture?"

"He's my son. I couldn't stand you not knowing I'd done this."

"Is there something wrong with him?"

"Is there something wrong with him?" Christopher sounded offended. "No. He's healthy, totally healthy. He's beautiful. He's ten-and-a-half weeks old now. I've wanted to tell you for so long. Do you know how hard—"

She lay on the floor, still not letting him near her. She stared at him. "What else do I need to know? Where is this baby?"

"They live in Nyack. That's why I've been there so much. I had to fix up the house. It's a mess, Nora. Her life, man, really. She needed the help."

"What do I *need* to know?"

"I'm not in any way and never was in love with her. I love Baby Don. I'm—"

"Just what I *need* to know, Christopher. Do you want a divorce?"

"Jesus, Nora. God, no. Do you? Do you want to divorce me?"

"Are you moving to Nyack? Who's supporting this baby?"

"She is. It's totally her deal. Totally. I signed a paper, she's the full parent. All rights are hers for every decision. I just try to help them—"

"You spent Christmas there, then."

"He was born on Wednesday, December sixth. I had to be there. It was a cesarean. I had to help him. And you were—"

"Never mind where I was. And don't make it sound like the doctor needed *you* there to perform a cesarean. You were there because you wanted to be. You saw some woman having a baby." They sat very still. Nora felt Christopher looking at her. She couldn't look at him. "What's going to happen now?" she asked.

"He's going to grow up. I hope, healthy and good. Happy, if he can."

"I mean with us."

"I don't know." A beat of silence. "Are you going to call 911 again?" She glanced over at him with enough anger to make him say, "Sorry."

"I can't sleep with you in this house," Nora said. "You're going to have to leave."

"There's no way I'm leaving you here alone when you're like this."

"I'll take responsibility for myself."

It went back and forth for half an hour. Finally, he put on his parka; finally, he left.

AS SOON as Christopher was gone, Nora chain-locked the door. Before long, the phone rang. She let the machine answer. Kevin's voice: "Nora, it's me. I know you fainted, he called me from the street. Pick up, I want to talk to you."

She picked up. "What did he tell you? What did that fucker say?"

"Nora?" Kevin's voice was incredulous; Nora didn't swear often. "He said nothing, just to call you because you fainted. What's going on with you two? This is getting too weird. Are you sick, Nora? Is that it? What?"

"That's all he told you? That's all—"

"Yes, what else is there? Tell me. Jesus, Nora."

"There's nothing else. Just stay out of it. I'm fine. I've got to go."

As soon as she hung up, she was trapped. She could not stand or sit or lie down and be still. Wandering the too-wide space of the loft, she forced herself to know what she knew. Walking into the bathroom, she thought, *Christopher has a baby. Christopher has a son.* In the living room, she stopped. *He had a child with someone.* Walking toward his old work space, she noticed the Harley parked there and she had to turn away, and as she did she got nauseous. *Nyack. Nyack?* When she reached the bedroom, Nora knew

383

she couldn't sleep in there that night. She went back to the couch, sat down. Her hand automatically went to the phone. *Christopher has a baby son.* This news needed to be told.

But to whom?

Whom could Nora call? Call Kevin back? Two years ago, even a year ago, that would have been the first call in a crisis, but slowly Nora had managed to cut her brother out. Mary or Giulia? Abe? For an odd moment, she thought of calling Lotte. Then an even odder moment when she thought of Giulia's father, a psychiatrist in Ohio. Nora had met him only twice. She took her hand from the phone, and said aloud to her mother, "Mommy, Christopher had a baby with some woman who's not me."

Nora sat on the couch.

It was too late to call her friend Candice. She had those twins now, and was never free to talk on the phone.

Nora sat on the couch.

All night, from midnight to one, to two, past three o'clock, she sat on the couch and thought about Christopher's odd, odd news. Over and over she had to deep-breathe to calm the palpitations in her chest.

All night she sat awake with the news. *I knew he had a secret.* Nora sat against the couch cushions and said aloud, "Christopher has a son." She got no further than that. No further than *Christopher has a baby.* That sentence was a wall. There was nothing to do with it, no way past it, or around it, or anything. All night, eight hours, and Nora sat and thought it, then thought it again. The words *Christopher* and *son*, and *Christopher* and *baby*, but nothing beyond those words. Nora didn't cry or throw things or scream. She didn't want to call Christopher to come back. She didn't want to file for divorce, or kill him. There was no action. There was just the one stunning fact.

Now what? The view out the window was lightening. Morning. In that scary physical phenomenon that happens sometimes after a night without sleep, Nora felt extra-strong when she stood up to get dressed for work, energized, but she couldn't eat or drink anything. She understood that her life had changed profoundly, as after a death. The days right after her parents' deaths had felt something like this. Now she just needed to act. *Wool socks, my boots. It's cold out. A long sweater.*

She wasn't aware of leaving the loft, or getting the bus, or arriving at her office. She did all her morning appointments, and they went well. Fine. No problem. At lunchtime, Nora pulled out the Yellow Pages and dialed real-estate agents. No one could show her any apartments at lunchtime. Nora's afternoon appointments were more difficult to sit through than the morning sessions had been. Exhaustion was kicking in. But she set up a meeting with a real-estate agent for tomorrow, at noon, which helped her get through the afternoon, get home, get to bed, fall into exhausted sleep.

The next day, Nora sat in the real-estate office filling out forms and, as she had anticipated, she began to want to kill Christopher. What if she didn't manage to move before people started to find out about this baby, find out that Christopher had stopped loving Nora and begun caring for someone else? Her friends would find out. Her patients. People.

The real-estate office was on the third floor of a walk-up and had huge greasy windows plugged up with grimy AC units. Looking over Nora's completed forms, the guy at the dented, tan metal desk said, "Wow. Well, you got a pretty low highest-possible-rent here. I don't know what I might have for you, not in this market."

Nora kicked his desk with her boot. "Just show me an apartment." Christopher had left two pleading messages on the phone machine telling Nora that it wasn't what she thought, he still loved Nora, not the Nyack widow. But that baby. That baby existed, and it was Christopher's baby, and the baby had nothing at all to do with Nora. "Show me anything," she told the real-estate guy. "Today. I need to move. Now."

Nobody ever talks about how truly strange it is to look for a new place to live. As Nora taxied with her real-estate agent, Gavin Grey, from an apartment on East Ninety-first Street, to a place on West Ninety-sixth Street, to another on West Sixty-eighth, trying to see as many places as possible in the hour and twenty minutes she'd given herself for a lunch break, Nora was beginning to understand something about her patients. When they came in weeping and wailing about the hardships of apartment-hunting in the city, no wonder it was nearly impossible to jolt them into a deeper plane of contemplation. The minute you began an apartment search, you stepped into an Alice in Wonderland world, in which you were comically too large for the space available to you, and your resources ludicrously too small.

An Upper East Side studio a half-block east of Park Avenue: one room with a cracked picture window looking out on the backside of an institutional high-rise; a stove, microwave, refrigerator, and sink along one wall; a bathroom with a stained plastic shower stall, no tub; all for $980 a month, plus 15 percent of the annual rent up front for the agent's fee. This, Gavin Grey said, was the best deal of the day. "Under a thousand."

An Upper West Side fourth-floor walk-up in a brownstone a half-block west of Central Park: two rooms, neither large enough for a queen-sized mattress; a closet-kitchen with mice feces on the counter; an arched northern-exposure window facing the street—"Classic," Gavin said—which brought the rent to $1,345 a month plus $2,421 agent's fee.

Apartment-hunting in New York City was, Nora learned, like reading Jonathan Swift. A pull-all-stops satire. You could get lost in the outrageous details, and therefore never give yourself a chance to consider fully the surreal nature of the act itself: dismantling your home; piling your belongings into a dirty rented truck; unloading your furniture, your precious tidbits and contraptions, onto your new street—literally, *onto* the sidewalk, or among the double-parked cars—a street or an avenue on which dogs shat and deliverymen spat and doormen stamped out cigars and cigarettes. And then, finally, hauling the whole deal up flights of steps, or crunching it into an elevator, to the new *space*, where you would spend weeks or months or years creating it again: your home.

But even before that stage—the actual move—there was the equally weird stage during which you opened doors and entered strangers' homes. People you'd never meet, and there you were with your head in their overstuffed clothes closets, lifting the little rugs under their pile of shoes to examine the quality of the wood floor (terrible, hence the rug). Your hand pulling aside their shower curtains, seeing their personal products, their still-dripping washcloths, sponges, loofahs. Their medicine cabinets. Their toilet seats. Seeing that their cats sat all day with their butts on the bed pillows, seeing underpants left on bedroom floors, on kitchen floors. Seeing filthy sponges floating in sinks of grease-dotted dishwater. Seeing the dust of strangers' lives. Nora could barely swallow the terror that someday she might be examined this closely herself.

The day of Nora's search with Gavin Grey, the air was full of wetness that wouldn't let you get warm, the worst kind of late-winter day. No new snow. The streets nothing but sludge; crusty, soiled, ossified snow underfoot. At the crosswalks, at the corners of buildings, old snow was dotted yellow with the urine of dogs and people.

"Gavin, you've got to have something better to show me." Nora was waiting with him at a pay phone on a street corner while he called ahead to see if a place he referred to as "a real find" was still available. "I need something quick. Now," Nora lied. She had the loft, but she needed to know that she could move quickly, start a new life, get away from

Christopher if he began to fight her. I have a baby, he had said, a son. Nora had never felt so afraid for her safety. *What if he wants to move his baby and the widow into the loft?* After what Christopher had done, he might do anything. "By the end of this week, Gavin, I have to have a new place."

"I'm doing my best for you, sweetheart." He was shuffling through a stack of index cards.

"This week, Gavin," she said, "and please don't call me sweetheart."

"All right, doll."

Asshole. And yet she had to stand on that cold corner waiting for him to flirt on the phone with the secretary in his office before getting the low-down on the "real find." Wetness was leaking into Nora's boots, through her socks and stockings. She tilted her chin down deep into the scarf around her neck, until her face was covered in mohair up to her nose. What if she ran into someone who knew her and Christopher? What if someone saw her standing here with this good-looking moron in a fake leather jacket?

What did people do who really did have to relocate in one week, people without a loft? People whose husbands didn't have a painting studio to sleep in? Or a second family in Nyack to stay with? From her patients, Nora had heard about husbands who turned violent when asked to leave. What did they do, the people without trust funds that could, if necessary, be tapped for $1,300 first month's rent, $1,300 security deposit, $2,340 agent's fee, plus the cost of movers, whatever it cost to get a new phone hooked up, and a couple days off from work? A friend had mentioned recently that the packing materials to move himself from one studio to another had cost more than one hundred dollars.

My next patient who needs to move, I'm giving them a free session.

Gavin slammed the phone and Nora asked, "Yeah?"

"It's gone. Somebody put money on it already."

"Doorman?"

"Yeah, but I told you, it's gone."

"If it was such a deal, we should have gone there first instead of—"

"Hey, the deal might fall through," Gavin said, tucking his stack of cards into the inner pocket of his jacket. "Nothing's gone until it's gone. Where can I reach you if something else comes up?"

Nora couldn't wait for the workday to be over so she could go back to her own miserable downtown life. It's bad, she thought, but it's mine. Her own pillows, her own furniture, her own shampoo. Probably, eventually, she'd have to fight Christopher for all of it. But better to wrestle with him than with strangers, better to be ripped off by him than by strangers. As she walked up the street to her office, Nora told herself not to feel defeated because she'd failed to leave Christopher today. It would take time.

But Nora did feel defeated.

SOMEHOW SHE MADE her way through the rest of Tuesday, all of Wednesday, Thursday, and Friday without canceling any appointments, without making any huge mistakes with her patients, though she did lose focus when a young playwright going through a divorce mentioned that he and his wife were deciding to put their small co-op on the market, and she almost began to weep when another man described the weekend from his childhood when his father moved out of the family's home. Nora had arrived now at Saturday morning, seven o'clock, after five hours' sleep, the most she'd managed all week. Sitting on the couch again—this was now her "post," a protective trench on the edge of a battlefield—she held a mug of hot coffee in one hand and with the other hand was touching a paper-towel-wrapped ice cube to the puffiness under her eyes. *Take care of yourself.* This is what she would have advised a patient in her condition. She dialed a locksmith to see about changing the locks on the loft, but when they put her on hold she hung up.

A LITTLE AFTER NINE O'CLOCK, the telephone rang. After four rings, Nora heard through the answering machine the voice of Gavin Grey. "Nora, it's me. Pick up if you're there."

You arrogant—

"Well, Nor, I was right. As usual. The deal on West Seventy-fifth fell through. I knew it would. If you're still looking, we should jump on this imme—"

"Nora Conolly speaking. Is this about an apartment?"

"Hey, yeah, sweetie, it's me, Gavin. Wake you? Good. No. Listen, how fast can you get uptown? Just off Broadway, Seventy-fifth Street."

"If it's a low floor close to Broadway," Nora complained, "it's going to be noisy."

"Do you want a place to live or not?"

IT WAS A PREWAR BUILDING, more worn out than charming. There was a doorman, but he wouldn't be on duty until four in the afternoon, and he'd leave at two in the morning. As Nora and Gavin entered, the main door was unlocked and wide open. The lobby smelled of fish with hints of a gas leak underneath. "Nice old slate floor," Gavin said as they waited for the elevator, and Nora stared at his lizard-skin cowboy boots.

Feeling she should make an attempt, she said, "Laundry in the building, right?"

"Absolutely, in the basement. This is a full-service building."

"What's the rent?"

"He's asking sixteen fifty. We could maybe get that down a bit if we show him you're the ideal tenant."

Upstairs, the sixth-floor hallway felt sinister—dimly lit with Gothic sconces, and the walls had that oily film left from insecticide—but the apartment itself, 6H, was a clean one. It was the tiny, overtended one-bedroom home of newlyweds. "These tenants bought a house in Jersey," Gavin said. "Weird coincidence. Turns out this guy's the brother of a girl I knew at Williams."

"You went to Williams?"

"Yeah, for a while."

Yeah, like maybe two weeks.

The couple's boxes were marked PANTRY, DEN, GUEST ROOM, COM- PUTER ROOM (did people in the suburbs actually have special rooms for their computers?), and stacked neatly along the walls, reaching the ceiling in some spots. Despite all the packed boxes, the two rooms were still stuffed with *stuff*, highly decorated in a way that made Nora lose heart. *Such terrible taste, and yet they can move out of a place I can't afford to move into.*

On every surface, there were brass-framed photos of the couple's wedding. Bride wearing a ruffle around her neck *and* a necklace. And the tables on which the photos rested were covered with flowered cloths *and* crocheted doilies. In the bedroom, Nora's eye caught a set of big shoulder pads on the bureau and she looked away, more embarrassed than if she'd seen a stranger's bra. The newlyweds' bed had a mound of decorative pillows on it, and stuffed kittens, and a crocheted quilt folded across the bottom of the lace-eyelet bedspread. The room was stuffed with Ethan Allen oak furniture, the regulation newlywed bedroom suite.

Standing in the cramped room, Nora assumed her own marriage was over, and, oddly, by now, that news really felt quite small. Sort of like getting used to the idea that Daddy had been in jail. The useful thing about the fact of Christopher's baby was that it canceled out every other worry, made a mockery of any effort. The word *Natassia* no longer bit.

"What do you think?" Gavin asked.

Feeling clammy, as in a déjà vu, Nora walked through the rooms a second time. GameBoy. Commemorative mugs. Photo albums. In the kitchen, a lineup of blender, mixer, food processor, electric grill, toaster, waffle iron, all covered with matching ruffled covers. Duck motif in the kitchen. In the bathroom, pandas. The toilet seat had a ruffled cover. The Kleenex box and spare roll of toilet paper had ruffled covers. So much effort.

"This building is co-op, you know," Gavin said, "so you'll have to be approved by the board. Two months' security up front, nonnegotiable. Plus the first month's rent."

"Plus your fee."

"Plus the fee." Gavin read over the card. "You'll have to give something to the super, too, it says here."

"So we're talking over eight thousand dollars."

"In this market . . ."

Nora interrupted him. "I'm going to think about this one."

"If you're serious, decide fast. I'd hate for you to lose it."

"You really think . . . ?"

"Yeah," he told her.

And that's how Nora found herself reaching into her big leather sack purse, pulling out her checkbook, writing out checks.

"Just three checks for now," Gavin instructed, "all made out to the agency. The super can wait till later. He gets cash. And you need to fill out this form so we can check with your employer and do a credit check. Your credit good, Nora? And now the owner, it says here, he wants three personal references in addition to the employer's reference."

Nora was leaning her checkbook up against the wall to write out her checks, even though Gavin had invited her to sit down on the young couple's sectional sofa and use their glass-topped coffee table.

"Nora, hon, you're making the right decision. In a year or so, with the market the way it is, you're going to have a very enviable rent." Gavin had stayed silent while she'd looked the apartment over, but now he was chattering. In the elevator: "Definitely the right thing for you. Nicest neighborhood in the city. Hell, I wish I could afford it."

By the time they got downstairs and out onto the street, Nora, to her great relief, heard herself saying, "I changed my mind. I don't want that apartment."

"But you just said . . ." All Gavin's chitchat had stopped, and for one naked moment his blue hound-dog eyes showed her exactly how much she'd been annoying him for the past forty-five minutes.

"Yeah, but I don't know. My gut. I think I'm going to give this apartment search a break for a while."

"Suit yourself," Gavin said, smiling, pretending again. "You're the one who has to be happy. I just hope . . ."

Tearing up the three checks and tossing them into a big trash can at the corner of Broadway was the first action in days that made any sense to Nora, but it wasn't even eleven o'clock yet, and she couldn't think what she should do next. Saturday, then Sunday lay ahead of her, and then the rest of her life.

Nora walked. All afternoon. Into shops, out of shops. As usual, sales clerks rushed to her; apparently Nora gave the impression of someone who was going to buy, and buy big. She spent fifteen minutes in the pews of a Catholic church somewhere, ten minutes in the ladies' lounge at Saks. She could have gone into the public library, but she didn't. It was late, and she was on the last leg of her hike home, headed east on West Twenty-third Street, and she glanced across the street and noticed a man standing behind his pretzel cart, and at just the moment Nora's eye passed over him, the vendor stepped out of his sneakers and, with white-athletic-socked feet, onto a patch of carpet spread between the curb and his cart. Nora saw the man get down on his knees, turn to face the East Side. He crouched, lowering his head to the carpet. The sun was setting, the Saturday-evening streets were high-strung. People rushing—many of them hungry, probably ready to grab a bite anywhere—but this vendor had stopped his business, turned his back, and given himself over to something essential to him that he could not see. Nora knew nothing about this vendor's God, knew nothing of what he prayed for, but she watched—her hands were inside the pockets of her coat, her fingers gently stroking her palms—and what she saw was a man acknowledging the powerful mystery that carried his life. Continuing down the street, Nora bowed her head and did the same.

CHAPTER 35:

FEBRUARY—MARCH

1990

Wednesday, a few days after her failure to find a new place to live, Nora was in session with her pregnant patient and heard something shocking. With just about one week until her due date, the woman was fanning herself with a folded-up *New York*, and she told Nora, "I have good news."

"Great," Nora said, "tell me."

"He left his wife. He decided he wants to be with me and the baby. He chose us."

Nora's facial expression must have shown her confusion.

"The baby's father, of course. He moved into my apartment this weekend."

Nora leaned forward in her chair. "What?"

"He's taken a room at the Yale Club, just, you know, so his wife won't feel so bad. But he's with us. He'll be there for the birth. He reserved a private room for me at the hospital."

Nora was floored. There'd been no mention of the man for months, nothing to suggest they'd even been communicating, but what was truly shocking was the sound of Nora's own voice saying, "That's your good news? You're kidding me, aren't you?"

She actually said that, to a patient.

And still Nora couldn't stop herself. "After everything you've said about him, you're letting the man near your child? You've taken him into your home? Are you nuts?"

The patient was very smart and, after just a moment of stunned silence, switched into her polished, professional mode. "I think there's something here that has more to do with you than with me. I'm leaving early today." And she walked out.

Nora was still leaning forward in her leather chair, her pendant bobbing against her knees. *I'm not doing well. I'm not well. I need help.*

FIVE DAYS LATER, to Nora's enormous relief, the patient left a phone message, her voice happy and excited: "Dr. Conolly, it's a girl. She was born Saturday morning. She's fine, everything was amazing. We named her Frida. We're all really, really happy."

Nora was relieved on several counts: (1) the patient was still communicating with her; (2) the birth had gone well; (3) it was a girl. Research suggested that unmarried fathers stuck around less often for daughters than they did for sons. If Frida was lucky, her bad-news father would ditch soon. If Nora was lucky, her patient would come back and give Nora a chance to say what she knew she needed to say: "I made a mistake. I never should have said to you what I said. I never should have reacted in such a judgmental way. I'm sorry."

I'm truly not doing well.

Nora knew it was time to call someone. She had lots of therapists' names she offered as references to other people, but for herself, who to call? Had someone mentioned a Cather? Dr. Cather? Where had she heard that? Nora had no idea where to begin. And so she considered it a gift from the universe when she got home that evening and found this phone message: "Nora, it's me. Candice. Are you still talking to me? I'm sorry I've been a lousy friend. I've been wanting to invite you and Christopher over for dinner, to see the girls. They're so big since you saw them at the hospital, but I can't even tell you, this whole twin business is—God . . . Anyway, would you meet me and the girls for coffee? This Saturday morning? Jacques has to work, which means we're switching our usual brunch with his family, which means the girls and I are free. And don't hate me for asking you this, but could you swing it to meet us in our neighborhood? That would help me a lot. The babies and I would love to see you."

Candice. No, I don't hate you.

There were a few back-and-forth phone messages and it was arranged: ten-thirty Saturday morning, for coffee at a French bakery on Madison Avenue in the Eighties. For the next five days, Nora clung to those details. She had high hopes for this visit.

CHRISTOPHER HAS A *baby son who lives in Nyack.*

Nora had not yet said those words to anyone. She'd been holding the news inside herself for three weeks. Would she tell Candice? Probably not, but Nora was ready for some kind of disclosure, an unburdening. *I made a big mistake in a session.* Probably she wouldn't tell Candice that, not a good move professionally, but Candice and her husband did own a maid's room on the top floor of their building, and Nora was ready to ask if they would rent it to her; this request would, of course, bring on further questions, and Nora would eventually be saying that she and Christopher were, basically, separated. Probably Nora should begin to get that news out herself, before Christopher started going around telling people he'd gone behind Nora's back, had a baby on his own. Nora wondered if she should tell Candice everything, the truth about Christopher, Baby Natassia, all of it. *Ten years we've been friends and I've managed not to tell her; I'm not telling now.*

Nora and Candice had met during their first semester of psychoanalytic training. For a while they were casual friends, talking before and after lectures. Candice was in the heart-wrecking last stages of divorce from her first husband, and she talked to Nora about that sometimes, but they never even exchanged phone numbers. So Nora was completely surprised one school night when Candice called the loft to ask if she could come over. "My family's great, but they're just worn out listening to me, and it's too late to call my therapist. You just seem really empathic," she told Nora, "and I'm hurting so much I don't think I can do tonight alone." What could Nora say? Candice lived a few blocks uptown. It was almost midnight; Christopher offered to meet Candice halfway (he was proud that his wife was already so skilled at her profession that other students were call-

ing for help). After that night, for several weeks, Candice had many sleep-
overs at the loft. Christopher was turned off by how forthright she was
about her misery; usually he went to bed. But Nora, from the start of this
friendship, admired Candice's ability to ask for what she needed. Eventually, Nora benefited greatly from these late-night sessions. She had never
met anyone as willing as Candice was to talk long and deep about grief. At
that point, eight years had passed since Nora had lost her parents. Kevin,
Mary, Christopher—none of them had offered Nora the chance to talk—
and be heard—the way Candice did. It was Candice who took the first
trip back to Greenport with Nora, literally held her hand when she cried.

You can get something done talking to Candice. That Saturday morning of
their coffee date, Nora felt calmed enough to go down into the subway.
Sitting in an uncrowded car on her way uptown, leafing through *Street
News* to distract herself, Nora realized she'd have to be a little bit organized
about this visit. In the past, she'd always had Candice's full attention, but
now there were babies. Two of them. Still, Candice was not the kind of
person to let babies get in the way of an important talk.

WHEN NORA REACHED the entrance to the bakery, she looked up and a
huge pram was less than half a block away and being pushed by Candice,
who was wearing a leopard-print fake-fur coat. Her hair was now several
different shades of red and looked like a babysitter's—pulled up in a ponytail on the top of her head and flopping over to one side. "Hi, sweetie!"
Candice called loudly down the sidewalk.

Nora never raised her voice in public. She smiled and waited until the
pram was in front of her, and Candice was close enough for a hug. Nora
wasn't a big social hugger or kisser, but she found herself relieved to hug
Candice, the first person she'd had physical contact with in two weeks.
Nora made a move to look inside the pram, but Candice put her finger to
her lips and whispered, "Our only chance to talk is if they keep sleeping."

And without knowing why she was saying it, Nora lied, "I have a cold
anyway. I shouldn't get too close to them." And then, because she felt
guilty about her lie, she said, "Wow. What a coat!" She didn't remember
Candice dressing like such a teenager before.

"Isn't it fun? My sister-in-law wore it over from Paris when she came for Christmas. I made her leave it here when she left. One of her boyfriends designed it."

Inside, as they stood waiting to be seated, Candice said, "It's good to see you, Nor. You look great."

"You're being kind. I'm big as a house."

"You. Are. Not—"

A waiter in a crisp shirt interrupted, spoke French as he led them to a table. Two old-lady customers fussed over the pretty pram and tried to look in, but Candice walked on, leading with her chin. At the table, Candice told the waiter, in French, she wanted to be farther from the window—it was too cold for the babies. Just after they were seated at an interior table, she called the waiter over. "The overhead fan, please, could it be turned off? The babies," Candice said with a pinched worried face, "the draft."

"Oui, oui, madame."

The minute her coat was off, Nora covered her own lap with the big cloth napkin, hoping to hide her hips. Candice had always had a skinny little body, stiff and not too appealing, but today she was wearing leggings and, boldly, a short-cropped sweater. Nora used to be able to dress that way. No more. Candice fussed with blankets and bags, finally took her seat, and shook her head, her ponytail spinning to the other side. She put her hand over Nora's hand on the table. "How *are* you?"

"These babies. They're beautiful, Candice." In truth, the twins weren't great-looking. Pimply, scaly. As Nora turned toward the pram, there was a funny smell. Something medicinal. But the clothes were showpieces: tiny hand-knit sweaters with pearl buttons, fleecy tights with ruffled bottoms. It was an odd, European way of dressing babies that Nora would never have thought of. She had a block about remembering the babies' names, which were French and referred back to Greek goddesses. Lots of vowels. Christopher's baby was named something like Ronald McDonald, and it was extremely likely, highly possible, that if Nora called Christopher and said, "I need you right now," he could say, "I can't come right now. My baby needs me."

This visit with Candice was a big mistake. I wish I weren't here.

"So how's Christopher?" Candice asked. "And the loft? And—"

"Not good. With Christopher, I mean. The loft is fine."

"Christopher?" The features of Candice's face, especially as she listened, were tiny and squished tight, and Christopher had once said it might not be easy for her to hook up with someone again, implying she wasn't pretty enough.

Candice was whispering, so Nora did, too. "It's not Christopher. It's me."

"What?" Candice took a guess: "You met somebody?"

"Sort of."

Candice brushed her bangs away from her tiny eyes.

"He's a writer," Nora said, as if this information were clarifying.

"Journalist?" Candice asked, hopeful. Then the waiter was at the table, and Candice, in French, ordered a café au lait, insisting on decaf, and a croissant, insisting that it be hot. She told Nora she really should have a hot croissant, too, because they were the best in town, so Nora let Candice order for her, and she promised herself she would not, under any circumstances, say the name Abe.

"He's a novelist."

"Oh no," Candice said.

"What?"

"Well, just that . . . Remember Greta in grad school who had that guy? He never did finish his book, and he used up all her money."

"But, no, this guy," Nora said, "it wasn't serious. It's not serious."

"It's still going on?"

"It— The truth is, it never took off. It was an attraction. It went nowhere. He is, he was, a symptom, I guess. He's not the real issue."

"Well, that's good. You sound really clear. . . ."

Nora allowed the conversation to go on this way, as if her problems really were about another man, which was easy, and freed Nora up to take in deeply all that she was observing. For example, Candice, good listener as always, maintained solid eye contact, but her hand never left the side of the pram. One baby flinched, woke, but before she even completed her first cry, Candice had the baby up and out, without disturbing the sleeping twin. It was as if Candice were playing a skilled game of jacks or Pick-Up Sticks. Her foot kept the pram in a slow rock while she adjusted the awake baby onto her shoulder. Her kisses on her baby's head were as unconscious as breath.

The baby didn't want the shoulder. "Does this guy, this novelist, know?

Do you think he senses your detachment from the situation? Is he pressing for more?" Candice's moves were deft, getting a cashmere shawl around her shoulders, reaching in to unbutton her sweater, lifting, lowering, and within the time it took to complete a sentence, the baby was nursing and quiet, and Nora watched her skinny pale fist unfurl as she relaxed.

The one time Nora had been pregnant, for six weeks when she was nineteen years old, her breasts had got enormous and they hurt enormously. She could still remember the particular quality of the bruised ache within her breasts, the way hot pain radiated outward, into her clothes and beyond, so that when her boyfriend even tried to come near her Nora crossed her arms in front of herself, made a shield. He showed up loyally, every night, at her apartment very late (he was studying to take the LSATs). "Nora, let's get married, I'm not kidding. I love you. We can do it." The ache in her breasts was so much more powerful than his voice. Now she had to stop a minute to remember his full name—a clear indication that she'd made the right choice all those years ago. She couldn't even remember exactly how it was when they broke up; what she remembered was sitting in a class one day and realizing that her breasts no longer felt bruised, no longer felt like anything. That's when she had to go to student services to ask about counseling.

Nora asked Candice, "Does it hurt?"

"What? This?" She nodded toward the baby on her chest. "No. Not now. At first they weren't latching on right and it hurt like hell. But now it's okay."

"What's it feel like, physically?"

Candice hesitated. "I don't know. Like nothing." Pause. "That's not true. It's a nice little tug. Suckling. It feels just like *that*. What do you call that, onomatopoeia, when the word sounds exactly like what it's describing? But I do it so many times a day."

"How many?"

"Hundreds. Thousands." They laughed. The baby fussed, and Candice shifted her onto a shoulder. "I don't know, but, no, it doesn't hurt. What hurts is their crying in the middle of the night."

"They cry a lot, huh?"

"It goes on for hours sometimes. Oops." The baby spit up on Candice's shoulder. There was a smell. "First you feed one, then the other."

"How do you do it all, Candice?"

"Well, I'd be lost without my mother. She comes in from New Jersey a lot. My sister comes over a lot. Then Jacques's sister was here for a while. God, I hated to see her go—she's just a stitch. And I have a nanny every afternoon for five hours. But even with all that help, I just end up weeping sometimes."

Weeping, suckling. Ancient words, Biblical language. *Widow.*

That woman in Nyack, Christopher was probably seeing her breasts all the time.

"When she's done feeding, do you want to hold her?" Candice asked.

"No!" Nora said very quickly. "I better not. My cold. Germs." She had never so intensely wanted something and at the same time not wanted it.

"Oh, okay," Candice said, and to the baby she said, "Next time Auntie Nora will hold you, next time. We need to see Auntie Nora more often."

Nora had disappointed Candice. Forgive me, Nora wanted to say, but I'm one of those women who come along sometimes in the history of women, an aberration who is just not able to latch on.

AT THE END of their visit, out on the sidewalk in front of the bakery, Nora and Candice spent ten minutes remembering last things they wanted to tell each other while Candice rocked the pram. "I saw your friend the dancer a few months ago. On Broadway. God, her daughter's all grown up now."

"Natassia." Nora hadn't said the name aloud to anyone in weeks. "Yeah."

"She's always fascinated me. Just the level of excellence—"

"Natassia or Mary?"

"Mary, with her dance. I remember you telling me how she performs even when she's sick and injured and all that. I think of her sometimes now, with the babies, when they've kept me up all night and I have to wake up and do the next day. She danced jet-lagged, all of it. The contradiction. Her work's all about body, and she goes about it as if she has no body. Nora, are you okay?"

"Yeah, just—"

And then Candice's voice shifted; she reached a hand and clutched

Nora's coat sleeve. "I've missed talking to you. Nora, I really need these talks with you."

As always, Candice's ability to know what she needed, and to ask for it, muted Nora. "I really like our talks, too," Nora said, but in a way that revealed nothing.

Then the babies were crying, first one, then the other. "Oh dear, I've relied on their patience for too long," Candice said, "I should go."

Nora, panicked, hugged her purse to her chest.

"We'll do this again?" Candice said. "Call me?" She was turning the pram around.

"Wait," Nora said. "I have to tell you something. I, this week, I made a really bad mistake in a session." Candice's face pinched with worry again. "With a patient," Nora said. "I yelled at her, I completely rejected a decision she'd made. A big decision. A bad one, but still—"

"Oh, Nora, I'm sorry." Both babies were crying now.

"You better go," Nora said.

Candice leaned on the handle of the pram. "There are no mistakes in therapy, Nora, there's just information, remember that?"

"What I keep remembering," Nora said, "is Winnicott—if there is a mistake, it's the therapist's."

Baby cries were all over the sidewalk; passersby were trying to look into the pram. Nora was hugging her purse tightly, afraid to let Candice go, but also embarrassed about the noise. Candice really did need to get going. "You're being too hard on yourself, Nora. You just need to sit with it, like with any countertransference, and figure out, you know . . ."

"What was going on with me."

"Right, what was going on inside that moment for you." Candice had never actually worked at her profession, but somehow she'd managed to turn education into wisdom. "And then, Nora, you'll talk with the patient, work it out."

"If she comes back." One baby howled, then another baby. "Go, Candice, go."

"You know what, call me, later today. I'll try to make sure we have a minute to talk. We should talk about this more." Candice offered a good-bye hug, but Nora didn't move her purse or open her arms, so Candice tossed a kiss into the air. The two women began walking away from each other in opposite directions. "Let's get together again soon," Candice called.

And Nora nodded and waved.

And then she turned away, letting her friend get lost in the sidewalk crowds, letting Candice become just another wealthy new mother with a nice stroller. It had happened with other friends, and now it would happen with Candice. Spending time with people who had babies left you feeling lonelier than you had before. Nora stopped at a corner and waited for a bus to race through a yellow light. As she stepped out into the street, a bunch of teenagers were approaching her, crossing the street from the other direction. About seven of them, city kids, all different skin tones and hair textures, talking loud. "My mom's going to kill my ass when she finds out," a girl said, laughing, and they all laughed, all of them involved in the same big conversation, and a boy from far back in the crowd said, "Your mama. My uncle, man . . ." When they intersected with Nora, she felt a little panic, the need to lower her sunglasses from the top of her head to cover her eyes. Young Mary had known how to be part of a group like that. Even Kevin. But Nora had always been off somewhere, alone with some exclusive boyfriend, some guy who kept telling her she was pretty, beautiful, great, the best. Seventh grade, eighth grade, high school. Even now, the group had ignored her, passed around Nora like water around a rock.

A FEW HOURS LATER, when Nora finally got back to the loft after walking all the way from uptown, there was one message on the answering machine. Slipping off her coat and scarf, she hit the red button and heard, "Nora, hi, this is Lotte Stein." *Natassia?* "It's David, Nora." Lotte was crying. "All of a sudden, after a lunch meeting today, back at his desk. It happened in a second. I'm reeling here, Nora, I'm just . . ." Lotte was crying hard into the phone. "The doctor said there was nothing anyone could have done. Nora, please, I have to ask you to do something for me. Would you, please, go up to Hiliard to tell Mary and Natassia? I want them to get this news in person. I'll pay for you to take a car service up there. It'll take you a couple hours. But, please, go soon. Tonight. Before Ross gets it in his head to call Natassia from an airport. He's on his way home now. I wouldn't bother you with this, Nora, but I don't know what this news will do to Natassia. What's going to happen to our girl when she hears her poppy died?"

CHAPTER 36:

MARCH

1990

Christopher was in Grand Central Station and had just bought his train tickets. The weather still wasn't good enough to start going up to Nyack on his motorcycle, which would have been so much faster. He was thinking about that, walking away from the ticket window, when his eye caught a woman in a black wool coat who looked like Nora. It wasn't Nora. But then, five steps farther, just at the base of the big marble staircase, he walked right toward Nora—actually her—in her good camel-hair coat. She was carrying her leather purse and a canvas bag. She was the classiest woman in the crowd.

"Nora." She saw him just as he was saying her name. Their quick halt sent people spilling to the left and right of them.

As soon as they had hugged, he realized that something serious was wrong, or Nora wouldn't have let him touch her. He began to ask, "Where—"

"I've been up at Hiliard." Her voice was full of troubles.

"Is Natassia—"

"Fine. It's David, Christopher. He died. David died. I had to go up there last night to tell Mary and Natassia. Lotte didn't want them to hear it on the phone."

"David? David Stein's dead? No. Wait—"

"Instant. In his office."

"My God. Is Natassia—? Wow, she was close to him."

"I can't even tell you— Christopher, I need to talk to you. Now."

He made a quick decision that wasn't really a decision—of course, if Nora wanted to talk, he'd talk. "Sure, come on. I'll buy you lunch."

"But"—she looked up at the huge schedule board, where the track numbers and departure times and town names were flipping—"your train?"

"I'll catch my next one. Come on, let's get a drink."

THEY SAT at a bar where it was dark and the lunch-rush crowd was thinning out. It was after two o'clock. They waited for their beers, though Christopher knew he wouldn't be able to drink his. He needed to find a pay phone so he could call Denise to tell her he'd be getting a later train. He needed to sit still and take in Nora.

She looked more afraid of him than angry at him, and her fear of him made him so sad he almost wished to see her angry again. As soon as she unbuttoned her coat, Christopher could see she'd gained more weight, and he tried to imagine her pregnant, but that game didn't feel good anymore. Baby Don was too real now. Christopher was on his way up to Nyack for one of his twice-weekly trips. He was building a half-bath in the basement of Denise's house. Her original baby-care plan hadn't worked. The Haitian woman she'd planned to swap child care with had made too many comments about Denise's mothering, and Denise had chewed her out. So now Denise had a nanny living in the house, which was working fairly well. Except they really needed another bathroom. The nanny was a young girl, also Haitian, barely twenty, but smart and breezy with Baby Don, just what was needed in that house to even out the unpredictable weather that was Denise. The girl smelled of patchouli. Christopher still couldn't pronounce her name. She wore skintight clothes over a great little body, and he wished he could ask her to model for him. He couldn't remember the last time he'd painted a whole painting. He couldn't remember when he'd last had sex. Those weeks in January, that early-spring thaw between him and Nora when he was back in the loft. Until that stupid Sunday he got the stupid idea to work on their stupid taxes. Now he looked at Nora, who was on the verge of crying. Let's stop this, he wanted to say; he wanted to insist, No more separation. You're my wife, you're the person I love, we have to stop this.

"Christopher," she said.

He took her hand. "Talk to me, sweetheart, what?"

There were tears. Her eyes were swollen, her gorgeous high cheek-bones bloated.

"Nora, before you start, can I just say something? Can I just say how much I love you, how much I miss you. Nora, you're the only person I'll ever love."

"Christopher, Mary flipped out on me. Mary and Natassia both flipped last night. We had an argument, a bad one. Yelling, everything. Christopher, I told them."

"About David? And they got mad at *you*?"

"I told them about France. I told."

He thought he understood but wasn't sure, and he didn't want to appear to be stupid. "France, you mean."

"The baby. When Natassia was a baby. When you—"

"When Natassia was a baby and they visited."

"I told them, Christopher."

"And now?"

CHAPTER 37:

MARCH

1990

David's dead was one thought Mary couldn't shake that Sunday morning as the Communicar sedan taking her and Natassia into the city from Hiliard was speeding down the Saw Mill River Parkway; the other thought was more shocking: *I can't trust Nora anymore.* The driver was in the passing lane; the road was bendy and sad, lined with winter-dead brown trees. Mary recognized the road as the one David used to drive to their country house—Mary had gone as infrequently as possible, only when Natassia begged. This was the road where Lotte nagged David, telling him it was the worst road he could have picked. And he'd grip the steering wheel and scream, "I'm trying to goddamn drive, can you see that? This is the fucking last time, Lotte, these weekends aren't worth it."

And Lotte would say, "I'll take the train next time. I'll take the bus."

And David would yell, "Good, take the bus. Ride in the bus like the goddamn peasant you are."

They had done it for years, and now he was dead.

Mary looked over at Natassia huddled into the maroon corner of the sedan, staring out the rain-specked window. "You okay?" The kid just nodded. She was sucking her index finger. Her violin case was on her lap. Natassia hadn't touched the violin once up at Hiliard, but she wanted to play it at her grandfather's funeral. Earlier that morning, as Nora was leaving the cottage, Natassia had told her, "Don't you and Christopher dare come to my grandfather's funeral." Mary wasn't going to disagree with that. Mary wanted never to see Nora or Christopher again, except maybe in court, to send them to jail.

Up front, the driver lifted his radio speaker and said, "Dropping off in ten."

Mary dreaded the moment when the Communicar would pull up in front of the building and she and Natassia would have to get out, see Lotte, do stuff, say things. And the whole time, Mary would have to be guarding Natassia, monitoring the telephone. But what a joke, the idea that Mary was capable of protecting her daughter. She had failed so long ago and failed so seriously.

Fuck.

Inside herself, Mary could not catch up with everything that had happened in the past twenty-four hours. First David died. Then Nora showed up. Then Natassia was molested when she was a baby. Then it was Christopher who had done it.

Jesus.

Mary tried to think it through again, reordering the events. First Nora had shown up at the door of the cottage. The thing Mary noticed was that Nora looked even heavier and more worn out than she had last fall. Mary had thought, Nora! And then, Do I owe her more money?

Nora had stepped inside the cottage, taken off her coat. She sat down on the couch, asked, "Where's Natassia?" just as Natassia came out of the bathroom tying her sweatpants up under her Hiliard School T-shirt. "Hey, hi," Natassia had said. Nora stood up. Mary remembered watching them hug, feeling that jab of jealousy, but, more than that, feeling relief to see Nora not angry anymore and wrapping Natassia in a good, long hug.

Then Natassia stepped back and raised her arms to gather up her loose, wild hair into a scrunchy, and Nora said, "Natassia, there's no good way to say this."

Natassia's hands stayed raised, holding up her hair. "Daddy?" she asked in a panicked voice. Nora shook her head. Quickly, Natassia demanded, "It's not Grammy?"

"It's David. Sweetie, he had an attack of some kind this afternoon. He was in his office. He passed away . . . instantly."

"Pop-py," Natassia whispered as her hands let go of her hair and slid onto her face. She pressed the polka-dotted scrunchy to her mouth.

Then Nora said, "Lotte called me and asked me to—"

"Who's going to tell Daddy?"

Oh, shit, this is going to make her want to call the BF again. Damn it, David.

"Your father is on his way home," Nora told Natassia.

"Poor Daddy. He can't take this."

"He's traveling with Harriet, so—"

The scrunchy slipped from Natassia's hand, and her fingers went into her mouth. Mary could see Natassia's teeth biting her fingertips, and no one seemed to know what to do. Natassia pulled her fingers out of her mouth and reached for Mary, grabbed her sweatshirt sleeve, and Mary covered Natassia's hands with her own—clumped together, their hands were tremoring. (Mary was aware of feeling, oddly, not sad about David, but she did feel afraid.) And then Natassia shuddered, started to cry, lowered her head to Mary's neck, and Mary's face was covered by Natassia's hair. "I didn't see Poppy at Christmastime. I never saw him after—"

"Sweetie, there's no way you could have known."

And then Nora said, "Natassia, I'm afraid you're going to have to try . . ."

And then the weight of Natassia's head was gone from Mary's shoulder. Mary would never forget that lightning-fast transition, that transfer of weight. She had had to work with the Hiliard students for weeks and weeks to get them to make a move that clean: on-*off*, on-*off*. The rage in the kid's voice was a shock, one more thing Mary wouldn't forget for a long time. "*Don't* you," Natassia said, with more of a grunt than a voice, "tell me what I have to try to do." And then Natassia continued yelling, and the bad news of David's death was over and something worse began to happen. "Nora, you're such a bitch to everybody. Like, why'd you drive my mom so crazy about that phone bill? You have so much more money than she ever will."

Natassia snatched a box of Kleenex off the coffee table, pulled out a handful, swiped at her face, and threw the cardboard box hard onto the floor, very close to Nora's feet. "You've always been so mean to me. You always"—Natassia retrieved the Kleenex box, grabbed more tissues, and pounded the box against the edge of the table—"always tell me what to do, you watch everything I do, it's like you're looking for bad stuff and you can't wait to tell me about it. You're so superior. You don't care about anybody else. You treat my mother like shit. You even treat your own brother like shit. You stood him up for Christmas. You drive Christopher crazy. I don't know how he puts up with you."

"Hey, hey," Mary said, "enough of that." Mary had stayed out of it as long as she could—recently Dr. Cather had been pushing the point that Natassia had relationships with lots of other adults besides her mother, and it was important for Mary to step back and give Natassia room to work things out on her own—but the kid could get so insulting, just like Ross, just like David. "Apologize to Nora," Mary demanded.

Natassia said, "No fucking way," and left the room. Mary followed her into her bedroom, where Natassia knelt on her bed and rolled her head to her knees and started crying full-speed. "Pop-py. Pop-py."

"It's not Nora's fault."

"I didn't see him, I didn't . . ." Natassia's words were muffled into her mess of sheets and blankets. The thin, sharp bones of her spine raised the back of her white T-shirt into a tent.

"Honey."

It took almost an hour. Mary went and got the mobile phone and they tried to call Lotte, but the line was busy and busy and busy again. They dialed Ross's number in Spokane and left a message on his machine. Natassia cried. It had been months since Mary had held Natassia the way she had to hold her that night, supporting Natassia's body to keep her from shaking, rocking her, saying over and over, "I'm sorry, Natassia. I'm so sorry." At least now Natassia's limbs felt more substantial, her body was a bit heftier, which was not to say that she wasn't still skinny, but there was more to her now than when Mary had held her in the fall. When Natassia finally wore herself down and was asleep, Mary lowered the kid's head onto the folded quilt she liked to use as a pillow, covered her feet with blankets, tucked a bed pillow up against her back, left the door open, and went down the hall, back to Nora, who was in the living room with her feet up on the couch and her chin resting on her raised knees. She, too, was rocking. Mary was sitting down next to her, pulling out a cigarette, before she realized that Nora's face was wet with tears. "I'm sorry she said all that shit to you," Mary said.

"It's all right."

"No," Mary said, "it's not. It's rude. I'm getting a beer. Do you want a beer?"

"No."

Walking into the kitchen, Mary was thinking about asking Nora, Why *are* you so hard on Natassia? Do you just not like her, or what? But what could Nora say? *Your kid bugs me and she always has.* Nora would never admit that. Even if it was the truth. This was exactly what Mary was thinking as she sat back down on the couch with a cold Rolling Rock, so it really weirded her out when Nora said, "Mary, I want to tell you. About Natassia, I want to tell you the truth."

"You don't have to, Nora. She can be a brat. I know that."

"No, she's not a brat. I've always felt—"

"Nora, not now."

"I have to, Mary. It's time."

Silence.

Mary yawned a big aching yawn. When Nora got on a psychology talking binge, there was no stopping her. The beer didn't taste that good after all. Mary put the bottle on the coffee table, picked up a notebook, found a blank page, and started a list of what she'd have to take care of for her classes before she left for the city in the morning. There'd be a funeral and sitting shivah and who knows what else. She'd have to tell the office, "Death in the family," and "I'll be gone a few days." Just a few weeks earlier, she'd signed a new three-year contract that gave her a raise and expanded her duties ("Good," Ross had said, "the more they're depending on you for, the less likely they are to fire you"), so she didn't have to worry too much anymore about losing her job, but she did have to take care of business.

Nora, not far from Mary on the couch, kept insisting on talking. "In a way that's difficult to explain, I've always felt, well, *close* to Natassia, too close."

Mary was writing: *(1) type up research homework assignment; (2) make copies, leave with secretary; (3) call substitute for studio classes.*

"Christopher used to tell me I was hard on Natassia, but I couldn't see it. I was so worried about her, wanting to look out for her. Always. Christopher said I was turning . . . harsh."

Still writing her list, Mary asked, "Does Natassia just get on your nerves?"

"No." Nora began rocking again, which shifted the pillows on the couch, made it difficult for Mary to write. Nora kept rocking.

What the hell did David have to go to his office on Saturday afternoon for, anyway?

Nora said, "I think I have to tell you now."

"Oh, Nora, don't worry about it. You and Natassia, maybe you're just too much alike to get along. Maybe it's a two-peas-in-a-pod thing."

"Mary, when Natassia was a baby"—Nora turned and faced Mary, forcing Mary to look up from her list—"do you remember how beautiful she was, how sweet? Remember when you and Ross hitchhiked with her all the way to France from Rome?"

Mary was lighting another cigarette, wishing for a pipe, but she smiled at the memory, even though she'd heard a little accusation in *hitchhiked all the way*. Mary was thinking, I never told Cather about that trip, did I? "Christopher's loft." Mary's hand shooed smoke away. "*That* was a really good time."

"Do you remember how—God, I don't know—how we were? So . . . loose, happy, free, in love. So totally in love—"

"You and Christopher, man, you were—"

"No, but you and Ross, too, and all of us, with each other, and with ourselves, and we were totally in love with your amazing baby—"

"She was a little pumpkin, wasn't she?" Mary inhaled deeply.

"And we were—"

"Young." Mary shook her head. "So, so, so young. And dumb."

"Lately, when I think about that time, I just keep thinking that we were in love. In every possible way, we were in love. I mean, there you were in Rome, performing. I was on the beach in France. Mary, we'd finally got past Albany. So much past Albany and all that misery when we were kids. Mary, you and I, by twenty, we'd been through hell."

"You can say that again."

"And then there we were all together in France, and it just felt like—well, to me it did, anyway—that we'd managed, we'd survived, and we'd found these great men who were good to us. For a change. You had Ross and the baby. And Christopher was so—"

"He still is, Nora. You got a great husband."

Nora's tears started up. "Do you remember how beautiful he was, so

413

absolutely gorgeous to look at? And I just . . . I liked watching his eyes when he talked. His lips."

"Oh, Nor." Mary got up on her knees and crawled over to Nora's end of the couch, sat next to her, put an arm around her. Nora really was crying hard now. She had to breathe deep to keep herself from gasping. Eventually, she reached for Mary's cigarette and took a drag.

"Are you going to tell me something," Mary asked, "about what's going on with you and Christopher? I've been trying to mind my own business, but, Nora, something big is not right with you two. Even Kevin feels like something's wrong, but you won't tell him. It's really pissing him off."

Nora looked at Mary. "Do you talk to Kevin a lot? Is he okay?"

"He's worried about you, Nora. But, listen, just tell me, are you guys going to divorce or something?"

Mary lit a new cigarette with the butt of her old one, and handed the new one to Nora, who took it and smoked.

"You look good with a cigarette, Nor. I think you'd feel better if you started smoking."

They looked at each other. Nora wouldn't laugh, not even a smile. Mary felt cold air and smelled the orange-blossom smoke from the bathroom candle. The bathroom window must have been opened, spreading the scent of the orange-blossom candle, and Nora was saying, "I do want to tell you about Christopher and me, but what's going on now has to do with something that happened a long time ago, that summer in France. It was that week you visited us."

The cottage was undeniably full of something that was just about to happen. Mary suddenly understood that she needed to defend herself. "We came because you invited us." She had an urge to say, Don't tell me! She knew she was going to hear something bad, and not just about Nora's marriage. Quickly, Mary tried to psych out the possibilities. "While Ross and I went away those couple days? You were mad at Christopher when we got back. Something happened."

"I didn't know what to do, Mary. I did everything wrong."

Mary took the cigarette from Nora's hand, stubbed it out in the ashtray on her lap. She turned sideways and sat cross-legged facing Nora, needing the distance, needing to make sure their legs and arms and hair weren't touching.

Nora could barely whisper as she said, "I'm really sorry."

"Something happened to Natassia while we were gone. What? Did you drop her?"

Nora shook her head no. She said, "Christopher."

"Did Christopher feed her something bad and you had to take her to the hospital? Was her stomach pumped? Goddamn it, Nor, what?" By now Mary was rocking, mimicking Nora's rocking. Nora was sobbing, and Mary wanted to slap her. "Nora, she was only six weeks old. Did he hit her, did he beat her or something?"

"I didn't know what to do, Mary."

Inside Mary's body, everything was turned on high, heart pumping crazily, blood pounding. Before she could stop herself, she reached out and slapped Nora on the arm. Not a smack, but a solid slap, fingers on arm flesh. "*Tell* me. *Tell* me."

"He didn't know what he was doing. He was taking care of her, changing her diaper."

Mary had no breath.

"He molested her, Mary."

Mary scampered up onto the arm of the couch to get away from Nora.

"He kissed her. That's all I saw. That's all I know." Nora's eyes left Mary's face. "I walked in from the bathroom, where I was getting her bathwater ready. We were trying to do everything right. And I saw him holding her up to his mouth, and she was naked."

Mary whispered, "And?"

"I screamed at him," Nora whispered, "to stop."

"Did he stop? Did he drop her?"

"Yes, he stopped. No. No, he never dropped her."

"Was he dressed?" Mary's hands were vised between her knees. "Did he have pants on?"

"Yes."

"Was he putting anything into her?"

"No."

Mary, rocking, stared at Nora. "Fucking tell me the truth."

Nora said, "His tongue. Maybe he put his tongue into her. I don't know. He says no, he didn't. I just saw his tongue out, and her body, and then I screamed."

"Christopher didn't do that." Mary's voice was begging now. "Tell me he didn't."

"He did it. He did do it."

"No. No, no, no, he didn't."

"I grabbed the baby from him—"

"That was *Natassia*."

"—and I ran into the bathroom with her. She cried really loud when I grabbed her."

"He didn't do that, he didn't. . . ."

"It wasn't like she was crying because of Christopher; I think I scared her. She hadn't been crying when I first walked into the kitchen."

"Are you fucking saying he didn't hurt her?"

"Mary, I have to finish. Please, let me finish."

"No-RA!"

"She *cried*," Nora insisted. "And then I grabbed her, and then I held her. I held her, Mary, for two solid days until you and Ross got back. I made Christopher leave the loft. I made him leave. He wanted to explain. I said, 'I never want you here again.' After he left, I washed her. The bath was ready, and I soaked her a long, long time. I put a clean diaper on and dressed her, and she kept crying because I was crying. When she finally fell asleep, I took off her diaper to see if there was anything. Any rash or—"

"Was there?"

"Nothing. I didn't sleep. I did nothing. I just watched her. When she was awake, I held her. Christopher came back. I had the door barred shut and I wouldn't let him in."

"You never fucking told me this, you never—"

"Mary, I need you to know we've been fighting about this for fifteen years. I made him go to counseling. I tried to leave him. I make sure he's never alone with her. Ever."

"But you never told me. Jesus, you're a therapist. You know how this stuff messes a person up. You know better than I do. That's why she tried to kill herself in September, isn't it? You knew that, and you didn't say anything. That whole night at the hospital, you never told anybody. None of the doctors."

"We don't know that, Mary. We don't know why Natassia hurt herself in September. We don't know, and may never know, if what Christopher did to her when she was a baby had any effect on her at all."

"I did what I did with the Cuisinart blade," Natassia said, "because I felt like it." Mary had caught Natassia's presence in the corner of her eye just the second before Natassia began to speak. "I hated myself that night. I couldn't tell anybody."

"How long have you been standing there?" Mary asked Natassia.

"I heard it all, Mom. You guys get louder than you think."

"You heard—"

"About Christopher and the baby thing and his tongue and all of it."

"Sweetie," Mary said, climbing over the back of the couch to go to Natassia. Before Mary reached her, Natassia said, "HJJ and I have been trying to figure out who it was. I was afraid it was Daddy. Don't look at me like that, Mom. I guess I just had the feeling that something like that had happened to me. And then talking with HJJ about the BF and stuff, stuff he did and I let him do to me and stuff."

"What?"

"Nothing I'm telling you. I told HJJ." Natassia, wrapped in a quilt, stepped away from her mother.

"Natassia," Nora said, "when did you begin to think that maybe you'd been molested as a baby?"

"Don't play shrink with me, Nora. You're a total coward. Not only do you not tell me this thing that any decent shrink would know was an important thing to tell, but you treat me like shit."

"Cut that out, Natassia," Mary said. "This is serious."

"Well, she does treat me like shit. At least Christopher was always nice to me. And, no, he never did anything to me again. I don't remember him hurting me. I don't remember anybody ever hurting me or molesting me or abusing me. Except Poppy used to tease me to death, and now he's dead." Natassia hugged the quilt tighter around herself. "All I had was these symptoms that added up to me being messed around with when I was a kid, before I could remember. I was so afraid it was Daddy."

"Honey, Daddy would never hurt you."

"But, Mom, you don't know half the stuff. After you left him and started touring, he used to get so messed up sometimes. Not a lot. But sometimes Poppy wouldn't let Daddy into the house. Once Dad was drunk and he tried to take me with him from the apartment. The doorman had to stop him. Grammy took me with her to work for, like, a whole week after that."

"How old were you?"

"First grade."

"You never told me, Natassia."

"Grammy said it'd worry you."

"Je-sus Christ."

The three of them—Natassia, Mary, and Nora—from their different standing positions, all stared at the coffee table, where a cigarette steamed in the ashtray.

So much time passed without anyone's saying anything; then, out of nowhere, Nora said, "It's beautiful up here, Mary. Kevin told me, and it really is. You two have found a good place."

"Yeah," Mary said. "Great."

Another long stretch of silence.

"You can sleep on the couch tonight," Mary told Nora, "but tomorrow you get out. Early."

"Thank you."

And then Natassia, still wrapped in her quilt, said, "My poppy is dead. My grandmother's a widow. Daddy doesn't have a father anymore."

I CAN'T TRUST Nora anymore. That wasn't the worst piece of news, but it was the one that kept knocking Mary over every time she tried to take a breath and straighten out her head. Jesus, now they were taking the curve of the exit off the West Side Highway. In a couple blocks they'd be at Lotte's. I'm not ready. I can't do this. That orange-blossom scent was with Mary again, floating through her panic, returning her to the moment when Nora had turned bad on her. "Do you smell anything?" she asked Natassia. "Like flowers or something?"

Natassia shook her head no.

Before leaving Hiliard, they had gone to Heather's office for an emergency appointment. Mary had sat in the waiting room while Natassia went in alone for forty minutes. Then Heather had wanted to see Natassia and Mary together for fifteen minutes. "How do you feel, Mary, now, about this terrible news you received last night, this information Nora brought you?"

Like shit. What do you think?

"Natassia told me," Heather said, "this morning she told me, that she doesn't know yet how she wants to handle this information about Christopher. She's asked me to ask you not to tell her grandmother or her father right now."

"Great," Mary said. "So, once again, I get to know all the bad news, and Ross doesn't have to know anything that'll make him feel bad."

Heather gave Mary that sympathetic-shrink look. "You *are* right, Mary. Absolutely. You are being burdened now, alone, the only parent to know this ugly truth from your child's early life. And it would help you to have support from Ross. But Natassia feels, and I believe she is perceptive in this, that Ross and his mother will be too upset about David's death right now to handle this, at least to handle it in any way that would be productive for Natassia, helpful. I'm impressed with her growing ability to take care of herself."

"Heather," Mary said, "just tell me what I'm supposed to do."

"Well, let Natassia tell you at every point what she needs, how she wants to handle this with Christopher and Nora. I'm afraid there's little we can do, just wait and watch and give Natassia the chance to figure out what she needs in terms of restitution, how we can best create for her a sense of safety."

"Like, I don't want Nora and Christopher coming to the funeral or anything."

"Is that acceptable to you, Mary?"

"Yeah, sure."

"But Kevin can come," Natassia said. "I'll feel better if he's there."

Mary told Natassia, "I really screwed up for you, Natassia."

"Mom. Please don't make it so I have to make *you* feel better, too."

"Well, Natassia, please don't make it so I can't say how bad I feel and how sorry I am. I'll do anything that'll help you, Natassia."

A tired "Okay" from Natassia.

"I believe," Heather said, "that is helpful, Mary, for Natassia to hear."

CHAPTER 38:

MARCH–APRIL

1990

In the days after she ran into Christopher at Grand Central, there was so much going on that Nora had to stay in touch with him whether she was afraid of him or not, hated him or not. The day after returning from Hiliard, Nora received on her office phone machine a message from Mary. Nora called Christopher at his studio (because of his baby, he'd had a phone installed) and told him, "You have to hear this message. It's important."

Nora held the receiver close to the answering machine and hit PLAY. Mary began with a sharp exhale of smoke, then said, "Nor, it's Mary. Me and Natassia talked to her therapist, and we don't want you guys coming to the funeral or to Lotte's or anything. And another thing, Natassia doesn't want anybody else finding out right now about this shit Christopher did. We're not telling Ross, and we're not telling Lotte. Not Kevin, either. Nobody, you hear? But you can be sure we're going to talk about this later. That's all I'm saying to you right now, Nora. I'm really pissed."

Nora clicked off the machine, raised the receiver to her ear, and heard Christopher sigh. "Okay," he said, "so we don't go to the funeral."

About an hour later, Christopher called Nora to ask if he could come to the loft the next day to use the kitchen. He wanted to make food to send uptown to Lotte's apartment.

"You're being Italian," Nora told him. "You're acting like your grand-mother."

"I am Italian. When somebody dies, you make food for them."

"Think again. David's not going to be eating much of whatever you cook for him."

Nora herself didn't like the tone of her voice, but if she and Christopher were going to have to be together for an indefinite period of time—and it seemed they were—Nora needed to keep her distance.

Christopher made a lasagna with homemade noodles and a huge casserole of eggplant parmigiana. He filled his largest wooden salad bowl with an as-paragus-and-feta-cheese salad. He made three different kinds of coffee cake. He didn't break Natassia's request, didn't go near Lotte's apartment. He paid someone to drive uptown to deliver the food.

Watching him work in the kitchen, Nora wondered, Does it ever cross his mind that Mary might call the police? If the police called me at work, Nora wondered, what would I say? And then, as she did a million, billion times daily, she told herself, He has a son, he has a baby who isn't mine.

"Hey," Christopher called from the kitchen, "will you come taste this sauce?"

"It's fine," she told him, not getting up off the couch. "I'm sure it's fine."

"Thanks so much," he said, "for your help."

Nora sent flowers to Lotte's apartment. She and Christopher made a large memorial contribution in David's name to the Authors Guild Fund, to help writers in need. It was their first joint act since working on their tax returns that cursed Sunday in February. "By the way," Christopher reminded her, "you need to sign the taxes so we can mail them."

"I know."

There was no word yet from Mary about what was going to happen next. Monday, Tuesday, Wednesday evening when Nora got home from work, Christopher was in the loft. Cooking, or rewiring an old lamp, or scrubbing the kitchen cabinets. Nora didn't want him there, but she didn't want to be-gin the conversation that would get him to leave.

Really, she wanted him there.

There was nothing to do but wait for the repercussions to begin. Mary on the phone? Natassia in the hospital? The police at the door? Nora and Christo-pher tiptoed through their days. Not really talking to each other, yet not letting go of each other. She ate what he cooked, but she didn't sit with him at the table. She brought her plate to the couch and turned on PBS. By bedtime, he'd wrap up his busywork and be gone. At the end of the fourth day, as he was leaving, Nora was closing the door behind him when she stopped and he said, "I'll finish fixing those curtain rods tomorrow night," and before she could catch herself, Nora asked, "Don't you need to be going to Nyack?"

"Nah. They're managing. This week." Christopher immediately reached to his back pants pocket for his wallet. "Can I show you a new picture?"

"Not really. No."

"Sorry," Christopher said.

"No. I'm sorry. I just can't look right now."

"I understand. Hey, we're calling him Donby, short for Don Boy." He pushed the button to call the elevator. "Okay. Good night."

"Christopher, I'm sure he's a beautiful baby."

"He's a handsome dude, except, poor kid, he's got my ears."

"Your real ears?"

"Yeah! Whoa, here's the elevator. See you."

Christopher's Dumbo ears. All kinds of truth were spilling out with the secrets.

THE WEEKEND WAS a day away. What if Christopher hung out in the loft all weekend? What if he didn't come back? What if Mary called to yell some more? Or, worse, Ross. They might be lining up a lawyer. If she stayed in the loft, Nora would be the one to get the phone calls, not Christopher. Kevin had called Nora several times during the week to let her know how shocked he was that she hadn't shown up at David's funeral. Nora was afraid that if she stayed in town she'd end up telling Kevin something she wasn't supposed to tell anyone yet. Friday, before she left for work, Nora pulled out the train schedule and packed a bag.

WHEN SHE WOKE UP in Greenport on Saturday morning, with beach wind jiggling the windows, she noticed immediately how much nicer being there alone was than being there with Abe. She had not returned to the beach house since Christmastime, when she'd left in a snit, giving Abe the place to himself, which is probably what she should have done all along. Last night, wiping away two months' layer of dust, she'd spent some time inspecting Abe's parting touches. A coffee mug washed and resting in the dish rack, a clean bag in the kitchen garbage can, two Rolling Rocks in the fridge along with an almost empty jar of Skippy crunchy peanut butter. In the bathroom, Abe had hung a new roll of toilet paper on the roller, and he'd lowered the toilet seat. *Nice touch, Abe.* Better than Christopher and Kevin usually did. She had tried to dismiss Abe as a jerk, but he really wasn't. He just wanted to be left alone to do his work. He'd been up-front about that from their first meal together. *Abe, maybe someday you'll make somebody a good husband. If you manage to look up from your work long enough to notice someone's there with you.* He had finished his manuscript, though. Giulia had called Nora recently and mentioned Abe (which she'd never done before—what did Giulia know?), and said the two of them had actually taken a dinner break together, gone to a restaurant to celebrate, when the agent had agreed to take Abe on. From the wastebasket in the living room, Nora picked up a page Abe had crumpled and tossed. She tried to decipher a bit of his handwriting, then found she didn't care enough, just crumpled the page up again, tossed.

Nora sat at the table at the window where Abe had worked. There was no fair reason to be annoyed with Abe, except that she was. *Mommy, Daddy, Kevin, Nora Conolly.* Why had Abe started all that when he didn't intend to hang around to listen to Nora tell the whole story? *What is the whole story?* Outside, the morning was all sun and gusts. The house was encased in a skin of wind. Nora considered going for a walk, but never did.

As it turned out, she never left the house once during the two days she was there. Curled on the couch, she slept a sleep free of dreams. Or she sat at the table and watched the day, watched the light get batted about by the wind. At night, through the window, she saw a pale-white line across the belly of the moon. Was it possible that Christopher had become a father without her noticing? Was he that hidden from her? Was she that unobservant? He had done it like those teenage girls who go through a whole secret pregnancy under the noses of their families, who afterward say, "We had no idea!" Nora tried to tell herself it was necessary now to make a real decision about Christopher, about their marriage, but apparently they had decided long ago that it was okay to live together with a vast distance between them. In truth, Nora couldn't imagine their marriage without Baby Natassia in the midst of it, or, rather, without the gulf between them that had begun with Baby Natassia. Now added to their old bad secret was Christopher's new secret. "Mommy, Christopher had a baby without me."

"Honey. Nora. Are you that surprised?"

Saturday, then Sunday floated around Nora. She watched the trees' bare limbs wave and shake. Shadows of branches fell into the house, landed on Nora's lap. A red sunset roughed up the horizon. She sat still and let herself be held by the house, that light. At one point she opened a can of soup for dinner. She drank some old-tea-bag tea. Ate a yogurt. She desired nothing more than to sit. She could almost feel her body losing mass and weight.

THE NIGHT after Nora got back from Greenport, Kevin wanted to have dinner with her. Nora very much wanted to see her brother, but she didn't trust herself not to begin talking about Mary and Natassia, so she asked him, "How about if we go to a movie instead? I'm dieting, I better not go out to eat."

A few hours later, Nora and Kevin were standing on the subway platform at Astor Place to go uptown to see *Crimes and Misdemeanors*. A street musician was improvising "Mack the Knife" on a trumpet.

"You're looking good, Nor," Kevin said kindly.

"Kevin," Nora asked, "do you ever feel mad at Mommy?"

"For dying on us? Yeah, sure."

"I mean from before, for the way she was."

"How was she?"

"So . . . secret. Like, do you ever feel kind of cheated that we didn't know our grandparents or either of their families? I mean, in a way, it's a kind of lie to withhold that information. It's like saying, We come from nowhere."

"They always told us about Daddy's family." Kevin never held eye contact when Nora tried to talk about their parents. "They were in the Midwest and he hated them. What else was there to know? No way Daddy was going back to those people who let him end up in jail."

Nora stared, as Kevin was doing, into the black subway tunnel. "But he stole money from them. His own family. Did we ever think about that?"

Kevin laughed. "Yeah, isn't it weird?"

"And he got Mommy to cut us off from her family, too."

"He didn't do that. After Mommy got pregnant, her mother dumped *her*."

"Dumped her? No, she didn't. Mommy cut *her* off when she wasn't sup-portive of the marriage to Daddy." Nora had to raise her voice over the noise of the incoming train, and she didn't care who heard her. "Mommy and her mom were still close when she was in the unwed-mother home. Remember the story of how her mother sent her money the whole time, and then, after the adoption—don't you remember?—when her mother showed up and sur-prised her and brought her a case of California oranges, which was stupid, but at least she tried doing something." They pushed into the train car and found seats next to each other. "Then she helped Mommy pay for nursing school."

"No, no, it was when Mommy was pregnant with *you* that her mother cut her off. She never told you this?"

"I have no idea what you're talking about." Nora looked around. Really, no one seemed to be listening.

"Mommy's mother was so angry at her for marrying an ex-con that when she got pregnant her mother just cut her off. For good. She told Mommy, 'You had a chance to get out of it before, but now, with a baby, you're stuck with that crook.' Mommy sent her a picture of you, but that was it. She never wrote back."

"A crook? Mommy'd never let anybody say that about Daddy. Kevin, how did you ever hear this? I never heard any of this."

"One morning early, in the car, when Mommy was driving me to hockey practice."

"How'd you ever get into *this*?"

"Yeah, it weirded me out, too. We were talking about me getting serious with Bebe Tucker, and Mommy was saying I better not go all the way with her. Mommy said that—'Don't you go all the way with that girl!' And the next thing I know, I'm hearing all this ancient history. Oh, man, she even started crying. 'I'm a girl who screwed up in a major way, Kevin. Do you un-derstand that? Do you understand I had no choices then?'"

"Kevin, she really cried?"

"Ah, I shouldn't have told you. Hey, we're the next stop."

"Why didn't you ever tell me before?"

"It's just so sad and pathetic, the crazy stuff she was saying. 'Babies are seri-ous business, mister. You get that girl pregnant at your age, you got a couple of choices, and not one of them is any good. Anything you do will leave you feeling like shit.' And I'm like, 'Relax! She's hardly letting me up her shirt.'"

The movie was very long for Nora; she couldn't concentrate. *Mommy lost her mother because she had me. Her mother helped her and then stopped helping her— because she'd had a baby? Just when Mommy had had a baby? She believed Mommy was in danger and still she abandoned her?* Every time people laughed, Nora was annoyed. Once, she tugged on Kevin's sweater and whispered, "Mommy really said her mother *dumped* her?"

"I shouldn't ever have brought it up."

"Sssh," someone said from the row behind them, and Kevin muttered, "Oh, go shush yourself."

Afterward, on the subway going back downtown, close to Kevin's stop, he said, "So—you're okay riding to your stop alone?"

"Yeah, I'm okay." But she didn't want Kevin taking off into the city, where their lives rarely intersected. Not until he told her more about their mother, told her something, anything. "So," Nora said, "*did* you ever end up going all the way with Bebe Tucker?"

"Are you kidding? Of course. Whoa, here's my stop." They hugged for a quick moment, then she had to let him go.

Mommy talked to Kevin but not to me.

ON FRIDAY AND SATURDAY NIGHTS, Mommy used to come up to Nora's bedroom, which was huge, with high ceilings. She'd turn off the bold overhead lights, make the room dark, and carve out a small, intimate space by turning on a dim Tiffany lamp at the side of Nora's bed. Nora, Mary, and Mommy huddled under different corners of Nora's huge down comforter. Did any little girl ever have as much comfort in her life as Nora had when she was young? "So, my girls," is how Mommy always started. Sometimes Mommy came upstairs when it was just Nora, but she arrived more often and stayed longer when Mary was spending the night. "Mary Mudd, you remind me of myself," she used to say, especially when Jerry and Dorie were especially negligent. Mommy and Mary both had to make their way in the world without a mother, something Nora knew nothing about at that time. Nora was the daughter of a pretty, fun, present mother—so *present*—right there on Nora's bed, talking. But it made Nora dizzy sometimes with frustration: the only way to get closer to her mother's true heart, to her locked-in secrets, would have been to become a girl who had no mother. *Like Mary.* Often

Mommy had advice for Mary. "Listen, you are a dancer, you're going to be a star, but dancers need a next career, you hear me?"

Back at the loft after her visit with Kevin, Nora sat up for hours, nested into her corner of the couch, considering the news Kevin had just given her. *Mommy was a birth mother of an adopted child. We knew that but never talked about it. Never.* But apparently Mommy never stopped thinking of herself in that way. *And how could she? How stupid to think that she would.* And how stupid for Nora to have been jealous of Mary's and Mommy's motherlessness. And maybe how wrong, too. Maybe for Mommy bringing Mary into the Conollys' life had really been an offering to that baby boy she didn't get to bring home with her. How Mommy loved mothering Mary. "Promise me, Mary, that you will go to college. Say it."

"I promise, Mrs. C." Mary said it rolling her eyes, blushing, obviously savoring the coddling she never got at home. "I'll go to college."

"Both of you girls. Nora, you I don't worry about with college, not with your good grades, but, whatever you study, you turn that into a job that's a career that guarantees you steady income, benefits, savings. I don't care who you marry, how good he is, you make sure you keep savings for yourself off to the side. Nobody needs to know."

Nora had come to assume that Mommy held on to her self-sufficient privacy as a way to keep some distance from Daddy because he was a man who was less than completely trustworthy. At times during her own marriage, Nora had even allowed the thought: *Mommy, see, I'm like you now. I have a husband I don't trust, too.* But maybe it was in her privacy that Mommy managed to keep her lost baby close, maybe even closer than she held Nora and Kevin. How much in Mommy's life had really been about that baby boy?

For the first time in a long time, the word "eternally" slipped into Nora's mind. *Some losses linger and never really leave anybody out.*

DURING THE WEEK of sitting shivah, Lotte's apartment was swarming with people, and Mary grieved like everybody else. *Nora.* Mary had never been so wrong about anyone or anything. One afternoon up at Hiliard, she'd seen a raccoon staggering across the thawing circle driveway. The animal had obviously been hit by a vehicle or poisoned or attacked by something big. The raccoon wasn't quite dead yet, but it wasn't *right* in any way. That was exactly

how Mary felt now; meanwhile, she was stuck watching all these people acting like it was the end of the world that David was gone. *That mean old man.*
Mary had to get out of the apartment. She tossed leotard and sweatshirt and
sneakers into her backpack. She had two gym passes left over from Christmastime. "Natassia, come with me. It'll be good for you, change of scene,
change of air."

"I don't want to. I'm staying here with Daddy."

"Leave her alone, Mar," Ross said. "She wants to stay here with me."

Mary didn't like any of it. Ross and Natassia were now inseparable. Except for the hour or so when he left the apartment to go to a meeting. Or
took the phone into a bedroom to argue long-distance with Harriet, who
never did show up. Apparently, they'd had a fight in the Minneapolis airport
and she'd got on a plane back to Spokane.

People were pulling Natassia aside and asking her, urgently, "How's your
father doing, sweetheart?" Mary was almost tempted to give Natassia the
phone and say, "Here, start dialing, call some of those slutty old friends you
used to run around with. Go, ride the subway, just get away from your sick
father."

Mary really had to go out. She pulled Kevin from the crowd. "You have
to do something for me, Kev."

"Anything."

"Promise me you'll make sure Natassia doesn't leave this apartment while
I'm away. I need three hours."

Mary walked, from West End and Ninety-first Street to lower Broadway.
An hour of straight walking. At the gym, it was lunchtime. The Stairmasters
and stationary bikes were occupied, so was the treadmill. Mary found the
rowing machine and got started. It was almost unbearable, peaks and peaks
of guilt rising and falling and rising into the most distant landscape within her.
It truly was almost too much. How hurt her daughter had been—in baby-
hood, as an infant, in childhood, as a teenager. Hurt not only by Mary but
also by Christopher, Ross, Lotte and David, and Nora. *Nora!* Natassia, utterly
exposed to every whacked-out force in the world. Mary pushed the machine, punishing her arms and legs. It was a wonder Natassia hadn't been hurt
worse. Or maybe she had been. Maybe there was more bad news to find out.
Mary kept rowing.

On the wall in front of her was a pretty-landscape poster, and Mary rowed into the hills of the poster. Up and up, endless hills of green guilt. Occasional valleys, then up again into the thin atmosphere of self-hate, the unbreathable air. Down into the bleak, black shadows of failure. Gretel without Hansel. The hills went on, all across the long horizontal poster; in the center was the broken glass of a waterfall cracking over rocks.

Finally, the manager of the gym came over. "Lady, a few people have come talk to me. You been on this machine already for over an hour. What are you, in training to be a galley slave?"

Leaving, drenched, Mary passed under the poster, read the title of the photograph: "Taebaek Mountains."

Later, back at Lotte's apartment, Mary asked Ross, "Where's the Taebaek Mountains?"

"South Korea. Why?"

CHRISTOPHER AND KEVIN were in Christopher's studio in Chelsea. Christopher needed Kevin's help to set up a timed device for his newest piece: one canvas with another canvas laid over it. Christopher had four sets of these, and he wanted Kevin to help him figure out how to mechanize the top canvases so they would slide open and closed. He wanted the top canvases to be very slow-moving, so that at first the viewer wouldn't even know the movement was happening. "Okay, Kevin, what I want is, when we're all done, I want a total of nine sets of canvases, all of them moving in opposing times."

"You mean alternating times?"

"Whatever." The telephone rang. Christopher answered, "Yeah?"

"Sorry to bother you, but this is important."

"Hey, Nora, hi."

Christopher felt Kevin watching him, listening. Nora was saying that a note from Lotte had just arrived in the mail. "I have to read this to you."

"Yeah, go ahead, read it."

" 'Please come to my apartment this Saturday afternoon, April 7, around two o'clock. I'm moving from my apartment, into a little penthouse around the block on Riverside Drive. I'm getting this big place ready to put on the market. There are piles of David's art books, and Ross wants Christopher to have them. There are some French prints I want Nora to have. The grand distribution will take place this Saturday. It would mean a lot to me if you could be there. Much love to you both, Lotte.' "

"Okay, so we'll go," Christopher told Nora. "We'll have to go."

After he hung up, he said to Kevin, "Lotte's moving out of her apartment? What's up with that?"

"It's a big controversy. If you guys had gone to any of the funeral stuff last month, you would have heard about it."

"Kevin, don't. There's a thing going on between your sister and Mary, and it's just better this way right now. Mary hasn't said anything to you?"

"Out of nowhere, Lotte came up with this studio apartment. Turns out, she's owned it all along, for forty years. She never gave it up when she and David got married. She's rented it out all these years. She never even told Ross about it. She's been putting away a bucket in rent every year."

"Did David know?"

"Nobody really knows. Natassia's freaked out about the whole thing, moving out of the apartment she grew up in and all that. But Lotte's just like, 'It's my turn now. I'm living alone, the way I want to.' She gave Ross forty-eight hours to decide if he wanted to keep the big apartment. He decided to put it on the market. He gets half of the money."

"Who gets the rest?"

"Natassia. In a trust, till she's twenty-one. But she's set now, for graduate school or whatever. If she makes it that far."

"What do you mean, if she makes it? Natassia's not that messed up. Everybody exaggerates."

"She's a pretty messed-up kid. I don't know all of it. She's got a shitload of stuff to figure out. Mary won't tell me. Mary is so good at protecting Natassia. I tell you, when it comes to that kid, Mary's like a bear."

ON SATURDAY AFTERNOON, when Christopher and Nora arrived at Lotte's, there was in the apartment an air of euphoria, giddiness almost. The estate-sale lady had stuck little round yellow price tags on all the furniture. There were clothes racks in the dining room stuffed with Lotte's and David's clothes for sale. Bedspreads and sheets and towels were priced and stacked on the bookshelves. Costume jewelry was spread out on coffee tables and on card tables. Stacks of records on the radiator covers. Books and books and books.

Nora cringed. "This is embarrassing," Christopher whispered into her ear. "There's something really tacky going on here."

Making Nora and Christopher even more uncomfortable was Ross, who kept thanking them for all they'd done during the funeral. He knew about the food Christopher had sent, and with all the confusion of that time, he imagined he'd seen them at the funeral and at the apartment. He even apologized for not having had a chance to talk to them. "I'm sorry, but with everything going on . . . I didn't mean to blow you guys off."

"Ross, I'm really sorry about your dad," Nora said, and hugged him, and when she did she was sure she smelled stale beer. *Mary said he'd stopped drinking.* As always, she felt Ross's too-tight hug, that embrace that insisted that her breasts touch his chest. *Ross.*

And then, as always, a too-long hug for Christopher, too, as if to say, See, I hug everyone too close, not just your wife.

The hour Nora and Christopher spent in Lotte's apartment that day felt like participating in a performance-art piece done by amateurs, a bad play.

Until Mary walked them down the hallway to the door as they were leaving—then the afternoon turned more sinister, scarier. "I have to talk to you two," Mary said in a low voice. She kept staring up at Christopher, who kept looking away. "Natassia wants all of us to have a session with her therapist in Hiliard. That's how she wants Ross to find out."

"He doesn't know yet? Oh, Mary, how'd you get through all this—"

Mary cut Nora off. "You guys just need to show up."

"We'll be there," Christopher said. Nora watched him pull his date book from the inside pocket of his jacket. *Does Christopher know what he's in for?* "When?" he asked.

Mary handed over a business card. "Here's the address. Next Saturday at ten."

"We're there, Mary," Christopher said.

CHAPTER 39:

APRIL

1990

It was Saturday morning, ten o'clock sharp, and Nora was looking around the office of Heather Jamison Jonson, M.S.W. *Finally. This is it.* The day was too warm for April, and everyone was dressed inappropriately. Natassia was tugging her sweater away from her neck and puffing breaths down into her black turtleneck. Mary had on a long maroon Danskin skirt over black leggings and ankle boots, and a too-big gray sweater; she kept pushing up the sleeves, then pushing up the sleeves of the black leotard underneath. A ridiculous outfit, but Nora immediately understood: unsure of what to expect, Mary had done what felt safe, she'd dressed for dance. Nora knew Mary inside and out, and even if their friendship was over, probably *was* over, Nora would never stop carrying within her all she knew about Mary, who hadn't said a word to Nora yet or even glanced over at her.

Ross looked more professorial than medical in his chinos and tweed wool sports coat and dark-blue chamois shirt and brick-red tie; his collar seemed to be darkened with sweat. Christopher was sitting right next to Nora. She couldn't remember what he was wearing, and she was too nervous to look at him. She herself that morning, not knowing how to prepare for this event, had put on the evergreen jersey-knit wide pants and tunic she wore when she anticipated difficult or long days at her office. A silver pendant and silver-and-jade earrings went with this uniform. In the crotch of her evergreen pantyhose, Nora was sweating.

Natassia, Mary, Ross, Christopher, and Nora. They were assembled for a double session (one hour and forty minutes), so that all the important adults in Natassia's life (most of them) could be "brought up to speed" on Natassia's recovery.

"Why isn't my mother here?" Ross asked, turning to Mary. He gave a nod toward Nora and Christopher, who sat across the room from him. He said, "They're here, but my mother's not?"

"Your mother's tired, Ross. Her husband just died."

"Yes, I am sorry, Ross," Heather said, "about your loss. The loss of your father. Natassia. Mary. You've all had a significant loss recently. To do this now, meet as we are now, I know it's difficult for you. It must be difficult for you, and I appreciate how—"

The odd cadences of Heather's speech were hypnotic. It was a rhythmic repetition, a sort of stitching together, not of words but of phrases, moving through her sentences slowly, reaching back, picking up a few words, carrying them forward. *Priestess* was the word that came to Nora's mind.

For years, Nora had imagined how it might be when she and Christopher came together with Natassia and Mary and Ross to tell about that afternoon in France, but Nora had never imagined them in the charge of someone like Heather. When Mary had handed over Heather's business card that day at Lotte's, Nora, snob that she was, had thought, Oh no, a social worker? For *this*? Now, in the room, it was too early for Nora to tell if Heather was up to the job or not, but Heather certainly had authority. It surprised Nora to see how young she was, possibly younger than Nora, and she was even paler than Nora—invisible eyebrows, absolutely no makeup, or else a lot of pale pancake. Heather had a prettiness that wasn't contemporary: it was the wan translucence of madonnas in Flemish paintings. She had a wide koala-bear nose made prominent by the way her hair was pulled away from her face with a tortoiseshell headband so thick it looked like a crown. Her no-color hair hung all the way down her very straight back. *Regal.* Heather's long, tapered fingers rested on the thick carved-wood arms of her chair. *She's like Henry VIII.* And adding to Heather's authority was her obvious wealth.

The office was attached to the side of the rambling French country-

433

style house she lived in, probably with her husband. Nora had seen a toddler with a French-speaking redhead, probably the au pair, who was hos-
ing down the dog's bowls outside in the portico when she and Christopher
had driven up the long cobblestone driveway half an hour early for the appointment. They had parked next to a large marble urn, sat silently in their
rented Tempo, and looked up at a long slope of wild landscaping, then up
at the leaded windows three stories high. "Holy shit," Christopher had
said. From her passenger seat, Nora counted three discreetly placed lawn
sculptures—two made of metal (Nora recognized the work but couldn't
remember the name of the sculptor, some woman Christopher knew and
envied), one of wood. Since Heather clearly had more money, Nora was
hoping Heather wouldn't be as good a therapist. Then Nora took that
wish back—they really did need to be working with someone good.

It was dark in the wood-paneled office, but two leaded windows were
opened, letting in warm air and light. Heather had a fire going in the fireplace, but it must have been early-morning-made: the fire logs were now
almost charred out. The ceiling was very high, wood-beamed. A dog was
sitting at Heather's feet. *Very Henry VIII.* Heather made no apologies for
the dog, a huge, old, stinky St. Bernard with matted fur, missing an ear.
Julius, she called him. All she had said about the dog as she ushered everyone into her office was that Julius was sick and had to be in the room with
her—no apology. What if one of us was allergic to dogs? Now, as Julius
shifted in place, his ribs rippled prominently under his mangled fur. *He's
dying.*

"So, Natassia, we're here," Heather was saying. "We're here together
now, with thanks to your father for traveling cross-country, and thanks also
to Nora and Christopher, thanks to them for traveling up here from the
city. Natassia, where should we begin?"

"No," Natassia said right away, but smiling more girlishly than when
she was a little kid. "There's no way I'm starting, Heather. You start. I'll go
next, but you start."

"Fine," Heather said, nodding. There was a direct aisle of energy between Heather and Natassia. It was a good sign, Nora thought, that
Heather had gained Natassia's trust in a relatively short time. Nora's patient
had met with Nora through most of her pregnancy and beyond before revealing that her elderly parents and her two older brothers suffered serious

alcoholism. It was a few weeks after Baby Frida's birth. Nora, thank God, had had a chance to apologize for her inappropriate reaction to the news that Frida's father had moved in, and she and the patient were moving forward, dealing mostly with practical issues but at least talking, building trust. In that particular session, the woman was crying, seriously sleep-deprived. In a month she'd have to return to work, and her nanny had been called abruptly away. The father was in the apartment but useless, her friends were sympathetic but all had busy careers, and Nora had asked, "Is there any way your family can help you?"

"*Stop* with my family," the patient had snapped. "They're not an option, okay? They're drunks, a bunch of absolute alcoholics. Okay? That's why I can't tell them about the baby. They still don't even know I was pregnant."

"But"—Nora finally had an opening, she couldn't blow it—"what would happen if you did tell them?"

The patient's answer was immediate, undefended, calm: "I'd lose everything."

"You'd lose everything," Nora repeated.

"My ex-fiancé, the man who left me—it was because of my family. He couldn't accept the idea of raising kids in a family like mine."

"So," Nora said, "do you also have problems with alcohol?"

"Me? No. By the time I was born, all the alcoholic genes were used up. My mother was menopausal when I was born. She was five months' pregnant before she knew she was even pregnant. I'm telling you, my parents are old, geriatric."

"And still drinking?" Nora asked.

"Is the sky blue? Look, they're very sick people. There's no way I could have cut them off the way my ex-fiancé wanted me to. They're my family. I love them." The woman began to sob. "I feel so sorry for them. I don't know what would happen to them. Really. I mean, since I was a kid they've depended on me and worried so much about me."

"Worried?" Nora asked.

"We'd leave family holidays at night and they'd have to give me the car keys. They couldn't even trust themselves to drive. And they'd say, 'Slow, dear! Don't attract cops.' "

"And your brothers?"

"They were gone—college, married, whatever. It was just me."

"And their worry about the cops?" Nora asked. "If you weren't drinking?"

"Well, I was only thirteen. Maybe fourteen. What's wrong? Dr. Conolly, you have tears in your eyes. I'm sorry."

"That's a lot, way too much for a thirteen-year-old. To drive illegally, to care for two alcoholic parents. An age when a girl should be with friends—"

"Yeah, they couldn't help it." Then, "You're mad at me, aren't you, for waiting so long to tell you about them."

"Of course I'm not mad. I feel sad for what you've carried. All this, on top of your pregnancy. So much."

And then the patient was sobbing. "I really want Frida. I want my baby so much."

"You have her. She is yours. You gave birth to her. You're doing everything you can to take care of her. You are her mother. How could they take Frida from you?"

"Way in the beginning, when I started therapy with you, I knew I wanted the baby, I knew it, but on my own I couldn't have gone through with it."

"Why not?"

"Too afraid, too . . . I don't know."

"I'm glad, then, that you gave this to yourself. And that you're giving yourself this new opportunity. Here, now."

"Opportunity for what?"

"To unburden yourself."

"You know, *I'm* the one who called Frida's father. He didn't call me. Two weeks before my due date, I just couldn't stand the thought of her coming into the world without a father there. It's just sometimes, when my family's all together, it *feels* so good. I want Frida to have that, a whole family."

"Do you feel you've had a whole family?"

The woman didn't answer Nora's question, but she said, "Have you ever felt— Well, I hope you've never felt it, but it's like, no matter what I do or how careful I am . . . I can't bear even the beginning of the thought that I might lose Frida." The woman wiped away tears and tears with tissues from the box Nora had passed to her. After a long time, quieted, she passed the box back to Nora and said, "I don't know if I can explain to you what it feels like inside to lose so much and to be so afraid of losing even more."

"Okay, Natassia," Heather was saying now, "I will begin. I'll start us off. I'll begin by saying, saying to your parents, and to Nora and Christopher, that, yes, Natassia wanted you all here today, wanted us all here together, so that important information can be shared. And it is important to Natassia, she expressed this to me, that this information be shared in an environment that feels, to her, safe. Where there are controls in place, some boundaries, to ensure her safety. That will be my role, setting these limits. Together, we'll work in this way: Everyone will have an opportunity to speak as freely as he or she would like. As freely as you are able. It goes without saying that we are working here together with complete confidentiality. Nothing said here will leave this room. So, please, all of you, all of us, together, whatever feelings arise can be expressed. The only restriction is, of course, that there be no violence, no threatening acts toward others or toward oneself."

"The dog's staying in here?" Ross asked.

"Yes, as I mentioned earlier—"

"But he smells, Heather," Ross said. "He's farting to beat the band."

"Yes, poor thing, he's very sick."

Nora had been so focused on Heather, she hadn't noticed that all around Ross hung a jittery shimmer of bad energy. Maybe he was dressed like a professor, but he was slouched far down in his chair like an uncooperative student, elbows hanging off of the armrests, fingers tepeed in front of his face. *He's never looked this strung out before.*

Heather, delicately embroidering her words and phrases into sentences and full paragraphs, was moving toward the big moment, saying, "Natassia has recently learned some personal history, events from her very young life, some events—"

"Listen, I'll go first, Heather," Mary interrupted. She'd been staring at a patch of sunlight on the carpet. Mary looked up, finally looked across the room, straight at Christopher. "I feel like I should be the one to tell Ross."

"Tell me what?" Ross bolted straight up in his chair. "There's something everyone else here knows, and I don't. What's going on? Why'd you drag me up here for this inquisition?"

Heather leaned forward. "Ross, you could go on in that way, you could continue, but I don't think it will be useful. For Natassia, it won't be useful."

Mary cut in on Heather again. "Ross, listen. Just listen to me." Mary, too, was leaning forward. "Look. We have to tell you this. When Natassia was a baby, really tiny . . ."

"Mary," Ross demanded. "Be clear. When she was young, how young?"

Ross was the wild card. It occurred to Nora that maybe Heather had the dog in the room to protect her, in case Ross, or somebody else, did get violent, even though she'd issued her warning. Nora's clothes were much too warm.

Mary was saying, "She was six weeks old, okay? Tiny, infant—"

"Yeah? And what?" Listening to Mary, waiting, Ross was staring at Natassia, who was now staring at the blotch of sunlight on the carpet.

"She was mol-"—Mary's voice dropped—"-lested."

"What?" Ross demanded.

"I said Natassia was . . . I can't—"

"I was sexually molested, Dad, when I was a baby. In France."

Ross made a face and a sound. Spinning toward Natassia, he reached over and pulled her chair next to his, and the padded arms of their chairs bumped loudly together. Ross touched Natassia's cheek. "Who?" he asked her; then his voice pleaded, "Honey, who?"

Ross hugged Natassia's head as if to hide her. Natassia held on to his arms, tried to raise her face to him, but she couldn't. "Dad! My arm. Don't, that hurts."

"Who?" Still holding Natassia, Ross demanded from Mary, "Who fucking was it?"

And then Nora heard a whisper next to her. "Me," Christopher said. "It was me."

The shock in the room was how quickly Heather managed to step in to stop what was happening next. Ross had shot across the room in two strides and grabbed the arm of Christopher's chair. But then Heather was there, tall but thin as willow branches, her arms between Christopher hunkered down in his seat, and Ross standing over him. Heather said in a loud, even voice, "Down," as an owner would command its unruly dog, but added, "Please. Sit down, Ross." He wouldn't budge. "How will this help your daughter?"

And then Ross did go back to his own chair. He kicked it. He kicked it again, hard, until it hit the wood-paneled wall.

"Are you all right?" Heather asked Christopher, who had begun to cry. He sat up in his chair and crossed one leg over the other. Nora sensed his movement; she couldn't look at him. *There's a baby and a widow in Nyack.* "Christopher? Are you hurt?" Heather asked again.

Christopher shook his head no; he wasn't hurt. But he was crying hard now, and Nora, a little shocked by the nothingness she felt for him, just stared at the dog's paws. Caked with mud. When Nora's patients cried, she always kept her eyes on them, so that when they looked back up they'd feel her with them, they'd feel connected, not alone. *Christopher's crying sounds like a pork chop being sliced.* Then Nora almost smiled, almost laughed, at the absurdity of her thoughts. *This is my anger.* She almost laughed again at her outrageous detachment from the man she'd stayed married to for more than a dozen years. *He's pathological. He's a maniac. He's poop.* Now she had to bite on the ulcers on the insides of her cheeks to keep from laughing. *Stop. You're getting hysterical. I'm the wild card here. Not Ross. It's me. What if I kill somebody? My God, I have to pee, what if I wet my pants?*

Ross, across the room, was muttering.

Sobs were galloping out of Christopher's mouth, too fast, a stampede of sobbing. *Something bad is going to happen.* And, indeed, from across the room, Ross's voice was becoming audible, ". . . guinea fucking wop, you stupid bad painter . . ." Then, louder, ". . . you no-talent *dago nigger.*"

"Dad!" Natassia panicked. "Da-ad! Mom, make him stop."

"You hopeless *fuck,*" Ross shouted.

"Dad. Stop! Mo-om!"

"How do you *sleep* with such an ignorant peasant?" Ross was yelling. Nora realized, He's yelling at *me.* Ross spit onto Heather's carpet. He spit again. His hand was on Natassia's chair, rocking it, jerking it back and forth, and the look on Natassia's face was one of utter panic.

"Ross," Mary said, low. He wouldn't stop, so Mary stood, and as soon as she did, Ross let Natassia's chair rest. Immediately, Natassia stood and walked away from both her parents; she took the chair next to Heather's.

439

"Baby?" Ross begged.

"I don't want you to touch me," Natassia said, "not when you're talking like that."

Ross stood and walked to the paneled corner and leaned into it. Then, quick, he turned and landed a punch into the wall. He pounded the wall twice more. Everyone heard the crack of his finger as it broke. "Ah," he grunted.

"Ross," Heather commanded, "you must stop. Now."

Mary's back was to him, and she didn't turn to look, but Natassia, so worried, was watching Ross hug his hand and slide his back down the wall. There was a good hard thump when he landed on the floor. The injured hand was tucked inside his jacket; he was doubled over and shouting, "He hurt our daughter, that smelly piece of shit, that stink sitting over there, he hurt Natassia."

"We all hurt her, Ross," Mary said to him. She spoke quietly, like a wife confident she knew her husband better than anyone else in the room did; and, like a longtime husband, Ross stopped shouting as soon as Mary spoke. "Those days in France, Ross, we left her. She was six weeks old. She was breastfeeding, and I left her. We even stayed away an extra day longer than we said we would."

Silence. Then Ross, aiming his words to the back of Mary's head, said, "You never liked the breastfeeding."

"No, I didn't."

"You always complained."

"Yeah, I did."

"You had all that extra milk in your breasts. Remember? They were bursting. I drank all of it. I thought it tasted so fucking tasty, so—"

"And I should have been back at Christopher's feeding the baby."

"You had so much milk in your breasts." Ross was hugging his injured hand.

Nora watched Natassia, who was sucking both her thumbs.

Next to Nora, Christopher was blowing his nose into a handkerchief, a sound so disgusting to her, she looked over at him, but when she glanced, she almost gasped. Every handsomeness had faded from Christopher's face. There was an oily sheen of despair across his forehead and within the creases alongside his nose. Nora had a patient with HIV, and in the course of a few weeks, the drugs he was taking had transformed his looks so completely that, one day, stepping out into the waiting room, she hadn't recognized him. *Like that.* Christopher's face was suddenly that changed.

Out of a long silence, Ross said, "You'll never forget."

Who's Ross talking to?

"You'll never forget what I just said to you. The words I just called you."

"No," Christopher said. "But I always knew you thought it."

"Good," Ross said. "I'm glad you knew. I'm glad you knew."

"And Natassia will never forget what I did to her," Christopher said. Nora felt him shift in his chair, turn to face Natassia. "Natassia," Christopher said, "you deserve to know, I want to tell you exactly what—"

"No, no," Ross said in a mean imitation of a congenial voice, "no, asshole, you're the one who deserves to know exactly what you did. Show him your wrists, Natassia." With his unhurt hand, Ross was unbuttoning his sleeve, pushing up his cuff, holding out his own exposed wrist. "Show him, Natassia. You see, asshole, what you did to my daughter."

Natassia's face showed she was in agony. She was swallowing quick shallow breaths. Her eyes were saying, This isn't at all how it was supposed to go.

"Show him," Ross ordered her. "Show your wrists, so he sees what he did to you."

"We all did it," Nora said.

And Ross said, "I knew you'd defend him."

"Did you mean to defend Christopher, Nora?" Heather spoke kindly.

"No," Nora said, "but we're running out of time. I just want Natassia to know . . ."

Natassia was biting her thumbs.

Ross went on: "I'm telling you, Christopher, you're the first person in my life I've ever truly wanted to kill. With my hands. Besides my father, and he's already dead."

Heather, of course, doing her job, asked, "Why, Ross? Why would you want to kill him? Your father?"

"And Mary's father, too. And his wife, that bitch of a bitch. I'd like to kill them both for what they did to my daughter's mother. Natassia, you were born into a mess of bad people. Real worthless pieces of—"

"You're not *bad*, Daddy. Neither is Mom." Speaking, Natassia kept her thumbs close to her mouth. "You're just messed up."

"Yeah. Messed up is right."

Nora watched Heather, who right on cue asked Natassia, "Messed up, how? Can you say how you feel your mom and dad are messed up?"

"Messed up without getting good love when they were kids. Like Poppy. He was pretty good as a grandfather, except he could get really ugly when he got mad. And the things that made him angriest were Daddy, or sometimes publishing people, but mostly Dad made Poppy mad. All those words Daddy just called Christopher, all that ugly stuff he said? Those are Poppy's words. The scariest thing about you, Dad, is when you act like Poppy."

"Why do you think your grandfather got so angry at your father?" Heather asked.

"He's jealous." Natassia was keeping her grandfather in the present tense. "He's the most jealous person in the world."

"Who?" Ross asked, looking confused.

"Poppy. He's always jealous. Of everybody."

"Jealous of what? He always had the world by the balls."

"Dad, you're a doctor. Poppy is just an editor—that's how he sees himself. Get it? Plus, he always hates when people leave him. Like you left New York."

"It was a job. I had a job. I had to go with the job." Ross still sat on the floor.

"Yeah, but all Poppy knows is you left. Whenever Grammy has a business trip, Poppy always instigates a fight with her first. She always says, 'Why are you sending me off angry?' and he says . . . you know."

"What does he say, Natassia?" Heather wouldn't pass up one opportunity. She never stopped doing her job.

"I don't know. He's like, 'You're leaving, so goodbye to you.' I don't know, Dad. Poppy really loves you, more than anybody, even more than he loves me maybe, but he can never make himself stop saying that ugly stuff."

"Ross, what do you think about all that, what Natassia just said?"

"My dad was a wicked old fuck, wasn't he?" Ross turned to Mary. "Why *isn't* my mother here? She should be here."

"Ross," Mary scolded, "grow up. Your mother's in her new apartment."

"I believe," Heather said, "Natassia prefers that the three of you have the chance to work at things as a family."

"Tsh." Ross leaned against the wall. "Freaks. The Munsters. A family of freaks."

Nora watched Mary, Heather, and Natassia smile a tiny bit, a small crack of relief. "Maybe *you're* freaks," Natassia said, "but I'm not. I'm no freak."

Speaking very slowly now, pausing to look into each person's eyes, Heather said, "I think, truly, I don't think any one of you is a freak, not in any way a freak. What I think, what I'm thinking, what I'm feeling strongly right now, is that you're all people who have been hurt, you've all been hurt to an extreme degree." Natassia teared up. When Natassia sucked in the corners of her mouth to keep from crying, Mary immediately stood and went to sit next to her. They held hands. Ross tilted his head back against the wall, looked up at the ceiling, closed his eyes. Heather continued, "You're each, every one of you, everyone in this room, hurt in a different way, but all in serious ways. Some of the worst ways people can be damaged in this world."

Next to Nora, Christopher was giving off a scent of stale sweat.

"Abuse," Heather said, "there's been abuse. Of different types."

"Fucking Chri—" Ross tried to say, but Heather overrode him. "*Verbal* abuse," she said. "There's been physical abuse. Sexual abuse. There's been neglect. Many types of neglect. There's been rejection. Abandonment. And when I say these powerful words, I don't mean that these acts were committed by the four adults here against the one child. Perhaps. But it sounds as if at least a few of the adults here, as children, were also victims—excuse my use of that overused word, but it's appropriate here—as Natassia later became a victim."

Weirdly, suddenly, Nora remembered so clearly an afternoon when she and Mary were kids, around fourteen years old, sunbathing. It was one of the rare times when they were hanging out at the Mudds' house instead of at Nora's. Mary, Nora, and another friend were lying on their stomachs on ratty old towels spread on the weedy grass. Mary's father came out into the yard to dump garbage, then walked over to the girls, who were in bathing suits, stood above them a minute, and said to Mary, "Hey, you still got that mark on your back, how 'bout that."

"What mark?" Mary had asked. Nora had never mentioned it to Mary, but Nora's mother had explained to Nora that sometimes Asian babies were born with a sort of birthmark on their back, a patch of discoloration—a "Mongolian spot," it was called. "What d'you mean I have a mark?" Mary was trying to turn to see it, but, double-jointed as she was, there was no gyration that would give her a clear view of that one spot on her own back.

"Ah, it's just a mark you always had there, since you were a baby. It's like a pond right there on your back. You know, when I left Korea with you, I had to get a note from an army medic saying that was normal; otherwise they'd think I tried to bruise you up."

Suddenly, from out the kitchen window, they heard Mary's stepmother, Dorie, saying, "A pond? Jerry, it was more like a puddle. A muddy, dirty puddle. And I said, Where'd this baby get this dirty mark?" Dorie laughed. "It was just gross. I tried to scrub it, but it wouldn't come out."

Nora remembered Mary asking, "How hard did you scrub?"

But Jerry reached down and tousled Mary's hair, said, "My little Mudd puddle. Don't worry, hon, that puddle there makes you a real Mudd, like the rest of us."

"Jer-ry, really!" Dorie called out from the window. "Like the rest of us have marks on our backs! What if the boys heard you saying that?"

The boys, Mary's half-brothers, used to sing to Mary about her Asian eyes, "Jeepers, peepers, where'd you get those creepers?"

"Shut up," Nora yelled at them, defending Mary, who seemed less bothered by her brothers' insults than Nora was. When had Nora stopped being loyal to Mary? *When?*

"And now," Heather was saying, "on top of all these profound wounds, there is a very alive and recent and painful grief among you for the loss of David."

Nora could not imagine a future in which Mary was irretrievably gone, and she willed Mary to look across the room at her, but Mary had her eyes anchored on the growing patch of sunlight on the apricot-and-baby-blue-colored carpet. Julius yawned. Nora could smell his rotting teeth all the way across the room.

"I would guess, I think I'd have to guess, that for each of you, every one of you, this meeting is maybe the most difficult couple of hours in your lives. But what might be even worse, almost unfathomably painful, is to recall, truly feel again, those times when you were being hurt in the ways you've begun to describe here today."

There's a baby and a widow in Nyack.

"Ross, if you could talk to your father, I imagine you saying to him something like this, something like 'How dare you! How *dare* you claim to be my father, claim to love me as a father, and then say to me the things you say, terrible, ugly things that make me feel not good about my strengths, when what I want is approval from you. How dare you get unhappier as I grow smarter and more talented and more accomplished. How dare you take that from me—my own enjoyment of my strengths. How dare you.' "

Ross had buried his face in his arms, hidden his face. Nora wondered what he thought of Heather's speech. Was he crying now? Ross looked up—grinning.

But Heather went on, "Natassia, you do have the chance to talk to your parents. What do you want to say to them?"

"And then," Ross interrupted, "you get to sit back, Heather, and judge us, right?" His voice was loud, and it broke the trance of Heather's incantations.

"Daddy, that's mean."

"Mean." Ross laughed a hopeless laugh. "Yeah, that was mean. Heather, I'm sorry."

"I accept your apology."

"I'm sorry I was a meanie."

"Dad," Natassia moaned. "That's exactly the problem, *that's* what I want to say to you, Dad."

Everyone looked up. "What?" Ross asked.

"If you—"

"What, Natassia, if I what?" Ross stood, went back to a chair. His hand hung loose by his side, his broken finger three times the size of the others.

"If . . . I just, I don't know, but if, well, you keep saying you really want to help me, well, if you really do, Dad, you have to promise me you won't self-destruct. I'm really, really tired of seeing you hurt yourself. You know, like now, you just broke your finger, and this session is supposed to be helping me and now I'm sitting here worrying about your broken finger. I'm always worrying about you." Natassia started to cry again.

"Oh, honey. Oh, shit."

"That night when Nora showed up at the cottage to tell us about Poppy—Dad, I thought it was you. I was so scared that Nora was there because something happened to you, like you were drunk and got in a car accident, or you overdosed, or something really bad. Daddy, I don't want to worry about you anymore." She was crying with her hands up on her cheeks.

"Oh, Natassia." Ross walked over and gently pulled her up off her chair so he could sit in it, then he pulled Natassia onto his lap, hugged her, held her. Her face was in his neck, and her back was shaking. "Sweetie," Ross said.

"I can't keep you alive anymore, Dad. I don't want to worry about you all the time. Please, stay alive. Just, please, take care of yourself."

Ross tightened his hug.

Then Mary walked over to the chair where Natassia and Ross were huddled.

"I promise you, I promise, I promise," Ross was whispering to Natassia. Mary wrapped her arms around both their heads, buried her face in their hair.

How primitive. The thing has happened, Nora thought, that thing that's supposed to happen in therapy. The professional constructs had slipped away, and now they were all sitting around an ancient campfire having a pagan exorcism of the bad spirits that had got inside them and brought them bad luck.

Natassia's voice was muffled, but Nora could hear her: "I love you guys, and I'm so sick of being mad at you. You've just always been so, God, you're so messed up, and you always made me feel like I was the problem."

"How? No!" Ross whispered.

"Like I was in the way, and I was this big problem to be solved. I mean, I know you love me, I always knew you guys love me, but I just hate the way you act like I'm this big, messy problem. I was just a kid. I didn't ask to be born."

"No," Mary said, "you're right. We did bad."

For the first time, Nora spoke. "You haven't failed her completely, Mary. You're here now. She sees you're ready to help her."

"Nora, shut up," Mary said, and that was maybe the worst moment of the morning for Nora. "You're always so—you're effectless. I don't know if that's a word, but that's what you are. You have no effect. You're always ready to say the nice thing, with all your training, but you never have a solution. I can't believe you never told me. In fifteen years, Nora, fifteen frigging years. I was ready to make you guys her legal guardians."

"I told you, Mary," Ross said, "but you insisted—"

"Cut it *out*," Mary told Ross.

"Maybe *this* is the solution," Heather said. "Here, now, what you're all doing now. Saying things that up until now have been impossible, too painful, to say."

"You must love this," Ross said, looking across the room to Christopher. "You're the one that gets us here. You're the one who's the criminal, and you sit there like a dunce." Again, Natassia rose, left her father's lap, took a seat next to Heather. Mary, too, walked away. As if he didn't even notice, Ross continued to rant at Christopher, "I want you in jail for what you did. You should be getting your ass fucked in prison by a gang bang of cocksuckers dripping with AIDS. That's what should happen to you. Meanwhile, I'm sitting here getting nailed for every stupid, ignorant mistake I ever made."

Heather ignored this last outburst from Ross; weeks later, Nora would wonder if that was Heather's one big mistake, ignoring Ross's rage and turning to business, saying, "I need to alert you that we've got about ten minutes left in our session. We can continue as we are, or do you want to address the revelation of Christopher's actions when Natassia was an infant?"

"Yes," Ross said. "Yes, I do. I want to ask you this, you asshole—"

"Ross, I'm going to ask you, please, to refrain from the abusive language."

"Abusive language—give me a fucking break, Heather. Okay, Prince Valiant. What d'you want me to call you, Mr. Rogers? Gandhi? I have just one question for you. Why did you do it?"

"Because the baby was beautiful," Christopher said. "And I was greedy."

"You were greedy," Ross repeated. "He was greedy, so he fucked up my kid."

The room was silent. Time ticked.

"Nora," Heather said softly, "you look very thoughtful right now. We haven't heard much from you."

"I don't know. I guess I was thinking, yes, we were all greedy back then."

"I knew you'd defend him," Mary said.

"Of course she's defending him," Ross said.

"Is that true, Nora?" Heather asked. "Did you mean to be defending Christopher when you made that statement?"

"No." *I was defending myself.*

"Is there anything more you'd like to add, Nora?"

"Probably. But we don't have time today."

"Yes, you're right, we will have to stop for today, but we must meet again. I would say it is imperative. I realize how complicated it is for all of you to gather here, but—not only for Natassia, for each of you—I'd urge you to find a way to make another meeting possible. I could see you all in one week. Ross, can you be here next week?"

"No, but I will be." Heather looked at him, puzzled. "I have to be at work that Sunday, but I'll fly back next weekend."

"Excellent, and—"

"Yeah," Christopher said, "Nora and I will be here." Nora felt Christopher turn to look at her. "Right, Nor?" She nodded.

"Excellent. Now, before you leave. Please, I can't emphasize enough how important it is that you be gentle with yourselves this week. Do not underestimate the power of what happened here today. You're likely to feel quite battered emotionally over the next few days. If any of you—any one of you—feels the need, please call me. I do urge you not to talk with each other. Natassia and her parents, of course, must be in communication. Nora and Christopher, together, with each other. But I urge you, Nora and Christopher, not to be in touch with any of the three members of this family. Is that clear and acceptable to everyone? Nor with the grandmother." Mary, Christopher, and Nora nodded.

"Now, Ross, I'm concerned. Your hand, will you—"

"My sponsor drove me up here. He's probably outside waiting."

"Will you go to a hospital to have your hand treated?"

"No. I'm a doctor. I'll go home and put ice on it and make a splint and take Advil."

"These are difficult days for you, Ross. I'm concerned that—"

"Chill, Heather. I go to meetings every day. I'm helping my mother clear out the apartment. We're almost done. I told you, my sponsor—he's a retired Columbia professor—he's got nothing better to do than shadow me all day."

"Okay," Heather said, in a jolting, wrap-up kind of voice—the finger-snap that broke the hypnotic trance they'd been in for almost two hours. Julius yawned. "You all worked very hard here today. I'll look forward to meeting with you again next Saturday." Everyone stood up. "Nora, Christopher, I suggest you leave before the family leaves. To avoid seeing them in the waiting area."

"Oh," Nora said, "yes." She hated feeling like a rookie.

As they walked toward the door, Heather was asking Natassia, "It's such a beautiful day—will you be working in the gardens?"

Gardens?

"No, I have homework to do."

Nora was reaching for the doorknob when, behind her, Christopher stopped. "Natassia," he said, "I'm sorry for what I did to you. I need to say that."

Nora looked back, saw Natassia standing so tall, but holding her mother's hand, just like a little girl, and without thinking, Nora asked, "Natassia, can I hug you goodbye before we leave?"

"No," Natassia said, looking down at the floor. "I think right now I'd rather not get near you guys."

CHAPTER 40:

APRIL

1990

As soon as they had left the therapy session, Christopher could tell he was going to be sick, so he had asked Nora to drive. She hated driving into the city. He was letting her down. Again. One more small way. But he had to ask her. "I'm sorry, Nor. I can't drive."

"All right," she'd said in that way that meant it wasn't all right at all. "I'll drive." They were now about twenty miles north of the city, and he had just asked Nora to pull over. As soon as the car came to a stop, he leaned out the open window and vomited all over the outside of the passenger door. Holding on to the top of the lowered window, he felt like an animal in a bad zoo: unkempt, barely fed or watered, caged into a small space.

Nora was gawking. "God, are you all right?"

"No." And he chucked up another block of decomposed food. His innards felt like a freeze-dried pack of coffee that had just been punctured, so the air loosened up and sent things rolling.

"Here. Here, take this." Nora was shoving a bunch of Kleenex onto his lap.

Finally, he stopped retching. He wiped off his mouth and his chin, and sat back in his seat with his head against the headrest. "Thank you." Trucks were speeding past, lifting dirt, forcing Christopher to close his eyes tightly. He turned away from the traffic and looked out his window down at the gravel roadside, grateful for its stillness. It seemed that a long time passed. "You want a divorce from me, don't you?" he asked. She said nothing. "Are you going to say something, Nora?" Nothing. He said, "Divorce. Say it."

"I'm sorry," she told him, "that Ross said those things to you. I knew it would get ugly, but I never expected that."

"That? Shit, it was a relief. I always knew what he thought of me. I never imagined that's what David thought. Did you know? Did you ever think?"

"It's always been pretty clear to me that both David and Lotte were completely nuts. And, no, I don't know that I want a divorce. It's really not what I want."

"What do you want?"

"I don't know."

Forsythia were blooming. The weekend before, in Nyack, Christopher and Denise had taken pictures of Donby outside, in his little bouncy chair, in front of a blazing wall of forsythia in Denise's backyard. Husband Don had planted a whole row of bushes, to ease Denise's end-of-winter despair. He'd also planted patches of crocuses everywhere for her. Now, out here where Christopher and Nora were stopped on the roadside, there were beer cans and a dented, empty turpentine can and a dirty Kotex and a dirty diaper and a clump of clothes-dryer lint that was a startled shade of turquoise. *I wonder if I'll ever paint again.*

He said, "I keep seeing Natassia sitting there this morning, like— God, I see her, you know, trying so hard to make something reasonable with her father, who's such— He's a sick person, Nora. Did we ever realize that about him?"

"Actually," Nora said, "I was impressed with Natassia." She began to say more, then stopped herself. But then she did say more, very quietly. "I was, maybe, a little jealous."

"Jealous?" Christopher said. "Jesus."

"Natassia's still young and she's getting the chance—it's rare, you know— to see clearly what went wrong in her childhood. She's got time on her side. She's got her parents there, willing to help. Well, Mary is—"

"Ross, God—"

"Yeah, I know. But even that is good, for Natassia to see how Ross is, to see what he's obviously not capable of, what he can't give her."

"Did you see her letting him sit her on his lap, like now he's really going to take care of his little girl? That made me . . . I almost cried right then. She's so fucking smart, but this thing about her father, she can't see it."

Nora's profile was serious, quiet, her forehead wrinkled in concentration. He hated that she was so much smarter than he was. "Yes," she said, "it was sad. Even in the middle of Ross's acting out, Natassia couldn't stop wanting more from him." Nora stayed focused on some idea in front of her. "What was amazing, though, was how visible it was, right there in front of us, *tangible*. You could just *see* how incredibly impossible it is for the child *not* to love the parent. And how painful to hold that kind of love inside you. How much energy spent trying to change it, change it, get it right. But you *can't* change it, ever. So you end up either acting out your anger and your disappointment, or directing it at yourself and becoming self-destructive, like Natassia was last fall, or you lie to yourself and say nothing's wrong and become a false person."

Christopher pushed in the cigarette lighter. They both waited for it to pop. "You're a good psychologist," Christopher said.

"It's not because I'm a psychologist, it's because I've done all those things myself. Natassia reminds me of me."

"You're not like that."

"Like what?"

"Unhinged. God, what a dog-and-pony show up there this morning. I just keep seeing Natassia, all dressed up in black like some little hip bohemian beatnik, and this helpless baby-kid look on her face, sucking her thumb."

"Two thumbs."

"Did you see that? And Mary, just sitting there, like some kind of trailer-park mother who's lost her teeth and can't say a thing. I'm sorry, I don't know what I'm saying."

Christopher opened the glove compartment, closed it. *Why do people buy American cars when they could buy something nice and attractive?*

"Well, how did you think the meeting would go? What did you expect from it?" Nora asked.

"I don't know. I thought I'd say my bit, you'd say yours, then the police would come in." Christopher looked over, but Nora wasn't smiling. "I just keep seeing Natassia, and then I keep seeing the baby's face." Christopher decided just to go for it, say the name. "Donby's face. He's got all this strength in his hands. He's only, what, eighteen and a half weeks old"—Nora was letting him continue talking—"and he can put the squeeze on my fingers; Donby squeezes my nose until I'm, like, Hey, okay, baby. He can make this little fist— I'm sorry, Nora, you don't want to hear it." Haggard, she looked haggard. She'd lost some weight lately, but that wasn't helping her looks at all. "I'm sorry," he said again.

"I'm listening," Nora said.

Christopher noticed that she was. She was staring into the rearview mirror, looking for what might come up from behind, but she was listening to him talk about Donby. "He's one strong baby. And I can't keep from thinking, if anybody did—tried to do to him—what, you know, *I* did . . . to Natassia . . . Jesus, Nora, why didn't she push me away? Why does she *let*? I'm sorry, this isn't nice and correct, what I'm saying, but—"

"She was *six weeks old*, Christopher. She trusted you. For several days you consistently fed her. You cleaned her and held her and sang to her. She got used to your smells and sounds and touch. She trusted."

"She trusted me," Christopher said disdainfully. "That baby was dumb to trust me. She trusted me, and I went and— If some asshole did stuff to Donby like that . . ."

"What would Donby do?" Nora asked. Christopher couldn't believe he was hearing Nora say the name. With no hate in her voice. *Donby.*

"I'd have to kill anybody who hurt him."

"What would Donby do if someone he's around all the time, who takes good care of him, suddenly did something . . . that was, well, not so good?"

"He trusts me, and he trusts his mother. He trusts her friend Carole. She's like his grandmother. He's starting to like the nanny a lot. But he doesn't really like it if anybody else tries to pick him up."

Inside the car, all was quiet; outside was traffic.

Nora said, "It sounds as if he's developed a healthy attachment to his mother, and to you. All that sounds good."

"You think?" Christopher couldn't hide his eagerness to hear anything she'd tell him. When it came to his son, Christopher was shameless. "Am I doing good enough?"

"Sounds like," Nora reassured him.

This conversation was so much like the way he and Nora used to talk when they lay next to each other in the dark, in bed, talking without looking at each other. He wanted so much to reach over and hold on to her hand. "He's attached, but, Jesus . . ."

"What?" Nora asked.

"Nora, I'm in way over my head. I let this baby be born into a real mess of a situation. My baby's mother. Denise. Her name's Denise Wojciekowski. Nora, she's alcoholic. Poor Donby has an alcoholic mother, and he's got me for a father, and I'm just a part-time father and a full-time fuckup. What's going to happen to that boy? Is he going to end up like Natassia? What if it ends up like that?"

"What do you mean, she's alcoholic?" Nora was finally looking at him.

"She doesn't drink. She quit. But still."

"Did you know? Did you know when you agreed to father her child?"

"I knew. Yeah, I knew, but I didn't know what that meant. Recovered alcoholic. I figured the problem's done."

"Hardly."

"Fucking-A. And, you know, I did it for all the wrong reasons. I did it to get back at you. It just seemed so clean."

Christopher felt as close to Nora now as he ever had. She was like a settled pond right next to him. Unrippled until he tossed a stone. Waiting patiently for him to toss any stone, big or small, and then she'd ride out all the ripples. *Wife.* He had never felt more grateful to anyone for anything than he was grateful now to Nora for letting him say *Donby* and *Denise* and *alcoholic.* Now, he wanted to say *scared.*

"Maybe that's the worst you can do to a person," he said, just to say something. "Make them think you're good, then you turn bad on them. Like me with Natassia."

A cop car pulled up behind the Tempo. The cop came over. "Trouble here?" he asked. "Driver's license, registration, please."

Nora was quickly groping around in her big purse for the rental-car papers and her wallet, and Christopher leaned over and told the cop, "I'm HIV and I just started a new medication and I'm not doing too well with it. I had to throw up."

The policeman stepped away from the car, looked over Nora's license, handed everything back to her. "Well, feel better. Drive carefully." He returned to his squad car.

"Why'd you say that to him?" Nora asked. "HIV? What were you doing?"

"Did you want me to tell the truth? Fifteen years ago, Officer, I molested a baby, and now her father wants to tear my skin off."

Nora laughed.

"What?"

"That thing Ross said to you, about cocksuckers in jail dripping with . . . Oh dear, I wonder what Heather's going to do about him."

"Do you think she's any good? Heather, as a therapist?"

"We'll find out." Nora made a move to turn the ignition key. "Are you feeling better? Can we go on now?"

"Why was it so hard for me to listen to you, Nora? All those years, you tried to talk to me about all this stuff, and I wouldn't do it."

Nora's profile was close enough to kiss. Christopher was so grateful to find he still felt desire for her.

"Can you listen now?" she asked him, taking her hand away from the ignition.

"I don't know, Nora. I want to, I want to a lot, but, to tell you the truth, I don't know. I feel like a person who just woke up and lived their whole life wrong. You could find somebody else, Nora. You could."

"Yeah, I know," Nora said. "I could."

He looked out the window, away from her. "Have you?"

"No." She paused. He knew there was more, and then she said, "I thought maybe I had. But, no, I haven't."

"Was it— Never mind."

"Even if I had found someone, even if I do, I'd still need you to listen to me tell you what I need to tell you."

"I just can't stand to hear some of the stuff. I can't stand to see you so unhappy."

"Well, you've got to get over that, because I am unhappy. I have a lot of reasons to be unhappy, from way before you met me."

"Yeah, the house fire. I don't think I ever—"

"The fire, yes," Nora said, "but there were problems in my family way before the fire. That's what I'm up against now. Issues I'd have to deal with even if my parents were still alive." She turned to look at him. "You say you love me completely, but you've always rejected my unhappiness, and that makes me feel—I don't know—left behind."

"You're right, Nora. I don't like your unhappiness."

They both stared ahead. This was what he'd been told to do, talk straight flat-out truth to his wife. For a month now, he'd been part of a men's counseling group in Nyack. A domestic-abuse group. He'd almost flipped when the counselor had suggested it. Christopher had gone there to see about their sex-offenders' group—he really did want to do right by Donby, make sure he really was okay to be a father—but they screened him out of that—*Do you rage at your wife? Throw things?*—and steered him into this group of domestic-violence offenders. Christopher had serious doubts about the whole deal. How could anything good come of telling bad stuff to the woman you loved, stuff that would for sure hurt her? But the counselors and the guys in the group who'd marinated in recovery for a while kept saying stuff like, And you don't think it hurts your wife when you keep big secrets from her? Or when you blow up at her?

So Christopher told Nora now, in a voice as calm as he could make it, "It's an aesthetic problem." Nora looked at him; he could read the questions on her face. "Your unhappiness. In such a beautiful, beautiful woman as you." He grabbed her arm. "You're stunning, do you know that? Do you know how stunning you are? But it's always sort of offended me, aesthetics-wise, how unhappy you get."

"Fuck you, Christopher," she said, but in the mildest way. "Your grammar mistakes offend *my* aesthetics." Then she utterly surprised him by turning her face in to his shoulder, resting her head there. Her cedary hair-smell came up into his face, and he wanted to cry. Despite his vomit stink, she'd come close to him.

"You snob," he whispered, and kissed her hair once, then twice more.

"You smell like throw-up," she whispered back. She turned up her face. They still couldn't kiss, not on the mouth, but their cheeks rubbed together. "You smell like Candice's babies," Nora said. Christopher raised a hand and held her white head close. They stayed that way a long time. Then another cop drove by, slowed, went on.

"We should get going," Nora whispered.

"You want me to drive now?"

"No. I can do it." She started up the Tempo, shifted into DRIVE, then stopped.

"What?" he asked.

"Can you?" She shifted back into PARK. "Show me pictures of Donby. Show me. I'd like to see." She pulled the emergency brake on. "Especially his ears." Her voice slipped. She was trying hard to make it light, but Christopher saw Nora's fingers shaking as he put a photo in her hand. She started to cry.

"Oh, Nor. Oh, Jesus."

"I practiced asking for this, and looking at it, but I didn't think it would feel like this to actually see him."

"Feel like what? What, sweetie?"

"Frightening. He's really beautiful."

"Don't be scared, Nor. There's nothing to be scared—"

"He's beautiful," Nora repeated, "and he's yours." There wasn't a thing Christopher could say. "And he's not mine," Nora said. "You did this with someone else."

Every angry answer caught in Christopher's throat. *What the hell does she want from me?* Then he closed his lips together, sealed them with two fingertips, exhaled through his nose. *One two three four five six seven eight nine ten.* "Yes, I did that. And you got hurt. And I'm sorry." *One two three four—* "Nora, please. Don't leave me. Don't. Even if you left— Jesus, I'll never stop being married to you."

"So what you want is for me to make room in our marriage for your child."

"Yes," Christopher told Nora.

"I don't know if I can do that."

"Can you try? Nora?"

Nora told him, "I'm going to try."

The morning after the meeting with Heather, Mary was in the dance studio rehearsing the solo she was scheduled to perform in May at a show in
Albany. A year earlier, in that other life she used to live, she'd agreed to
perform with her company at a memorial performance in honor of the
company's founder. Mary would be in two ensemble pieces, and then
she'd do the solo she'd performed most of the years she toured. It was the
solo that was killing her now. Eight counts in the middle of the dance, a
quick run of turns interspersed with lightning-fast footwork that she just
was not getting right. Mary was feeling her age. She'd left Natassia in the
cottage doing equations for an upcoming calculus test. The kid had recently started talking about wanting to become a pharmacist. How convenient that would be for Ross, Mary thought. She couldn't remember
when she'd been this angry at Ross. *That nightmare therapy session.* What
she wanted more than anything was to call and scream and scream and
scream at him.

But at least Mary could leave Natassia in the cottage now. She was
studying with a friend. Mary felt sure Natassia wouldn't perform any acts
of violence against herself, not with exams so close. Mary rehearsed for
two hours that morning. Eventually, she came to the conclusion that it
was going to be impossible to get that string of turns and footwork as

quick-quick as when she'd been at the height of her performance career. She made peace with that by cutting out one turn and two counts of footwork. And still, at each transition, each pivot into a new direction, there was a brief lag, a reluctance that, try as she might, she could not compensate for. She did the only thing she could—she incorporated the lag into her dance.

Six weeks later, after her performance in Albany, a reviewer would write:

> There is an ache in this dance now that was not there when Mudd performed it four years ago. To have watched her then, and to see her now in the same dance, is to witness, for a flickeringly elusive moment, exactly what it is that the person who is the dancer brings to the dance. Last night, the aptly retitled "So-Lo" was beautiful to watch, and yet it was heartbreaking to see that this dancer has, in the past years, moved into a deeper understanding of the ravages of loss.

FOR THE SECOND GROUP SESSION at Heather's office, Ross didn't show up. He had called Mary the night before to say he'd missed his plane and there was no way he'd be able to make it on time. He said they should just go on without him.

"Ross, this is *family* counseling," Mary yelled into the phone. "Natassia needs us both there. Jesus, Ross, why're you screwing this up?"

Ross yelled back, "Christopher's the one who needs to be there to take the heat. I swear, Mary, if I'm in that room with him again, I'm afraid I'll really kill him. How's she been this week?"

"Miserable. Why haven't you called her?"

"Miserable to be with, or miserable-she-doesn't-feel-good?"

"Both. She's got these exams she's totally paranoid about. She's doing great in her classes, all her teachers told her so, and she keeps going nuts that she's going to flunk everything. She stays up late and gets up early and gives me orders right and left about how I'm making too much noise, how I'm bugging her while she needs to study."

"But about that meeting we had with her shrink, she's all right?"

"Jesus, Ross, no, she's not all right. She's paranoid and overreacting.

459

And, plus, she's driving me nuts. She needs you to be here, and—excuse me for being so blunt—*I* need you to help me with her. Fucking at least call us once in a while."

"Hey, Mary, I buried my father less than two months ago. I just helped my mother unload, sell off, and relocate our whole life's worth of stuff and move her into some shack-up studio my father and I never even knew she had. Then I had to sit in that woman's office last week with her stinking mongrel dog and hear that my only daughter was molested, sexually molested, by a longtime friend who, I have to remind you, *you* brought into our lives with that selfish ice-goddess bitch Nora, and now you're . . ."

SITTING IN HEATHER'S OFFICE for the second Saturday-morning meeting, Mary was feeling a mess of traffic inside herself, Mack trucks of emotion colliding within, especially as Heather talked about how regrettable it was that Natassia's father got tied up with work and stranded by the airlines and wasn't able to join them. "But perhaps we'll use this session to focus on what Natassia would like to say to Christopher and to Nora."

"I'll just say this right off," Natassia said, looking directly at Nora and Christopher, who sat across the room, "because I know you're freaking out about it. I decided not to take any legal action. And I'm not doing that to save you guys. I'm doing it for myself." Natassia's thumb rested on her chin, babylike, but Mary thought, She's taking care of herself. She's not letting those two get away with anything.

Christopher spoke up. "No, Natassia, we're not worried about that. We want—"

Nora cut in. "Thank you for telling us that. It is a relief to me to hear it."

"I guess what I want to say to Christopher is that I heard, from overhearing Nora tell my mom, about exactly what you did to me. You put your mouth on my genitals. You put your tongue in me. Is that right?" Christopher nodded. "You put your tongue into my vagina?" He nodded again. "If that's what you did, say it," Natassia demanded.

Christopher whispered it.

Mary was rapt now. The kid had the room. The sick dog was the only one not paying close attention. Natassia continued: "I'm not sure Nora wasn't lying—like, maybe there's more I haven't heard."

"Yes," Mary said. "That's what I want to know, too."

"There's *not*." Christopher leaned forward, far forward, until he was halted by the knot of his tie. "Nothing else," he whispered.

Heather said, "Christopher, it seems as if you want to say something more in response to Natassia's question."

"Yeah, but, you know . . ." He turned in his seat so he could look at Nora, and that's when Mary noticed the change in Nora. Yeah, she'd lost a little weight, but it was more than that. Nora was beautiful again, and she hadn't been beautiful for months and months, and Mary understood that Nora and Christopher were together again; their big problem, whatever it had been, had ended. Linked to Christopher, Nora was healthy again, and they were clear to walk away from the shit they'd created in Natassia's and Mary's lives. "Nora," Christopher was saying, "Nora tried hard, a lot of different times. She tried to make me tell your parents." Nora finally looked at him, and Christopher said, "Nora, you were right about all this stuff, and I really screwed up."

Natassia uncrossed her legs, stamped her leather sandal on the rug. When Mary looked over, Natassia was rolling her eyes. "Fuck you both. Here I am, trying to untangle my guts"—that's a Ross word, Mary thought—"and all you're interested in is your marriage." Natassia turned to Heather. "Did you see that? I told you, Heather, I told you."

"Ah, Natassia, no, wait," Christopher was saying, but he was holding Nora's hand on her armrest.

Heather said, "Natassia, I do see why Christopher's response disappointed you, I do see." Even that dog had his eyes open now. "Address Christopher and Nora, if you can. Can you say more clearly—"

"More clearly, my ass. How fucking clear do I have to be?" *Now she sounds like me, just like me.*

No longer adult, slumping down in her chair, Natassia rested the ankle of her right foot on her left knee—her bad-girl pose. "It's hopeless, it's useless."

"I don't see that it's hopeless at all," Heather said, petting her dog's head, and she was about to say more, but from down a hallway somewhere came the sound of a baby crying. Mary said, "The baby."

Heather said, "It's fine. The children are being cared for today by their father."

Natassia smiled. "I love when you ignore your baby to stay in here with me."

"Natassia!" Mary said.

"But it's the truth," Natassia said. "Heather wants me to say the truth."

"Christopher," Heather interrupted, "just now your face, when the baby cried—what were you thinking?"

"Oh, shit, you're going to make me?"

"I can't make you, but—"

"All right." He sat forward, on the edge of his seat, as if getting ready to leave. "I have to tell you something." Mary saw the look on Nora's face turn very strange. "Natassia, I don't know if it has anything to do with what we're doing, but, Heather, you keep asking what we're thinking, and I have to be honest that I'm not thinking about what I'm supposed to be thinking about."

"Which is?"

"I'm not thinking about Little Baby Natassia. I mean, I see you, Natassia, and you're this pretty grown-up girl, and you're in all this pain. And I did it. I know I didn't do all of it, but I did a bunch. And, Natassia, I'd do anything if I could take back what I did."

Natassia's face was all suspicion. Last week, Ross had taken the spotlight; this week—you could feel it in the room—Christopher was about to grab top bill.

"I'd do anything," he said. "And I promise you, all the rest of the time I'm alive, no matter what, if there's anything I ever can do for you— anything . . . And I have to tell you this. I have a baby son. Not with Nora. I have a son. I want to be the one to tell you, so you don't hear it from someone and think you can't trust me. I want you to trust me."

Nora had covered her face with her hands.

"What do you mean, Nora's not the mother?" Natassia had forgotten her thumb. Heather had moved up in her seat.

"This woman," Christopher started to say.

But Natassia asked, "Does she know about what you did to me? I want you to tell the mother what you did." *You go, Natassia, you stick up for yourself.*

"I did tell the mother. She knows. I told her way in the beginning, before, when she was deciding to let me be the baby's father. She—her name's Denise—she's the only person I ever told about when you were a baby. Really. Besides a couple of therapists Nora and I went to through the years."

"So you have worked on this event, this event that occurred in Natassia's infancy?" Heather asked.

"We've tried. Nora tried. I never worked hard enough."

"Are you in love with this woman?" Natassia said.

"Natassia!" Mary said.

"It's okay, Mary. She can ask me anything she wants. No, Natassia. I'm not in love with Denise. I'm in love with Nora. It never was a relationship like that with Denise. I care about her because, well, because she's a good person, but mostly she's my son's mother. Love, no. Nora is the person I love. I'm in love with Nora. That's it. It's Nora."

"And how did it happen," Heather asked, "your fathering this baby?"

"Long story, but, basically, Denise lost her husband. He died. Good guy. Artist. She was grieving bad and she wanted a kid and was looking for a donor and really wanted a painter, since her husband was a painter. Good painter. Anyway, she was interviewing various guys. And this friend of mine told me, and Nora and I, well, I really wanted a baby. So we just fit, me and Denise. It was all lab work. No sex. Never any sex."

"Nor, did you know about this baby business?" Mary asked.

Christopher had to answer for her. "Not till after he was born. The baby's four and a half months old now. His name's Donby. I lied to Nora a long time. He was born in December. I knew since last June, but I never told. I was afraid to. Plus—"

"You were angry at me," Nora whispered. "We were angry at each other."

"Yep, we were."

"We should stay with Natassia's concerns," Heather said. "Time's running out."

"Yeah, well, Natassia, this *is* about you. When I hurt you, I was greedy and untrustworthy. And I hurt Nora, and I was greedy again. Two people I love very much."

"Yeah," Mary said, "but listen. This baby news is wild and all, but the kid I care about is Natassia. Nora, *why* did you lie to me for so long? Why didn't you tell me?"

"I was afraid I'd lose you."

"We were so close, you were my . . ." All Mary could do was shake her head. "I mean, always, but after the fire especially."

"You had dance, you had Ross. Even my mother admired you."

"You had boyfriends all over the place, then you got Christopher."

"Mary, I've always needed you so much more than you ever needed anybody. You've always been so self-contained, so complete, confident—"

"If that's true, Nora, that you *need* like that, then I don't know who you are. Really, I never, ever saw you like that."

DRIVING CLAUDIA'S CAR back to the school, Mary said, "That was something."

"Christopher has a non-Nora baby. It's too weird, way too weird."

"Very, very weird," Mary agreed.

"Wait till Daddy hears. He'll flip."

CHAPTER 42:

MAY

1990

Natassia never did get to tell her father about Christopher's baby son. More than six months would pass before she spoke to her father again, more than a year before she saw him. By then Natassia would be headed for the University of Pennsylvania (after being accepted at Columbia and wait-listed at Harvard), because Penn offered her significant financial aid, and Natassia's father, a year into recovery and unemployed, couldn't be depended on, as in the past, for financial support—or for much else.

But in May 1990, all anyone knew was that Ross wasn't showing up for the group sessions with Natassia's therapist.

After he missed the second and third sessions, Mary called him and left a message giving him the date and time for the fourth. She added: "You *must* be there. There's no choice, there's nothing more important than this, Ross."

When Mary got a call from Harriet, she was surprised. She had assumed, after the arguments she overheard during the days of David's funeral, that Ross and Harriet had broken up, that Harriet had moved out. But maybe Ross had moved out, so Mary asked, "Where'd he move to?"

"Mary, he's gone."

"What do you mean, he's gone?"

"He hasn't been home for three days. I figured he was on a binge, but today the hospital called me: he faxed in a resignation letter. He quit his job."

"Three days? You're telling me now? Jesus, Harriet."

"Mary, let me finish. Just a few hours ago he called me. He's checked himself into a rehab program in a different state. He's been traveling by train for three days. I can't even think about it. The condition he's in . . ."

Mary had pencil and paper in hand. "Give me the phone number."

"I can't do that. He doesn't want anyone to know where he is."

Mary sighed. "Okay, Harriet, be that way. But he's got a daughter here who needs him. Lotte will tell me where he is if you won't."

"He specifically does not want his mother to know where he is. I refuse to talk to that woman. The level of abuse she allowed Ross to receive from his father—"

"But, like, what, Harriet? *What* did David do? Yeah, David was a prick—"

"How can you minimize it? You've seen— Well, all I know is that the destructive dynamic between David and Ross has left Ross with demons that are fierce, just terribly fierce."

What the hell does "destructive dynamic" mean? "Maybe Lotte never knew—"

"She's his *mother*. How could she not have known what was going on with her own child, with her husband, in her own apartment?"

Mary sighed a deep sigh. "Harriet, you don't have any kids, do you?"

"Don't you dare condescend to me."

"No, no, that's not how I meant it. No. What I meant is, there's this thing, and nobody talks about it, so you don't know it, you can't, until you're a mother, it's—"

"And what is that *thing* that I don't know because I'm not a mother?"

Mary had twice seen pictures of Harriet; she had big, out-of-style, shaggy hair and large breasts, and she smiled with her eyebrows raised up a little unnaturally, as if smiling didn't come easily to her. "Well," Mary said, "it's, like, mothers make a lot of mistakes. You really do. And you can't even help it. You don't even know sometimes when you're screwing up big-time. You're just trying to—"

"—do your best," Harriet said in a singsong voice. "Do the best you can."

"Exactly. And how much you fuck up doesn't have anything to do with how much you love your kid. Even when you love your kid like crazy, you fuck up and make mistakes. Lotte loves Ross a *lot*."

Long silence. "I think there's hope for Ross this time. I really do."

"Why?" Mary asked. "Why this time?"

"He has finally," Harriet said in a slow voice, "hit bottom."

"I'm really sorry, Harriet." Silence. "You really love him."

"Yeah," Harriet whispered, "I do. I had so much hoped . . ."

"What, Harriet?"

". . . hoped I could have a baby with him." A crack in Harriet's voice was an echo of how Natassia had sounded during the worst days of the BF mess.

FOR LOTTE, the news of Ross's inaccessibility was like news that he was gone forever, and it hit Natassia that way, too. It was May. Mary and Natassia were scheduled to go to the city for a memorial service for David, and they took the train down a day early. As expected, Lotte's small studio was filled with friends of David's, but all the talk was about Ross. His addiction, his disappearance. His brilliance. His job. Ross had finally managed to upstage his father.

"But the insurance," more than one person asked, "who's paying for his treatment?"

"The money he got from the sale of West End Avenue."

"Dear God, to make such a business decision, he's really lost his head, poor man."

Lotte and Natassia were inseparable, and they cried all the time. The Grieving Club, Mary thought as she sat in the mini-kitchen on a stool, looking out the tiny porthole window. In the main room of the studio, visitors were coming and going. Six people created a crowd, but there were dozens in attendance. First, David's friends. Then, because of Ross, a whole new crowd began showing up—young doctors, nurses, regulars from a local bar, Twelve Step friends. Everyone felt bad for Lotte. "How do I know he's not in a cult? I know nothing. Is he dead? Alive?" Lotte wept. And, really, on this count, Mary sympathized with Lotte. A kid who's disappeared—pretty much a mother's next-to-worst nightmare.

A window air-conditioning unit was going full-blast, and Mary, on the sidelines, was cocooned in a sheath of noise, apart. No one came in to talk to her. It was almost as if everyone assumed that Mary had moved her heart away from Ross long ago and wasn't available anymore to be hurt by him. But, man, everybody was wrong about that.

Even Mary was surprised by how much she was hurting. Seventeen years earlier, she and Ross had met, and for fourteen of those years they had been leaving each other, separating in every way possible, but nothing in the past had felt as bad or as irreversible as this. *He may as well be dead.* She tried to picture his skin—gone.

When Mary first knew Ross, it had taken two months of him pressing her before she gave him the time of day, and that only happened after he said to her, "You're coming home with me for Fall Break." Even as a kid, Ross had that power to announce to you what his plans were for you. "My mother's going to adore you. My father'll be so jealous."

"Wait," Mary had said. "Is he the kind that's going to hit on me when you're not in the room? I don't like that shit."

"No, the old ass knows his limits. Besides, he's totally into my mother. But he'll be like, Hey, son, how'd you get such a class act to go out with you? Who'd you bribe?"

"Nice guy," Mary said.

"Oh, my daddy's a piece of work."

Mary had almost canceled the trip. Four days with somebody's parents? What was she thinking? But it would be four days in New York City. His mother had bought tickets to take Mary to see Merce Cunningham. Anybody could survive four days in New York, no matter how bad the father was.

Turned out, the father was a smoker, and since Ross and Lotte weren't smokers, David was happy to have Mary's company. He dubbed the two of them "the Smoke Team." He called Lotte and Ross "the Wussies." David was always setting up sides.

Fathers were beside the point anyway. What got Mary from the start was the way being in the Steins' apartment, way up high above New York City, felt a lot like being in the Conollys' house. The Steins had too many books and a lousy TV (Mr. Conolly had had the best TV and stereo system). Lotte, David, and Ross ate funny foods. Their apartment was dark, with hardly any sunlight except in the kitchen, and not decorated anywhere as nicely as the Conollys' house had been. But whenever Lotte walked into a room, there was a hefty thump of connection; Mrs. Conolly could do that to a room. Even the back-and-forth bickering between David and Lotte felt familiar, just like the Conollys'. By that Thanksgiving, Mary and Ross were hot and heavy, and Mary brought Nora and Kevin to the Steins' for dinner, but Kevin acted bratty. A few times during the years, Nora joined the Steins for Passover seders, but the Steins' scene had never clicked for Nora, which pissed Mary off a bit. Nora could have at least tried, since Mary was making the effort to include her. Whatever, the Steins' became Mary's next home.

All these thoughts about the Conollys and the Steins had started coming up one day when Dr. Cather pushed Mary hard and asked her, "Can you remember what you were thinking or feeling when you decided to give birth to Natassia? What I mean, Mary, is that you are a very practical person. You've always had high expectations for yourself in terms of your dance career. To bring a baby into your life at the start of what was clearly going to be a successful career . . . What were your expectations?"

In other words, What the fuck were you thinking?

In the earliest days of that pregnancy, Mary had had a couple intense, more-real-than-life dreams that included her birth mother: the woman was there, spooking Mary but being nice to her, letting Mary move ahead of her while they were waiting in a long, long line to buy a car. Plus, Ross (idiot!) had called his parents long-distance from Rome and bragged to them that Mary's period was ten days late.

"Ross," Mary had yelled in the middle of some piazza, "why'd you call them?"

"It took my father years to get my mother pregnant. You should've heard him."

"What'd he say?"

"Nothing. Total transatlantic silence. He was so jealous he couldn't speak, that old faggot."

Within a week, a letter arrived from Lotte with a package containing a bottle of folic-acid tablets for Mary. "We support you," Lotte wrote, "whatever you decide." It was almost like having Mrs. Conolly alive again when Lotte wrote, "I will help you."

Alone in Lotte's tiny kitchen now, Mary stared out the window. There was nothing like sunsets on the Upper West Side, so bruised and beautiful. Cather had been pushing a discussion lately, something Mary didn't like talking about, but, sitting in the kitchen, she had the sick feeling that probably Cather was barking up the right tree. *Shit. Oh, shit.* Mary was crying now, needed to grab a paper towel off the rack. *It's Kevin's fault.*

Kevin had just not let things go with that Hiliard gardener, Tomio. Every time Kevin came upstate to visit—about once a week these days—he and Tomio had long talks in the gardens and in the garages, and so now, whenever Kevin and Mary were walking around and ran into Tomio, they had to stop. Usually they just talked polite bullshit, flowers and motors. But one night, Mary heard herself saying, "Can I ask you something? During the Korean War, did you ever hear of a big bridge blowup over this river, the Han River?"

"June 28, 1950," Tomio said.

"Yeah, it was like in the middle of the night, right? Some fat South Korean general who was a sumo wrestler planned the blowup as a way to keep the North Koreans from getting farther south, but the timing got messed up and the bridge was full of civilians when it exploded."

"Maybe eight hundred people died. Maybe more." Tomio was nodding his head, looking hard at Mary. "This is one terrible moment in terrible war."

"I guess my mother was crossing that bridge when that happened. She was the only one in her family who made it across."

Kevin said, "Jesus." Tomio looked at Mary with eyes so piercing she could not look away from him. Natassia asked, "How'd you know that, Mom? You never told me."

There were only two bits of information Mary had about her Korean mother. The story of the bridge explosion was one bit.

Tomio looked over at Kevin, as if for permission, then said to Mary, "I must speak and tell you this—it is very impossible your mother was what you think." Mary had to watch Tomio's mouth as he spoke. His English was difficult for her to understand, and he spoke quickly, as if embarrassed about his accent and wanting to get what he was saying out as fast as possible. Like a beginning dancer who races through the steps to get them over with. But she watched Tomio's mouth, and eventually his speech slowed down and she understood.

"True prostitute," Tomio said, "she knows how not have a baby. Especially then, in that war. There was no food. Truly." Tomio stomped his foot. "No. Food." He smiled broadly at this bad news. "In war, every person is prostitute. You"—he gave a laugh, confusing Mary about where this conversation was going—"you are true lucky. True, true lucky. Your American father, soldier? Officer?"

"Just your run-of-the-mill grunt," Mary told him.

"No officer?"

"No way."

"For him to go *back* to Korea—oh, this." Tomio shook his head. "Believe me, your mother happy all her days to send baby *daughter* to U.S. To send with U.S. father to feed and give education and give house. Your mother very good. True lucky mother."

The only other piece of information Mary had about her mother had come from Dorie, who had said, when Mary got pregnant the second time, at age eighteen, and was forced to ask for money for an abortion, "Right on schedule." And when Mary asked what Dorie meant by that, Dorie said, "How old do you think your Korean mother was when she got knocked up?" To Tomio that night, Mary said, "My mother was really young, like thirteen, when that bridge thing happened. I wasn't born till she was sixteen. Three years she was on her own. I mean, with no family, how else do you think she survived?"

Again, Tomio looked at Kevin. "Can I say?" Kevin shrugged, so Tomio continued. "I believe your mother—Korean—and your American father, they love. Maybe big love. Or little soldier, GI Joe, why go *back*?"

Mary was holding a cigarette burnt to the nub; she'd forgotten to smoke it. "That would explain why Dorie hated me."

"Mary," Kevin insisted, "did you hear him? It changes everything, even the idea, even the possibility."

Tomio's theory changed nothing for Mary that night, but as she sat now in Lotte's tiny kitchen, Mary felt a rocking at the pit of her stomach, as if a boulder that had been falling and falling and tumbling forever had finally, just recently, hit the ground. She'd found a book in the Hiliard library and begun reading about her mother's war, about the tragedy on the bridge. It was just Mary's luck that the prettiest story of her life—that her birth parents might have been in love—was so bad it was making Mary's asthma worse. Lately she'd been holding a cigarette between her teeth most of the day, but she couldn't light up. Imagine hauling yourself over that collapsing bridge, imagine no food. Truly, no food. A life so bad that the best card you had to play was letting your baby be taken halfway across the frigging globe, saying to a little GI twerp like Jerry Mudd, Here, take care of her. Knowing you'd never ever see your kid again.

Mary was crying so hard now, she didn't know how she was going to catch her breath. She looked down at her open palms in her lap, her shaking thirty-six-year-old hands, and within them, she saw baby hands. Tiny hands. And Mary knew that this time she was crying for herself. *Stop!* But she couldn't stop. And through the tears she saw adult hands again, a mother's hands, *her* mother's hands. And Mary was crying so hard she had to stand up and pace the six-foot-long kitchen. The cigarette slipped from her fingers, rolled somewhere. Mary crouched to the floor but she couldn't see.

Jesus, what was my mother—beautiful, or phenomenally sexy, or what? To get Jerry to do it? At this point in her life, Mary knew that it took more than a really good fuck to get a man like Jerry Mudd to be a better person than he really was. She thought it all the way through: Jerry would have had to tell his wife he'd cheated on her, then tell her he had a kid in Korea, then tell her he was bringing the kid back, moving the kid into their house. When he went overseas, Jerry and Dorie had been married only four months. *Poor Dorie, that bitch. No wonder she was so mean to me.* Jerry then had to tell the armed services what he'd done, and the U.S. government and the Korean government and the church. He told his neighbors and relatives. The guys at the warehouse, they all knew.

My mother. It's fucking amazing what she got Jerry to do. That young girl in Korea, so helpless, but she had managed to get herself over that burning, falling, exploding bridge, managed to stay alive with no family, and managed to get her baby out of a war zone and to upstate New York. True lucky, Tomio had said. True lucky.

"But it was shit," Mary whispered to the ugly linoleum kitchen floor. "Growing up with them was total shit." She leaned back against the oven door and tilted up her head. *Oh God.* The books Mary had found were full of pictures of peasants crying on roadsides, and Mary could picture that young girl, her mother, alone, curled up, small, squatting on haunches, just like Mary was now, just like Mary in starting position for her solo—*home base*—those moments when she was nothing but a pulsing heart behind a thirty-foot-high curtain, on a sixty-foot-wide stage, with an audience filling a fifteen-hundred-seat auditorium, and when the curtain went up Mary took off—maybe as fast as her mother crossing that bridge—both of them doing what they had to do to stay alive.

"You know what your problem is?" Ross had said to Mary years ago. "You know how to be mad, but you don't know how to be sad." *I'm sad now, Ross, I'm good and sad now.* With her face inside her cupped hands, Mary saw blackness, and it matched the terror she'd felt all year long for Natassia, which matched the terror she'd felt as a kid, and this was how she came to know the Korean woman who gave birth to her. *Terror.* After a while, Mary lowered her hands. Her cigarette appeared in front of her, just under the base of the refrigerator. She put the cigarette up to her nose, but the smell of it made her wince. It was a wonder, a frigging wonder, that she had managed to keep not only herself but also her daughter alive all these years. "Jesus," Mary whispered. "I'm amazing, I'm fucking amazing." She kept staring at her hands. "My mother. I bet anything she was a smoker."

CHAPTER 43:

MAY

1990

Back upstate after David's memorial service, Mary checked in with Harriet now and then, and she heard several disturbing stories about Ross's behavior in the weeks leading up to his disappearance: On his way back to Spokane after the first meeting in Heather's office, he'd been taken off the plane in Minneapolis. He was drunk and annoying people. Back home, he'd used a pellet gun to kill squirrels in the backyard, then skinned them and hung the skins on trees to "teach the rest of them a lesson." He'd had a string of nights of impotence, and he'd shaved his pubic hair and buried it under a tree, hoping to "reverse the bad spell."

WITH ROSS God knows where, Lotte wasn't managing well in the city. She was seeing lots of doctors, having all kinds of aches. "Listen, dear," she told Mary, "Natassia is so concerned about her exams, let's do this—instead of you dragging her with you to Albany for those days you're performing, why don't I come up to Hiliard to stay with her? Actually, Natassia's been hinting that she'd like me to see her school and all."

And at the same time, Natassia was whining, "Mom, I really don't want to go to Albany and sit through those rehearsals. Please, don't make me."

Mary called Kevin. "I don't feel good about leaving those two up here by themselves. Kevin, I hate to bother you—we've already relied on you too much—but—"

"I'd love to come stay with Natassia and Lotte while you're in Albany."

THE "BABYSITTING" was set up, but for a day or so Mary was dreading the trip to Albany. A respiratory infection had her coughing hacking coughs and sweating a fever, and it wouldn't go away. So many times in the past, she had performed in this condition, and she would do it next week, but Mary had really hoped the Hiliard job would mean never having to push her body around this way again. Antibiotics had her feeling woozy and dim. When she called Franklin's secretary to cancel her classes—Mary just could not get out of bed—the secretary said, "My, your family certainly is high-maintenance."

"It's me this time, Tracey. I'm the one who's sick this time. I might even be dead already, for all I know."

Then, the next day, day six of not being able to smoke any smokes at all, Mary woke up and her lungs felt as if they were two gigantic dance studios where rows of tall, open windows were letting in all kinds of extra air.

IN ALBANY, the dress rehearsal went as Mary and the other dancers had expected—not great, nowhere near perfect, but good enough. The dancers of the current company had just returned from an extended tour on the West Coast and Canada, and they were beat. There were only three rehearsals with the current dancers and former company members all together, so it was a surprise to none of them that there were some lapses—a couple entrances were delayed or too early, timing was a bit off here and there.

For Mary, the real surprise was how happy she felt onstage after her one-and-a-half-year absence. "So-Lo" began with Mary behind the curtain in a crouch. From the moment the curtain opened and she leaped up, Mary was aware—from the makeup on her face to the pumping of her heart—of only one sensation: *I love this, I love doing this.*

Except for the thirty minutes, total, that she was onstage, Mary had a toothpick in her mouth the whole time. Still, no cigarettes, not one pipe.

For the performance, Mary was afraid it wouldn't happen again like it had during the dress rehearsal, that thorough glee, that adrenaline-sharpened awareness that she was alive and doing exactly what she'd been born for.

But it did happen again. The dancers got a standing ovation; there were two curtain calls. Backstage afterward, everyone was giddy. The company manager came around with opened bottles of cheap champagne in each hand, pouring wherever she saw a glass or mug or paper cup. There were many toasts, including a toast for Mary, who didn't remember postperformance being this much fun. As she made her way to the pay phone to call Natassia, Mary felt weightless, hardly any guilt—tomorrow morning, early, she'd be driving back to Natassia. No question. Meanwhile, Mary didn't have to worry about what Ross might be doing or failing to do. And there was a delicious absence of fear in knowing that Kevin was with Natassia and Lotte. That night, when Mary got them on the phone, all three told her, "Everything here is okay."

"It went good here, too," Mary told them, "but I miss you."

Most of the dancers were heading out to a restaurant. One car was going back to the hotel, and that's what Mary decided to do.

For the first time ever, Mary had requested a nonsmoking room, so this trip smelled different from all the other times she'd traveled. Her roommate wasn't back yet, and Mary had the room all to herself, which would have been an unlikely bit of heaven on a tour. The room was chilly with air-conditioned air. The wallpaper was blue, and the room had an interior window that looked out on an indoor swimming pool. *Maybe I'll take a long swim later.* Two queen-sized beds. She clicked the remote to turn on the television.

Then she clicked it right off. "I want to go home," she said to the room.

In the bathroom, she brushed her teeth, didn't take a shower, cleared her stuff off the counter, and popped a fresh toothpick into her mouth. She grabbed her bag of dirty rehearsal clothes, stuffed everything into her backpack, wrote her roommate a short note. Then Mary got into Kevin's car, tucked two ice packs under her hips, and hit the road, with the front windows wide open. She was driving through nighttime mountains, taking the curves like a dance, her foot a tiny bit heavy on the pedal. Hiliard, New York, was the only place she wanted to be.

A couple hours outside of Albany, she stopped at an all-night convenience store to pee. There was a pay phone. Natassia answered. "Mom?" Quickly, on a different phone extension, Kevin picked up. "Mary?" Together, at the same time, Natassia and Kevin asked, "Are you okay?"

Mary laughed. "You two sound like parrots. Everything's fine."

"I'm beating his butt in this Scrabble game," Natassia said. "Where are you?"

"I'm on my way home. I just called to tell you that. Where's Lotte?"

"Asleep. Did the hotel have bedbugs or something?"

"I just missed you guys. I want to wake up at home, so I left."

"We'll wait up for you," Kevin said.

"He will," Natassia said. "I'm going to bed soon. My study group's meeting really early, at breakfast."

CHAPTER 44:

JUNE

1990

Memorial Day weekend Saturday, 1990, 10:47 p.m.

The thing about freedom is, if you use it randomly, for random action, you're a loser. Mom's been trying to talk to her students about this since last winter, when Charlie almost screwed things up for her with the naked dancing. The board of trustees made Franklin Fields bring in a therapist to have an "open talk session" with the students. Sometimes this place is so bogus. But Mom stayed and talked to them after the therapist left, and she's like, You guys have to use your freedom for some good reason. Like, onstage, you have to be free to dance but have enough discipline to know what you're doing. She keeps telling them this stuff, which I agree with. But, aside from my group of friends here, everybody's mostly morons. Poppy used to say, "You can maybe turn a brain surgeon into a dancer, but you'll never turn a dancer into a brain surgeon."

Fuck him, Mary said to herself. She was sitting out on the stoop of the cottage reading Natassia's journal. Week five of no smokes—not one—but tonight Mary was tempted. For the first time in nine months, Natassia was in the city without Mary, spending the night with Giulia, who had got tickets for some James Joyce thing at Symphony Space. Natassia's birthday gift, which had taken a lot of prep work.

Mary and Natassia, in a session with Heather, had talked the plan through. As Cather pointed out, there were lots of controls in place. Mary would put Natassia on the train, Giulia would meet her at the station. Giulia knew that Natassia was *not* to go to Lotte's apartment by herself. Natassia was not to be left to walk around by herself. No hooking up with friends on this trip. Giulia was paranoid enough to make sure there wouldn't be a slip. Kevin would drive Natassia back upstate the next day. "Do you feel all right in the car with him by yourself?" Mary had asked.

Heather said, "That is a very good question to ask, Mary."

"Kevin? He's a really good driver."

"Natassia, that's not what I mean."

"I know what you mean. No, Kevin's fine. With Kevin I feel safe."

Now, sitting on the stoop with the journal in her hands, Mary felt pretty shitty about herself, but if she didn't read the journal how else could she find out, really, how the kid was after everything that had gone down? First her grandfather dead, then the deal with Christopher and Nora, now her father disappeared. Mary wasn't taking any chances. She had a newspaper with her on the stoop, in case somebody came by and she had to hide the journal, which is exactly what she did now as Tomio drove by on the lawnmower. When he saw Mary, he raised his cap and nodded.

"Hey, Tomio, how're you doing? Nice night, huh?"

He nodded again and smiled and left her alone, turned his mower so he could cut a wider swath around the flower gardens. Mary uncovered the journal and read on.

I try to write, but it's like we're always waiting for the phone to ring. And then it doesn't. Or it does, but it's not Daddy. This is like, it's different from waiting for the BF. Maybe I feel different, not so desperate. I want to write about what I've been thinking. It's about context. My dad. HJJ tried saying the other day that he was, maybe, even with all his craziness, using his freedom for a purpose. Maybe all his "acting out" was for "the audience of his father," a "cry for help," and now the audience is gone and blah blah. I told HJJ to spare me the clichés. She's bugging me, even though she's probably right. I know she's right. I just hate to hear her saying it. I'd like to take a break from therapy, but Mom won't let me. It's so weird to see Ms. No-Vocabulary turn into Therapy Mom of the Year. I think she actually thinks I still don't know she's in therapy. Like, who're you making those private phone calls to all the time, your secret lover? She's hurting about Dad. She keeps telling me, they all do, that if Dad's using and drinking was his "cry for help" it wasn't my responsibility to be the one to hear the call and try to help him. "Tell that to my superego," I said to Mom, and she said, "Don't get smart with me."

Tuesday, 6:10 p.m.

HJJ keeps referring to Daddy as "Ross" instead of "your dad" or "your father," and I told her to quit it. But I get the point. I'm supposed to see him as a separate person.

Did you see how scared *and* sacred *are the same, just transposed? Scared/sacred. [A poem?] Daddy, I'm scared sacred without you. The sacred/profane scariness of my poppy.*

"Coping mechanisms," HJJ says.

Friday . . . after dinner, 7:13 p.m.

The words Mom *and* Dad *are both palindromes. Backward and forward, they're the same; you can't escape them.*

HJJ told me, "You have to be vigilant. Hold what you know, hold it in your hands. And look at it. This sadness, Natassia, this loss is not the only thing you know in your life, there is your writing talent, your intelligence, your ability to love, your good health, your growing relationship with your mother, your studies, your growing relationship with your creativity. There is all of that. And parallel to it, along with it, there is this darkness and sadness and loss and the damage your father and grandfather experienced, and your mother, too—and Christopher, of course, and Nora—that predated these current losses, predated the damage done to you."

I love how HJJ talks. Mom and Kevin love when I imitate HJJ.

It should have been enough for Mary that she'd arrived at a part of the journal that made her smile. But it wasn't. Mary flipped forward and read.

Daddy disappeared one month ago today. Every once in a while, I feel like I'm going to do the little cuts again. I was no way going to tell HJJ, but then, weirder than weird, she asks me, "The impulse to hurt yourself? Is

that part of these days for you?" I cried a bunch. HJJ said it's good I told
her. I was wearing a skirt, and she even made me show her my legs and roll
up my sleeves, but there wasn't a scratch. "I'm not doing it," I told her, it's
just that this pain is so always there. HJJ is teaching me that inside me
there's this pattern that happens when I feel overwhelmed. First sad, then
pissed off, then I feel like I hate myself and I turn on myself. It's a very
clear pattern. She says this pattern got set up because I didn't have anybody
really to talk to, and that's how I'll continue to handle it until we set up a
new way for me to cope. She asked me if I was going to hurt myself in New
York. I said no. So she said it was okay for me to go and we'd tell Mom at
the next session.

Mary stopped reading. "Shit." But she wasn't surprised. She'd had a
sense that's what she was going to find even before she picked up the pink
folder. That's *why* she had picked it up. *Instinct.* Gripping the bowl of an
empty pipe, Mary looked up from her lap and took a deep breath. The
days were getting so damn long now. She had been sitting on the stoop for
over an hour, and still there was light in the sky. In her mind, Mary raced
through the list of possible actions: She could find Tomio and get a key to
one of the school vans and rush down to the city. She could call Claudia
and ask her for a ride to the train—there were still two more trains that
night. She could call Giulia, but they were probably at the performance.
She could leave a phone message. *Urgent. Call me.* She could call Lotte and
ask her to go over to Giulia's and wait until Natassia got home. She could
call Ross.

The impossibility of the last idea made Mary see the ridiculousness of
the next-to-last idea, then the inappropriateness of all the others. What
would she say? I need the school van because my daughter wrote in her
journal?

Natassia had not cut herself.

Natassia had thought about cutting herself.

Natassia had talked to HJJ about the impulse to cut herself.

Then she'd written about it in her journal.

Tomorrow Natassia would be home. She was coming back in the early
afternoon, because she and Mary were scheduled for a session with
Heather. All together, they would talk about what Mary had read. Mary

would have to confess, finally, that she read the journal, that she'd always read the journal.

The smell of cut grass was everywhere. In the twilight, bugs were coming out. Mary thought about leaving a message on Cather's machine. She thought about it a good long couple of minutes. *I need a cigarette.* But there were none in the house, so Mary went inside to work on her income-tax returns. In April she'd had to file for an extension, but the cool thing was that this year she was able to list her daughter as her dependent.

MARY HAD FINISHED her taxes and was hitting the sack when the phone rang, and it was Giulia, who said, "Something amazing happened tonight, and I couldn't wait until tomorrow to tell you."

"Where's Natassia?"

"She fell asleep on the couch watching a video. She's fine. I just covered her up with a blanket. It's nice and cool here tonight."

"So what happened?" Mary asked.

"It's wild," Giulia said, "it's good. Wait'll you hear this."

Apparently, Natassia and Giulia had been walking on Seventy-ninth Street from Broadway to Amsterdam, on their way to get coffee and pastries at La Fortuna. They had just walked past the Dublin House, and Giulia was telling Natassia, "Your mom and dad and Nora and I used to spend lots of time in that bar when we all first came to New York. It was so cheap," and just then this guy standing at the curb, a handsome, shortish, very dark-haired guy eating out of a carton of Chinese food, called over to Natassia. Natassia looked up and said to Giulia, calmly, "Oh my God." Then she walked over to the guy. Giulia followed.

He was standing next to a dark-blue Lincoln Town Car with a big number sign hanging in the back window. He was a driver for a car service, and Giulia was wondering, How does she know this guy? When Natassia began talking to him, he tossed his carton of food down into the gutter and wiped his hands with a handkerchief. His accent was Russian. Giulia was taking this all in, and Natassia was conversing with him—she was noticeably taller than he was—and he said something about how she'd just vanished from sight, and Natassia told him, "Yeah, well, I switched schools."

And he said, "So—you left the Barnard?"

And Natassia told him, "No, I don't go to Barnard now. Listen, this is my mom's friend, and she's taking me out, and we've got to go."

And the guy said to Natassia, "You will call me?" and he pulled a business card out of his pocket and put it in her hand.

Natassia told him, "Yeah. Right."

And she and Giulia walked away, left the guy standing there. Giulia said nothing at first, but when she and Natassia reached the end of the block and were waiting for the light at Amsterdam, Giulia asked, "Who was that?"

And Natassia told her, "Remember last fall I was all upset about some guy?"

"Yeah."

"Well, that was him." There was a trash can at the corner. Natassia tore up the guy's business card, crumbled the pieces, and tossed them. The light to cross Amsterdam Avenue was flashing. Natassia grabbed Giulia's hand. "Come on, run," she said, "we can make this light."